Made for Houston

Sweet McKenna Book Five

Christine Young

Published by Rogue Phoenix Press, LLP
Copyright © 2022

ISBN: 978-1-62420-690-0

Editor: Sherry Derr-Wille
Cover Art: Designs by Ms G

Chapter One

Houston, Dr. Stuart, stepped back slanting a look at the little freckle faced, red headed boy sitting on his table. The boy wore a pained look on that cherubic face of his. He was barely five. It was the third time in the last month that Mrs. MacKay sat nearby, shaking her head. The boy was a little hellion except when he was asleep. At least that was what his mother continued to tell him.

"I've warned him a hundred times if not a thousand he was going to fall out of that tree. I tell him not to walk along the top of the fence. He's not supposed to go in the shed with the cows or the field with the bull. Does he listen to me? No. He thinks he can fly. Last time you saw him he had a concussion, the time before that a sprained ankle. Now he's got a broken arm. What next?" She threw up her hands in desperation as she stared at the little boy.

"I believe he has no fear along with the fact that I'll see him more as he grows older. For now, though, he'll be limited in what he can do."

Houston had a difficult time stopping the laughter that bubbled deep in his belly. His brother, Kit, was just like this boy. He didn't fear anything. In his life his brothers Kit and Riley along with his cousins, Roby and Brady, got into more scrapes than he could count. They defied all rules of common sense. They never listened to sage advice coming from the oldest.

"Don't know if anything will stop that *lad*. I tell him time and again not to push the limits. It's almost as if I'm puttin' ideas into his head by warning him not to do something." She was pointedly shaking one finger at him as if that would make a wit of difference. "Well, you can't be climbin' the trees for a while. Swingin' on them as if you were bein' a monkey."

"Make him keep the splint on his arm. He needs to rest the bone and muscle to assist the healing. You're absolutely right, he can't be using it to act like a little monkey. This is going to take some time to mend. You can give him willow bark tea to ease the pain but nothing stronger."

Dr. Houston helped the boy down from the table before patting him on his head. He shuffled to the cabinet where he kept medicine, handing her the willow bark. "Bring him back in two days. At that time, I'll rework the splint, check to make sure the arm is recovering properly. He'll most likely have the splint in tatters by then. Remember, rest and time are the most important factors for him to get back to normal."

Houston watched the woman with her child leave his office. Wondered if he would ever have a wife, family too. He sat down on a chair as he stretched his long legs out in front of him. His foot ached. It always did when there was a change in the weather. He figured they were in for snow soon if it wasn't falling already. When he peered outside, the sky was gray darkening as the seconds slowly ticked by. He pinched the bridge of his nose wishing for something illusive. Lights from the buildings cast an eerie glow on the surroundings.

He thought on the day five years ago when his toes were crushed in a steel trap. In his cat form, he'd been racing across a deserted part of the highlands. Agony tripped across his body, swirling through his veins to trigger all his nerves. His roar reverberated through the valley echoing in all the empty spaces. As his cat he couldn't spring the trap. Too many English soldier roamed the area for him to shift back to human. He had to take the risk. There was no other choice. He could hardly stay pinned to this spot while praying some kind soul would chance upon him. Houston wasn't sure if his prayers had been answered when a young girl found him. He recalled how soft and gentle her voice was, almost a whisper in the air. For her age she was a beauty. Deep down he knew she would grow up to be beautiful in every way.

Without a question in her eyes, she sprung the trap. When she touched his mangled foot, he felt a surge of protectiveness swamp him.

Nerve endings burned. Her caress gentle as it eased some of the pain. She brought out a vial of lavender oil, rubbed the essence on his paw. After that he would always recall the instant when he caught the unique scent of lavender.

After he limped back to his clothes where he could dress, he thought of that moment. With tenderness, she rubbed his head, scratched behind his ears. Told him all would be better. Her last words to him were to make sure the bones were set properly.

They had not been set correctly. At least he didn't think so. Believed to this very day if they had been, he would be able to walk without a limp. Without dragging one foot behind him when the pain overwhelmed the threshold he could tolerate. At the time, he knew nothing about doctoring. Apparently, the bone-setter didn't either.

Ah, Mrs. Mackay had four children, a fifth one on the way. He tried to explain to her that she should stop having children. Too many could cost her her life or that of a child. She laughed telling him he should talk to her husband about that *vera* important fact. How to approach a man to tell him he should only have sex with his wife at certain times of the month or that he should take his great rod from her body before he ejaculated?

It wasn't a conversation he would relish. Knew for the sake of her health, he should do so. Her husband would laugh then tell him he would never do such an outlandish thing. Withdrawing from a woman wasn't natural or right.

Actually, he knew it was a conversation he should initiate with Mr. McKay. Mayhap he loved his wife enough to listen.

Pondering on that thought further, maybe he would do just that. He knew her husband loved her. Wouldn't want to see anything happen to her. She told him paying attention to her cycle wouldn't work because she wasn't regular.

Oh, he closed his eyes for a moment thinking. Perhaps it was time to move on with his career. He received an invitation to study with one of the finest surgeons of his time in Edinburgh. His earlier apprenticeship taught him a great deal. He was more than just a bone-setter. He was a surgeon. He knew things. Understood how a human body worked better than most physicians. Never believed in bloodletting. Never thought it would cure a disease. What he did know was that people died when they lost too much blood.

Maybe for a short time he'd go to Edinburgh then to be close to his family as well as his extended family, the McKenna's. His mother, Brenna McKenna, wed his father Alistair Stuart. Both he and Kit had the raven black hair and silver blue eyes of the McKenna clan. His littlest brother, Riley, received the red hair and green eyes from their father. Riley's mischievous temperament fit the color of his hair perfectly.

More often than not he found himself homesick, wishing to be back in the highlands. He wasn't cut out for living in the city nor was he meant to live away from his clan. He missed the births as well as the marriages. He knew Crissie had two children, Brady and Lilly two babes as well. Roby was wed, a child on the way.

He was the oldest.

Yes, it was time to think about selling his practice so he could move home. When he first arrived here, living had been an adventure, the land almost as wild and untamed as his homeland. He couldn't remember the last time he shifted. With a long-drawn-out sigh, he realized it might be much longer before he was able to do so. Even in the lowlands there were Sassenach patrols. Now with his schooling and apprenticeship in Edinburgh coupled with the year he spent here, he'd been away from the highlands for a long time, far too long.

Houston wandered upstairs to his living quarters. It was three o'clock, almost time to close up shop unless there was an emergency or Sara Jane's baby decided to arrive early. If that happened, he would be gone most of the night, possibly into the morning hours. He flexed the toes on his bad foot, reminded himself he should not walk with a limp. He needed to do better. Concentration was the key to walking without a hobble.

A groan emanated from his belly at the sound of his office door being opened. It had been three days since the simpering Marie Hughes came to him with some imaginary complaint. Her family was the wealthiest family in the small town of Selkirk, Scotland. For some reason she decided she saw more in him than he wanted any woman to see, any woman except his mate. Marie wasn't his mate. He groaned again, his belly coiling. If he was to find his special woman, he would have to get out of Selkirk. Although Roby found his mate in the most remarkable manner, at the end of the hangman's noose. How Robby realized that fact from the tales he heard via the sight of her, head covered, noose dangling beside her was beyond him. Perhaps there would be a quickening of the blood. Maybe one just knew.

Making his way downstairs, he cursed the change in weather. The snow had not started yet. Nonetheless white flakes would tumble downward in minutes. If the snowflakes fell too quickly before he could give Marie a diagnosis, he would be obliged to walk her home. She would have thought of that, planned for that very scenario.

When he opened the door and saw her, she appeared suspiciously healthy. Her welcoming smile was coy, deliberate. Her head must be whirling as she sought symptoms for some imaginary illness. Just last week she had a strange ringing in her ears. Said she felt dizzy. Pretended to faint while she was sitting on his table.

That wasn't well thought out by her. She should have waited then fainted when she stood. He would have caught her in his arms. The devil, he was glad she did not. Today, he wondered what she would come up with. What fake illness assailed her? Her dark brown eyes gazed at him, trailed up then down his body as she took stock of him, lingering in strategic places meant to seduce him. Unable to help his disgust, he shuddered. He didn't know why she was putting her hopes on him. He wasn't rich although his family was. He did have funds to fall back on when necessary. For Christ sakes, he was a doctor. Hell, but there were dozens of wealthy young men in surrounding towns she could set her hooks into.

Why him?

The rush of air that passed his lips was meant to remind him that he was a professional. It didn't matter that he was the most eligible bachelor in this small out-of-the-way town. He was the only doctor. Marie wasn't the only unmarried lady who sought ways to meet him. He had to admit she was the prettiest as well as the most imaginative. Nonetheless, there was something about her nature that disgusted him.

"Well, hello Houston," she greeted him with the slight lisp she affected for reasons he couldn't understand. Her smile was brilliant though, her eyes shimmering with what seemed to be pleasure.

"Marie," he returned pleasantly all the while hoping this would not take overlong. "What can I do for you today?"

It wasn't worth getting into another argument. Miss Hughes was a much more appropriate way to address her. He just didn't have the energy to disagree. It wouldn't get him anywhere if he tried.

She nodded, walking by him to sit on the table. He wasn't going to examine her even though he was sure assessing her was exactly what she wanted. She leaned back placing her hands behind her for support. Her small sassy breasts pushed upward on display for him. She arched her back. He supposed she had practiced this move enticing the eligible lads in the surrounding villages.

"Do you have to be so formal?" she asked, lowering her dark lashes so they fanned out across her ivory cheekbones. She opened them while she waited for an answer. "I much prefer a bit of casualness. I mean to get to know you better."

He certainly didn't intend to know Marie better than he did. "I assume you're here with some sickness you want cured." His words held a wealth of sarcasm. As always, the tone slipped past Marie. "We should go about the business of curing you. What ails you this time?"

"Well, I've been having headaches. They hurt so badly. Why, at times I have to take to my bed." She looked straight at him as she narrowed her eyes feigning the pain that would go along with what she claimed. She rubbed her temples. "Very bad headaches. They happen most every day. I have to take to my bed when they occur." She had to tell him twice.

"Do you have one now?" he asked wondering what excuse she would give him as he knew she wasn't in pain.

She didn't know how to pretend the agony she was trying to attain. He didn't believe she'd ever felt true anguish. "I won't give you laudanum. Willow bark tea is the best. The taste is bitter. However, with enough honey the flavor is palatable. The tea will help without any lasting effects. I've some lavender oil you can massage on your temples that

6

might also help."

"The stuff is horrible," she told him grimacing. "I've still got the willow bark you gave me last time. I might try the lavender oil though. It smells divine."

"You didn't use the tea?" he inquired trying not to smirk at the look of utter distaste on her face. "So, then I won't be needing to give you anything else. You have a supply that will last." He extended a hand to help her down.

She slid from the table with a tiny puff of air as if she was exasperated with him. "My family is having a get together, well, a small celebration Saturday night if you'd like to come, I'd love to see you there. We could dance. It will be ever so much fun."

"Thank you," he told her, hesitating while knowing he would never attend.

Interesting though, before his accident he would have joined the party just to mingle, to meet new people. He didn't care any longer. That wasn't entirely true. It was just he didn't like small talk or flirting girls. His gimp foot made him a bit self-conscious. "That's actually quite nice of you to ask," he told her as he tried to think of a polite way to say no.

"Then you'll be there?" She smiled while she tossed her wealth of curls over her shoulder. This time it wasn't coy or affected just sincere. "I'll look forward to a dance or two."

He marveled at the nice change. She could be human when she tried. "Maybe. Sara Jane's baby is due anytime. You know I don't dance."

That was something else he missed, dancing. He thought it had been a long time since he held a woman in his arms while music played. The strange thing was he didn't have one inclination to hold Marie Hughes. If he met a woman he wanted to hold...to dance with...he might dance.

"Well, that doesn't make a wit of difference to me." She stared at his foot then back to his face. Leaning forward she placed her hand on his arm. "We can stroll through the gardens, hand in hand. You can kiss me if you like. I believe I would like that, a kiss." She closed her eyes.

"That's a bit premature, don't you think? Besides it's winter. The weather will be far too cold for a late-night stroll."

He was thinking that was a blatant invitation only a cad would take advantage of. He also didn't have one inclination to feel Marie's lips beneath his.

His foot wasn't diseased yet she always had such a look of distaste when the shape of his maligned foot was brought to attention. He wondered what she would think if he did take more notice of her or if she actually saw his foot without his shoe covering it. He didn't want to find out. She would have to hunt up some other poor man to finagle into marriage vows.

It wasn't going to be him.

On top of his disability if she knew he was a shifter, she'd most likely faint dead away.

The door banged open, shaking the walls along with the glass vials that were on the shelves around the room, startling both of them. He jumped at the sound, his mind reacting to the pending emergency. His heart thundered. He was thinking ahead.

"Stick!" Marie cried out stepping back. Her expression changed to abject hatred. "What are you doing here? Barging in like that?"

Stick ignored Marie then bent his attention toward him. "You've got to come, Doc. Got to come now! It's a matter of life or death."

Stick stood in the doorway. He was a young man, tall and skinny, blinding red hair. He was known around town as someone who didn't have all his wits about him. Stick was nice enough. Sometimes he didn't make a great deal of sense. This time there was no question about what he wanted. Someone was in dire peril.

Holding her elbow, Houston saw Marie to the door. When he peered outside, there was still enough light left for her to walk home in safety. *Thank God.* Snow wasn't falling, might not for the next five minutes or more. She would be fine. Her coat was warm. He felt as if he dodged something unsure of exactly what that was. Next, he felt as if he was about to meet his destiny head on. For no reason he could think of, he suddenly remembered the young girl who helped him so long ago. He shook the image from his head.

"Got to come, Doc. He's hurt real bad, somethin' terrible. Hurry!"

"Who's hurt?" Houston had his medical bag in hand as he strode toward Stick, his mind whirling with possibilities. "Who did you say?" Houston asked again. This time he pulled his hat from the coat stand.

Stick was backing out the doorway, turning toward the frozen rutted road. Houston slipped his coat on as he followed the gangly young man to an old wagon sitting across from his office. A young woman stood in front of the mule drawn cart. She was wringing her hands, the saddest look on her face he'd ever seen. Despite the despair etched vividly in her eyes, she was beautiful, ethereal in the fading afternoon light. Her golden blond hair was braided down her back, the tip brushing across her slim waist. Because of the brewing storm, the day was too dark to see the color of her eyes. His gut clenched when he saw the ribbons of tears sliding down her cheeks. Her sobs were silent. Not for a moment did he doubt the distress.

"It's Shadow," Stick said as if he thought the village doc could do anything. "Fix him up. Her *dah* kicked him in the ribs. He's real old. If you don't help, the dog might die."

"I don't..." He cleared his throat looking from the girl to Stick. "I don't fix dogs. I'm a human doctor." The devil, would he refuse to fix a black panther if one was brought to him? One of his own if the person was in cat form? *Nay,* he would have to try. If nothing else he could make the animal comfortable.

"Please just look at him. He needs you. I can't do anything more for him," she spoke softly, so softly he barely heard. It was a whisper in the chilling winter air.

Snow threatened.

Cold air burned his lungs with ice.

Beneath his breath he swore. A moment of thought, with another soft curse he climbed onto the back of the wagon. He was going against all of his training, all of his principles. He wondered at his decision as he ran his hand down the animal's side. He touched the dog's nose. The tip was dry and hot with fever. Bending close to the animal's side, he listened. It wasn't good news he'd give the girl. The dog was going to die. When was the only question?

"Grizzly kicked him. Hard. He got in his way." She spoke again a soft sigh caught in the chill. "Can you fix his rib?"

"Grizzly?" Houston looked up. "Is that someone?"

He had too many questions at the moment. He supposed it could have been the mule or a horse. Was Grizzly her *dah*? Did she live with a man who would kick an old dog instead of step around him?

"Her *dah*," Stick said offering answers before she could.

The lad was eager where she was reticent. "Her *dah* gets mean drunk every night. Got to stay out of his way. Sometimes she has to sleep outside. Shadow was sleeping that's all. Didn't see him coming so he could get out of his way."

Houston wanted to hear from her even though she held back. Still, he digested every word Stick uttered. He looked at her. This time his question was meant for Stick. "Were you there?" Houston asked staring at the girl who didn't seem to want to say anything more. He found he wanted to hear her voice again. The sound reminded him of another time, another place.

He just couldn't remember.

In time he would.

"No, he wasn't," she said as she settled down beside her old dog. Her hand rested gently on his back. "He met me on my way here. I don't mind if he talks for me. Stick knows the story. He likes to talk. I don't."

"Don't work on animals," Houston said again, wishing he didn't have to tell her no. What did he know about mending dogs? It couldn't be too different. There were basics. Since he understood these were the dogs last moments, he could ease him across the rainbows into another land.

I can at least try.

"Can't be much different from humans," Stick spoke again not wanting him to give up.

Nervous energy abounded around the young man as he shifted from one foot to the next, his hands waving wildly with every word he spoke. "You got to do this for Leah. Shadow's one of her only friends besides me. She can't lose him. Who will she have if Shadow's gone? A person ought to have more than one friend."

Leah, it was a nice name. Seemed to fit her. Stick was her only friend. A girl as beautiful as Leah should have lots of friends. He hadn't seen her in the village or heard of her. She swiped away tears. Maybe she was as elusive as her voice.

"I'll take a look."

He was a damn fool for giving in to emotions better left alone. For some reason, he couldn't resist.

Just from what little he saw of the poor animal, he wasn't going to be able to help. He didn't want to get her hopes up. This just wasn't something he needed at the moment. Bending over, he swept up the dog. His foot ached as he stumbled slightly on his way to the building. Stick rushed in front, opening the door as he reached his office then standing in the way as he tried to navigate through the slight opening that was left.

After he set Shadow by the wood stove, he rubbed the dog's ears. He didn't understand how. Nevertheless, he felt Leah's pain as if it was his own. It seemed to touch his soul. She sat next to him stroking her dog, murmuring soft endearments to the animal. After that, she stood, looking at him, silently questioning. He didn't know how to tell her the dog wasn't going to make it through the night.

Her eyes were blue, the color of a summer sky, her lips a soft pink against pure white skin.

Next to him, she was cold, her breathing shallow. He wanted to fold her into his arms in order to warm her. Needed to find a means to do away with the pain freezing her. Chasing away her agony was a task that couldn't be accomplished. The feeling was also something that went deeper than the possible loss of her dog.

"He has two broken ribs. At least one has punctured his lung. There isn't anything I can do for him except make him comfortable. I'll give him something to ease the pain. Keep water by his side if he wants to drink. He won't want to eat."

She wasn't sobbing. Although tears were sliding faster down her cheeks, she cried without making a sound. He hated what he told her. She thanked him with that soft whispery voice he would never get used to but wanted to hear until he remembered exactly where he heard the sound before. It sounded as if it hurt her to talk. She should have someone to confide in besides a mean drunk along with this young man who meant well however...

"Don't think he'll make it through the night." Houston dropped a blanket over the scruffy dog, his muzzle white with age. The animal's breathing was labored. Nevertheless, after the small amount of opium he gave the dog, he breathed easier. Shadow would sleep until the end.

"Can she stay here with him?" Stick asked as he took her hands in his. "I'll go up the mountain to tell Grizzly she's staying so he won't be worrying none about her."

"Grizzly won't worry about me. He's not really my *dah*. Just my step-*dah*. What he will be is angry about is if I don't get his supper ready. I have to go."

"It wouldn't look good if she stayed the night. Would ruin her."

Houston had the strange feeling she wouldn't care. He would though. Somehow, he understood she was special.

"She can't go home," Stick insisted, seemingly worried about her as he looked outside.

It was obvious how much the young man cared for the girl. He was still standing in the open doorway. Behind him the snow began to fall. "It's too far and too cold."

"Where do you live?" Houston asked wondering how long it would take her to get home, a few minutes or an hour or two. He had a gut feeling that with the old mule pulling the wagon it would take her more than an hour.

"She lives up the mountain. Just her and her *dah*, Grizzly," Stick spoke up again looking from the darkening sky to the animal in front of the stove.

Leah placed her hand on his. The touch was light and warmed him even though her fingers were cold. Houston didn't want to think about her riding up the mountain all by herself or with just Stick beside her.

"It's alright," she spoke again sensing his fears. "I've got a pistol."

Hell, the woods were filled with predators, man along with beasts. He stood, stretching as his tired muscles pulled and ached. He thought of the lost sleep. "I'll go with you."

She shrunk away from him seemingly appalled at his suggestion. "No, no, that won't be necessary. I've taken care of myself for too many years to count. I don't need anyone."

He had the distinct feeling she believed her words. "I'm going with her to the turnoff," Stick offered with a lift to his shoulders. "We don't need you to go all the way to her house."

He wasn't at all sure this was the right decision. Didn't want to be afraid for her though he was. She slanted him a wan smile as she sat down on the floor next to Shadow. It seemed she intended to say goodbye. As she placed her face on the dog's head, a small sob erupted from her body, her shoulders shaking with the pain she must feel.

"I'll miss you," he heard the soft murmur of words. "You've been a dear friend."

His eyes clouded with tears. She truly loved this animal, cared for him deeply.

"You can come back tomorrow," he offered believing the dog would die during the night. He told her he would make Shadow comfortable. The only thing that would truthfully ease the dog's pain would be death. He didn't know if he wanted his passing to come before she arrived in the morning or after. Houston supposed she would want to hold his head in her lap when he sipped in his last breath from the air.

He found he wanted to see her again.

"Thank you," she told him before turning to look at Stick. "We should go now. What time?"

"I'm usually up by six."

She nodded. It was her invitation to Stick to follow her out as well as her commitment to return to see Shadow journey to another life. Houston lightly held her elbow as he walked her to the door then across the road to her wagon. He helped her up. "You take care now."

A chilling wind gust caught him by surprise. Snow fell, swirled around him. She would have a cold drive home. He didn't like sending her home by herself. He watched as the unlikely pair boarded the wagon. She held the reigns lightly in her hands as slowly the old mule started down the road, the wagon wheels crunching snow as they made their way along the deserted route.

Houston watched them as they disappeared into the night. Why he waited for a few more minutes he didn't know. He drew in a long draught of air before stuffing his hands in his pockets. He ran to the door. This time he'd neglected his coat.

Standing inside the door, he brushed snow from his trousers then rubbed his hands together to warm them. She didn't wear gloves. Her hands would freeze. He wondered if she owned a pair of gloves. The concern he felt for this ethereal woman was unusual. The sensation was something he'd never before experienced.

Shadow moaned softly. It was a ghostly sound. He shivered. He knew the old dog was ready to say goodbye to the world. Ready to face new challenges. Houston sat down beside him, stroking the rough fur. It seemed to make the dog feel better. His gaze turned toward him, his lids lowered for a moment almost as if he thanked him.

Houston tucked the blanket around Shadow before heading upstairs to his rooms. The cook left dinner for him as always. He sat down to the venison stew provided for him by one of the families. He didn't get paid much. Instead of groats, the people of the parish provided him with fresh game, some with baked bread, biscuits along with muffins straight from their ovens in the mornings. Sometimes he would find a pie sitting inside his office door. More often than not he'd find wheels of cheese in the waiting room when he walked downstairs.

It wasn't a bad life.

However, he needed to start over. As he slipped off his shoes and socks, he stared at his feet, his mangled foot. Rubbing his hand across the bones that had not been set well, he wondered if he could break them again, in the process making the foot right. The pain would be excruciating. The days of recovery too many. Was healing his foot worth the price he would have to pay in time along with the excruciating pain?

From the side table he uncorked a bottle of lavender oil then rubbed it on the mangled toes. The massage felt good, the scent relaxing. Once again, he thought of the girl so long ago who freed him from the steel trap. She carried lavender oil with her that day. She rubbed the medicine on his foot while she cared for an animal, a stranger to her.

Something about Leah reminded him of the girl. That had been more than five years ago. She must have been fourteen or fifteen then...

~ * ~

Leah understood Shadow was going to die. She supposed she'd known that truth since she left with him in her wagon. There was nothing she could do for the dog so she tried the only thing she could think of.

She brought him to Doc Houston.

Thinking of Grizzly as her *dah* never sat right with her. He was cruel, an ornery son of a bitch. Had never treated her mother right, barely tolerated her. She was nothing to him when she was younger. Now that she was older, she'd become his servant, his housekeeper as well as cook.

She never could figure out why her mother married that man. Her mother always told her she needed his protection. Told her that a woman needed a man to keep her safe. Leah didn't believe a woman had to have a man's protection to get on with her life. She always wished her ma had more faith in herself. The two of them would have been better off if they stayed in the highlands. The McKenna clan would have helped them with anything they needed, would have made sure they wanted for nothing. McKennas were good people.

She would have offered to work in the kitchen at the McKenna keep. Her mother could sew. She was an excellent seamstress. Could have supplemented their income with her work. Instead, she married a no good, mean drunk who had a hard time keeping a job.

She didn't mind living so far away from the village. It was peaceful when Grizzly wasn't around. Grizzly wasn't his real name. They used to call him Bear, but someone who went to the colonies, a trapper, came back and dubbed him Grizzly. Said it was the biggest nastiest old bear he'd ever encountered. Had been lucky to get away with his life. Bear was more a grizzly than just a bear. He even had a hump on his back like a big grizzly had. Of course, Bear probably wasn't his real name either.

Leah hoped that when she got up to the cabin, he would be asleep. She didn't want to talk to him. He would want to talk if he was awake. She didn't have anything to say to him. If he would just tell her he was sorry for what happened, she could forgive him.

He wouldn't.

The man never apologized for anything. He was always cursing her, telling her she was no good, telling her she should speak up. Wasn't normal for a woman to be so quiet. She didn't want to talk louder. Didn't want to talk to him at all. What she wanted was to visit her sanctuary. It would be too cold for that. Perhaps in the morning if the weather let up a bit, if it stopped snowing. From past experience she knew it wouldn't.

"What you thinkin' about. Leah? Shadow? He's going to be alright, you know," Stick asked as if her silence was getting to him.

He didn't like it when she didn't talk to him. Sometimes she just wanted to think. Stick never understood any of that.

"Yes and no. Mostly thinking I'd like the sky to stop churning out the snowflakes and warm up a bit."

She tugged her coat sleeves lower so they would cover her fingers. They felt like ice. Might be ice by the time she made it home. She was glad before she left she made sure dinner was simmering over the fire. Fixing a meal was one less thing she had to think about. She told Doc a small fib so she would have an excuse to leave. She hoped he would forgive her for it.

"How come you told Doc Houston you had a pistol when you don't?"

Stick was rummaging in the back just to make sure, she supposed. He wouldn't find one. True, she lied a second time. If she hadn't, he would have felt obligated to escort her home.

Leah shrugged her shoulders pondering the question. "I suppose to make him feel better. Didn't need him taking me home or feeling obliged to do so. I'm not some fragile flower that will wilt if the going gets tough."

"You look pretty fragile to me. You *ken* you always smell like wildflowers."

She slanted him a look of reproach sending him a message that if he asked her a question, he should honor her in the process let her answer. "Don't want to be indebted to any man more than I have to be. He's helping Shadow just by keeping him warm as well as free of pain. Doc doesn't need to do anything else for me. Nothing I might have to repay. Don't have any funds to repay the man."

Stick didn't have anything to say to that. He held his tongue behind his teeth simply because he couldn't refute anything she said. Men were creeps. Except for Stick. That was because he didn't think or act like a man. Didn't think like anyone except himself, which was refreshing. Stick cared about her. As far as she could tell, she was the only living breathing person in the small village of Selkirk who cared about Stick.

She probably saw Michael Graham as well as his two buddies before Stick sighted them only a second or two later. She squared her shoulders. Stick started quivering. He should leave now, hightail it home before Michael joined with his friends got closer. They would torment him if given a chance.

"Michael won't hurt you. I won't let him. If you want, you should leave now before they get too close," she told him even though she knew he didn't believe her while at the same time, she wasn't entirely sure she believed herself.

Stick didn't move. He whimpered. Over the years Michael changed from an arrogant bully to an arrogant bastard. The same could be said for his friends, only worse if that was possible. She wasn't quite sure what the difference was, nevertheless she knew there was a difference.

Stick seemed frozen solid to the seat.

When they were abreast of the men, Michael stopped the mule before taking the reins from her hand. He looked into her eyes, held her attention too long while her breath caught in the back of her throat. She didn't like the feelings that look from him generated. He wanted more from her than she was willing to give.

"What are you doing, Michael? Give those back to me. It's cold out here. All I want right now is to get home before I freeze."

She found herself breathing hard, her heart ricocheting beneath her ribs. Her body trembled.

"What are you doing in the village? It's a little late don't you think?" Michael moved closer to the wagon, to her. "Not safe for you to be out by yourself after dark."

"Shadow was hurt. I took him to Doc Houston," she said in her paper-thin voice. "Need to be going before the snow gets falling too fast."

She didn't want to talk to Michael. Didn't want to be late getting back up the mountain. She was already late. Grizzly would be swearing at her. If he wasn't dead asleep drunk.

"Not going to let you go, at least not until you grant me a few seconds of your time. Want to talk to you, Leah. It's important, you know. You've got to have a few seconds for me. Need to ask you something important. Could change your life."

He set one of his large hands on her knee and squeezed. She felt a moment of fear. Pushed it aside telling herself he wouldn't hurt her. No, he wanted something else from her. Something she wasn't willing to give. He wouldn't force her. At least she didn't belief so.

Resigned, she knew he would hold onto the reins until he had his way. She was helpless to stop him. All she could do was brace for whatever he wanted. So far, he'd not hurt her. In fact, he stopped his friends from hurting her once several years ago. It was at that time he seemed to change, at least his attitude toward her altered.

She'd been trying to walk across a bridge down by the old mill. He, with his friends saw her, teased her. Blocking her way, they kept her from the other side. She told him how mean he was. Informed him also that she thought he was better than acting the bully. It was then a strange look came over his face. He stabbed his hands into his hair. After a pause, he told his buddies to stop. With that said from the leader of the little gang, they allowed her to cross. Now, it seemed he was always trying to collect on that day. Told her she owed him.

"Can you make it fast. I've a ways to go." She wrapped her arms around herself. "It's cold out here. By the time I get up that mountain, the snow could be knee deep." She felt as if she was repeating herself. She was. He wasn't listening.

"Well, I'd be happy to go with you. If I was driving on that seat next to you, I could make sure to keep you warm," he said his grin growing wider as he said the words. "I'd wrap my arms around you, let you slip your tiny little hands inside my coat. Maybe anywhere else you'd like to glide them. Lower if you like."

She shivered and clenched her teeth. She wasn't at all sure about what he meant. Ignoring his comment, she went on to ask, "What is it you want to talk about?"

He cleared his throat. For a brief moment, she thought he might be nervous as she watched him shuffle his feet. "My father has promoted me, Leah. I've a room of my own now. It's over the tavern. The room, well, it's not just one but a suite of rooms. There is even a bathing room just for me along with my wife when I have one. Just got me a big feather bed, big enough my feet won't hang over the edge when I sleep. Plenty of room for you, too, when you say I do to me."

She didn't know what to tell him. It all sounded very nice for him. However, Leah didn't understand what his news had to do with her or why she might do any of those things he suggested. She'd never given him a single indication she was interested in spending her life with him as his wife or in any other capacity. She was growing more and more impatient. "Michael, is that it? Are you done?"

"No," he responded quickly giving her knee another quick squeeze. "You know how much I like you. We could get married, live in those rooms, have children. I'm sure my father will be giving me more promotions. The inn is doing well. We'll have plenty of money. I could give you things you don't have now. You wouldn't have to live with ol' Grizzly."

He touched her arm as if she would like the caress. She jerked away. He scowled at her. "You shouldn't be lurching away from me, Leah. Who else is giving you an offer of marriage?" He looked to the Doc's office down the street. "Certainly not Houston Stuart the town doc."

"I can't marry you, Michael. We don't love each other."

If there was one thing her mother inadvertently taught her was that she should love the man she married. Nothing else would do. Nor could she ever wed a man who made her skin crawl, even if he would be able to give her things. She didn't need monetary things. She craved an intimacy that would permeate soul deep, a relationship that would fill her heart with love as well as happiness.

"If you won't marry me, will you go to Marie's party with me on Saturday night? I would come up the mountain to get you, bring you home too if you'd like. You'd be safe with me."

"You *ken* I cannot. Grizzly would never let me go anywhere with

19

a man." She reached for the reins. He tugged them away making it harder for her. "Michael, please, let me go. I need to get home."

"I don't know anything of the sort. You can't stay up on the mountain for the rest of your life. You need a man to protect you. Grizzly is going to make your life harder and harder. He's not going to be around for many more years. Don't turn down my offers. You might not ever get another one."

"I cannot go to the party or anything else with you."

She felt her exasperation all the way to the pit of her belly. She didn't know what to do. Didn't know how to make him understand.

Michael continued on ignoring her requests, repeating himself as if she didn't hear the first time. "Grizzly's not going to be around forever, you know. One of these days he's going to drink himself to death. You can count on that. I won't be a free man forever offering to make you an honest woman. You *ken* there are other women in this village, women who would like to marry me."

Once more Leah grabbed for the reins to no avail. "I am an honest woman. No man can change that fact one way or the other. Why don't you become an honest man and..." she heaved in a long breath of air searching for the right words.

"...and?" One of his dark brown eyebrows arched upward in question.

She let out a long-exasperated sigh. "I don't know. Leave me alone. I can't go to the party with you or anyone. Now, let me go. It's getting colder by the minute. I don't want to freeze before I get home. How many times do I have to say the words before you'll listen to me?"

She had stuffed her hands in her pockets a few minutes ago. They warmed. A few seconds exposed to the frigid air they would once again feel like ice.

"You boys go on to the tavern. Think I'll ride a ways with Leah. Want to make sure she stays safe. I'll catch up to you later."

His boys immediately left. They always did what Michael said. When Michael turned his attention to Stick, he leapt off the wagon intent on getting as far away from Michael as he could get as fast as possible. She watched as he disappeared down the street, the falling snow finally hiding him from view.

Michael still held the reins in his hands. He leapt onto the seat sitting close to her, closer than she felt comfortable. At his instruction, the mule started plodding down the road. She turned her face away from him, afraid now that they would be alone together. Leah didn't want to be alone with a man, not now not ever. Unless perhaps, it was the doc. She paused staring back the way they'd come, looked toward Doc Houston's place. A tiny quiver whipped through her belly. Heat pooled inside.

She didn't know what to make of the feeling.

"You can't stay with Grizzly all your life. You're a grown woman. I want you to think about me. Think about the proposal along with all the other things I've told you." He wrapped one of his arms around her, tugged her closer. He was strong and tall, a well-built man. She knew trying to distance herself was futile. He was right. There were other girls in Selkirk who would like his attention. She just wasn't one of those girls.

They rode in silence for a while. She heard the crunch of the snow beneath the mule's feet coupled with the wagon wheels the sound was soothing. She didn't have anything more to say. He didn't seem to, either. The flakes were freezing to the ground as soon as they fell. The weather smelled cold combined with the scent of the surrounding pines if that was possible. They passed by the MacKay house. Lights blazed in all the downstairs rooms. Brenda was pregnant again. She would be kneading bread and setting it aside to rise for the night. Her mouth watered thinking about the yeasty taste of the fresh baked bread.

He turned left toward the mountain. The winding trail in front of them would take her home. Grizzly would be angry if she showed up with a man. He told her more than once she wasn't to go gettin' herself with child. He wasn't going to pay to bring up some man's bastard. Michael would have to get off soon.

Her stepfather didn't have to worry about anything like that. She wasn't going to give herself to some man then find herself in the family way. She knew what was right from what was wrong.

"You should join your friends before they start rumors about us. You can't ride with me all the way home." She turned to Michael, for the first time looking at him, his profile.

21

He was a handsome man with chestnut colored hair. She couldn't see his eyes now. Though she knew they were a deep, dark brown almost matching the color of his hair. His nose straight, his jaw hard and unyielding, she didn't doubt he'd make some woman a good husband. That female just wasn't going to be her. She tugged in a long breath of frigid air.

"No rumors. I won't let that happen, Leah. If you haven't figured it out yet, I care about you." He pulled on the reins before hopping from the wagon. "Don't like the outcome of the conversation. Fact of the matter is, even if I don't like what you're telling me, your no will have to do for now. You going to be alright?"

"I won't change my mind. You deserve a woman who can love you. That isn't me." She would never lie to him, or take something she didn't want.

"I've been told love can grow when given time." He was making another argument then he'd most likely think of some other reason to present to her.

She wasn't going to argue with the man. Quarreling wouldn't get her anywhere. "Thank you for taking me this far. It will only take me about fifteen minutes now to get home. I'll be fine."

"You're welcome. I'm not going to stop asking, Leah. You can count on it. There isn't anyone else around that I'd like to be my wife."

After he jumped from the wagon, he gave the backside of the mule a swat then whistling, showed her his back as he headed into town, after that on to the tavern. With a tiny shake to her head, she watched him saunter down the old trail. No, he probably would not quit asking anytime soon. She was sure, though, in time he would turn his attention to someone else.

The snow let up a minute as she moved farther into the forested area. Somewhere in the wintery sky an owl hooted. Another answered. A wolf howled in the thick stormy air. Wind shrilled through barren trees. She passed by the rundown Fletcher place. Even with the moisture cleansing the air, she smelled the garbage along with the ill-kept pens that housed the hogs. They had one horse. Its stable was muddied, mired in goop. One light burned in a back room. They had two children. Friendly little mites even if they were always dirty.

If she had children...

She stifled her laughter. She didn't think she would ever have children even though she wanted at least one. Sometimes she didn't think she would ever come down off the mountain even though she yearned to return to the highlands. She didn't suppose there would be much left of her home now after five years of emptiness. Maybe if she could save a few coins, she could return and see what was still standing. If she were lucky, no one would have moved into the abandoned home. She could clean up the dirt, make it habitable.

Leah saw the light from the fireplace in their tiny hut. The golden-red flames glowed in the darkness. Shadow would have heard the wagon lumber up the road. He would have greeted her with barks if he weren't staying comfortable in Doc Houston's office. He rested by the fire. He was warm. Comfortable. Tears welled in her eyes. She pushed them back.

After taking care of the mule, she walked into the house. Truthfully, she didn't want to go inside. Wouldn't if it weren't so darn cold. She swallowed hard before stiffening her shoulders to brace herself for her stepfather's spewing of his wrath. Sometime before marrying her mother and now he found religion. Of course, he was pious only when it suited him.

"Where you been, Girl?" Grizzly was sitting at the table, drinking from the jug. A dirty plate sat in front of him. At least he had dinner. She would only have to wait a short amount of time for him to sleep.

"Took Shadow to the village. Thought maybe Doc Houston could mend him." She wanted to hear an apology from the man. He wouldn't apologize. "You hurt him real bad."

"Can he fix him up?"

He drank long and deep before wiping his mouth with the back of his hand. His fierce scowl told her he'd already heard enough about her dog.

"Don't think so," she murmured as she bent over to stir the stew she left. "Have you eaten?" she asked even though she saw the dirty plate sitting in front of him.

Sometimes he wanted more. Problem was he was too lazy to dish up the food himself. She would have to get it for him.

"*Aye.* You be goin' back tomorrow to bring the mangy cur home? That dog's not worth your time. He's old and worn out, good for nothin' if you ask me. Don't suppose you would be askin' though. Can't even move to get out of my way. Nearly killed myself trippin' over the mutt." Grizzly pounded his fist on the table, rocking the spoon that was resting in his plate.

Leah ignored him as she tried to keep the evil thoughts from pounding into her head. Sometimes her mind spun in the wrong directions. At this moment, she didn't have one good thought for her stepfather. She pulled in a sip of air to steady herself. Let it out slowly as she fought for the patience she needed to deal with this irascible old man.

"Yes. I've got to see Shadow in the morning." *Before he dies or help bury him if he doesn't make it through the night. From the look on Houston's face when he told her he would make him comfortable, she didn't think Shadow would see another day.*

She understood she needed to stay out of Grizzly's way. He would badger her until she would have to leave, go outside to wait until he fell asleep. She dished up a bowl of stew for herself then sat down in the tiny alcove where her bed was fastened. She ate until she was satisfied. She cleaned up the dishes. Scooped what was left of the stew into a jar before setting the container in a cold room just off the back porch.

Grizzly spent an hour mumbling while drinking before he stripped to his underwear. He settled in his bed, the jug of whiskey dangling from his fingers. When he started snoring, Leah let out a tiny sigh of relief. He would still be asleep when she left to go down the mountain in the morning.

She curled up on her bed, her hands under her cheek. Her fingers were still cold. She rose to put another log on the fire then returned to the bed.

Shadow...

Doc Houston didn't lie to her. Didn't come right out and tell her the truth either. He would keep her dog comfortable. She understood what that meant. After she thought of shadow along with the fact he would be in a better place where there was no pain and no Grizzly, all she could think about was Houston's strong gentle hands, his kind silver-blue eyes.

~ * ~

"She loves me. I can hear it in her voice." Michael sat down with his friends, Quaid and Ryan. He wasn't going to tell his friends the real reason for his apparent attraction to Leah Kennedy. The devil he was enamored of what she could bring him. Leah possessed a willowy grace along with a kindness that touched his soul, even started to heal his jaded heart. He'd always been mean. Had a chip on his shoulder from all the beatings his father administered. He thought that was the way to treat everyone, hurt them before they hurt him. As far as girls were concerned, he had no respect for them.

Until he encountered Leah.

Leah was different. Her very difference would give him what he wanted. He grinned.

It wasn't because she was the most beautiful girl he ever set his eyes on. The amazing part of that was she didn't know nor did she seem to care. She wasn't anything like Marie Hughes who flaunted herself around all the young men. If he wanted to, he was sure he could coax Marie into bed. He was also sure she wasn't a virgin. There had been rumors last summer that her innocence had been stolen by some gent in Edinburgh. Now, it seemed she had her sights set on the doc despite his disability. He didn't know why all the ladies thought Doc Houston was such a good catch. Everyone knew doctors were poor.

Leah was a virgin though. He was sure of that. He wanted her not just to bed her but to have her for his amusements. She was his. He would make sure of that. He'd be the envy of every man around Selkirk to Edinburgh then on to Glasgow. What he didn't know was how to convince her he was the right man for her. Hell, what choices did she have here? Just the Doc. Houston Stuart wouldn't want such a fey creature.

He was educated.

More than most.

Leah seemed to be pretty smart too. He didn't know if she could read and write. Most women around these parts couldn't do either. If she married him, she could help out in the inn, wait on tables when needed. She could do the books if she could cipher numbers.

"Leah is going to the party with you then," Quaid asked with a smirk then looked at Ryan. "You going to let the rest of the village know she's yours?"

"No, seems she doesn't want to. I'm making progress though. I think she almost said yes. The look in her eyes told me she wanted to even though she's afraid of Grizzly." Michael waved his hand in the air to get the bar maid's attention. She waltzed over then plopped on his lap. She smoothed the front of his shirt while she leaned into him, pressing her breasts against him in invitation. He liked the way she felt all warm and soft just like a woman should feel.

"Yeah, he's a mean devil, that one," Ryan said.

"What can I get for you?" she purred as she stroked his cheek.

She kissed him where her fingers lingered, her little tongue lightly touching his skin.

He pulled her close. His mouth slanting over hers, he wrapped his tongue around hers. Michael liked the lady. Betsy was her name. Slept with her several nights ago. He would do so again if he wanted, if she was willing. He didn't have any doubts. Tonight, maybe if she didn't have another customer waiting for her. She didn't charge him though. Momentarily, he thought of Leah. He shrugged. A man had needs.

There were other women besides Betsy. He wasn't sure if he'd curb his desires when he married Leah. One woman was never enough for him. He didn't think that would change in the future. Perhaps Leah would prove to be so passionate in bed he wouldn't want another woman. That brought a chuckle rumbling up from deep in his lungs. He didn't think so.

"A glass of ale along with some of that warm bread I smell baking. After that I want you, darling, that's what I want." He pinched her fanny as he thought of other parts of her he would also enjoy toying with.

She squeaked. "Me? You want me? Well, if you like you can have all your wishes."

"Later," he said as he gave her nearly barred breast a soft squeeze before putting her on the floor. "I'm starving."

"After my hours are done. You know where to find me. Don't have anyone else waiting for me."

Michael leaned back in his chair, his long legs stretched out in front of him, his arms crossed over his chest while he watched little Betsy sashay her pretty fanny to the bar to bring him his drink. He hardened thinking about later tonight. Wished it was Leah he would be bedding tonight. He would have her soon. Damn but he was a lucky man, no denying that fact.

"So, who you going to take to the party?"

He kept his eyes on the barmaid. "Don't know. Have to do some serious thinking. Not going to show up there alone. Maybe little Elisa, if I can stand all that carrot red hair for an evening." He thought about that some more. Yes, Elisa would never turn him down, never did. He could bring her up to his rooms over the inn after the dance and make love to her. He'd had her there before. She was easy. Not like Leah.

Leah was a challenge. Maybe that was why he wanted her so desperately. No, there were other more important reasons he wanted Leah.

The threesome stayed at the tavern for several hours. Nearing midnight his friends left with some of the other serving maids. When Betsy served him, he pulled her onto his thighs, one hand firmly around her breast, sliding the fabric lower so he could rub his thumb over the hard tip.

"I'm your only customer now. Should we leave?" His other hand roamed the length of her leg. Giggling, she squirmed against him.

"You have to wait," she laughed then nipped him on the ear.

"Don't want to wait."

"I'll ask the boss."

He let her go, watching her again, wishing she was Leah. When he swept her off her feet to carry her up the steps to her room above, she giggled again. By the time they reached the small bed where they would sleep, she was half undressed as was he.

He let the clothing he'd taken off her fall to the floor as he set her on the bed before spreading her legs. He was inside her. She was hot and swollen, slick with her need. He roared his pleasure as he left his seed inside her hot, moist sheath.

"You can take it a bit slower next time," Betsy purred rubbing her hands along his sweat sheened back. "What had you so desperate you couldn't wait?"

"You know," he murmured.

"Leah."

Chapter Two

I've no intention of nagging you. You must understand how much we miss you here at home. As you well ken there is a village near the McKenna keep. You can be a doctor, deliver your brother's and cousin's babies. While the midwife is great, I'm sure the clan would rather have you tend to them. Roby has one child on the way, you know. You're the oldest. You've yet to wed. I do understand that you can't marry anyone until you find your mate. She does exist somewhere out there. All you need do is be patient and come home. You're just as likely to find that special person here as you are in Selkirk.

Roby McKenna even says you can tease him about his gallows bride if it makes you laugh. He's right. You don't laugh enough. Since the accident you are far too somber. Not since you hurt your foot have you been the same. We all worry about you, Houston. It's been far too long since you've been home. If I didn't know you better, I might believe you are hiding from your family. You can only stay hidden from everyone for so many years before you start missing out on what's most important in your life.

Kit hasn't found his mate either or Riley for that matter. As you must recall Kit even travelled to America in search of that special someone. I'm not saying you should do that. Riley is still young. He has plenty of time. No, you are responsible now. You won't shift in the process get caught by some Sassenach soldier to be displayed as a freak. Kit as well as Roby both needed to grow up have adventures. What better place than away from their family and friends. If you hear the sarcasm in my words, please ignore them. Alistair is pleased by the result of their endeavor. Says Kit left as a boy and came back as a man.

If he ever tells you how the two of them ran the gauntlet, I pray you don't encourage them to continue with their frightening tales. While Scotsmen can be brutal, their ways don't compare to the natives in America. I pray every night that the two of them don't do something so childishly foolish again. Of course, that is not likely to happen for Roby since he's wed with responsibilities. Then there is Riley. I've heard my two boys with their heads together talking about riding to Glasgow in order to see if there are any ladies there who might suit their fancy. While it's much better than heading off to that wild untamed land across the ocean, I'm afraid the talk doesn't make me happy.

Alistair says they have to do what they think is best. They are men not little boys to be coddled by their mother then he laughs and kisses me. After that he takes me to bed. Well, they are still my little boys as you are as well.

Now, when are you coming home for a visit? You didn't grace us with your presence for Christmas. It is well into January now. If you recall, we haven't seen you in nearly a year. I'm not getting any younger. Although your father still insists on chasing me around the bedroom from time to time. I do put up with his antics because I love him so dearly. That was probably too much for me to tell you. Nevertheless, you will have a wife someday. I pray you will continue to love her when the two of you are our age.

Crissie seems happy in Ireland. They visited last summer with the two children, Ian and Ilene. Have to say Connal and Wynnie still watch him with anger in their eyes, probably their hearts as well. What Walker did is hard to forgive. In time I suppose, they will find some way to except him wholly into the family. Crissie does dote on him. She loves that man with all of her heart.

I digress. Your father sends his love as do I. Let me know when you might come for a visit.

Love,

Your Mother

With a drawn-out sigh, Houston set the letter on the table. His foot ached with the chill of the night. His heart ached for Leah. She would lose her dog soon. He wished he encouraged her to stay the remainder of the night so she would be near when Shadow drew his last breath. He understood that was what she wanted.

He stumbled across the room to the kitchen table where a pot of tea sat on a tray waiting for him. Mrs. MacKay left freshly made stew this afternoon as a thank you for patching up her little boy. After he sat down, Houston heaped his bowl full to the brim while thinking about the letter from his mother.

He did miss everyone.

The hot tea felt good in his belly. Nevertheless, a brandy would feel even better. With his eyes closed he waited until he felt a burst of energy pool through his body. The devil, yesterday as well as the day before had been grueling both emotionally and physically. He could use help with the practice. Needed someone to make some of the house calls that weren't emergencies just necessities. Help wasn't coming anytime soon. If he left Selkirk, everyone would have to travel to Edinburgh to see a doctor. He couldn't let that fact influence his life. For him it was far past time for a change.

Hawk, Hawkins should join him soon. The man traveled through here monthly. Hawk needed to settle down and take on half of his practice, half of his obligations. Hawk liked his life the way it was. He lived for the adventure. Didn't want permanence of any kind. He was due in today. Should have been here by now. The inclement weather would have slowed him if not that, a willing wench.

Brandy, he held the glass to the light twirling the amber liquid inside the glass. He sipped. As the liquid slipped down his throat he felt better. Didn't take long for the fiery stuff to take effect. He looked to the small stove. Shadow still slept. He could see the gentle rise and fall of the blanket the animal was wrapped in. How much longer did the dog have?

Leah would be here in the morning.

She understood Shadow was not going to heal.

He heard the footsteps. While he listened, he prayed the man making the noise up his stairs was Hawk and not a patient or Mary Jane's husband telling him it was time for the baby to be born. He listened and waited while he held the breath he just drew into his lungs.

The door burst open. Hawk stood in the doorway a grin above the growth of hair on his chin. "Houston, you look like an old man all stretched out in front of that fireplace a glass of brandy in your hand." Hawk's powerful strides ushered him into the room. "Got one of those for me?"

"Help yourself." Houston raised his glass in greeting before nodding his head in the direction of the brandy and glasses. Not that Hawk needed help finding what he sought. Hawk was familiar with his home. "What took you so long? Expected you this afternoon."

"Didn't you notice it was snowing outside? Seems your eyesight might be as deficient as those toes of yours. Still think we could do something about them if you'd let me." Hawk poured his brandy then sat down in a chair beside him.

"Anything you could do wouldn't be worth the pain involved. Don't even know if breaking them again then setting them would help. Not sure I'm willing to try." Houston had thought of the procedure many times. Had remembered the incompetence of the bone-setter who did the original job. That fact was all part of why he became a doctor.

"You and I both believe resetting the bones would help. We both understand much better how to set bones now than we did five years ago. The man who you went to for help didn't have the sense God tried to give him."

Houston drank down his glass. "It's easy for you to suggest the procedure when you don't have to live through the agony. The first time was pure torture. How do you suppose we would go about breaking them again? Hit my toes with a steel mallet?"

"I'd rather hit your stubborn head with one," Hawk laughed as he perused the room, taking in the changes that had been made over the last month. "No, we could always spring a steel trap. You kept the one that got you the first time. We could use that one, break all the bones in exactly the same place."

Houston's gut curled with the thought of sticking his foot in a trap on purpose. Even if the intent was so that he could walk again without a limp. No matter how he tried he was never as surefooted as he used to be. He couldn't will himself to ignore the pain when he put pressure on the foot. No was his answer, as long as he had a choice, he'd keep rubbing the lavender oil on his toes. The oil always helped.

Ignoring Hawk's stare simply because he knew the man wanted an answer, he turned his attention to the fireplace, to Leah's dog. Houston watched the dog, looking for signs that he might need more opium. Shadow didn't stir.

"What's that?" For a moment Hawk studied the dog from his chair. In one easy move, he was by the animal's side, lifting the blanket. "That's Shadow." He looked up concern in his eyes, his brows narrowed. "It's Leah's dog, isn't it? What happened?"

Houston wondered how Hawk knew Leah, how he knew the dog. He shrugged it off. Hawk was always off in the backcountry to see to his patients. "She brought him by this afternoon. Seems Grizzly kicked the dog when he didn't get out of the way fast enough. You know Leah?"

He felt a bit of jealousy at the thought. He didn't know why. Hawk had his traveling practice in this area of Scotland longer than he'd been in Selkirk. Of course, he would know her.

"Sure do. She's been in these parts for five years now. Moved down from the highlands with her mother along with Grizzly. "Bout the time you got your foot caught in the trap." He stroked the dog's head watching the animal, concern written clearly in his eyes.

"What do you know about her father?"

He wanted to learn everything he could about Leah Kennedy. She fascinated him. Despite her height or perhaps because of it, she moved with a willowy grace. Her smile reached her heart. He wanted to see it more often. He was certain she was true and honest. Women with those qualities were rare.

"Not her father for one thing. Grizzly is her stepfather. She could leave him. However, her heart is too kind. As long as she thinks he needs her, she'll stay. Don't *ken* where she'd go though."

Hawk moved back to his chair to help himself to his brandy. He leaned forward his forearms on his thighs, moving the glass between the palms of his hands as he watched both the dog as well as him.

Houston waited for his friend to continue with the story. He knew the man was thinking in his mind what he should say. Leah was a private woman, very private. He recalled seeing her once before from a distance.

Other than that one time she remained an elusive figure to him. Her blue eyes the color of the sky just before a summer storm, pulled him to her in an indefinable way.

"Leah's mother wed him so she would have his protection. Grizzly used to hold down a good job at the print shop. He could set type as well as clean the machines. Now Mr. MacKay only lets him sweep the floor as well as tidy up the room. He's drunk most every day along with every night. Didn't help when his wife, Leah's mother, died. At the funeral, he showed up drunk ranting and raving at Leah that it was all her fault."

"Why would he think it was Leah's fault? That was putting a lot of pressure on a young girl."

"Her mother was chasing after her one day. She slipped and fell. The embankment was steep. She shouldn't have been up the mountain though she was. She was looking for her daughter. Never did find out why. Suppose it was never my business to ask more questions."

"Does he hurt Leah?" Houston asked concern for the willowy girl foremost in his mind. Didn't know what he would do if the answer was yes.

She was tall. Moved with an easy grace. He wanted to see her again. Needed to hear the truth from her for himself.

"No. Doesn't mean he won't in some drunken stupor though. He's wiry, strong too. Everything Leah is not. When he's nasty drunk she disappears for the night. She can't do that in weather like this."

"I should have insisted she stay here with her dog," Houston mumbled softly as he stared at the flames. "She shouldn't be riding up the mountain at night by herself."

"Would have gone worse for her with Grizzly if she stayed in town without letting him know what she was doing. She could have stayed with Brenda."

One dark eyebrow lifted. "Mrs. MacKay?"

"*Aye.* Leah takes care of everyone up the mountain. Sometimes she forgets to take care of herself. The Fletchers live half way to her place. They'd starve without her. She brings them food when Grizzly isn't watching. He might beat her if he ever discovered the truth about that.

He's a miserly old man. What's his is his. He doesn't share."

"There's Stick too. I see him around town from time to time but he avoids me. This afternoon he was the one doing all the talking," Houston said, downing what was left of his brandy.

"*Aye*, Leah is shy. Doesn't like to talk to people. If she spoke to you, you're one of the lucky ones." Hawk rose, striding into the kitchen. "Got anything good to eat? I'm starving."

"There's some stew left in the pot that Mrs. MacKay brought over."

He did feel lucky. She was so soft spoken he had to listen hard to hear what she was saying. He could just imagine hearing that soft sultry voice whisper to him in bed. Who was he fooling? He didn't need to get involved with a fey lady who wasn't his mate, who wasn't his special person. He wasn't going to sleep with a virgin because there wasn't a single doubt in his mind that was what she was. He cursed his unruly brain for even thinking about lying with Leah Kennedy. She deserved better than that. The unruly thoughts reminded him of his cousin and Walker. He took her innocence. Got her with child first and only one time. After that he didn't show up for a year. Ian, his child, was three months old before Walker even knew the baby existed. When he discovered the truth, he hauled Ian off to Ireland telling Crissie she could come if she wanted.

"She helps out with Mrs. MacKay too. Babysits for her so Brenda can have a few moments alone. The MacKays have to stop having a baby almost every year. Told Brenda I'd talk to her husband about that. She doesn't think it will do any good."

"I had almost the same conversation with the lady today." He cleared his throat thinking over what Hawk told him. "Leah seems to be a saint," Houston mused although he sensed the goodness in her the first second he saw her. All the clan could sense good and evil. It was a sixth sense that helped keep them from trouble most of the time. Too bad he couldn't have sensed the animal trap that day.

"Leah would never let you call her a saint. She says she does what she does because it's the right thing to do. Her care for others is genuine. She also has her wildlings to look after. They're very special to her."

Hawk set his finished bowl on the table before he sat back, relaxing and stretching his long legs out in front of him.

"Wildlings?" Houston was still riveted to the tale Hawk was telling. "What the devil are wildlings?"

His mind spun as he thought of her with wild animals while his heart caught in his throat with real fear. She was taking chances with her life and it would have to stop.

He didn't have the right to stop her. Hell, he understood he had no rights where she was concerned.

"Somewhere above their house she has a refuge of sorts, farther up the mountain. I've been there once. She never shows it to anyone. She keeps the wildlings there. Grizzly doesn't know about the place or I'm sure he would destroy the little sanctuary she built."

"Refuge?" he queried. More questions that needed answers spun in his head. Now more than ever he wanted to get to know this woman who was so different from any woman or person he'd ever encountered.

"Yes, she takes care of wounded animals along with the strays. Seems to do the same with people too. Probably why she still takes care of Grizzly. She can't help herself. If she can, she sets the wildlings free once they are healed. There was a hawk once," he laughed softly, "who had a broken wing. She mended the wing. When it was all better, she set the bird free. She's had mice. One year a skunk with a sore paw stayed with her. They aren't afraid of her. She even helped a fawn who'd been shot recover."

"The wildlings...wouldn't have anything to do with you, would they? Are you her friend or something more?" Houston asked watching his friend of so many years.

He knew a lady wounded Hawk's heart at one time, wounded and betrayed him. He'd been devastated for the longest time. Hawk left. Was gone for over a month. When he returned, he was better. No longer looked like the walking dead. "Did she have anything to do with your healing?"

"A lot, but not the way you're thinking right now. You should go back to your first thoughts about her. She's innocent when it comes to men as well as most things. Are you interested in her? If you are, make sure you don't hurt her. I'd hate to have to come looking for you."

He laughed softly. Hell, for a few seconds every other hour since he met her, he was interested in the lady. It was, however, time to change the subject to something less personal. He needed to get some questions answered, if nothing else, set Hawk to thinking about settling down in Selkirk. "You should consider the end to your roaming days." Houston decided to change topics. "I can use the help here." He stopped talking for several seconds. "The truth is I'm thinking about another apprenticeship in Edinburgh then going home to the highlands. I've had my moment of rebellion along with a tiny bit of adventure. I miss my family. Think I might like to look for the young lady who freed me from the trap. She lived in the highlands, a small cottage That was a long time ago. She might not even be there."

Hawk sipped his brandy as he brought in a long breath of air. "She might be closer than you think," he spoke softly his eyes seeming to hold more information than he was willing to give.

"What the devil is that supposed to mean?" Hawk's words had Houston sitting up, staring at him. "You're implying something. If you don't want to clarify..."

"Nothing to clarify. I'm not sure of anything. Not certain why I spoke out of turn though. It's just a gut feeling."

He needed to change the subject from Leah. "Would you consider buying my practice? It wouldn't cost much." It was time for Houston to pursue his original question. "Understand you don't want to be tied down to anything. Don't you think it's about time to stop wandering so you can put down some roots? This would be a great place for you as you know the inhabitants. You could still visit some of the closer villages."

"Don't know," Hawk said as he stepped to the window his hands clasped behind his back. He stood silent for a long time before he turned. "Don't much like the cold and the snow. Been on the trail, slept outside when I'd rather have a warm fire in front of me, like tonight. I'll have to think on it."

Houston felt a surge of relicf sweep through him. His only regret would be leaving Leah behind without getting the chance to know her. Perhaps he should do something about that before he left. "Don't want to leave the folks in Selkirk without a doctor. It would be nice that when I do leave, they'll have someone they can count on to look after them. You could have this office and home or set up another one. There is an empty house on Hasting Street"

"I do know most of the good folk here."

"You do. You know them better than I do."

He thought about Leah along with all Hawk told him about her. Perhaps he should pay a visit to her. Ride up the mountain to see her surroundings. Maybe she would show him her sanctuary. He did want to be part of her life. What would it take to win her trust?

The devil, he felt as if he already was part of her life.

Sensed he'd known her forever.

None of that made sense. He'd known her for a few hours.

He was leaving.

In any case, the connection he felt for her ran strong and deep. How deep did it truly go? Deep enough that he might consider her for his mate? Did one choose his mate or did it just happen? Thoughts of Roby, his hasty marriage to Pippa struck him. He wasn't sure Roby knew at the time? Roby didn't know. Nonetheless he sensed the connection then acted on his gut feelings.

The devil, he sensed that same connection with the girl who freed him from the trap, sensed the same thing with Leah. There couldn't be two women who held his heart.

Could there be?

No, he needed to find that girl, a young woman now, after that he needed to find out if his senses spoke true. As soon as his apprenticeship was over, he would travel north. He would find the cottage she once lived in. She might still be there.

"You look far away. What are you thinking about?" Hawk asked as he ran his fingers through his mahogany reddish hair leaving it a disheveled mess.

"You look tired. How far did you travel today?" Houston wasn't ready to let Hawk into those self-contained thoughts. He needed to mull them over in his rattled brain for a while before they could be anything except private.

"I am tired. You're changing the subject. I've gone farther some days and didn't have a roof over my head when I went to sleep. Tonight, there is a roof. I'm blessed. What are you thinking?"

It seemed Hawk meant to persist. If he had a second person to run his thoughts by, he might be able to clarify some things.

"You've given me a great deal to think about. If you would do more than just consider taking over this practice, I'd be grateful."

"Only if you consider the only possible remedy to your foot."

"It's a deal."

Houston wanted to take back the words as soon as they were out of his mouth. If the bones were broken again, he would have weeks of recovery time. He trusted Hawk with the task though. It would be heaven to be able to walk without a limp. What did he have to lose?

"When?" Houston asked.

"After your time in Edinburgh? You could rest in the city before you return to the McKenna keep and a new practice."

The night took a long time to change to morning. Shadow didn't suffer before he passed on. He would have to see about burying the dog. He hoped Leah would return before the animal crossed over to a better place. He wasn't sure he believed that but the animal was in pain. Shadow fell asleep that was all. He would never wake up again. It was for the best.

Hawk left with a promise to return in a couple of months.

~ * ~

Leah couldn't take the wagon down the trail into town this morning. Too much snow covered the narrow path. She would have to walk. It wouldn't take her anymore time walking than riding on the old rickety mule drawn wagon. The cold would nip at her feet though. They would feel numb by the time she was half way down the mountain. She put on her warmest socks along with thick boots then slipped into her heavy coat. She should have worn it last night. She had been in too much of a hurry to get Shadow to the doctor to take the time for warm clothes.

Michael gave her a lot to think about, going to a party. She would have liked to dance with Houston. He was tall and strong, his shoulders broad. He smelled of the soap he used as well as the lavender oil he massaged into his foot. She didn't know why he walked with a limp. She'd heard it had something to do with broken bones not being set properly.

She remembered the beautiful black panther she rescued from the steel jaws of the hunter's trap. The memory of the animal, his eyes huge with pain never failed to put tears in her eyes.

She hated the traps, despised what they did to animals. Would like to do the same to any man who set a trap such as that one. She also knew the panther wasn't what he pretended to be. The animal was a shifter, most likely from the clan Chattan. He wasn't a McKenna though. She learned his last name was Stuart as in Doctor Houston Stuart.

Her thoughts traveled in the wrong directions again. She was truly sorry she had such wicked thoughts. She tried to be better. Reading the good book every night before she went to bed was supposed to keep her mean thoughts at bay. At least that was what Grizzly always told her. Too bad she couldn't read.

Reading wasn't something she excelled at. It was just too hard for her. She still hated the men who set the traps. She knew they were Sassenach soldiers trying to catch one of the shape shifters. If she had not come along when she did, the big cat could have been theirs. They would have caged him. Taken him to London to show off as if he had no feelings. She felt sure the cat would have been trapped forever. He would have died in the tiny cage they intended for him. She'd seen one when she was in the village near the McKenna keep. What she'd never thought was that she would be able to help one of the shifters.

She thought she might be afraid of the big cat. She learned quickly there was nothing to be afraid of. Now, she wanted to see a man shift, to once more meet his cat form. He wouldn't admit to being a shifter. If she asked, she would shock him to the core.

If she did, she knew she would recognize the cat then know the man. At the moment she just had guesses. She wanted proof.

Didn't dare.

The snow from last night was slowing her down. In places the drifts came up to her knees. Her skirt would be soaked by the time she got to his office. She was sure Shadow passed on early this morning. The terrible feeling of loss swept over her when he left this world.

His passing was for the best.

Shadow wouldn't suffer any longer. The doctor promised he would feel no more pain. She trusted him implicitly. He would keep Shadow content. She believed him with all her heart. Selfishly, she thought about her loyal companion. She wouldn't have anyone to go to her refuge with her.

More than an hour passed before she saw the village houses below her. When she passed by the MacKay house, Brenda was at the sink washing dishes. She waved to her, calling her inside.

Leah didn't want to spend the extra time to say hello. She knew she should do that. Brenda was always so nice to her. Brenda would want her to have a cup of tea and chat for a time. She could do that on the way home. Brenda would understand when she told her what happened to her dog.

When Brenda opened the door with the youngest baby on one hip, the scent of yeasty fresh baked bread wafted out to her. Leah's stomach grumbled. She'd not eaten this morning. It wasn't because she forgot. It was because she didn't want to take the precious seconds for food.

"Come inside," Brenda waved her in. "Have a cup of tea with me along with a slice of warm bread, some honey also. You look near to frozen to death."

"Can it wait for an hour or so? Have to go see the doctor." Leah knew Brenda heard the sound of her stomach as it growled. There wasn't anything she could do about that.

"You're not sick, are you?" With her free hand, Brenda touched her forehead. "Shouldn't be going to see the doc unless you're sick. You're not warm." Brenda bounced her youngest on her hip while she stepped back as if she hoped Leah would walk inside.

"No, he took care of Shadow for me. I think my dog is gone now." Leah couldn't stop the rise of tears to her throat. "Have to go see if he made it through the night or if I need to help bury him."

"Well, you can hurry back. We'll have tea. You can talk about it if you want. Tell me what happened. He was an older dog. Nevertheless, he didn't seem sick to me," Brenda said softly a hand on her arm. "It was that nasty old man you call your stepfather, wasn't it?"

"No, he wasn't sick. We can talk after I see to him. Say my goodbyes you know. He was the dearest animal to me. I've had him for as long as I can remember."

"Here, you just wait a second." Brenda hurried to the loaf of bread sitting on the kitchen table. After slicing a large chunk then slathering the bread with butter, she handed it to Leah. "There now your stomach won't be grumbling the rest of the morning."

"Thank you, I'm certain this is delicious," she said softly. "I'll be back as soon as I can. If you don't have the time then, I'll understand."

Leah didn't look back as she ate and walked. She thought of the dog. Thought of Houston. He seemed so familiar to her. She wished she could figure out how she knew him, if he was indeed the shifter she freed. He was from that part of the highlands. All the facts pointed to that supposition. The cat could have been any one of his brothers. No matter how hard she tried, she couldn't make all the ends meet. Maybe she should ask him.

No, she didn't think that would be very ladylike. In any case, she didn't know how to pose the question. One didn't just ask a man if they knew them or if they could change from man to cat then back again. Her mother would certainly die a second time if she thought she was doing something so forward.

Her mother always told her she was different. She supposed she was. Just like Stick was different. No, Stick was strange.

Stop it, Leah. You're being small minded. Stick is your friend.

She didn't understand why she had mean thoughts about a friend. She didn't tease him like the others in the village. She would never do that. Others in the town were terrible to him. Called him names behind his back. She supposed calling him Stick was teasing.

She never knew his real name.

Perhaps she should ask him. Leah wondered if Stick even knew his real name.

Finishing the bread, she picked up her skirts, hustling down the street toward Doc's office. She passed by the newspaper. When she peered inside, she didn't see Grizzly. When she left he wasn't at home as she'd expected. She hoped he was at work somewhere in the building. They could use the money. Although Grizzly usually picked up the supplies they needed. At least he did that once a week. They weren't starving. She made a few coins when she babysat for Brenda.

Brenda gave her eggs to take home when they had extras. That wasn't very often with her growing nest of children. A child, that was a wish of hers. She wanted a baby someday. She didn't think that would happen, at least not anytime soon. The prospects of a husband here in Selkirk weren't good. Except for Michael Graham, there weren't any men for her. She wasn't going to wed Michael despite his overtures.

She didn't love him.

She learned from her mother you didn't wed someone unless you loved him.

There was Houston though. She felt a lot of things for him. Things she shouldn't be thinking about. After all, she'd only spoken to him once. He told her he didn't fix animals, only people. Certain he was a shifter, she thought perhaps he might have to use his abilities to that end.

When she knocked on the door to his office, there was no answer. She walked around the building then into his yard. The yard was large. He was at the very back. He was bent over, shoveling dirt. She knew then what she felt early this morning was Shadow's death. The dull pain in her stomach throbbed again. Unshed tears spiked her lashes. Damnation!

Houston kept him comfortable. Now he was digging his grave. She needed to help. She swallowed a shaky breath of air. Now those tears slipped down her cheeks again. It seemed she'd been crying off and on for hours.

His eyes were closed. He was leaning on the shovel. Shadow's body was wrapped in the blanket Houston covered him with last night. She set her hand on Houston's back. Heat along with other sensations radiated from him into her. She gasped and stepped back. The strong energy between them surprised as well as confused her.

When he stiffened then turned, his silver-blue eyes simmered for an instant boring into hers. He arched an eyebrow. "Leah, I'm sorry. Shadow was comfortable. Passed on early this morning. He didn't suffer."

"You kept him snug and happy..."

"Yes," he spoke softly.

She had this strange feeling he wanted to hug her to comfort her. She wanted that too but understood he wouldn't act on the feeling. "I sensed his passing. Knew what I would find when I could make it down the mountain."

"You did? Now why am I not surprised?"

His smile was slow and infectious. Even now with all the sadness, the grin was warm as if he understood her grief and wanted to help. "Would you like to say goodbye?"

Unable to form words, she nodded then kneeled down next to the covered form. She pulled back the blanket. Her fingers stroked Shadow for the last time. She touched a knuckle to the corner of her eye in a feeble attempt to sop up the moisture threatening. It was a useless act. Ribbons of water slid down her cheeks.

Houston stepped back seeming to give her the space she needed. When she stood, she nodded to him again. "I had hoped. When you spoke to me before I left last night, I understood he wouldn't live until morning. He's not in pain now. That's good. I should help."

"No, it's almost done."

"All right." She thanked him again then started to leave. Leah turned back, "I forgot something." A rumpled package was in her hand. She handed it to him. "For you. It's just a small thank you for your kindness."

"Stay. Come inside where you can warm up before you start up the mountain again. You are going home after this." He turned back to the chore of burying Shadow.

"Yes. Brenda asked me to stop and talk. I can come inside with you first, at least until you have a patient. I'd like someone to talk to."

She wanted to be with him for a bit longer. He gave comfort to her just by being. She knew she shouldn't think anything about it. He was a man. She didn't understand so much about men and women. She thought perhaps she should talk to Brenda so she could find out what these emotions might mean.

"Go on now. I'll finish here then meet you upstairs in the sitting room. If you like you can put a pot of water on to boil. I've muffins Mrs. MacKay left yesterday. You can have some. Help yourself. Whatever you want."

Leah looked one last time at the covered form then turned. She walked up the porch steps to his home. He lived above the office. There were two ways to go. She chose to walk through the office then up the inside stairs to the sitting room. She'd been there last night when he covered Shadow and gave him the opium to keep him comfortable.

She set the pot of water that was on the stove to heat before she sat down in the kitchen. Restless, she stood, walked around the room. There wasn't much to see. She supposed he didn't cook much. Some of his patients paid him with money, some with food or other services. She picked up a portrait of a beautiful dark-haired woman with blue eyes.

"It's a portrait of my mother," from behind her, he spoke softly.

Startled, she dropped the portrait to the table feeling foolish and jealous. She didn't like that feeling. There was nothing to feel jealous about. She didn't mean anything to Houston. She was glad the woman was his mother and not a girlfriend. "I'm sorry. I didn't mean to snoop. Thought she might be a girl friend or fiancée."

"I agree. Brenna Stuart is beautiful. My father thinks so too. He's very possessive, you understand." He unwrapped the scarf around his neck then took off his coat. He helped her with her coat before hanging the coat on the stand by the door. She found that he was staring at the hem of her dress. Embarrassment flooded her cheeks. He would see all the lines around the bottom, would know the number of times she let the hem down. There was no more fabric to do so again. She caught his gaze with her own. Flush heated her cheeks.

"Of course, he would think that," she murmured softly while she wondered what was truly going on in his head.

"You're a beautiful woman," he told her. At her second round of heated cheeks, she looked down, "I'm sorry, that was too bold of me. Sometimes I say what's on my mind without thinking that my words might be embarrassing. Will you forgive me?"

To Leah, Houston looked as if he wasn't the least bit contrite. "At times I do the same," she said smiling at him. She felt silly as well as a little girlish as she didn't know how to talk to a man. "Don't see how you can think I'm beautiful. I'm such a mess." She pressed her hands along the sides of her dress.

He touched the bottom of her chin, lifting slightly, his eyes shining with something indefinable to Leah. "You're the most beautiful woman I've ever set eyes on. Who are you truly, Leah Kennedy?" His voice was soft when he asked the question, his eyes darkening now with a light she didn't ken.

The question as well as the look startled her. She didn't know how to answer anything like that. The question seemed personal yet the answer was obvious. "Leah Kennedy, that's all. That's who I am. I'm just a girl who lives up on craggy mountain."

"No, it's more than that. I'm going to make it my mission to learn about you. Everything about you. You know things others do not. I've this sixth sense about you. Even though I'm a doctor and I'm not supposed to believe in things beyond the five senses, I do."

At his words a tremor swept through her. She thought she should tell him what she *kenned* about him. Perhaps it was too soon. Shifters didn't like it when others they didn't trust knew about their abilities, could identify them. Houston wouldn't be different. He had no reason to trust her. She could uproot his life in a blink, if he let himself become vulnerable.

From her experience shifters were suspicious. They had to be. That was why when she helped the panther from the steel trap, she didn't go with him. Never saw him in his human form. She would have liked to though. The other reason she didn't follow him was that she would have seen him naked. Once again heat flooded her cheeks.

"A penny for your thoughts, Leah. That time I didn't say or do anything to cause the color to rise on your cheeks. What are you thinking about?" His knuckles grazed her cheek.

Shivery sensations filled her. It seemed he might well be able to read her mind. She prayed he could not. "Could not tell you. In the telling I would embarrass myself again."

He roared with laughter, clearly enjoying her discomfort. "I would not have that even though I laughed. Laughing was not well done of me.

Nonetheless, you amuse me in a tender sort of way. It was the expression that swept your angelic features when you said the words that made me laugh. You are a rare gem of a woman. Did you have wicked thoughts about me? For some unfathomable reason I'd like to believe so."

His words came way to close to the correct conclusion. The devil, she was in over her head and drowning fast. If wanting to see him naked constituted a wicked thought then yes, she did. She looked up from her clutched hands. "I believe the water is boiling."

"That it is. Sit down. I'll serve you. Have a muffin. I won't be able to eat all those before they spoil. Mrs. MacKay is way too generous. Either that or she truly believes my stomach is larger than it is."

"Brenda is one of the sweetest, nicest women I've ever met." She thought she should try one before her stomach started to grumble again. "I *ken* they will be delicious. Brenda is also a marvelous cook. She tells me that is why her husband fell in love with her and married her." Leah was thrilled to have a change of subject.

Houston set the cups filled with tea on the table. "It's hot. Be careful. Wouldn't want you to burn yourself."

Leah picked up a muffin, slowly breaking it apart. It was delicious. Holding her breath for a moment, she wondered at her decision to pry into Houston's life. Before she asked, she slowly let the air out of her lungs. It was a precious question to her. One she desperately wanted to learn the answer to, "How did you hurt your foot?"

She felt his pain as if it was hers. His gaze narrowed as his lips thinned. It was obvious to her he didn't want to answer the query. He drew in a long-ragged breath of air, held the precious oxygen for what seemed an eternity to her before letting it go.

He waved his hand in the air, dismissing the request. "It was nothing. I was a foolish young man. Did something I was warned against."

"You limp. The accident or whatever happened must have been horrendous. Painful."

She meant to continue on this vein until she learned more. Meant to discover the truth he didn't want to reveal.

If not today mayhap another one.

His voice harsh now, he pulled in a deep draught of air. "It was nothing. Makes no difference any longer. I limp. That's a fact. There is little I can do to change my circumstances."

The cut was deep and quick. Still, she persisted. "Were the bones broken? How many?"

"If you must know. Yes. Bones on all five toes on some of the smaller toes, more than one." His answer was curt, dismissive. It was obvious he was finished.

Leah understood she outstayed her welcome in his home. She should leave before he tossed her out. "I'm sorry. I'll go."

She was too upfront too uncaring. The pain she inflicted by her abusive question was obviously intense. He didn't like the fact he walked with a limp.

"Finish your tea. The accident happened a long time ago. The bones were set poorly. Never truly healed. That's why I hobble."

"An incompetent bone-setter," she murmured remembering the one in the highlands who often did more harm than good. She was certain the man set the panther's bones, the one she rescued.

Are you Houston? Are you the panther I rescued?

"Yes. Did that accident have anything to do with your wanting to become a doctor?" she asked understanding the great sense of worth when a patient was healed.

There were the losses though. That was different.

"I suppose in part. From the time I could walk, I wanted to make everyone better. I would take in animals who were hurt."

Just like me.

He stopped smiling at her. "I know I said I didn't heal animals. That's all true. I don't any longer. Now what about you? What do you do day to day up there on your craggy mountain?"

The air she sucked inside hurt. He was too astute by far. Had someone told him about her refuge or implied she healed wounded animals? About the animals she healed before sending them on their way? This time she understood her private space was invaded. Somehow with Houston she didn't mind.

"I..."

This time his grin was wide showing even white teeth. She felt a delicious tremor of something shuffle languidly through her body. The need to reach out and touch his mouth swamped her. She wondered if he had similar feelings.

"I?"

"Should be going now." She stood up so quickly her chair toppled. With fumbling hands, she turned to right the damage. He was beside her, propping up the chair.

"Let me."

He stood so close to her. His breath ruffled across her face. She caught his scent. Everyone, person or animal had its unique smell. She remembered this one. It was pleasant, filling her senses. She swallowed the lump that hovered in the back of her throat while wondering what it would feel like if he kissed her.

His cook and house cleaner walked into the room. Her scowl of disapproval sent Leah scrambling for her coat.

"Best be going." She was out the door before he could say or do anything to stop her.

~ * ~

Her cheeks were still flushed when she sat at Brenda's kitchen table sipping tea. Brenda stared at her for the longest time wondering what had her so over heated. She'd never seen Leah quite like this. She was fumbling with her napkin. Her hand shook when she brought the cup of tea to her lips.

"If I didn't know better, I'd be thinking that you're in love with someone," Brenda said as she set a plate of muffins in front of her. "Oh my, it's not Michael Graham, is it? He would never do for you, although from what you've told me, he seems to think otherwise."

Leah choked on her tea. "I don't *ken* why you'd be saying something like that. You know how I feel about Michael as well as his friends. They aren't very nice. You better than anyone knows I won't wed someone I don't love." She picked a part another muffin, the crumbs falling on the napkin.

"Then whom do you have your eyes set on?" Brenda asked as she waggled a finger at her. "I know by the look in your eyes linked to the way you're acting there is someone."

"Have you ever had this feeling you've met someone before?" Leah asked, her sigh causing Brenda to look more closely.

"Like as a few months before or years?" She handed a quarter of a muffin to one of her toddlers who promptly sat down on the floor to eat. "Sometimes, Leah, you say things I've no understanding. You are so different, unique. This rareness is what makes you so very special."

Leah pulled her braid over her shoulder, running her hand down its length. "More like in another life time."

"Speak o' the devil, something like that's not possible. Who do you think you might have known in another life?" Brenda had her hands on her hips as she was tapping one foot. Now shaking her head, "You're a fey creature, Leah. I've no idea what you could be rambling on about. Still, I love you as if you were my own daughter."

Leah brushed some of the crumbs into the palm of her hands before taking them to the sink. "I didn't say I knew someone in another lifetime. It's just I've this feeling I can't shake. I feel as if there is a closeness that can only come from knowing someone before this lifetime. I don't understand it either."

"Who is it?"

Leah looked down the road toward Houston's office. "The doctor. There is something so familiar about him. I can't shake the feeling I've met him before. I understand it's not possible. Until he came to the village, I'd never seen him."

"You're in love with the doc? Isn't he a little old for you?" Brenda asked before shaking her head. "No, probably not. I keep on forgetting that you aren't the wee little mite who came here five years ago. You're a grown woman. Doc Houston is older though."

"No, I'm not. I'm twenty. That's old enough to be in love. He would have to return that sentiment. Wouldn't he? He doesn't." Leah looked down then up to meet her gaze a challenge in her eyes. "What's it like to have a man kiss you? I *ken* you must know."

Brenda was thinking Miss Leah was in over her head if she was thinking about kissing. Yes, she did know a lot about kissing. Her husband could never keep his hands to himself or his wickedness in his pants. "Well, it's real nice. Despite what I say about kissing, don't you be getting any notions in that pretty little head of yours. That man is experienced. I'm certain of that fact. He's had more than one woman as a lover in his lifetime. You're an innocent in every way. He could use you. After that take advantage of the fact you don't *ken* anything about how a man and woman go about things."

Shrugging, it looked as though she thought about her future. "One can't stay innocent forever. I know I'd like him to kiss me. Perhaps more except I don't know what more is. Maybe you could tell me." Leah was looking at her with wide, hopeful eyes.

Brenda set the baby down in the little pen she used to keep the child from getting into too much mischief while she worked. "You don't have a mum to talk with about these things. I'm not sure how helpful I can be. Never spoke about lovemaking with an innocent *lass*."

Leah lifted her slim shoulders in a gesture that went straight to Brenda's heart. "No, I don't, as you *ken* I lost my mother. Obviously, you know what goes on between a man and a woman. I'm not stupid. I've seen how animals mate. For starters, I'd like to know if it's the same between a man and a woman."

"It's not. Well, it can be. No, this isn't what I'm trying to say. You've put me in a very uncomfortable position. One I didn't think I would be in until Fiona got a few years older. Haven't given it much thought. Not really sure what should be said along with what shouldn't be said to a young woman. A man wants to play a part in educating his woman. Now, what I am going to tell you is that you're not under any circumstances getting into bed with Houston Stuart. That would be a grave mistake. Doing so might have repercussion you would come to regret."

Leah was nodding, her eyes wide seeming to take in everything she told her. "So, if I don't get into bed with a man...then nothing bad will happen. Is that right?"

"Now, I didn't quite say that. I did say that but you shouldn't lie down with a man anywhere," She was getting more flustered by the second. "You can even do it standing up." The devil, her man had made love to her everywhere including the kitchen table. She could never say no to him. He never took precautions. Both docs told him he would have to start doing that, taking precautions. A woman's body just couldn't take having that many babies.

"You're confusing me. I haven't even been kissed yet. There is no reason to think Houston even wants to kiss me. He did lift my chin so he could look into my eyes. Thought at that moment he might kiss me. He didn't."

"Perhaps we should go at this from a different direction," Brenda said, sipping in a bit of air as she thought. She found herself totally embarrassed by the topic at hand yet she supposed it was good practice for when her daughter was older.

"What direction would that be? I'd like to know?" Leah was leaning on the table, her forearms stretched out in front of her.

"What you can let a man who is not your husband do as well as what you should not let him do."

That felt better. Brenda understood how her husband coaxed her so very gently the first few times they were together. She knew he loved her. He still took advantage of her innocence. Sometimes, she wondered how she could be innocent still after having so many children.

"I'm interested in what I can let him do. That is if he even wants to do anything," Leah said her eyes simmering and eager to learn.

"You can let him kiss you. Kisses are fine." She shook her finger, "However, don't let him think he can kiss you anywhere except above your shoulders. If he goes lower and tells you he's not kissing you just caressing, you've got to tell him no. When he does something like that the kisses can lead to other things including a possible baby in your belly."

"What if I don't want him to stop? I'm thinking about the way that would feel. Thinking about his lips on me makes me quiver. Why, I've got goose bumps on my arms."

"You just remember what I told you. Same goes for his hands. Don't let them go beneath your skirt or...don't let him touch your breasts. If you do, it will be harder to make him stop. Once you pass a certain point, saying no becomes very nearly impossible."

"Can't I just say the words?"

"The devil, I remember the first times Seamus tried that. I nearly swooned. I just managed to tell him no but I didn't want him to stop. He chuckled then told me next time all I would be able to say is please."

"Was he right?" she asked, smiling as if she was thinking about Houston touching her.

"No, he wasn't. The time after that though..."

"I *ken* a man you like a lot is hard to resist. A man as handsome as Houston must be impossible."

"Seamus was impossible. Managed to keep my innocence almost until the wedding night. Just barely."

Brenda felt a little dreamy at the moment thinking back all those years ago. Sometimes when he made love to her, it still felt like the first time.

"I don't know if I would want to stop Houston. Seems I'm not going to have a husband. If I could have those feelings just once, I'd be content for the rest of my life."

Brenda poked her finger at her. "Don't go thinking that way. What would you do if you got with child? Old Grizzly would set you out on your arse. You *ken* it. That pious old man wouldn't give you one consideration. Would think the devil spawned the child. Where would you go? What would you do?"

"I don't know. Guess it's pretty silly of me to be thinking along those lines when I've nowhere of my own to call home. Always said I don't want to need a man to take care of me. Don't want to do what my mother did."

"No, you don't. Now, it's not so farfetched to think Doc Houston might be interested in you. You're a beautiful girl. You be careful though. Sometimes men of wealth use girls who are poor to ease their bodies. I'm not saying the doctor would do that though it's always a possibility."

"He wouldn't do that, use me."

Brenna knew Leah was sure that was the truth. He would never use her to get what he wanted. "Hawk would hurt him if he did. I've known Hawk for as long as I've been here. He is the nicest and handsomest man I know except for Houston."

"If you come to him willing and eager, he might not think he's using you, that's a fact. Men don't think very well when they're around a woman they want." Brenda saw the dreamy look in Leah's eyes. Knew if Houston took a shine to Leah, she was in trouble.

"I've listened to you, Brenda, every word. If anything like that happens, I'll do as you say."

"I certainly hope so." But she had a bad feeling about this.

Chapter Three

Houston wondered where the month and a half slipped by. It was the middle of February. Hawk visited two weeks ago, telling him he was wrapping up his plans to take over the practice here in Selkirk. It might be another month or more before he could stay here permanently. They decided Houston should wait another month after that before he left for Edinburgh.

All that time Houston thought constantly about Leah Kennedy. She was in his mind most every second of the day. He hadn't seen her though. Didn't think she'd come down from the mountain. One time he was sure he saw her walking along Downy Street.

Other than that...

It wasn't her. He missed her. He wasn't sure why. Perhaps it was her smile. Maybe it was just the way she looked at him with those bluer than blue eyes.

Time was running out for him. The only way he was going to get to know her better was to go up the mountain. A house call might be in order. He wanted to see how she was doing after the death of her dog. His was a flimsy excuse. Nevertheless, Houston knew the fact for what it was. She would still be mourning the dog.

Today was Valentine's Day. A little gift might be appropriate. When he unwrapped the package she gave him the day Shadow passed on, he found a bouquet of wild flowers along with a coin for payment. He wouldn't have taken the coin had he known the money was part of the package. He assumed what was in the tiny bundle was something else to eat.

From the village store he bought an assortment of hard candy as well as sugared nuts he thought she might like. He found a paper covered box his mother sent him that once held candies. He put the things he bought inside the box before tying the gift with colored ribbon, blue ribbon, the shade of her eyes.

In the field behind his house, he picked a bouquet of Daphne then tied them with the left-over ribbon. His heart pounded in his chest. His palms were sweaty. He didn't ever remember being this nervous when he courted a girl. The devil, he was thirty-one. He shouldn't be feeling this way.

This beautiful lady was different though.

She meant something to him he didn't understand. When he was with her, he always had this distinct sensation she knew something about him. Now that his time here in Selkirk was running out, he needed to figure out just what it was she meant to him if anything.

Houston dressed in his doeskins along with a white shirt that was laced in front. It was warm out, the sun shining. Not one cloud appeared in the sky. The day was perfect for whatever transpired. He knew the temperature would drop with the sunset. For now, he carried his heavy coat under his arm. He rode his horse up the mountain. He passed the Fletcher house. Twice he'd been there to see to the children. After that he understood why Leah gave them food. She didn't have that much herself yet she was generous to a fault.

When he reached her home, all was silent. She had to be there. Where the devil would she be if she wasn't home? Before he headed up the mountain, he checked at the MacKay household for her. Dismounting then tying the reins to the rail of the small house, he walked up the porch to knock on the door.

No one answered. He swore softly to himself, thinking she might be at her refuge. He didn't know where that was. Couldn't be too hard to find though. A path had to be close by that would lead him there.

He was right. When he heard the soft footfalls, he saw her. She was striding toward the cabin, her legs long, her skirt swirling around her showing off slim ankles.

"Miss Leah," he said his voice gruff.

She jumped startled to see him. "Houston? She blushed.

He heard the part she didn't say which was what are you doing here? "Thought you might want to go for a walk. It's a nice day. I brought something for you, a small gift. Is Grizzly here?" He stretched out his hand to give the small package to her.

"No, he's still at work or...or somewhere else. He doesn't come home much anymore. When he's here, he's meaner than before." Her shoulders quivered as she accepted the gift. "What is it?"

"Open and see." He couldn't help the besotted grin he bestowed upon her.

She did, her eyes shining. "I don't get many gifts." There was a pause while she finished with the ribbons. "Candy?"

"Do you like sweets? It's Valentine's Day you know."

She looked down. "I didn't expect anything. Yes, I do like sweets. I don't have anything for you. Will you share?"

"One, the rest are for you."

"A hard candy or a nut?" She popped one of the sugared nuts into her mouth chewing slowly while her eyes seemed to cross with pleasure.

"Hard." When she picked one up, he opened his mouth. Hesitating, she placed it on his lips. He touched her fingers with his lips and tongue before the candy made its way into his mouth. He sucked thinking he would like to suck her fingers, her breasts along with every other part of her. "Now, why don't you put that box somewhere Grizzly can't find it?"

"Yes, I don't want to share with him." She stopped on her way into the house then turned, "That's not very nice of me, is it?"

"They are meant for you not your stepfather," he told her thinking she looked adorable when she frowned. Even when she received a gift she was thinking of others.

"Yes, well..."

When she returned, he held out his hand to her, ginning, "A walk maybe? Where can we go?" He was still holding out hope she would take him to her healing spot. Wanted to see her wildlings as Hawk called them. Jealousy that she trusted Hawk more than she did him filled him even while he told himself he was with her now. Hawk didn't seem to have a romantic interest in her. Perhaps she wasn't attracted to Hawk either.

"By the river would be nice. There is a path leading up the mountain that's easy to follow. If you're here when Grizzly gets home, he'll be madder than a hornet. Maybe a walk isn't such a good idea."

"Would you rather go into town? I could buy you dinner."

He wouldn't mind holding her in front of him on his horse. Her being close to him was something he lost sleep over. He thought if he could just hold her or kiss her, he would remember how he knew her. The memory plagued him waking as well as sleeping.

"That might be better." She was quick to say as she started back inside. "I'll get my coat."

"He doesn't hurt you, does he? I know I've asked that before..."

She held back answering for a few seconds. He didn't like the look of fear he saw in her eyes. She was holding truths inside her. "I'm afraid of him."

"Has he hurt you?" He meant to persist until he heard a viable answer.

"If he does, I'll leave. He doesn't want me here. He doesn't like me either. All he wants is his dinner on the table. Thought I might go to the highlands where I used to live before we came here."

"Where was that?" he asked, hoping her answer would shed more light on his feelings for her that sense they'd met sometime before. He didn't think he could leave her if he didn't figure this out. Sometimes when he thought on it, he wasn't sure he could leave her at all.

"Between Balvaird and Inverness."

He smiled wide. She lived near the McKenna keep. Most likely knew of them. Maybe he'd seen her in the nearby village or when he was out with his brothers or when he...when he found himself caught in a steel trap. He couldn't shake the feeling. That thought bothered him more than any other possibility. It also served to make him feel confident she wouldn't reject him if she discovered he was a shifter. If that was the case, she was not afraid of big cats. Perhaps she knew he was a shifter. Forcing himself to stop the wild wanderings of his brain, he returned his attention to the moment at hand.

"Let me help you up, *lass*."

He did so. Then he was behind her. They were heading toward the village. His hands spanned her waist. Heat from her pulsed between them sliding from her into him then back whispering against him. Giving him thoughts he shouldn't have.

Enticing.

Fascinating.

Intriguing.

She was all that. He understood this contact was more than it should be. He swallowed the lump growing in the back of his throat. He was leaving. He couldn't have her. He certainly wasn't going to make love to her then abandon her to fend for herself if he got her with child. Not like Walker Endicott did with his cousin, Crissie. No, he couldn't do that.

"I was talking to Brenda MacKay the other day," she murmured softly, the back of her head resting on his chest. He never thought a contact like that could feel so intimate, so very right. He wanted to hang on to this moment forever. "She told me some things. I suppose I'm being too bold. Nevertheless, I heard you were leaving here, selling your practice to Hawk."

"And what were the two of you speaking of? It wasn't just my practice, was it?" Gently he squeezed her waist, gauging her reaction. Thinking they might have spoken of other things.

She pressed her body closer to him. "Hmm...what a woman should let a man do and what she shouldn't." Her voice trailed off evolving into a whisper of air.

He chuckled thinking he might enjoy this conversation. In her own way she was exploring her sexuality while questioning. He was certain she was innocent. What he did know was that she didn't have anyone except Brenda to talk to about lovemaking. "What is that? I'd truly like to know."

"Told her I wanted to be kissed sometime. Is that outrageous? Too bold? Am I brazen? Grizzly would yell at me if he knew." She sighed and the sound was wistful. "A kiss or two would be nice from the right man. I'd have to find somebody who wanted to kiss me."

He wanted to kiss her and more. "It's natural for a woman to want a man, the right man, to kiss her. You have someone picked out? Or are you just fantasizing?" He hoped if she did have a suitor picked out the man would be him. Today, he meant to kiss her, taste the sweetness that was Leah Kennedy if she would allow him to do so. He'd thought of little else for over a month now.

It was Valentine's Day.

She was in his arms.

"Yes..."

What more could he want? He rubbed gentle circles at her waist, pressing slightly wondering too what she would allow. "Care to tell me who?"

"No."

"That's not very neighborly of you since I brought you candy and flowers. I hope you did put the box somewhere Grizzly won't find it." He wanted the conversation to return to kissing.

"He'll be too drunk when he comes home. If he comes home. All he'll want is the stew I left for him along with his whisky."

"For your sake I hope he doesn't come home. You don't need him. You should find some other place to stay." Somehow the conversation got off track. He meant to shoo the topic in the right direction if he could. "What else did Brenda tell you?"

It seemed she was softening, melting into him.

"She said I should never let a man kiss me or touch me below my shoulders. Seems as if you're doing that very thing right now." She squirmed slightly between his legs, pushing back against him.

He shrugged. Wondered if she could feel the movement of his fingers as they made gentle circles just above her waist. With great effort he kept them from roaming higher. "What I'm doing is harmless. You don't have to worry."

"Not so sure about that...harmless. What you're doing is making all these butterflies dance around in my belly."

"So," he spoke softly smiling at her reaction along with her innocence. "Is this something a man can do?" He moved her long braid to the side before brushing his lips on the back of her neck. He swept this tongue lightly across the space where his mouth rested. Shivers wracked her slender body pulsing against his chest as her fingers clung to his

60

forearms. Tiny nails bit into his flesh. He stopped as suddenly as he began.

"Well?" He wanted an answer to his question. If the answer was the right one, he would continue in this manner. If it was not, he would search out something else that would excite her.

"Y-yes..."

"...and? I *ken* there is something more you would like to say?"

"I didn't want you to stop. Could not tell you no. If it's alright, what will things that are not acceptable make me feel?"

"I don't know. How do my kisses make you feel?"

Ach, but he wanted to hear the words. He guessed more than she would say. However, she'd been honest about her conversation. Perhaps she would be just as honest about the sensations he created.

"So, tell me, sweet one." He wanted to push her to open up to him. "Should we try again so you can figure everything out?"

She nodded.

He laughed softly as he continued with the gentle exploration of her neck, turning her head with a finger so he could proceed along her jawline to a small ear. He bit then laved. His tongue swirled inside. She shivered against him, pressing back against his arousal. A soft purr rose from the back of her throat.

He knew then before he left her at home this evening, he would give her that kiss she wanted. His hand rose to beneath her breast. Touched the underside. Felt the soft movement as the horse caused her small breast to move lightly against his hand. He was hard pressed to keep the groan rumbling from his belly suppressed.

He stopped.

His hand drifted to the curve of her hip. He meant to prolong this delicate play for the entire night. She would know more with each passing second. Some of her questions would be answered before he left her at her door but not all. "You haven't answered. How did that make you feel?"

"I *dinna ken* if I can say. *Dinna* know if I have the words, the right ones in any case." Her voice trembled; shivered whisper thin into the soft breeze blowing around them.

"Tell me..." he coaxed knowing she would eventually say the words. "Please, I need to know if I'm doing this right. You would tell me if you don't like the way my hand feels."

"You couldn't do what you are doing any better if you tried," Her voice was thin and thready, barely there.

His smile widened as his heart pounded. His erection pulsed against his tight-fitting trousers. He adjusted slightly in the saddle to ease the pressure. These moments with her were both heaven and hell. He didn't remember if he'd ever denied himself his pleasure.

"Tell me," he continued smoothly, anticipating an answer he would appreciate. "Do my lips and teeth as well as my tongue make you hot or cold?"

He heard her sift in a deep breath of air. Felt her sweet little arse move against him, "H-hot."

His breathing hitched. "Good, that's very good. It's how it is supposed to make you feel. What else did Brenda tell you a man shouldn't do?" He bit gently on the side of her neck, sucked then laved before biting again. A soft pink spot appeared. He gave that same spot more attention while her body quivered and pulsed sending waves of pleasure into him.

She didn't answer. He wondered if she could remember or if he could slip his hand beneath her skirt. No, that would have to wait for another time. He was a patient man. He could wait.

"Well, he asked?"

"A man should not put his hand beneath my skirt." She could barely speak.

He wondered if he inched the skirt up so his hand wasn't beneath actual fabric if that would count. That would also wait for another time. He bent to give more attention to the spot on her neck that would remind her she was his at least for the time being.

"Besides hot how do you feel? Wet?"

"Wet?" she queried with a shaky voice. "I *dinna ken...*"

"If I touched you between your legs, would you be slick with moisture?" He understood he was embarrassing her, telling her things she might not fully comprehend. "Did Brenda tell you why you might find yourself wet after my kisses?"

"No, but I ache there. Is that what you want to know?"

"Yes, you've done very well. Perhaps we will continue this conversation over dinner or on the ride back to your home."

This was enough for the time being. If he didn't stop now, they would never make dinner. He was ready to explode.

"You aren't going to kiss me?"

She sounded so disappointed he thought for a moment he would relent, diverge from his plans of seduction. Sweet-talking was one thing, coaxing something else but seduction...not tonight. However, in the very near future if he had his way. He reminded himself he could tease and flirt. Reminded himself taking her innocence was unacceptable. Without feeling a moment of guilt, he could give her, her woman's pleasure though.

"We are here." He squeezed her waist.

"Oh."

"Are you disappointed?

"No, well yes, maybe."

He laughed then kissed her neck again, slowly sucked then bathed the spot one more time with his tongue. "We'll take this a bit farther after we eat. Would you like that? Hmm...?"

The one restaurant in the tiny village was in front of them. He dismounted then helped her down. She fit nicely against his body. Soft curves, rounded in all the right spots. The devil but he was enamored of her. Couldn't help himself. He held her a moment too long, pressing her belly against his swollen erection. He wasn't at all certain she understood what was happening to him or to her. Slowly she was softening while swelling, turning to liquid heat. He hadn't been celibate over the years. Suddenly, he felt as if all he wanted was to find a deserted alley, push her against the side of the nearest building then thrust himself into her secret depths. Needed to feel the rhythm of her body when he was inside her.

"Promise."

"Yes, now..."

He led her inside to a table near the back where he hoped they could continue the private conversation they started on their way down the mountain. Finding out what other interesting tid-bits Brenda MacKay told her would fill his curious brain. Houston decided he would have to stay within the bounds Brenda dictated the best he could.

He ordered.

Platters of food arrived filled to the top with bread and cheese, salmon, a variety of spring vegetables along with roasted potatoes. He enjoyed watching her eat. Willow thin, he knew she would fill out a bit if she had good food at her disposal. He wondered if she ate three times a day or just once.

She drank the wine he ordered then filled her plate a second time. He did the same.

"I've never eaten in a restaurant before," she told him, her smile reaching her eyes.

It was an experience he was thrilled to give her for the first time. There were other things he wanted to be the first to teach her. He wanted to show her the highlands where he grew up. Needed to give her a tour of Edinburgh and perhaps Inverness. Somehow, he thought, she might be his mate. He'd also thought the young lady who rescued him five years ago might be his mate.

Time would tell the true tale.

"What else did Brenda tell you?" he queried as he sat back, relaxed and replete, not wishing for the afternoon to turn to evening then end. As he turned his wine glass between his fingers he watched her carefully, trying to read all the subtle nuances that made up Leah Kennedy.

She stopped chewing then set her fork down. She sipped the wine, watching him over the rim. Seeming to think and speak clearer now that she didn't sit on his legs.

In a whispered voice she spoke, "Brenda told me not to lie down with a man. She got all flustered and confused before she told me she and Seamus had made love all kinds of ways; standing, on the kitchen table as well. I'm not supposed to do any of those things with a man. With you..." Her voice cracked with the last words.

He wanted to let his head fall back then howl with laughter. "But you would like to?" He arched a brow upward, understanding why Brenda and Seamus had so many children. The man couldn't keep his hands off his wife. In his defense, she couldn't tell him no either. He wanted the same when he wed. The need for this woman was growing at an outstanding pace.

"I don't know," Leah said. "I didn't *ken* most of what she was telling me. I might if you were willing to teach me."

He was more than willing. At the moment the evidence would be hard to conceal when he stood. The conversation was doing nothing to ease his lust for her. "It's because you're innocent. You should listen to her advice. She didn't tell you that you couldn't sit on a man's lap when they were riding? Did she?"

"No."

Thoughts of Leah riding him swamped him. If he wasn't sitting, the notions sifting through his poor man's brain would have sent him to his knees.

"Perhaps on the way home you could face me. Would you like that? It would be easier for me to kiss you."

She sucked in a long breath of air. "Y-yes I think I would like that? Can we go now?"

"We haven't had desert," he told her looking to the waiter. "I want this evening to be perfect. You must have your sweets."

"I don't think I can eat another bite of food," she said, "you ordered so much. I'm not even sure I can walk."

"I will carry you to the horse. You won't have to do anything."

~ * ~

"What are you doing here with doctor Stuart? It's not proper, Leah Kennedy. Since you're going to be my wife, I have to insist you act appropriately."

Michael's voice sounded harsh to Leah's ears. She didn't want to see Michael or talk to him. Didn't see why it was any of his business. At his words, heat flooded her cheeks.

Houston looked at her, a quizzical look in his eyes, "Leah is eating dinner with me. Not that it's anyone's business except hers and mine. I think she would have told me if she was engaged."

The tone in Houston's voice changed. The quality was no longer tender and gentle but harsh, harsher than Michael's. One black eyebrow arched toward the sky as he questioned.

She didn't want Houston fighting her battles for her. Not that this should be a battle. "Michael, I don't owe you an explanation. You and I both *ken* I turned you down for the party. What makes you think I would want to marry you?"

"Grizzly is not going to like you being with a man." Michael stomped back and forth between her seat and Houston's. "You *ken* I want you for my wife. You can't be seeing other men. I won't stand for it."

Exasperated, she looked from one man to the other. Houston now sat back, his long legs stretched out in front of him, arms crossed over his chest. His eyes were narrowed nevertheless she didn't think he was angry or concerned. It seemed he meant to let her tell Michael what she wanted.

His reaction pleased her.

"Michael," she began in a tone that sounded as if she talked to a child, "listen to me. I told you I didn't want to go to a party with you. Now I'm telling you I'll never be your wife. You've got to find someone else. You don't want a woman who doesn't love you."

"You could learn. Most people don't love each other when they marry." He still paced as he glowered at Houston then tried to smile at her.

Frist hand knowledge told her he spoke true. "No, I can't. It's not going to happen," Leah said adamantly. She hoped it wasn't to convince herself. "I don't love you."

Seeming to change tactics Michael spoke again, "What do you see in him?" He pointed a finger at the doctor. "What's he got that I don't? I certainly make more money than he does. Half the time he gets paid with food."

Her spine stiffened. She was truly angry at him now. What business did he have asking questions as well as maligning Houston? "I don't have a reason to tell you anything. Please go."

She wanted him to leave. He ruined this tiny bit of time she was treasuring with Houston. She didn't know when she would get more precious minutes with him. He wasn't going to change the best afternoon in her life or change the fact that Houston might kiss her tonight.

The devil, she wanted that kiss and maybe more if she liked the way his lips felt on hers. She knew she'd like the way his lips would feel after what they shared today.

"Need to protect you from him. He's too old for you. He's a poor man. He's going to take advantage of you, use you then leave. Everyone knows he's sold his practice to doctor Hawkins. Hawk's going to be here in a matter of days. What are you going to do then when he's gone?" His hands were waving in the air as he angrily pointed out things she never considered before.

Startled she turned to look at Houston. Had not known he was leaving in a few days. While she knew he sold his practice, she didn't expect him to vanish in the next day or two.

He nodded though the expression on his face told her he meant to talk with her about that. "I would have told you how soon I was leaving on the way down the mountain. However, we got sidetracked. My departure won't be in a couple of days, possibly weeks. I've too many things to take care of before I can leave. Michael will not be the first to know of my plans. I can promise you that," he said blandly as he looked pointedly at Michael.

Michael turned red seeming to understand what Houston was speaking of. He chose to ignore Houston's brief words.

"Just how sidetracked did the two of you get? I'm shocked at you, Leah. You're not that kind of girl. You are still innocent, aren't you? Never mind, it makes no difference to me. I still want you. Would want you if you'd had a dozen lovers. We both *ken* you have not."

"What kind of girl do you think I am?" she queried, her voice taking on a hard edge.

What right did he have to judge her? Everyone in town new he slept with Betsy on a regular basis. If the rumors were true, he also bedded Marie Hughes a week ago. How dare he question her morals?

"One who doesn't give her favors away to just anyone."

"I don't." She turned to Houston. "It's time to leave. Obviously, Michael believes he has a vested interest in me. He doesn't. I'm no longer comfortable here." She was boiling with anger along with mean thoughts.

She couldn't help herself though. They simmered and churned in her head. She wanted to tamp then down but couldn't.

Houston rose then slipped around to her chair. While she'd been talking with Michael, he paid the bill. There was nothing keeping them here. He placed her hand in his before leading her out the door. His hand holding hers comforted and warmed the ice Michael created. Her confidence grew a notch.

"I'm sorry," she told him, leaning into him as if that contact slight as it was would give her courage. "Didn't mean to ruin the evening for you. Don't understand why Michael is acting that way."

He squeezed her fingers then brought her hand to his lips to kiss the back. "No reason to make apologies. Although I'm curious why the young man believes you will be his wife. What do you say? Is there a reason? Is there something I should know?"

"I've never given him cause to think on those lines. Never." She grit the words out still furious with the man.

He rescued her once a long time ago. Now he thought he had rights.

He didn't.

"I believe you," he spoke softly as he helped her up then mounted behind her. She pressed back against him, reveling in the hard muscular planes of his chest. Her fingers wrapped around his forearms while he steadied the horse. The breath she pulled in was ragged and deep as she thought on the way Houston's touch made her feel. She was scared he would leave too soon. Terrified she would be left alone here on the mountain. The devil, she'd only known him for a short time. She had no right to think he might want something from her other than a dinner on Valentine's Day.

"I thought I was going to face you then you were going to kiss me," she spoke softly turning her head to look into the depth of his crystal-clear silver-blue eyes.

Finding herself melting beneath his gaze, she caught her lower lip beneath her teeth. Good Lord, she thought she was turning to mush inside. Her brain must be made of cobwebs. She couldn't think only feel. Paying attention to Brenda's words seemed more important now than ever before. She didn't want to heed them. Didn't want to think about them.

He kissed the tip of her ear then the tender sensitive spot behind it. A place she never knew existed. The caress sent heated shivers down her spine. "We are, just not until we get out of town. Don't want to ruin your reputation. What would the good people of the village think? If they saw us kissing?"

"I think Michael will make sure everyone knows we were dining together. He will also follow us at least a short distance."

"That my sweet innocent will not ruin your reputation. However, if the entire village saw us riding out of town with you straddled on my lap facing me, that would. Do you really think Michael will follow?"

"No, well, yes." She was hesitant to say the words. However, she was quite sure Michael was single minded when it came to her. He was proving to be just that. She turned to look around Houston's shoulder. "Yes."

Leah felt the stiffening of his shoulders. Heard the quick indrawn breath of air. "How far do you think he will go?"

With her eyes closed, she imagined Michael following them all the way to her place. He was a stubborn man, bent on his pleasures. Thought he could do and have anything he wanted. "I *dinna ken* why he thinks I'll change my mind." Most likely because she was so different from Houston.

They had nothing in common except their love of healing. He was educated. She couldn't read or write. His family wasn't like hers at least she didn't believe so since her's were dirt poor. Houston came from a loving family filled with doting parents who loved their children. He had siblings as well as cousins. Now that both her mother and father passed on, she had no one, not one sibling or cousin. Grizzly didn't count. She had no idea what a family should look like. Her's was certainly not an example to be shared.

Michael never failed to point those facts out to her when he was attempting to make his case for marriage. She was different from Michael too. It was just that he failed to acknowledge that point.

"How long do you think he'll stay close and watch us?" Houston repeated the question as his fingers tightened around her waist.

"Maybe to the Fletcher place. I doubt if he'll go farther. He's afraid of Grizzly and his shotgun. Of course, it might do for you to let me off at the Fletcher place. I could walk home. It's not far. Don't want Grizzly threatening you with that gun of his."

Houston chuckled softly.

She felt the deep rumbles from his chest vibrate her back. The feeling was pleasant not like the other sensations his lips and hands evoked. This man tapped energy within her.

"Would never do that. Grizzly won't hurt the only man in these parts who can help him ease his arthritis. Getting worse every time he comes to see me. So, you don't need to worry about his shooting me."

"You're pretty cocky. Grizzly might be smashed out of his mind. In that case he might not know who he's shooting at until after the fact. If our follower leaves, are you still going to kiss me?" For some reason she couldn't get that notion from her mind. All through dinner she thought of little else besides his lips on hers. Most of the time she watched them. Couldn't take her gaze away from his mouth.

"When he leaves, maybe after we pass the Fletcher place, I'll kiss you. Wanted to since I first picked you up this afternoon." He swept her long braid away from her neck.

She felt the soft touch of his lips, the moisture, a quick flick of his tongue. Her breath caught. Fingers that had been relaxed a second past, dug into his flesh. She squirmed back against him, her body coiling into his in anticipation.

"Houston..." She didn't *ken* what to say. Didn't have the slightest notion why he affected her the way he did. What she did understand was that she wanted him to keep doing what he was doing. Needed the feeling he generated within her as she also felt his reaction to her.

"What?" he asked sounding pleased as well as amused.

He understood what he did. That was something else that set them apart. He was experienced. She wasn't.

"I *dinna* think I can tell you." She couldn't because she didn't have the words.

"Ah, sweet *lass*, you can tell me anything. Speak to your heart's content. Will never judge."

He squeezed gently, squeezed her waist as he also stroked with his thumbs. Telling her he wanted more too.

"I don't have the words," she told him.

For the longest time they rode in silence. Her head rested against his chest.

She heard the beating of his heart, thought his melded with hers. For a small moment in time, she almost felt as one with him. Believed once she'd had the same sensations. The scent of pines filled the air then wood smoke as they neared the Fletcher cottage.

The fletchers were caught up in an argument. That was normal. A loud bang rippled through the air followed by swearing.

Leah shuddered, hating the arguments linked to the hurtful words that were always a part of them. Her mother and Grizzly fought all the time.

"You don't like confrontations?" he asked as he spurred the horse a bit faster as if he too wished to put as much distance between them along with the harsh words.

"No, I would just as soon avoid them whenever possible."

By the time they rounded the next curve soft forest silence met them, except for the usual sounds of the breeze moaning in the trees nothing else greeted them.

The scents changed to those of spring and warming weather. People didn't believe she could catch the scent of the changing season on the wind. The fragrance was there. All one had to do was breathe deeply while allowing their inner self to absorb nature within. Perhaps that was why so many called her a fey creature.

"Michael is gone, isn't he?" Houston asked, touching her nape once again with his lips, teasing her with the tip of his tongue, grazing her with his teeth. "He wouldn't fall back just to show himself later, would he?"

"Where he is concerned, I would never be surprised. He might even return to town and find his pals to come up the mountain with him. I doubt it though. He's more likely to ease his frustrations with Betsy tonight. Don't know what he expected to get from me."

Perhaps a little of what you're giving Houston which isn't much.

She understood from what Brenda told her there were a lot of things men and women did together.

"Come, *lass,* I'm going to turn you around. Help me."

He lifted. She swung her legs over his. Now she sat astride him. Her body seemed to be open to his. His gaze burned hot and fierce when he looked into her eyes. Her dress rose on her legs, leaving them bared from her thighs down to her feet.

A lump of apprehension rose in the back of her throat. She tried to recite in her head all the things Brenda told her not to do. Every last one of those things vanished in a brain filled with mush. Her gaze was fixed on his simmering silver-blue eyes. They were liquid heat, a fire seemed to blaze from them into her.

It seemed he focused on her lips. She swept her tongue between them and across, leaving moisture behind.

"Do you want that kiss now?" Lightly, he touched her bottom lip with his thumb. "You made yourself ready for me. Your mouth is moist and dewy. Do you *ken* how much I want to taste you?"

She felt ribbons of his warm breath whisper across her lips, leaving the taste of him. Sensed the heat sift through the air to her, moving from him into her. He was close so close. She didn't feel the pressure of his lips on hers. Knew the caress would come soon. Where her tongue ran across her mouth it was moist, slick. She did the same again. Couldn't help herself.

"What you do to me." Instead of his mouth on her, his thumb slipped along her bottom lip. "It's so plump and full. Where you wetted it, moonbeams glint off the moisture, shimmering with untold promise. You best keep Mrs. MacKay's advice at the forefront of your agile mind. The way I feel you'll be the one needing to tell me the words to stop me from doing as we both please."

"Advice?" she murmured questioning him.

His laughter wafted across her cheeks. He closed his teeth gently on her bottom lip, nipping then soothing with his tongue nipping again before pulling it deeply into his mouth. His taste was dark and sultry. When he pulled away to look at her, he was grinning.

"Was that a kiss?" She was disappointed it ended so soon.

"Thought there would be more."

Houston didn't answer. His brows drew together as he watched her with intensity that burned. This time he bathed her lips with his, claiming them, pulling them deeper into his mouth only to do the same again and again. Kissing his way across her mouth, running his tongue across the middle, seeming to ask for something from her.

When his hand settled on her naked thigh, she gasped sucking in air, attempting to breathe. Heat curled deep in the most intimate parts of her. He slipped his tongue inside her. It touched hers. An aching need of want settled into her between her legs where she was open to him. She pushed against him. Felt what she was sure was his member.

He sucked, pulling her tongue into the heat of his mouth. Her breath was tiny pants, sipping oxygen gingerly as she coiled against him, needing to feel more of what made Houston unique from her. Her fingers wound into his silken hair, tugging him closer. He could never be close enough. She closed her eyes, imagining all that he might do even though she had little to go on except what he wasn't supposed to do.

His lips opened wider, his tongue delving deeper. The wet slick moisture lingered everywhere.

It was decadent.

Enchanting.

Delicious.

One more time, he pulled away, breathing heavily, moving strands of her hair that escaped to lie across her face as well as her mouth so they were behind her ears. His lips were wet from the kiss. His fingers traced the shell of her ear. He followed with his lips, touching on every part even behind her ear. She tried to hold back the sounds of pleasure.

Could not do so.

"You taste so sweet," he murmured as he bathed her neck with the tender kisses he placed on her lips. He traveled across her collarbone, lower. The wetness left behind from his kisses lingered above the top of her corsage the soft breeze blowing down from the mountain touching the moisture cooling where his touch heated. He pressed lower, well below her shoulders.

She didn't care.

Could never tell him no. She understood that now. It was exactly what Brenda had been afraid of for her.

As if he recalled Brenda's advice, he was kissing her again. His mouth enfolded hers beneath his, sucked and pulled, teased and nibbled. With his fingers he found tender sensitive skin on her thigh, rose higher to her hip then back. She wanted him to never stop. Suddenly, her gown was pulled lower. The heat from his mouth possessing hers vanished to find purchase lower.

Her body shuddered deep inside understanding this magical enchantment would come to a halt.

"You're home. It's a good thing Grizzly is not on the front porch waiting for you. However, I've only compromised you a little." His chuckle reached into the *verra* marrow of her bones.

The sound pleased her.

"Perhaps you are right about Grizzly. You're a *verra* wicked *mon*, Houston Stuart. It seems you've done much of what Brenda warned me about. I've not one regret."

The sensation spawned by his coaxing caresses made her yearn for more. Now, he would leave her. Go back down the mountain. Soon he would be gone from the territory.

She would be alone with her thoughts.

Her memories would help her survive the rest of her life. If that was all, she was meant to experience more than a few stolen kisses.

"I never touched you beneath your gown and just barely below your shoulders. I've enlisted a great deal of strength of will to hold back. You entice me to be wicked, Leah Kennedy. Indeed, you do."

He helped her dismount, setting his hands on her waist. The emptiness of the ensuing days tugged at her soul. She no longer wanted to stay in this cottage with Grizzly. New adventures awaited her if she would act fast. She would have to be bold and brash.

Bold and brash was not in her nature. She was shy, reclusive.

If she stayed here without Houston, she was terrified she would end up wed to Michael, a man she could never love. She would be just like her mother. So many years ago, she vowed to live her life different from her mother.

When she looked at the small hut, she called home she cringed. What must Houston think? The door hung loosely by its hinges. Grizzly broke the front window two months ago in a drunken rage. She hung an oilskin over it to keep some of the cold along with the nastier weather outside. The steps to the porch were slanted and crooked. The first blush of embarrassment heated her cheeks.

"I suppose you can pat yourself on the back for all your restraint," she told him sweetly turning her face from him in the hope her skin would cool before he saw the effect he had on her. "I for one would have preferred it if you had been a *wee* bit bolder."

Houston tossed his head back roaring with laughter. "I can do that now if you're saying to me the truth." He grasped her by the waist then set her on the porch railing, which, thankfully was not falling apart or she'd find herself on her arse on the ground.

"Spread your legs, *lassie* so I can come closer. I find I don't want to leave you quite yet," he told her his voice throaty with what she assumed was desire.

He didn't sound like himself. His voice was dark, dangerous as well.

She did. He pressed against her. Once again, the fabric of her gown rose to her knees then a bit higher. His lips fell upon her neck as she arched to give him better access. She clung to his neck as he pushed her back farther. She didn't want to fall. Would most assuredly do so if he continued, bathing her with his kisses, holding her bottom in his hands, enfolding them squeezing.

Leah wanted to absorb all the magic of this evening she could. She was afraid she would never feel the wickedness again. He still didn't do anything except lave kisses along her neck, across her collarbone. She wanted him to possess her mouth again, suck her tongue inside the velvet warmth of his mouth. If she could taste him once more, caress his teeth then feel him plunge deeper, she would be happy.

A tiny moan of pure female pleasure rumbled up from deep in her belly. Ribbons of shivers quivered inside sensitive places that until now, until Houston, she never knew existed. Yearned for this delicious pleasure to go on forever.

This was heaven.

She prayed Grizzly would not come along to stop the sensual play between them. Grizzly might shoot first then ask questions.

He pulled back, smoothing her dress down her legs, looking with a simmering passion in her eyes at her lips. All he'd done was kiss her then make her want more, so much more.

"We need to stop before this goes too far. If that happens, you might come to regret what we've done," he murmured as his eyes blazed with unspoken desire.

"I *dinna* want to stop," her voice was paper-thin, needy in the extreme.

"I have to get home before it gets dark. Don't want to go down the mountain when I can't see what's in front of my face," he said his voice tender while he brushed his knuckles across her cheeks. "I don't like the fact you're staying way out here. It's dangerous. Would feel much better if you came down off the mountain, came into town."

She lifted her shoulders slightly. Often, she felt the same, "I've nowhere else to stay. Nowhere to go."

"The small one room house behind Seamus MacKay's house. You could stay there. I'm sure Brenda would tell you yes."

"No, they use it for guests. Because of his work, Seamus has them all of the time. I would only be in the way as well as an inconvenience. Besides, I've no money to pay them rent."

"I could give you a job."

"Doing what? There is nothing I can do for you. You've a cook and a housekeeper. *Ye* cannot fire either one." Leah didn't want her voice to tremble and shake. She couldn't stop it.

"I don't like this situation you're in. It's not right for a beautiful young woman."

She didn't either. Nonetheless, the mountain was her life. "I have to make do with who I am. I've no prospects at the moment. You *ken,* that except for Hawk I've no one to turn to. He's so seldom around."

At her words his eyes blazed. His fingers tightened where they still held her. She didn't understand the emotion she saw in the dark simmer of his eyes.

"Would you consider my suggestion if I lent you money to travel back to McKenna land. I could write a letter to my father. I'm sure there is work at the keep. He would speak to my uncle. You would have a safe place to sleep. A small room to call your own."

One moment her heart soared, the next it fluttered, falling to the ground. She wanted more than that. Needed to hear words that might make Houston a part of her life. All he wanted was for her to be safe. Nothing more. "*Aye*, but what would people think? I'm not going to compromise myself or your reputation."

"Nothing. They would believe you to be a friend who needed a job, a place to stay. You could work in the kitchen or cleaning. We employ many people."

"Where would you be?"

"In a week or two, I hope to be in Edinburgh. I believe you knew that."

"Then you're going home."

"*Aye.*"

"I'll consider your proposition." The thought was bold even while she understood for his sake, she would have to turn his suggestion down.

~ * ~

Houston spent the next two days showing Hawk around the area. He introduced the soon to be resident doctor to the people who would be his new patients. Leah was constantly on his mind. His beautiful fey, Leah. He couldn't leave her here to fend for herself. He didn't think she would take his money to go to his family home in northern Scotland. He didn't *ken* what to do.

So, how was he to solve this problem?

She needed to learn to trust him, not just Hawk. He well knew, he didn't offer her anything of himself had not shared his truth with her. Why would he hope for her trust? Telling her he wanted more from her than just kisses would not suit well with her. Even though from her reaction to him the other night he was certain she felt the same lustful stirrings. She would want love. At the moment, he didn't know what he had to offer her. When he moved back to the highlands, he would have to set up his practice. Start from the beginning.

Positive in one thing, he needed to find some way to coax her to use the groats he could provide for her. Thoughts of her staying here and wedding Michael turned his stomach sour. That just wasn't to be. He couldn't let that happen. She was his mate. As his mate anything except her coming to the highlands was untenable. Deep in the pit of his stomach he knew it to be true.

Leah was his.

She just didn't know it yet.

He didn't know how to tell her.

His current plans were put in motion before he met her, before he held her and kissed her. Before he knew he wanted her in his arms as well as his life for all eternity. She didn't believe she was good enough for him. What she thought was that they were far too different. In his family, wealth and privilege didn't count for much. In the scope of one's life it wasn't important. What was in a person's heart was the heart and soul that made up a relationship. Her heart was pure. From almost the first moment he saw her, he understood she was his mate. Now he needed to find a way to bind her to him before he left for his apprenticeship. Once his foot was healed, Hawk could see her to the highlands.

Hawk, the man who she told about her wildling, her refuge, the man she told him she could rely on to help her if she needed someone.

That man was supposed to be him.

He was jealous even though he knew Hawk never kissed her or touched her. Never sat on a railing while she spread her legs for him while she wrapped her arms around him sharing kisses.

No man save him had kissed her. He'd meant to see her sooner, yesterday to be exact. That wasn't to happen because he found himself caught up in delivering a baby who didn't want to leave the womb. The little tyke took more than twenty-four hours to make his way into the world.

Before he left, he had to have time with her. Needed some way to diminish her insecurity about herself. The devil, she was the most beautiful woman he'd ever seen.

Now he was heading home, with a puppy for payment in tow. Laughter bubbled up from his lungs. With all his skills, he was paid with a puppy he didn't want. He hoped Leah would cherish the dog. She loved animals. He also hoped Grizzly wouldn't be there when he arrived at the cottage or anyone else for that matter. He needed to be alone for two reasons. A private conversation with her about what she was going to do when he left as well as sharing another kiss or two.

When he sat down to eat, the puppy bounded around the kitchen. The little dog smelled everything. Houston gave him some of the prepared meet. She ate it up quickly then set herself down in front of the fire and promptly fell asleep on the rug. He stretched out on his chair, thinking.

Putting a plan in place was uppermost on his mind. First, he needed to speak with Hawk about his surgery as well as his place in Leah's life. He was sure Hawke's feelings for Leah were only friendship, platonic. He was certain that also was all Leah felt for Hawk.

Keeping Michael away from her was another matter entirely. The man craved her. Thought with perseverance she would be his.

When he left here, he would have no way to communicate with Leah, except through Hawk. He needed to make sure he could trust Hawk with her. He also prayed the new doc would understand his feelings. Hawk would be reading his letters to her. Until now he trusted the man implicitly.

The knock on the door surprised him. For a flash of a hopeful second, he thought it might be Leah. When he opened the door, Hawk stood on the porch, hands stuffed into his trouser pockets.

"I was just thinking about you," Houston said as he stepped aside to let Hawk inside.

"Were you now? Well, that poses some serious questions. "Good or bad?"

"Maybe a little of both," Houston said as he followed the man inside. "Want a drink?"

"Oh?" One of Hawk's brows lifted into a perfect arch. "Brandy would be fine since you're offering."

"One can image I was thinking of the surgery. In addition, I was also wondering if you would look after Leah while I'm gone."

"You trust me with her? I'm flattered." Hawk chuckled softly as he sipped the brandy he gave him.

"More than I could ever trust Michael. He's persistent when it comes to Leah. I don't trust him with her or anywhere near her."

"Maybe it's you who isn't trustworthy," Hawk's tone changed as he implied so much with those few words.

"What?" Houston bristled.

He'd done nothing to warrant that comment. What was in his mind when it came to Leah didn't count. She was his mate. What they did together on her front porch didn't count either.

"Around this town, gossip about you and Leah is spreading faster than one would expect." Hawk eyed him critically.

"Gossip? What kind of gossip?" He asked though he suddenly had a pretty good idea.

Anger sifted through him, pooling in his gut. How dare he?

"Someone saw the two of you kissing. Is there more to the story as was implied?"

"We had dinner then I took her home. I kissed her on her front porch. Damn, but Michael must have followed us all the way to her house. Michael spreading gossip about the woman he thinks he will marry isn't a wise idea. That fact could hurt his chances with her. Hell, it's a good thing for me."

"No, but I heard he thinks it will help his cause by dissuading you. He doesn't believe you could possibly want her. Are you using her?" Hawk asked his voice low, threatening. "If you are, I'll have to do something about that. She deserves better than abuse."

"Hawk, she's, my mate. I don't have doubt of that fact."

~ * ~

In a different part of the village, Michael paced the room jabbing his hands through his hair. He'd seen the two of them kissing. Had wanted to wrench them apart. When she spread her legs for him, he nearly cried out his rage. He wasn't a damn peeping Tom, but by gosh she was his. The problem was she didn't know it yet. How to convince her was beyond his wildest imaginings.

His heart thundering in his chest, he slammed his fist on the card table. Glasses and cards bounced at the impact.

"Whoa...what's got you blinded with rage?"

"The devil take that man then toss him in hell!" Michael shouted.

Houston couldn't get out of town soon enough to suit him. As soon as he did, he would have clear field to Leah. She would kiss him not Houston. Would spread her legs for him just as she did for Doc Stuart while she sat on the front porch railing. He would make sure she understood that she would never do so again.

He would give her a chance to say yes to his proposal. If she didn't, he could go to Grizzly. He would tell the old man his daughter spread her legs for him.

They would wed.

"You're strung so tight, you're going to make yourself do something you'll regret. On second thought you might just need to react in order to get whatever is bothering you out of your system. Go bed her."

"She's giving him what she should be giving me. Have to ease my needs with Betsy instead of the woman I want to make my wife. Don't want to do anything to make her angry with me." His ranting wasn't making him feel better, his erection hard and pressing against his trousers. He needed relief tonight.

"Sit down and play or go up the mountain so you can take what you want," Quaid said his voice bland as he studied the cards in his hand. "Take what you think you deserve. My God, no one else would have waited this long for a tiny piece of muslin, especially a *fey* one. Don't *ken* what you see in her. She's a strange *lass*, beautiful but damn strange."

"You need to show her who's the man," Ryan said with a chuckle at his predicament. He spread his cards on the table. "I'm out."

"I'm the man," Michael spoke through gritted teeth as he poked his thumb on his chest. "Not Houston."

"Wouldn't do that until Stuart left town though, take her. If you do, there might be nasty repercussions. Heard the doc has power as well as wealth in his family. Suppose the rumor could be true. If he thought you forced her in anyway there might be more problems created than you have answers for." Ryan was shuffling the cards now, looking at Quaid then Michael. "She seems to have a thing for Houston. Maybe she doesn't want you. Have you thought of that? Maybe she doesn't want you for a husband."

"You could be patient and wait until the good doctor leaves. Would be much easier to seduce her with him gone. Get her so she's increasing. She won't have a chance without you then. Houston won't be coming back here. So, I've heard. Old Grizzly isn't going to be around much longer. Even if he is. the pious son of a bitch would disown her if she got with child. She'll be all yours. If she's thinking with her purty little head, she'll know she's not good enough for that family of Doc's. They would turn her out on her nose if she showed up there expecting something she's never going to get."

"They would, wouldn't they? Leah can't read or write, at least I don't think so. I'm sure all those women in his family have book learning. If she's wanting a ring, I'm the only man who's going to put one on her finger," Michael said, however he wasn't sure at all. Few women got an education. What made him so sure the Stuarts would provide that kind of learning to their women.

"The two of you are confusing the hell out of me," Quaid said with a grin. "Go up the damn mountain and take her or be patient and wait until he's out of town, your advice is muddled."

Michael sat down head in his hands thinking over what his friends told him. He was tempted to ride up the mountain. If he took her, she would be his. Houston wouldn't want her any longer if she wasn't a virgin.

He drank his ale.

Burped.

It was delicious. Almost as delicious as Leah would be when he finally tasted her. He wasn't going to force her though. If he did something like that, she would never give herself to him of her own volition. He would have to force her every time. The only way he wanted her was wiling. Having come to some conclusions, he was ready to move on to something more fun. Somehow, he felt better now. True, he wanted her with an ever-growing ache in his groin. He was patient though. He could wait until she was alone and vulnerable. She would come to learn he would always have his dalliances.

He sat down, concentrating on the cards in his hand as well as Betsy. Betsy would keep him sane while he waited for Leah to agree to becoming his wife until Stuart left town. A long breath of air filled his lungs. Slowly, he let it go then he breathed deeply again as he tried to form a plan. His groin bulged with so much lust thinking straight was nearly impossible.

His friends were right. Seducing Leah to his way of thinking would be easier when Houston was long gone and not coming back. It would also be easier if she had no means to live, if Grizzly was gone. Hell, Grizzly disappeared for days on end. Perhaps he could arrange something more permanent.

He could wait as long as it took. He realized then if she was pregnant with Stuart's child, he would raise the baby. It made no difference to him. He would have double the rewards. Having Leah as his for a short time was the important thing here. He meant to enjoy every second.

Chapter Four

The poor bird was floundering, flapping his wings as hard as he could while he went nowhere. Desperately, the bird fought for freedom. Leah managed to calm the sparrow hawk. She had to cover his eyes with a sock then keep his wings from getting in the way so she could set his broken leg. The endeavor was time consuming needing delicate precision.

He was such a pretty bird, strong, resilient courageous as he fought for life. The wire he caught himself in terrified him, which made the situation worse. When she found him, he was frantic. A wild creature was difficult to contain. Houston was like that, wild and free. She would never enclose him.

Sometimes she was sure she was struggling here, so out of her depths. This wasn't the life she imagined for herself. In her dreams, she thought she might find love. Her dreams deserted her. That had been a long time ago when she still lived in the highlands when she had a loving mother as well as a father. She yearned for things she couldn't have.

After the night of shared kisses with Houston, she found some of those dreams surfacing in her imagination. In time, perhaps she could learn to hope again. Ah, her mother told her she was a dreamer as she was. Women like them could not expect the type of life they dreamt about. There was no such thing as love. She supposed she was just that, a dreamer hoping for love.

She half expected to see Houston the next day. Nay, she fully expected to see him.

He didn't show up.

She didn't know if that meant anything.

She'd like to believe his lack of attention was because of an unexpected patient or a birthing. That he wasn't distancing himself from her because of his move. That didn't matter to her. She stole a wobbly breath from the sweet-scented air around her. The warm February sun hitting her face heated her all the way down to her bones filling her soul. This sunny weather wouldn't last for long. It was still winter. She supposed this could be considered false spring. Rain would come soon followed by more dreary days until spring finally arrived. As far as weather was concerned, Scotland never behaved itself.

Leah turned her attention back to her wildling. Safe now, the bird was in a small box she rigged to keep him from moving until he healed. She would let him go when he could survive on his own. Once she almost named one of her rescued birds. Naming wasn't a good idea. Naming gave her reason to want to keep the animal, to think of the wildling as hers. These animals were wild and didn't belong to a human, never would. They needed to have their freedom. So, she kept herself from giving any of these creatures a name. She had no hold on them. Even though Houston was wild, he needed his freedom. The problem was he had a name.

She sat back, watching the hawk as she pulled out her sketchpad along with her charcoal. Every wildling she helped she drew. Her collection was growing. Now, she had nearly thirty drawings of animals. More drawings if one counted the flora in this part of Scotland. Before she left the highlands five years ago, she had a stack of illustrations. In their haste they were left behind. Hawk told her she might be able to make a book of these then sell them. She didn't believe anyone would pay to see the pictures. She had no means or ideas how to go about Hawk's suggestion. It was another dream that would never happen. She let a small puff of air slip from her lungs.

Hawk helped her with the names of the animals and flowers she drew. He would look each one up in all the books he had, then write the name at the bottom of the drawing. She tried to memorize the names. Those few words were all she could read since she knew the designations of the plants from memory as well as the animals. At times she attempted to copy the letters. Her skills fell short.

Sometime she sat and memorized what he'd written for her as she tried to recall each one as well as the letters that made up their names. She didn't know the names of the letters. Nevertheless, she had the symbols memorized for each plant and animal. Well, she knew some of the symbols because there were ones that were more difficult. Hawk tried to teach her except everything looked backward to her. Sometimes he told her it was a b and she was sure it was a d. There were other letters she had trouble with also as she turned them around in her mind.

Once he swore not understanding why she had so much difficulty with the letters. He told her she was so smart, talented as well; that learning the letters should be easy for her. Small children learned the letters that eluded her. Here she was having turned twenty. She couldn't absorb into her mind what a small child had no problem with.

It wasn't easy at all. Learning the letters was the most difficult thing she'd ever tried. She didn't know why. Didn't think she would ever learn how to read. A lone tear slipped down her cheek. Furious with herself for giving in to her emotions she swiped the moisture away with the back of her hand. You're too old to cry over something so silly.

For a few minutes, she checked on the other wildling that was in her hospital. The small creature was a rabbit who had the bad luck to run into some animal that wanted to take a bite out of its hind leg. Lucky for the rabbit, he found a place to hide. She discovered the animal badly traumatized beneath a thorn-filled berry bush. When she picked the tiny thing up, the rabbit's body was trembling and shaking so hard it scared her. So distressed she wasn't sure if she would be able to save his life.

"There you go, little fellow," she said as she stroked it's back. "In a few days you'll be ready to brave the world again. I hope you have the good sense to stay away from the mean ones who want to eat you."

The bunny's nose was sniffing the air, its whiskers tickling her fingers. She let out a delighted laugh.

A flash of Michael's image swept through her mind. He did. He wanted to eat her, control her life. She couldn't allow that to happen. She needed to stay out of his way. *Nay*, she would figure out something, some plan to make him understand she wouldn't marry him. Nothing could make her marry him. A feeling of fear settled in her stomach. Terror that she was slowly losing control of her life swamped her.

She couldn't let that happen.

She had to stay strong, determined too.

For a few precious minutes, she kneeled on the ground, her head in her hands, her life as well as her future flashing in poignant images in her mind. While everything seemed to be changing around her, she didn't know what her future would bring. As long as she had this home, she could remain here. She could dictate her life the way she wanted it. Relying on someone wouldn't be necessary.

What if she left to seek out something else? She would have nothing. Her existence would be in jeopardy. She sucked in a life-giving breath of air, reeling in the sensation. Realizing she couldn't leave the security of this mountain, this home, she trembled, her body shaking as fear swamped her. Houston wouldn't want an uneducated backwoods girl for a wife a woman who couldn't read and write. She couldn't even write her name. She always formed the first and last letters backward. It made no difference that she was the daughter of a woman who was born a lady. Her mother was the daughter of an earl, an impoverished earl but an earl no less. Her mother once had been the daughter of a countess.

She held a title. Her mother told her so many times.

Did that mean she was a lady?

She laughed softly then bitterly, amazed at her question. It was a small sound that held no meaning. Leah looked at her dress. It was threadbare, the color faded from so many washings. She didn't care. She'd never hungered for the finer things money could buy. To her, other things in life made a difference, like the way one treated another human. The way one treated an animal. The earth along with its inhabitants was more important than anything one could buy, more important than power. Men seemed to want power. She never understood men.

She shuddered. Houston thought much the same about life. In that, she was positive. That one fact might be all they held in common. He was a healer after all. Could it be enough?

Houston...

He wasn't coming to see her. It was best she forget about him then set her sights on a future that might be possible for her. She acknowledged that for a few moments of her life, he made her happy. Touched a part of her heart she didn't believe would ever be touched.

Leaving the secluded area behind her, she felt as if she garnered some answers for herself even though she still didn't know what she was going to do with those answers. There were too many variables, too many factors that terrified her. It seemed to her all she wanted now that Houston would not be here was to leave this place behind and seek something new.

I've no groats to get myself to the highlands. Grizzly certainly isn't going to give me any money. Houston offered though. She couldn't take his money.

By the time she left the tiny trail behind her, she realized the path she used was getting too easy to see. She didn't want Grizzly finding the refuge. He would take great delight in tearing the small sanctuary apart, killing any wildlings in her tiny hospital. No one other than her except for Hawk knew of her private secluded place, a place where she could dream and imagine a different life, one that included love.

Houston should know of it.

Why though?

He was going away. She didn't believe he would ever return, not even for her. He would leave her behind. In the process, never have a second thought. A tear slid down her throat as pain ripped at her heart.

When she rounded the huge oak tree near her home, she heard voices. Her heart leapt. It was Houston. She picked up her pace, breathless with anticipation. He came to see her. The problem was that Grizzly was home.

She placed a fingertip on her lips, remembering the heated sensual kisses they shared two days ago. Her body felt the flush of desire for the man who coaxed her to feel in ways she never imagined.

She wanted to be alone with him. Feel his tender caress, the sultry glide of his tongue against hers.

That was impossible today.

"What are you doing here?" she asked breathless from excitement when she saw them. "I wasn't expecting you."

Of course, you weren't expecting him but you were hoping?

A little ball of fur jumped from Houston's arms. The puppy ran up to her, sniffing, running around in circles before the obnoxious beast jumped on her legs begging to be in her arms. She reached down. The dog squirmed as she looked up, her big brown eyes imploring her to love her. The dog licked her chin. She melted.

"Thought you might like a puppy. He was in payment of services rendered," Houston spoke softly as he watched her.

His eyes focused on her, on the dog in her arms.

With all her heart Leah wanted to tell him, yes. She needed a companion to love. Grizzly wouldn't welcome the puppy.

"She can't have a dog. No need for another mouth to feed. Just got rid of one damn dog, not going to have another," Grizzly told them as he drank his whiskey. "You got chores to do, girl?" he asked her.

Thankfully that was a question and not a command. She finished everything before she left to tend to her wildlings. Everything was done for the day.

"No," she told him snuggling with the dog who was now squirming so fast and furious, she flipped from her arms. "Does she have a name?"

"Not yet. Thought I'd let you name her, that is if you were going to take her off my hands. You still can if you like." He got down then walked slowly toward her, the silver steel of his gaze penetrating her telling her a myriad of things yet leaving her with unanswered questions. The breath she stole from the air clung to the back of her throat before the air finally found its way to her lungs.

"Best you be getting back down the mountain," Grizzly called out.

He seemed to have lost interest as he ambled into the house. The door banged shut behind him.

Leah was glad he left. She didn't want to share time with Houston. "At least he doesn't have his rifle," she murmured feeling the beginnings of a smile as she watched Houston's grin widen.

"No, however, he could be walking inside to retrieve it as we speak. Would you like to go for a walk?" he asked, as he leaned casually against the side of his buggy.

Hesitant, she bit the inside of her mouth as she peered inside wondering what Grizzly would do if she told Houston yes to his question. She did want to go for a walk with him. Did want him to kiss her one more time. Needed to find out when he would leave.

"Yes," she told him. "I suppose Grizzly will stay in the house. Supper is ready. He'll start to drink..."

Houston stuffed his hands in his pockets, rocking on the balls of his feet as his intense stare sent a shiver down her spine. She wanted to know exactly what he was thinking.

"Know I've asked you this before. Going to ask again. Does he hurt you if you don't do exactly what he wants? If he does, you're not staying here. I'll figure something out for you."

"This might be the first time. He didn't say so. Nonetheless, he wants me to send you on your way. I'm going for that walk. So, in a way I'm disobeying his wishes."

She wasn't going to give Houston a chance to back down from the walk. She led the way to the river running near their house.

He caught up, his hand on her shoulder stopping her as he turned her in a quick fluid motion to look at him. "I don't like the idea that a walk would cause him to hurt you."

Letting out a leisurely breath of air as she searched for the words, "I don't think he will give me a second thought except that I'm with you. He believes you're a threat to his meals, however you can't possibly be a threat to me. You're not what he thinks."

"A threat to his meals? Not sure I'm understanding what you're trying to tell me." He laughed though as if perhaps he figured it out.

"He doesn't want anyone to take me away. He wants me here to wait on him then make sure he has dinner ready for him when he gets home. He won't hurt me. At least I don't think he will. For now, his dinner is prepared, warm for his stomach. By the time we return he'll be drunk and asleep. He's halfway there now. Shall we?"

This was not what she wanted her life to be like. She was too terrified to take the only way out she could think of. The courage she needed to take the first bold moves she didn't possess. A shudder swept through her.

"If, you're sure."

"*Verra.*"

The puppy seeming to know they where they were going bounded along the river trail in front of them returning to circle their legs before dashing away again. Leah had so many questions to ask him she didn't know where to begin.

He settled his hand around her waist pulling her closer. His chest pressed against her breasts. She wondered what it would feel like if they wore no clothing. Brenda would tell her it wasn't something she should be wondering about. After the ride with him along with his kisses she couldn't help but speculate.

"What are you thinking? You're so quiet, Leah."

His low husky voice sent a shiver of sensual anticipation sweeping inside. She understood how the slow glide of his tongue felt, vividly recalled the sensation.

Heat raced to her cheeks, her heart pulsing through her veins until she could barely breathe let alone answer. Her feelings were wayward. She thought of things that would get her into trouble if she carried through with them.

She didn't care.

"What has created that pretty blush on your cheeks? Tell me."

He coaxed his lips so close to her, his warm breath washed across her cheek settled into her core.

She had every reason to tell him yet she remained mute. Words stuck in her throat. His hand roamed the curve of her hip then back to her waist then a bit higher until she felt the weight of her breast below his hand. Did that caress feel the same to him as it did to her?

They stopped walking. He turned her, his hands resting on her bottom as he pulled her close, so close she felt the same hard bulge as before when he kissed her when he held her in front of him while they rode when she straddled him.

"I want to kiss you. Do you suppose it's safe today or would...?" he asked as he bent lower, his mint-scented breath once again sweeping across her face.

The glide of her tongue across her top lip left wetness behind.

He was so close she absorbed his warmth, saw the movement of his tongue across his lips as he moistened them. Anticipation for the heated rush of desire he generated when his mouth touched hers smoldered waiting to be ignited. Slowly, she nodded her head telling him what he wanted to know.

Her knees weakened.

The puppy played around them seeking their attention.

"Do you want to feel me inside you?" His throaty question was left unanswered. She thought for a moment he might mean something besides his tongue in her mouth.

Once again, she nodded seeking the same. It seemed he teased heartlessly. Contact was sweet, slicked with the wetness of his mouth, everything she imagined. Pulses of energy dark and inviting flooded her, swept to every part of her body to settle in the most intimate private part of her. He showered her face with his kisses, touching everywhere, teasing her lips apart so he could delve inside.

The strokes he laved upon her were everything a girl could want from a man's kiss and more. She met him with desire as well as passion that was both hot as well as sweet as she accepted the same from him. The rumble of pleasure surging from his belly delighted her. She had not thought she could do something like that to him. The simple power she had over him surprised her. While he controlled the intricate dance they played, she could give him more than she'd thought. He was not immune to her kisses even though she was sure he was experienced.

He rested his head on her forehead ending the carnal delights. She didn't want him to stop. His breathing was heavy, harsh to her ears. Leah understood it matched hers. In this they had something in common. She was certain he must want more than just kisses as she did.

"We need to stop, Leah," he told her as he placed her hand in his. "Come, let's walk a bit farther. It will be dark soon. I do need to get back to town before the night is so black I can't see the next pothole on the road."

He brought her hand to his lips, placing a tender kiss on the back before turning it over to do the same on the palm.

The tiny mew of pleasure escaped. "I don't see why."

She didn't either. Grizzly would be drunk by the time they returned. Disappointingly, he wouldn't be passed out, not yet. He still had a few hours of drinking left before that would happen. She would be left alone to avoid him. If she had to spend time outside before he fell into a drunken stupor, she'd just as soon be with Houston.

"People have been talking about our Valentine's Day dinner, none of it good. I would not have more of the same gossip tomorrow. Don't *ken* how anyone would know I was here except..." He brushed strands of hair from her face, lightly grazed her cheek with the back of his hand. "You're wellbeing means a lot to me. Seeing you hurt is not something I want to be responsible for."

"Who? Who would be saying anything?"

She knew. The air she forced inside stalled in her throat, ached. Michael was working the people of the village against her so he could make it right. He would be her hero when he saved her from shame. Only he could change their minds about her if she married him. He was directing her down a path she wasn't about to follow.

"I think you know," he spoke softly. "This shadow hanging over your head is not something I want to leave here without finding a solution. Hawk tells me he needs another month to set all in motion for him to start a new practice in this village. He needs to see some people before he moves here permanently. Told me this process might take longer or it could be less time."

Running her tongue across the front of her teeth, she spoke softly as she searched for words, "Michael. He is planning my demise so he can run to my rescue. I'm not going to let that happen."

"Is that it? I wondered at the reason he would seek to hurt you. So, it's for his gain, has nothing to do with your feelings. Leah." He placed both of his large hands on either side of her face. "You cannot wed that man, not ever. Promise me."

She slipped her tongue across her lips, her eyes closing as she knew the answer would be forthcoming. "I've no intention of ever marrying especially not to that man."

He jerked as if he'd been burned. It seemed her words stung. If she couldn't wed Houston, she wasn't going to marry anyone.

"Promise. You never know what might happen. Whatever you do wait for me. Promise me. I'll come for you. I'll take care of you."

Wait for him? What did that mean? He gave her no promises, no commitments. *Wait for him?* Why on earth should she do that? *Because you love him.* "I promise. Houston, you should realize, he has been nice to me where others have made fun of me. You *ken* I cannot read or write." She was telling him things he needed to know about her, things she didn't want him to know. Yet she blurted the words without thought to the repercussions.

"No, Hawk never told me about that." His voice was bitter now. "You should trust me too, Leah. I've always your interests at heart. Can you trust me at my word?"

"What are you saying?" she asked, her mind a whirl of things Hawk knew about her that he might tell Houston. "What has Hawk told you? If he did, everything he said were confidences he had no right to betray."

She felt herself bristle. Absorbed the anger to the tips of her toes. Of all the people she knew, she didn't expect Hawk's betrayal.

He turned away from her then, pinching the bridge of his nose, his broad shoulders rising and falling with unspoken agitation. "I should not have said anything. Forget it." He waved a hand in the air, his eyes darkening to deepest gray. The difference in him frightened her. She'd never seen him look so black and dangerous.

Shaking, with confusion swirling beneath the serenity that had once been, she tried desperately to hold on to. "I cannot forget." The small sip of air she sucked into her lungs was not enough. She sipped again and again wishing she could see into his head. In that process she craved to understand his words as well as what he thought. She should not have shared that bit of information. If he left now, she would not be surprised.

Silence stretched between them, caught in her mind, torturing her. She needed to find a way to broach the subject once more; as it was obvious, he wasn't going to speak of it again. He'd turned inward.

"If Hawk is talking about me, it's just like all the other people in the village. I thought he was my friend." Tears spiked her lashes, threatened to fall. How dare he share her secret thoughts she only told to him? How dare he?

"Leah, he is my friend as well as yours. Don't ever doubt it. It's just that..." He drew her against his chest, held her tightly. His heart thundered next to hers. Unable to resist the startling temptation, she placed her hand where she could feel the steady, strong beat of his heart that melded with hers.

"Just that what?" she queried still confused at his outburst that made no sense to her or to him it seemed.

"You're not going to let this go, are you? It would be better if we did not speak of this again. I was impulsive. Should have considered consequences before I said anything."

"No...no, I want an answer." She needed him to tell her the truth, tell him his thoughts. Her trust in this man went beyond anything she'd ever felt for another person, even her mother and father especially Hawk.

He kissed her lightly. She thought it was an apology of sorts.

"If you must know, I'm jealous of the man."

~ * ~

Awnings were set up in the field behind the Hughes mansion. For the last few days, the women folk in the village were busy cooking, preparing lavish, delicious platters of food for the celebration. Upstairs the ballroom was prepared for those who were invited into the Hughes home. The celebration was staged to welcome the new doctor to the village while sending the old one a thank you on his way out the door.

The atmosphere this evening was magical. The people came alive as music filled the air. Games of brawn were played beyond the awnings that were meant to keep out the rain if the sky clouded over. So far, the weather held. It was a perfect afternoon for the celebration that would stretch into the evening.

Pipes and drums played. People danced to lively Scottish music. Leah stood on the outskirts tapping her toes to the rhythm, wishing she could disappear. She knew she wouldn't be missed. She only came so she could see Houston and welcome Hawk. After that she intended to leave. This wasn't the type of place where she belonged.

She was wearing her best dress, a faded threadbare yellow muslin. She wasn't sure the color could actually be considered yellow any longer. If she could she would have liked to impress Houston. Appearing in this old gown would hardly do that.

"Well, little lady, you managed to sequester yourself where no one will see you or ask you to dance." Brenda laughed as she tugged on her arm in an attempt to move her where she could be seen. "Why did you come if not to dance and eat?"

"I *dinna* want to dance," she murmured unable to stand firm against one of the only friends she had. "You *ken verra* well I've two left feet."

"If you stay hidden, your favorite doctor won't see you. If he doesn't see you, he won't ask you to dance. He won't come talk to you or smile at you," Brenda heaved a sigh of discontent. "I don't know what to do about you, child."

"You know I don't know how to dance." Leah did look around, saw the couples their feet moving so rapidly she couldn't keep track. She couldn't deny the fact she might like to learn. Now wasn't the time.

"You don't have to know. Just let your partner swirl you around until you're breathless then he'll stop so he can kiss you. You'd like that. A kiss that's appropriate for a young girl and her beau."

"Yes, that would be nice in theory. Houston isn't here. He's most likely upstairs in the grand ballroom, drinking sweet wine while talking with the lovely Marie. I'm certain he was invited into the house."

She did feel the bitterness in her voice. Thoughts of Marie flirting with Houston left a sour taste in her belly. She was jealous. It was a strange sensation to feel about a man she'd known for such a short time. While she thought of Houston as hers, he wasn't. She had to accept that fact.

Brenda patted her on the arm, "He'll be down. You just wait and see. I'm sure he'd rather be dancing with you than talking gibberish to Marie even though she does bat her lashes at the man."

"Just about every man. From what I've seen, she doesn't much care who she's with as long as it's a man."

"Do I detect a note of jealousy?" Brenda asked softly her eyes showing concern while they also seemed to demand answers. "I've heard the rumors floating around the village about you and Houston. Are any of them true?"

"Just the kissing part. Took heed to your words. Even told Houston what you said. He was a perfect gentleman."

He was more of a gentleman than she wanted him to be. If he was leaving, she wanted to know what it would be like to have him make love to her. It would be something she could hold on to in her dreams.

When he left that was all she would have left to her, dreams.

"Come let's get something to eat. The food is delicious. Much different fare than you are used to having. You can treat yourself." Brenda slipped her arm through hers chatting merrily as they walked.

When she saw the concoctions on the tables, her stomach rumbled. She was hungry. Seemed she was always hungry. Brenda was right, she wasn't used to anything like this. There were all kinds of pastries for the sweet tooth she had. Salmon and chicken along with roasted pig were in abundance. On another table little cakes were adorned with all types of frostings including chocolate, which she adored.

Both women filled their plates then found a spot where they could sit and watch the dancers while they ate.

"I didn't expect to see you here." Houston stood in front of them with three pints of ale. "Thirsty anyone?" He set a glass in front of her as well as Brenda before he pulled up a chair.

Leah lifted her shoulders in a small movement that meant she'd been talked into attending this affair. "Brenda thought I should stay for a short time."

She looked away for a second, unwilling to give away her thoughts. Feelings for Houston muddled her mind. Where he was concerned, she felt too many different emotions. At the moment, thinking of him leaving, walking out of her life, her heart felt ripped to shreds. She didn't know the exact date. Nevertheless, she did know his departure grew closer with each passing second. This party was proof of that. Hawk was getting ready to begin his practice while Houston was preparing to leave all this behind.

Somehow, she thought she would have a little more time with him. If the party was an indication, more time wasn't to be.

"How is the food?" he asked watching her with intensity in his silver eyes.

"Delicious," she told him her voice soft nearly a whisper. "Nothing like I'm used to eating."

The fact she'd never had anything that was sitting on her plate before this evening was another reason why the two of them were far from suited for each other. She didn't drink. Until I met you, I'd never had wine or ale. "The ale is good also."

"Would you like to dance?" He stood, holding out his hand to her the expression on his face heart warming.

Dancing?

She'd never danced.

A ripple of fear gripped her heart. She swallowed hard as she searched Brenda's eyes as if she could answer for her. Brenda nodded as if telling her Houston wouldn't let her down.

The air she drew choked inside her throat. She coughed yet she managed to nod in agreement. Leah put her hand in his. He pulled her into his arms.

"For a moment there, I thought you weren't going to agree." He bent low to whisper close to her ear. Touched the lobe with the tip of his tongue. "Was certain you would tell me a resounding no."

He would know the affect that action had on her body. Playing her was something he did with ease.

When he took her in his arms, twirling her in circles, she stumbled. His hands gripped her waist, keeping her on her feet. Music flowed through him into her giving her confidence. She caught the rhythm, delighting in the changing sounds as they began to move as one around the dancing area.

When they were breathless, they stopped at the table where Brenda still sat watching the festivities. He lifted his pint, drank deeply, turned to Brenda then smoothly bowed low, "Would you like to dance?"

"I would. However, Seamus would not like another man dancing with me, holding me in his arms. Dance with Leah again." She smiled shooing them away with her hands.

The evening went on like this. They would dance then stop for a drink again and again. He danced his way from the lighted area into the darkness of the woods beyond the home. Pine scent filled the air coupled with this man whose scent stirred every part of her with intrigue

"Are you having a good time?" Houston asked as he set her against a tree.

His lips hovered close to hers. His whispered breath floated across her cheeks. He was so close she felt the heat emanate from him into her.

She smiled at him, slowly lifting a finger to run it across his bottom lip. "Are you?"

She wanted to ask when he was leaving or if he even knew. Didn't dare be so bold.

"Yes, now that I found you. Before that..." He lifted strong shoulders a crooked grin on his face. "Before that I spent most my time trying to guard my poor body from Marie's attention."

She giggled. "Marie fancies herself in love with whoever is closest to her."

"*Ach, lass* you wound my pride. Thought she wanted only me."

"Well, she told me you weren't rich enough. Doctors, while they are good for what ails a person, don't get paid enough to keep her in the things she loves." Leah said on a wistful note.

She didn't care about any of that. It would have been best for her if he was just a poor country doctor. While she didn't know for certain, rumor had it that he came from wealth. He would expect the woman he married to be refined, knowledgeable. "I'm glad Marie doesn't *ken* what is important in this life."

Leah's hand rested on his shoulder, smoothed the fabric. She let a few dreams slip through her mind. When she looked at him his eyes told her how much he wanted her. She wanted him too. Her lips quivered slightly while she thought about the way his lips fit so nicely against hers.

"You should not be walking up that mountain alone tonight. I see Michael has been staring your way for quite some time, which is why I wanted to go out here where we might find a small measure of privacy. You need to stay in the village this evening where it is safe."

"It's dark now."

"You know you shouldn't walk that trail by yourself."

"Can you think of an option? I can't."

"You can stay with me." His lips brushed softly against her

forehead. "I would be good, follow Brenda's directions."

"We both *ken* that can't happen, especially not tonight when half the village would see me walk into your house. When you leave to pursue a different life, I will still be living here," she reminded him.

"If you will accept my help, I'll give you the groats to get you to the highlands and my family. I'll send a message. They will give you a job. In the process, they will keep you safe. You won't have to worry about Michael along with his ill-conceived plans."

A sting of tears clouded her eyes. She found herself shaking her head. "*Ye ken I canna* do something like that. People would talk. While I understand you have my interest at heart, other's will not."

He placed a tender kiss at the corner of her mouth. "No one will know what we've done because you won't be here. My family won't care. They will accept you into their lives as I have accepted you into mine." He moved to the other side of her mouth. Warmth followed his lips everywhere he touched upon her. His touch was damp and heated.

A small trembling flooded her. Oh, how she wanted to accept his help, needed to believe in him along with his intentions to be noble and good. She wasn't noble or good. She wanted things he couldn't give her. If she traveled to the highlands, she would ache for what she couldn't have.

"You never told me when you were leaving." When she asked again her heart nearly stopped beating while she held her breath.

"Will you accept the coin?" he asked before he answered the question.

"I'll have to think about it. Doesn't seem right of me to take money from you unless we make provisions for me to pay it back. I could do that. If your family did give me work, I could return the money."

He shook his head. "It's not my intention to have you repay me. However, if it's the only way for you to accept my offer then I accept your conditions."

"Now then can you answer my question?" The words came out both brisk and angry. She had not meant the words to be so. Frustration at his reticence swamped her. She worried about this for too many days to count. A simple answer would help her come to terms.

He lifted his broad shoulders, shrugging thoughtfully, "Maybe a couple of weeks. The doctor I'm to practice with is in Glasgow now. I'm not sure when he'll return to Edinburgh. Hawk and I will share the practice until that time. My workload will not be so intense. I can spend time with you if you like. You could show me places you like to go."

"I believe I would like that. Perhaps you can come see me tomorrow. I'll show you a place that is very special to me."

The only other person to see her sanctuary was Hawk.

His smile surprised her. The throaty sound of his voice came as a shock. "I'd like that. I feel as if I've waited a lifetime for you to share a part of you with me. You keep everything hidden deep inside you."

The realization that he knew more than he let her know. "You know about the refuge, my sanctuary?"

"Hawk told me, let it slip. I've got to tell you it's another reason why I've been jealous of the man." He placed a finger on her lips as she thought to reply. "I know he's not kissed you. *Ken* you don't return feelings for him as you do for me. Still, when a man knows the woman he's coming to adore trusts another man more...well, it doesn't help his ego one bit."

"I don't trust him more than you."

He adores me?

He ran his finger across her bottom lip, his thumb beneath her chin. The ache for him increased with each small caress each touch of his hand. Heat rose to an inferno sliding through her to inflame all of her as he brushed his lips gently across hers.

"You have no idea how that makes me feel."

She caught her bottom lip between her teeth as she sought to tell him the most damning peace of information about her. The sip of air turned to a tiny pant then another one. She closed her eyes trying desperately to slow her pounding heart while she evened her breathing. Nothing worked. "It's just that he is only a friend. I *ken* he will never pass judgment. You on the other hand..."

He cut her off with angry words along with a slashing of his hand in the air, "You think I would judge you?"

"Yes...well no...it's just that I'm ashamed."

She was terribly humiliated with herself. More than anything she'd always wanted to learn how to read and write. She always felt deficient because no matter how hard she tried she failed.

"What could you possibly have to be embarrassed about?"

Her eyes crossed while every nerve in her body seemed to be stretched to the breaking point. She had to tell him now before she lost the courage. "I cannot do something that the smallest child can do easily. I've tried and I've tried again to no avail."

"What would that be?" He sounded both angry and perplexed.

She watched as she drew circles in the dirt with the tip of her boot. His thumb once more settled beneath her chin while he lifted her face so she had no choice but to stare into his silver-blue eyes. Pity was something she didn't want.

"I cannot read or write. I cannot even learn to write my name. When I try, it comes out all backward and funny."

Fear rose in her innards. The breath she held in her lungs waiting for a response scorched.

"I did not expect that. You can learn. It should not be hard."

Wayward tears slipped from her eyes, wetting her cheeks then her lips with the salty taste. She was shaking her head, denying his words. "Hawk has tried to teach me without succeeding. I cannot learn the simplest of things."

Leah knew then he would turn away from her, reject any love he might feel for her if he indeed felt love. Hawk told her to be careful of men who might use her for their own purpose, Brenda as well. She didn't dare look at him. Didn't want to see the disgust in his eyes even though she understood many women never learned to read and write. It wasn't such a simple thing. It was just something she longed for.

Hawk tried to teach.

She failed.

"You are not alone in this. Backward, you say? *'Tis* not uncommon. I've read about this issue in medical journals."

"I *dinna ken* what you're trying to tell me."

"It's just something I've heard of before. He reached in his pocket, swore softly. I've no paper or pen. If you go with me to my office, I can show you. Will you do that?"

"People will see. They will talk some more. I need to go up the mountain tonight where I belong."

"No. It's not where you belong. The mountain with Grizzly is no fitting place for you." He jammed his hands into his hair leaving it an endearing mess. He looked as if he wanted to argue with her.

Leah reached up, smoothed some of the wayward locks. The strands were soft just as she remembered. She didn't know what to do. How to make him love her as she loved him? "I adore it when you do that to your hair."

He swore again, breathed deeply. His chest rose and fell with each breath. "Do your bs look like ds? Is everything pointed the wrong direction. We can get through this together. I promise you. Hawk didn't understand how to help you. I do."

A glimmer of hope shot through her. She tried to push the sensation down except the expectation of a dream come true clung to her heart. "You can help me learn to read?" she asked in one whoosh of air that seemed to flash by in less than a second.

"I believe so. We might even make some progress before I have to go. Afterward, when you come to the highlands, we'll continue to learn. You will go to my family home where you will wait for me. You will work at the McKenna keep so you can pay your way."

His last statement sounded to her like a command. Under the circumstances she could do nothing of the sort even though she yearned to do just that with all her heart. Perhaps there was a way.

"Yes, yes I'll go but only if I can repay you the coin."

She felt breathless and happy beyond anything she felt before. She looked at him wide eyed as if he could do anything for her.

She pushed away from the tree. "I'm going home now. We both know more gossip isn't good for either of us. You're not going to walk with me." She placed her hand on his chest. "I'll be fine. It's something I've done hundreds of times, probably more. Will do so again and again."

"No."

"Yes." She was adamant in this. He could not dictate to her. She had to look out for his reputation more than her own. He could not afford to be sullied by gossip. "Don't follow me. You understand you can't."

"I understand nothing."

When she turned to look over her shoulder, he didn't move. His hands were fisted at his sides, his expression grim. She thought for a moment he wanted to throttle her. To get to the trail up the mountain she needed to walk through the village. She thought he would have walked with her at least to the path she took. That much would have been appropriate. Disappointment clouded her mind to the extent she wondered if the conversation they just had was in her imagination.

If he wasn't following her, she didn't want to know. Her emotions were so mixed up and scrambled in her head she couldn't think straight. The first touch on her shoulder led her to believe he had a change of heart. The second touch, which spun her around, sent terror into her veins.

"No!" She pushed away from the man holding her shoulders.

"Leah, what are you saying? It's just me. Don't be afraid. I don't mean you any harm."

"Michael." For a swift moment, terror changed to relief. She knew he spoke true, "What do you want?"

Slowly, he grinned, a lazy confident smile that frightened her when it should have reassured, "Why, I want what you give the good doctor. I saw you on your porch. You didn't know it."

"What would that be? What do you think I give him that I can give to you?" She brushed off his hands to walk away. He was beside her then in front of her stopping her. Dear Lord, where was Houston? If he watched her leave, he should have been beside her now.

"Your friend is with Marie. He doesn't care about you as I do. He doesn't want to make you his wife, just use you until he leaves."

He pulled her close. His lips found hers in a bruising kiss she wanted nothing to do with. She didn't like the way it felt or how he tasted.

She was both confused and angry at Houston, an emotion that seemed to hover in her mind all night. Too many times he contradicted himself in his actions joined with what he told her. Why wasn't he here when she needed him?

Michael's tongue pushed between her lips. One hand cupped her breast his thumb caressing a nipple. She pounded on his chest trying to wrench her mouth away from his so she could scream for help. If not Houston then Seamus would come help her.

In desperation, she bit his lip.

He pushed her slightly. "Why'd you do that? I was just kissing you," he asked as he held two fingers over his bleeding mouth. "You never bit Houston."

"You didn't give me a chance to tell you no. You didn't ask, just took. I don't want you to kiss me, Michael. Don't want anything from you."

"You're lying, Leah. You're going to marry me. We're going to kiss every night for the rest of our lives. I'm going to hold you in my arms. We're going to make babies together."

"You need any help here?" Houston asked as she felt his male strength and the heat of his body so close to her.

His hands were on her shoulders, his chest pressed against her back.

He'd gone home for his big stallion. He didn't abandon her. She wasn't going to have to walk up the mountain by herself.

"Yes," she spoke softly. "You can convince Michael I didn't appreciate his kiss. I don't want him to touch me."

"You tell him. The words will hold more meaning if they come from you." His voice was soft yet angry too. No one could argue the intensity or the unsaid meaning behind the tone. She shivered.

He was letting her solve the problem. For that she was grateful. Nevertheless, she also knew nothing was going to deter Michael. She had to use Houston's money to leave here. She had to do it as soon as Houston left for Edinburgh. If she waited, she might end up in Michael's bed.

"I did tell him," she whispered softly as she leaned into him, absorbing his heat and strength.

"Come, I'll take you home."

"Yes. I'd like that." Whatever energy she might have had before Michael confronted her was drained from her now.

"He doesn't want you, Leah. Not like I do."

~ * ~

Michael stood on the road watching the two lovers ride away from him, his gut churning. He clenched his fist, wishing he could hit the guy, knock him out of the running then take what he wanted. He didn't know how to make her willing. Didn't have trouble with any of the other ladies he bedded. They were lined up waiting for him. All he had to do was crook his little finger. Why wasn't the one woman he wanted to make his wife willing? He would find a way. He had to be the one who had her.

He didn't mean to force the kiss. Well, perhaps he did. He'd thought a kiss might be the only way to convince her. When he pulled her into his arms, he lost rational thought. All he could think of was what she would bring him when she was finally his.

She would be willing when Stuart left and there was no one else. He could wait. During that time, he would have to think of a way to coax her along.

Tonight, his need for her so strong, he couldn't stop himself when she started to fight. He understood he needed to woo her gently and sweet-talk her so she would beg. Couldn't do so until Houston was out of the picture. His erection throbbed. The devil, she was a sassy piece even though she couldn't learn to read and write.

What did he care? Her skills in bed were what was important. He could teach her those enjoy her then reap the rewards.

What he wanted was the use of her beautiful body. She was the most attractive woman in these parts even though she was a little bit fey. She was going to be his.

Patience man, lots of patience is what I need.

He also heard her agree to use Houston's money to help her get to his family. It was odd to think of a man bringing a mistress home to his family. He would have to find a means to keep her from using the coin.

"You should forget about her for tonight. Come back to the celebration. Marie has been asking about you," Quaid said as he stepped beside him. "She'll give you what you're looking for from Miss Leah. She *kens* she's better than everyone else."

"Don't want anything from Marie I haven't already had. Don't want her pregnant with my child although if it were to happen, I'd deny

106

it. She's given herself to both you and Ryan. Why, she could be carrying your child or Ryan's. No one would know and no would claim the *bairn*. Even though she's rich every one *kens* she's no better than Betsy."

"Could be. That's the beauty of it. No one's going to know. If she claims you or me as the father, it's easy enough to deny."

"Maybe I will visit her instead of Betsy. Last time I went to see Betsy I had to wait in line to taste her favors. Don't like waiting when my trousers are bruising my cock. Besides Betsy's not worth the wait."

The only woman worth waiting for as far as Michael was concerned was Leah.

"No, she's not. By my estimation neither is Leah Kennedy." He shrugged then with a wry grin, "What do I know? You're the one who wants her. Although I certainly don't understand why."

"Don't know much that's for sure. In time you'll see my reasoning. Might even share some of the rewards when the time comes."

By the time the pair reached the lighted field the population was thinning, people leaving for home. Hawk lifted his ale glass in a toast of some sort while he was speaking to a group of four. Marie sat alone at a table, a glass of wine in front of her. It seemed all her prospects for the night had also left.

Michael sat down beside her, his hand resting on her thigh. "You look tired and perhaps bored. Want to liven things up a little?"

She looked up, smiled before batting long dark lashes at him. For a second, her sooty lashes arched across pale, alabaster cheeks. When she opened them, "Not at all. Did you come sit with me for a reason?"

He traced her jawline, felt the shiver of heated response to the caress. So unlike Leah. Yet, he still needed Leah. "I want you tonight. Do you want me?" he whispered as his thumb slid down her neck massaging tiny circles coaxing and enticing. Felt the pulse of desire at the base grow.

He rose before holding out his hand. She accepted his help. He wrapped an arm around her shoulder. "Where are we going?"

"To my apartment above the store, unless you have a better place."

Chapter Five

Houston stopped at the Fletcher place on the way up the mountain to see Leah. The night before she gave him the invitation. He was going to see her refuge, her sanctuary against the world. After that, he was going to start teaching her the letters she so wanted to learn. During the night while his overheated body couldn't sleep, he'd gone over all the different ways he'd heard of to teach children who saw everything backward.

She would learn quickly.

When he went inside to see the Fletcher children, the place was just as disgusting as it always was. Mired in filth along with garbage, the home stunk. He didn't know how anyone could live in these conditions. Mrs. Fletcher did have six children all under the age of ten. It must be terribly hard to keep a home clean with all the babies. The oldest, however, was perfectly capable of helping out even if it was just to hold the newborn while his mother washed dishes or clothing or even picked up the garbage tossed on the floor.

He gave his usual lecture about protection to her husband. He told her a woman's body was not created to carry so many children. Eventually, it would give out. He didn't have to tell the man that he didn't have the coin to feed so many mouths. Mr. Fletcher didn't listen to anything Houston told the man. All he did was grunt. Mrs. Fletcher told him the lecture was useless, that his words fell upon deaf ears. The man wasn't about to take his rod out of her and lose the pleasure as well as the satisfaction. Tried a condom once but didn't like the way it felt. She didn't either.

Houston drew in a shaky breath of air as he thought about Leah, the kisses they shared. Not last night though, last night he was terribly afraid if he kissed her, he wouldn't leave. Grizzly wasn't around. The place was empty and far too inviting. He didn't know how much longer he could see her, kiss her and not make love to her. He would have to listen to his own lectures.

He would have to wait until she believed in herself to tell her she was his mate, to claim her. If she learned to write a few things, the accomplishment would go a long way to helping her with her confidence. He understood she didn't think she was good enough for him. When he gave her coin to go to the highlands, she would have to make sure Grizzly couldn't find the money or all would be lost. Houston didn't doubt for one second the man would steal the groats if he found them.

Ah, Leah, she was so sweet and kind, too caring for her best interest. Mrs. Fletcher told him she brought water for them every day since their well turned foul. Perhaps that was a reason why the house was such a mess. They didn't have water for cleaning. He didn't think so. Mrs. Fletcher was just too exhausted to do chores while Mr. Fletcher wasn't about to lend a hand.

Leah's dilapidated home was in front of him. He could hardly wait to see her gone from here. She would be safe in his mother and father's home. He could relax. The letter he intended to write his mother would explain how she was his mate. He didn't want her to have to work. Although he knew she would insist. That was probably for the best. He couldn't imagine her idle. After they were wed, she could help him with his practice.

Now he wished he hadn't committed to this apprenticeship even though he would garner much needed knowledge. Working with another physician, sharing ideas along with theories always proved to be productive. This was a man who, like him, looked for new ideas for treatment rather than using all the old ways.

She must have heard his approach. By the time he dismounted and tied the reins to her porch railing, she stood in front of him, her smile brilliant. She wore the same lavender dress she'd worn the day he took her to dinner. A shawl was wrapped around her shoulders.

"You came, Houston?"

His name broke in the back of her throat. She sounded breathless as well as eager for the day. Her blue eyes were alight with anticipation.

"You didn't think I would?" He wanted to pull her into his arms and after that was accomplished kiss her senseless, send the heat along with the taste of her through his veins to his soul. "Told you my schedule was empty for the afternoon. Hawk will take any emergencies."

He needed to look his fill. Her heated blush enthralled him. She was so very innocent. Had no idea what her sultry smile did to him.

For a moment she looked to her toes, seemed to want to see him as she slowly brought her gaze upward to meet his. She smiled softly. "As I told you last night, I've got something to show you. It's important to me. You said you wanted to see my place, a place that is just mine, no one else's. I'll share the space with you if you wish."

He did. He was pleased she trusted him enough to show him, not just Hawk, this place that was special to her heart. "I will be happy to share. Show me."

Even to his ears his voice sounded deep and dark, husky with simmering passion burning him. With just the single look, the slight lowering of her lashes, she made him that way.

She led the way as she lifted the front of her gown to move more easily down the too well traveled path. If she didn't want Grizzly or anyone else for that matter to discover this trail, she would have to do something to make it less obvious.

As if reading his mind, she turned. "I have to find another way up. After today I'll use the path from two years ago. Every few months I change the way in. If you know where the refuge is, it's easy to find it without a path."

He supposed she might be right. It seemed to him she was going to the top of the crag. "How far is it?"

"Are you winded already?" she asked laughing as she danced in front of him, backing up the path as if she possessed eyes in the back of her head.

"If this is the path, I'll race you." He swept by her before he turned to look back at her. When she reached him, he picked her up, twirled her around a few times then followed the path, keeping her in his arms drawing her close.

She laughed at his antics as she pounded him on the arm. "Put me down!"

"Not until we get there," he told her stopping long enough to place a chaste kiss on her forehead. He didn't ever want to let her go. "I'll give you winded."

"I take the words back," she told him solemnly. "You don't have to carry me to prove a point. I must weigh as much as a whale."

"Two whales," he told her as he pretended to stagger under her weight.

"Monster," she whispered then hit him again. He dutifully grunted. "A girl doesn't want to hear she's fat. Two whales..."

"Maybe two feathers," he told her, as it seemed they reached the sanctuary she spoke of. "Are we here?"

"You *ken* we are. Isn't it beautiful?"

He let her slide slowly down the length of him, reveling in the feel of every soft curve she possessed as it encountered every part of his hardness. "Not as beautiful as you."

She seemed to be breathless when he let her go. "Flatterer. Are you using me, Houston Stuart? Is that you working your wiles on me as Brenda warned me against."

Houston stuffed his hands through his hair. "Just speaking the truth." He turned in a circle memorizing the clearing, noting where it stood in comparison to her home. He needed to be able to find his way here again if need be.

She kneeled in a corner. "I've a sparrow hawk here. He's almost ready to be set free. The bird got caught in some wire. The hawk was so frantic to get out, he broke his leg."

Houston remembered another time, a place where he had that same feeling until a fey little girl with an angelic smile rescued him. He'd been frantic, fearing discovery, fearing capture.

He crouched beside her, studying the bird then her face. Tears sat on the bottoms of her eyelids. Her kindness and caring never ceased to amaze him. He never met anyone like her. When he recalled the tears she shed for him when she pried him from the steel trap he'd been caught in, the memory stole his breath. If he closed his eyes thinking hard, he could see her eyes, her face. The encounter had been horrific for her, nearly as terrible as it had been for him. On that day it seemed to him she shared his pain, stole some of it from him to wrap herself in what he felt.

"What is it?" he asked her placing a hand on her back, soothing her, hoping he could make the pain go away.

"I cannot stand to see an animal suffer." She sniffed back the moisture clogging her throat. "He will fly away soon. I *dinna* believe he is afraid of me anymore. He was at first. All wild animals are afraid when they first meet you."

When she looked at him her eyes were wide, questioning almost as if she was asking him if he was afraid when he first encountered her.

He had not been. He wasn't a wild animal either, just wild for Leah. With every encounter he was more certain, Leah was his rescuer that day five years ago. She would have been fifteen then.

She went on to tell him, "There is a rabbit over here. Something tried to take a bite out of him. By the end of the summer, I'll have more creatures. Sometimes the boys who go to the forests to explore hurt them on purpose."

She stood, sliding her hands down her dress, pressing the fabric against her willowy curves. Every feminine part of her stood out for his inspection.

He sucked in air as he watched, mesmerized by her, by the way she moved, the roundness of her hips, the slight swell of her breasts. He wanted to see her with nothing on. He would someday. "This is amazing."

They had healing in common along with a strong sense of right from wrong. He'd always been taught all animals have a purpose. They should be revered.

"No..." she denied his words. "It is just how it should be."

"Would you like to try your hand at the letters in your name? I'm willing to show you what you need to know."

He was changing the direction of the afternoon. When the time was right, he would change it again. Today at least he would like to show her what her name looked like the way she saw the letters. Reading for her should be simple when she learned a few tricks that might come in handy.

She smiled wide, "Truly, you think you can do such a daunting task when everyone else who has tried has failed?"

"I'm going to show you the way you see your name." He sat down with her next to him as he pulled out paper and charcoal. Painstakingly he wrote each letter backward. Then he held it to her. "That is your name the way you see the letters when it is written properly. Now you see your name backward. What you will have to do first is learn the letters that make up your name." He pointed to each one telling her what they were called.

She repeated them. "That isn't what Hawk showed me."

At the mention of Hawk, he sucked in a breath of flower-scented air that came from Leah. "That's because he didn't understand why you were having difficulty. I do."

"You do?"

"Can you form the letters?" He handed the writing utensils to her. "Say each letter as you write it."

She did.

"Very good, now I'm going to show you how most people see your name. You do have a difficult task because you have to learn two things when practically everyone else only has to learn one." He set about showing her the way her name, Leah, looked to most.

"That's what Hawk showed me. As you said, all the letters are turned around. Now it looks like the first one you wrote. How peculiar."

"Say the letters again."

She did. The lesson went on for another hour or so. The sun shone bright upon them heating the small space. There was a slight breeze in the enclosed area, just enough to keep the sanctuary cool. With Leah sitting close to him, her breasts pushing against the wall of his chest, he decided the lesson should come to an end. Perhaps one of a different nature should begin.

Houston leaned against a rock, his legs stretched out in front of him, his hands behind his head. She sat with her legs folded under her.

"What would you like to do now?" He wasn't at all ready to end the afternoon. Kissing was on his mind as well as a bit of subtle coaxing to see if they dared get past Brenda's instructions.

Her impish grin sent a sizzle of heat down his body straight to his groin. What the devil was she about to blurt now? He didn't want to wait. Nonetheless, she seemed hesitant. So, he decided patience would serve him well.

"Brenda told us where as well as how a man could touch a woman. I want to know what the rules are for me touching you. Is there anywhere I can't put my hands on you?"

If he had anything in his mouth, he would have spewed it out. No, as far as he was concerned, she could touch him or kiss him anywhere she wanted. He wasn't sure he could tell her that. If he did and she touched him wherever she wanted, they would be in huge trouble.

"Think maybe you could show me something else. Did you have a sketch book?"

She didn't seem pleased. "Yes, though I gather you don't want to answer me."

"No, I just have to think about what I should say."

She'd withdrawn from him. The devil, he didn't want her withdrawal. He liked her spouting whatever crazy question or notion came to her mind.

"I suppose you don't want me to touch you." She folded her hands in her lap. "Fair enough."

She was staring at his mouth. His body hardened. This was not what he expected from the afternoon.

"That's not true, not true at all."

How was he going to explain any of what he wanted without hurting her feelings?

Her head tilted slightly to one side then the other as if once again she studied him. "Tell me then. I'll show you the sketch book later, after I've touched you everywhere it's alright."

He swallowed down the lump in his throat. She was going to be the death of him. "I suppose you can touch me anywhere above the waistband of my trousers."

"Truly?" She sounded so eager he could barely keep the groan from rumbling forth.

He should have the mush in his brain cleaned away. "Truly."

"Can you take off your shirt so I can see you better?"

The breath he just sucked in stuck half way between his mouth and his lungs. "If you would like."

When he tried to untie the laces, she pushed his hands aside, seemingly eager to see him. Lord, but he wanted to see her without her gown covering her breasts. That was taboo. At her urging he lifted his arms as she kneeled to move the shirt over his head. She tossed the fabric to the ground then sat back looking her fill. At least that was what he thought she was doing.

It was strange to be seen like this. She was sweeping her gaze over him, studying him he supposed more like devouring him.

"Do you like what you see?" he asked, his voice so husky he wasn't sure it was his.

For a few more seconds she didn't say anything. "You're nothing like me. I *dinna ken* why it's alright for me to look at as well as touch you when you *canna* do the same to me."

"How so? How am I so different? Perhaps then you'll have your answer."

He was utterly curious what she would say. Finding out through her eyes how she saw him was intriguing.

She cleared her throat as if she was having trouble forming words. "You're hard where I'm soft." She reached out as she moved closer to him. Touched his stomach. His muscles jerked. Her tongue ran across her lips before she bit the bottom one. "How did you get so hard here?"

He tried not to let the rumble of sound leave his belly where she was slowly tormenting his rise of passion to a point where it would overpower his control. His erection pulsed against fabric. He prayed she would not let her gaze drift lower. For now, he had his wish.

Exquisitely, her fingers roamed higher although he might have wanted her to explore closer to his waistband, perhaps dip a bit below. Instead, he told her not below his waist. A man could dream. He lurched to attention when her tiny fingers, caressed one hardened nipple then the other. For several seconds her fingers explored from one to the other.

"Did that hurt?"

He could tell her about ache between his legs, about how she could ease both of them. There was not one doubt in his head that she was feeling much the same.

She let her tongue touch her upper lip for the longest time. "You are very different here. So tiny, but still hard, your muscles... I'm soft and much larger, rounded where you are...flat. I *dinna* have the words to describe what I'm thinking."

"Do you have any idea the risks you are taking? You tempt me, Leah." His knuckles grazed her cheek. With wide eyes she stared at him. "You are teasing me out of control."

"Risks?"

"I should not have... Never mind."

It was all he could think about. How Leah saw him. Where she touched him.

"Your neck is larger." She placed wet slick lips at the pulse that throbbed with the need for more of the same, for more of Leah. He would give her whatever she asked for. Soon he intended more. For now, he didn't wish to scare her or intimidate.

He closed his eyes certain this was almost heaven. Her lips closed over one nipple. Her tongue wrapped around the hardness, caressed, nipped then did the same on the other hard peak. "I wonder what this feels like. Would it feel the same if you did that to me?"

His voice cracked. Every muscle and sinew he possessed tightened beyond anything he felt before. The sensations delicious. "Don't think we'll be discovering that any time soon even though I'd like to suck your nipple along with your tiny breast deep into my mouth. Would love to hear the small sweet sounds you would make."

She sat back, a strange expression of annoyance on her lovely face. For a moment her lashes closed over her eyes. "My breasts are not tiny." She sounded indignant, almost as if he offended her. He reached out then brought his hand back before he could touch her.

He could not help the rush of curiosity. Against Brenda's courting advice, he ran his hand along the curve of her ribs up her side until he brushed the side of one breast. "Doesn't seem more than just a bit. Not that the size of your breasts matters to me." He was sure her breasts would be beautifully sensitive even though they were small. Didn't understand why what he thought the size was seemed so important to her.

She blinked several times. Still piqued. "You wouldn't know." She turned a stiff back to him.

"I can tell..."

She returned her gaze, eyes blazing, darkening with her scrutiny. "Since I bind my breasts, there is no way you can tell."

He felt a sudden hot rage while he wasn't certain why it was there pounding at him. "You do what?" Despite his best efforts he couldn't keep the anger behind his teeth.

"They hurt sometimes. It's much better for me to wrap cloth around them to hold them in place so they don't bounce when I walk or even do the smallest task."

"That's not good for you."

He sounded as if he knew. Nothing in any of his reading mentioned this particular problem for women. Often women as separate entities from men were overlooked in the medical journals. He meant to discover more.

"How would you, a man, *ken* this? You do not have this problem. I do what helps me. I don't care what you think or believe in this matter."

He groaned unable to stop the low, raw rumble. The devil, he'd like to see these breasts, not that it mattered to him. *The size of her breasts.* No, he didn't care but a man could...hell what could he do. Leah was his mate. He didn't care about the size of her breasts. Often enough he'd thought more than a mouthful was a waste. He was intrigued though. Curiosity goaded him to see more of her.

"I don't. You're right. It just surprised me. Sometimes what one sees is not the truth, now is it?" Houston asked.

"I'd let you see but...of course..."

"Brenda."

"Yes," she agreed.

"She wouldn't know. We wouldn't tell her." Where the devil did that come from? "Maybe we should continue where we just left off. Perhaps this isn't fair. You do want this to be fair."

How would he ever consider fairness with the opposite sex? Leah was vulnerable. He was not. Life for women was hardly ever fair.

Expectations for their chastity ran high while a man could seek his sexual needs anywhere he pleased.

"I do like touching you. Love the dreamy look that fills your eyes. Did you know you have tiny marks on your chest?" She was tracing one with a fingertip. "They are dark and all different shapes. Why do you suppose they are there? Do all men have these kinds of marks?"

She looked at him as if she knew something about him she couldn't possibly know. "I do?" he asked understanding that if she did know something this was by far the worst thing he could say.

He shouldn't feign ignorance, neither could he give himself away. This was too soon. He didn't know if he had her complete trust. Didn't know if she would think of him as a freak of nature if she discovered his truth.

"Yes, you *ken* it too." She trailed kisses down the middle of his chest to his belly then up to circle both nipples one at a time.

His body shuddered in response, "I do?" he stammered again unable to say anything else. "Perhaps we should have another reading lesson."

"*Nay,*" she spoke softly. "I want you to answer my questions."

"No? Well, when you're ready I'll tell you all that I know."

She was shaking her head, running both hands along his chest. He had to stop this before it went too far. Before he was mindless and had no control left to him.

"I know who you are as well as what you are. I *ken* some of what you can do. You've no reason to lie to me or pretend ignorance."

~ * ~

When her hand settled just above his waist, she felt the ripples surge in his powerful body. Perhaps she asked too much of him. His scent filled her with longing. The spring day made her bold. Touching sent silvery shimmers through her, heating her until her core ached. Touching him was almost as intense as when he caressed her, raw and delicious, mercuric in nature. He understood what would enflame her.

She did not.

One of his hands settled on top of hers where it rested on his stomach. He moved her fingers lower. The bulge beneath her hands and the fabric of his trousers came to life, pulsing throbbing. She understood he wanted something primal, exciting.

Questions shuddering through her she gazed at him. She'd seen pictures. Knew this was a part of him completely different from her. Yet this did not feel like any of the pictures she'd seen.

"Houston." His name broke from her on a soft sigh coupled with a whimper. She touched her lip with her tongue as she inhaled a wavering breath of air.

He moved her hand back to his stomach. "I should not have done that. Another time perhaps." His dark silver eyes burned into her, heating her, promising sensual passion.

"You'll be leaving. When will another time happen? If not today, when?" Leah wanted everything now. Needed to show him that her breasts were not tiny. She didn't understand why his words hurt, stung in a way she couldn't define.

"I can't answer that. Perhaps in a day or two, possibly another week. I'm not in a hurry." It seemed he was as impatient as she was to learn more.

In a quick move that stole her breath while capturing her heart, he was on top of her, kissing her, his lips touching and tracing intricate patterns along her neck to her lips then back again. She was enthralled by the magic he elicited. Her fingers stroked through his thick dark hair down to his nape then back. The moisture from his lips slicked a path down her neck to the opening of her gown. The fastenings dissolved beneath his teeth, left her dress open.

"I wish you wouldn't wrap your breasts when you will be with me. I'm trying to understand why you would want to at all. No matter, your reasons elude me," he murmured softly as he gazed down at her.

"Why?"

"I want to see the curves, imagine the way they will taste," he rasped out huskily while his hands bracketed her face.

Something told her he was going to discover that today. She wouldn't stop him. Nimble fingers found purchase where she fastened the cloth. Quickly, she was lifted and turned until the wrapping vanished then tossed aside.

Vulnerable as well as open to his perusal, she almost covered herself with her hands until she reminded herself this was what she wanted. His gaze remained fixed on her while the golden sun beat down, warming her hands where they were pressed against his back. His weight pushed into her while he lifted her, turned her so she sat on his lap.

Soft, gentle kisses rained down upon her lips, trembled down her neck to the valley between her breasts. Silver shivers of delight swamped her while she soaked up his heat. His lips traveled across the ivory flesh until he met the hard pink tip. As his tongue curled around the peak, the crest hardened even more. An ache deep inside rippled through her. Needing him, she lifted her hips until they met his hard erection.

"Houston," his name broke from her lips in a rush of desire so intense she would have fallen if she'd been standing.

His ardent attention with his lips as well as his tongue moved to her other breast, touching, tasting until she writhed coiling against him, needing something she didn't understand. She ran her hands over the heat of his muscled chest.

"Is this heaven?" she asked in a whispered soft puff of air she wasn't sure he heard.

"For me it is."

"I feel so hot..."

"This is why you were told not to let me touch you below your shoulders." He nipped at her ear while his hands cupped and held her breasts, his thumbs running across the nipples he drew to tight harder buds.

"Why do I want you to never stop?" Tiny sounds of pleasure rushed from her, begging him. She made a broken sound in the back of her throat.

"We shouldn't go any farther. We should stop now while I still can. The devil, I do want you, Leah." He kissed the tip of her nose then her lips. "God knows I don't want to stop."

"Then don't," she whispered while his fingers stroked her from her waist to slowly caress her collarbone.

"You're right. You are far from tiny. Is that why you sounded so indignant when I said differently?" He was smiling at her.

"I didn't want to be thought lacking." This time she knew she sounded annoyed. "You sounded as if you thought of me as a little girl, not the grown woman I am."

"Never," he laughed softly cupping each breast in one of his large hands, rubbing his cheek against each one.

The blatant sensuality of this tanned hands holding her breasts brought more questions to her mind. Breasts were meant to suckle children. It seemed strange to her they could be so sensitive to a man's caress.

"I'd like to touch you where you are most different from me."

"Right now, that would be a huge mistake. One we might suffer consequences for if we indulged," he told her as he continued to kiss and nip along her neck then her lips.

When she looked beyond him, he turned her to look at him. "It's my responsibility to make sure nothing happens that we'll regret no matter how much we want each other right now."

She stiffened, understanding he thought her an innocent, perhaps even not capable of taking care of another living soul. She wasn't. "I would never regret having your baby. *Ye dinna* have to worry yourself about me, Houston Stuart."

"We are not wed."

They never would marry. Their differences would keep them a part. What they had in common could never make up for the disparities between them. She understood that. If she had his child, she would be censured. She could not travel to the highlands to meet his parents. That might be a regret for her, but not the *wee* babe.

"Does it matter so much?" The reasons she could think of did not outweigh her desire for his child.

"Yes, you *ken* it does." His voice changed tenor, no longer hungry with desire, rather annoyed at her insistence to continue the conversation. "You don't have the coin to raise a child. I'm going to be gone for more than a month, possibly two or three. I've no idea how long it will take my foot to heal. Grizzly wouldn't want another mouth to feed even though he would not have to worry about it for a few months."

Even if she conceded to him, it didn't change the fact she wanted his child. It might be all she would have to remember him by as the years passed.

"You could take precautions," she told him still hoping for a change of heart from him. That would not help her have his baby. Nonetheless if he changed his mind, it would give her a memory she could hold close to her heart.

"I could." He ran his knuckles gently down her cheek then lower to one exposed breast teasing the hard tip.

She should have covered herself. Now that she understood she couldn't sway him, she felt vulnerable, even deficient.

"What type of precautions does a man take?" she queried softly hope rising once more.

"If you were pregnant with my child, I would insist you go to my parents as well as seek their help. Leah, it's not going to happen. The last thing I want is to burden you with a child out of wedlock."

Slowly, he pulled her gown together, fastening it as he did so. His fingers brushed against her bared breasts. The cloth she bound her breasts with was in his hands. He held the fabric to her.

"Don't put this on until I'm gone."

Disappointment swamped her. She wished she understood more about men. Hawk might explain to her why he didn't want to make love to her. Men did it all the time without repercussions.

That's because they don't get pregnant.

He was touching her face again, her lips. She swept her tongue across them. All she wanted to do was vanish down the mountain. "It's not that I don't want you. The devil, I've never wanted anyone more. Yes, we could make love. Odds are there would be no baby. It's always possible though whether precautions are taken or not."

She wanted to hear other words. Words that might tell her he wanted her, needed her. They wouldn't come from his lips. She knew that just as certainly that she knew her heart would keep beating.

"Perhaps you could show me your sketchbook. I'd like to see what you've drawn."

By demanding things she'd put a damper on the day. All the sunshine seemed to turn grey. She nodded. His hands on her waist, he helped her stand.

"Suppose it's for the best." From her hiding place near the sparrow hawk's home, she retrieved a satchel.

"It is, Leah. Where you are concerned, I've only a limited amount of control. If we go too far, I cannot make promises that would be kept."

She couldn't tell him she didn't care if he didn't have any control at all. She was twenty. Most girls were wed and had at least one child by the time they were her age. She wasn't most girls. She was still innocent. She wanted to change that with Houston. She would survive just as she always did.

"You know about protection. I heard...well Brenda says you've talked to Seamus about that so she won't keep getting pregnant."

His expression changed as his brows narrowed almost forming one line. Houston cleared his throat, his brows coming together. "Yes, I've given Seamus some ways to keep from getting Brenda pregnant, Mr. Fletcher as well."

"Then you could do that. What you told them." She pursued this despite his obvious displeasure.

He jabbed his hands through his hair before he slipped on his shirt. "I could." There was a long pause as his breath hovered in the stagnant air around them. "As I told you before, nothing is guaranteed. Even with precautions there are chances of pregnancy."

"Do you have any children? I'm sure neither you nor Hawk have been celibate. Hawk doesn't have children. Do you?" She heard the breath catch in his throat.

"No, I don't have children. That doesn't mean anything. As I told you before, with you I've little to no control. There are no guarantees."

"Is that why you stopped because you can't control yourself? Seems you either don't care that much for me or you've got more control than necessary. You're always able to stop when I just want you to keep kissing me."

Tension radiated around his eyes as they darkened to stormy grey. She pushed him too far. She understood you could only push a man so far. After that there would be anger as well as shouting.

"I've control when you are still clothed, when I'm not looking at you with not one stich between the two of us. When and if that happens, I don't know..."

Leah needed to tell him that would happen. She would be naked as well as in his arms. His words also planted some ideas in her head that she might try out next time they were alone. She didn't know when that would be. She certainly hoped sooner than later. In this she was going to have to take the initiative. If left to Houston, they would never be together. He would never make love to her then he would be gone from her life. She wanted to have a memory with him, one she could hold on to when she was alone in the cold and the dark. He would just have to make sure he had enough control. Whatever that meant.

He was going to see her naked.

It would be her pleasure as well as his.

In this she was determined, more so than ever before.

"I haven't seen that book yet." He looked pointedly at the satchel. "Now would be a good time."

"Very well." She showed him the drawings. Told him how Hawk used all his books to find out the names of all the plants as well as the animals she drew. How he wrote them on the drawing and how she memorized the names so she knew what they were called.

"These are very good, Leah. You should be proud of what you can do."

One at a time, he was looking through all the drawings.

His fingers stopped sifting through the pages. When she saw what brought a startled shift of air from his lungs, she understood why. The picture of him as she remembered him when his foot was caught in the steel trap stared back at him. He knew it was him. All black panthers were different. None looked the same.

He stared at her, his gaze piercing then burning into hers. She understood he wanted answers. Until he was able to tell her who he really was, she could not say a word.

Although a few hours ago, she nearly gave it away.

"What is this?" he asked as his gaze fell back to the panther. When he asked, he sounded incredulous, questioning. "You've seen a black panther."

"Just something I drew. Saw a drawing once a long time ago." She shrugged, her unfettered breasts rubbing against the fabric of her gown.

His gaze fell upon her, watched as she moved. She saw that he was interested in her once again. Saw his erection she'd felt earlier grow beneath his trousers. He noticed the direction in which she was looking. A flush painted his face. It made her smile. She'd never seen him blush before.

It seemed he tried to ignore her as well as the growing erection he was unable to hide. "Did someone tell you about this? From what I've seen in your sketchbook, I'm positive you could draw this from another's description. What picture did you see? Where were you?" He said the words but she didn't think he was speaking truthfully.

"No." Leah supposed it was too late for lies but silence might work in this situation. Where she came from, paintings of black panthers would be rare. He would know. Her nerves were unraveling just as they did when he kissed her. Somehow this was different. She felt no pleasure.

"How?"

It didn't seem he meant to let the question go. She turned from him, shuffling through the drawings, placing them back inside the satchel before putting them in their secret place as she tried desperately to ignore him. "It's getting late. We should go now. I'll take you down the new path so you can find this place again. If you want to that is."

"Leah, tell me." His hand rested on her shoulder, his long lean fingers squeezing lightly. "It's something I need to know, should know."

She swallowed the growing lump in her throat. "I don't know what you want me to say."

"The truth, only the truth," he murmured as he seemed to study her, searching her eyes. "Where did you see a black panther?"

"I promised myself I'd never tell anyone. Promised someone else too." She hesitated for a few seconds that to her seemed to stretch into eternity and back. "A long time ago, when I was wandering in the highlands, I came across an animal that needed help. I helped him. It was nothing. Anyone would have done the same."

She hoped he would tell her the animal was him.

He didn't.

"Just as you did the sparrow hawk, you helped the big cat. You could have been hurt. Did you think of that? Of course, you didn't," he murmured as his molten gaze drifted toward the bird with the broken leg.

"Yes. Except I understood the animal wasn't dangerous. He meant me no harm."

That was all. Nothing more was said as he placed her hand in his. "Lead the way."

Silence followed them down the mountain. He was angry with her. She didn't know why. She tried to push her thoughts away from him along with the sketch he saw which told a tale she didn't want him to know until she knew a few more truths.

She tried to concentrate on the day while forgetting his anger. Leah soaked in the scents and sounds while wishing for something that might not ever come to pass. When they reached the house, Grizzly wasn't at home. She didn't expect him, yet she did. He'd been away for two days now. It was past his normal dinnertime. He would be hungry. She left a vegetable stew simmering slowly over the fire. She hated cooking with meat. Though meat was what he wanted. She was thankful he rarely provided it.

Once again Houston set her on the porch rail, his hands around her waist. A half smile graced his lips. "I believe you should never wrap your breasts again," he murmured as he placed silver kisses along her lips. It seemed he put the drawing from his mind.

"Grizzly would ogle them. I don't know what Michael would do. I would feel terribly uncomfortable in their presence."

Leah watched as he set his hand on top of one breast. Her nipple hardened with the soft caress of his palm in the place where it was so very sensitive. She shivered as her nails dug into the nape of his neck.

"You have sharp little claws," he murmured, sliding his tongue across her lips, seeming to beg her to open for him. "I *dinna* like the idea of Michael seeing you like this or Grizzly. I guess you'll have to keep binding them." His breath against her cheek was raspy and warm. Mint scented the places where the air he breathed out bathed her.

126

"Neither do I," she whispered the words even while she shuddered at the thought Michael might see her, take something from her she meant only for Houston. "I only want you to see me, no one else."

Needing more she opened for him, pushed her tongue across his mouth until she slipped inside. She wanted to see him shift almost as much as she wanted him to make love to her. As much as she needed to tell him what she knew, she was also terrified that the information would change their relationship irrevocably.

She wasn't willing to jeopardize what they had.

Unable to stop herself, she ran her tongue across his teeth, feeling the smoothness, wondering if he had fangs in his cat form. There was so much she needed to know, yearned to discover about him. With time she could learn everything. They only had a few weeks a month at best maybe even less. For them time slipped away too rapidly.

Stroking his soft fur was something she thought he might enjoy. She certainly would. Deep in the back of her throat she purred softly.

She gasped when he suckled one breast through the thin fabric of her gown then grazed his teeth across the hardened tip. Her gown was so threadbare it was almost as if she was naked. Her eyes closed as she arched back giving him more access while sensual energy created magic inside. Her body came to life as only Houston could make it happen.

When he lifted his head, he grinned. "Did Brenda say anything about kisses with your gown covering your breasts? If she did, you didn't tell me. Do you suppose it breaks the rules?"

Breathless with exquisite pleasure, "I'm sure she probably did. At the moment, I cannot recall. So, no you didn't break one, it must be within the rules."

He laughed, chuckling in the back of his throat as he stared at the wet mark his mouth created as well as the tight bud so obvious now. "If we cannot remember, is it still a rule?" he asked as his teeth traveled to entice the other tip. "I would surely like to know. Don't know if I could stop because this is certainly heaven."

With her hands woven through his hair she held him close, begging him for more and more.

~ * ~

Brenda set a cup of mint tea in front of Leah. "How is your romance with Houston going?"

She sat down at the kitchen table watching and contemplating her friend. In the few weeks since she'd known Houston, Leah changed. She wasn't as withdrawn. She smiled and laughed more often. What would happen to her when he left? When all the happiness drained from her.

Brenda knew Leah fancied herself in love with Houston. She was so afraid Leah would do something she would come to regret. "You have to be careful not to let things go too far."

"What if I want them to go farther than Houston? He always stops," Leah murmured unhappily while she swirled a spoon in her tea.

"Then the doctor is thinking of you. He is doing the right thing by you. He cannot leave you increasing and alone when he goes off to Edinburgh. Heard he was going to see if Hawk can fix his foot. Whatever happened to it?" Brenda asked while she looked at Leah over the rim of her cup hoping she would see answers in her eyes.

Leah set her cup that had been half way to her mouth on the saucer. "His injury happened a while back. He didn't see the trap and stepped into it. Broke all the bones in his foot. When the bonesetter took care of him, the man didn't do a very good job. That's why he limps."

"He told you?"

"No, well, yes, he did tell me." Leah stared into her cup seeming to avoid looking at her.

There were stories behind Leah's silence. Something in the way Leah looked sparked more curiosity in Brenda. She knew from past experiences one couldn't draw words from Leah's mouth she didn't want to share.

"Grizzly hasn't come home in three days," Leah volunteered after a lengthy silence. "I don't know what to think."

"Bless the lord," Brenda murmured her voice soft as she tried to think of the ramifications that might come from his death. "You could get along just fine without that mean, old man."

"It's true but..."

"But what? What has he ever done for you?" Brenda asked even though she understood Grizzly was the provider. Leah could fend for herself. She was an amazing seamstress. The dressmaker here in town could use the help if all Leah needed was a bit of coin to put supper on her table. While it wasn't the best, she had a place to stay, a home.

"Nothing. I don't like wishing bad things on anyone. It's true I would be happier without my stepfather. The only reason he wouldn't come home would be if he was dead or hurt."

Brenda leaned forward, patting her on the hand. "You're too kind. Always thinking of others instead of yourself. How did God ever make such a perfect human?"

Brenda would never understand how Leah always felt for the underdog when she was just as much of an underdog as anyone in this place. She knew a change of subject was necessary. She wanted to learn more about Leah's relationship with Michael. After all the rumors, Leah should know what had been said.

Bluntly, "What about Michael? I've heard some things, gossip that isn't flattering to you or Houston. Is any of it true?"

She watched the puffy little sigh Leah gave. "Michael is angry with me. Told him I wouldn't marry him. Also told the man that I didn't like his kiss. Guess he reacted to it by insults."

"Why on earth did you let that man kiss you?" she asked as she rose to put on another pot of tea.

On her way to the stove, she peeked into the main room to check on the children who were strangely silent.

"I didn't," Leah fiddled with the cup. "He forced me to kiss him. I wasn't strong enough to stop him. It was nothing Like Houston's kisses which I love."

"Well, that boy needs to listen to the woman he wants to kiss. He's so head over heels for you, he can't think straight. What about your doctor? Does he think straight when he's with you?"

"Too straight," Leah murmured.

"What's that supposed to mean?" Brenda was suddenly worried. "Tell me you've been abiding by my rules."

"Well yes, but...mostly"

"But...mostly?"

"You told me everything about what he could do. Nevertheless, not about what I could do. I wanted to know if I could touch him without a shirt?"

"You did. No, no, no..." Brenda was shaking her head, knowing full well that would lead to things that just shouldn't happen.

Leah clamped her hands on her mouth. "It's too late. He almost didn't stop. Oh my, we agreed I wouldn't say anything to you. He might not forgive me."

Brenda had a bad feeling about this, a very bad feeling. Leah was rushing headlong into something she might always regret.

Chapter Six

Houston stumbled up the path he thought at first was the one he and Leah traversed yesterday. It wasn't. Brambles and cobwebs caught him in the face. Tree branches tripped him. He must be half crazy. He should have taken the path he knew would lead him to the top.

Hell, he didn't even know if Leah was there. Hawk was taking over more duties each day so he decided he would come see her this afternoon. She wasn't in the house, neither was Grizzly. Grizzly hadn't been at work either. That situation didn't bode well for Leah.

He tripped. Swore. His hands and knees were on the ground. This would be so much easier if he shifted. Knew he couldn't do that. In his cat form, if Leah was at the refuge, what would he tell her? The devil, he'd terrify her if she wasn't the girl who saved him so long ago. Send her running down the mountain.

That wasn't something he could live with.

Inhaling a long, deep breath of heather scented air, he stood. A few birds flitted from branch to branch. He wished he knew their names, as he was sure Leah could tell him the names of most every animal as well as plant on the crag. With the back of his forearm, he swiped the sweat off his forehead. His shirt clung to his chest and back. When he started out, he never imagined the day was this hot. He always believed it to be cooler up the mountain.

The path was airless. Maybe it wasn't so hot. Here, though, it was wretched.

Shading his eyes with his hand, he looked upward. What there was of a path continued seemingly without end. He was lost. It would be interesting news when the next paper was printed. Doctor Stuart lost on

131

the mountain. Found sitting in a pool of his sweat.

Houston pulled in a long draught of air wishing he'd thought to bring a skin of water with him. When he started out, he would never have thought he would come to this. Believed the trek would be easy. It certainly was yesterday.

"Leah," he said softly to the bushes and brambles surrounding him, "you better be there. I've something important to show you."

Well, he should tell her first then if she doesn't run down the mountain screaming perhaps, he could show her. It was about time she knew more about him as well as his family.

He wanted her to see his cat. When she did, he prayed she would still want him in her life. Wasn't at all sure what he would do if she was afraid of him, if she didn't want anything to do with him. He'd never heard of anyone's mate turning them down.

"No, that never happens," he murmured as he tried to reassure himself. "At least it never happened in his family."

He certainly didn't want to be the first to lose his mate. What happened to a man if his soul mate didn't want him? Would that mean they would never travel through eternity together. They would never meet in another time? He wanted Leah. He didn't want to chance losing her.

Houston let a low growl rumble from his gut through his throat. He jabbed his hands through his sweat-damp hair. His heart thundering, he pushed his way up the last part of the trail. He jerked to a halt when he stepped into the refuge.

His mind reeled with the sight that greeted him.

Leah?

The small panther was lying down, her back to him. She was tawny and spotted beautifully, not black like he was. She didn't know he was in the glade watching her, mesmerized by the vision. All types of scenarios danced in his mind. His heart soared to his throat.

Why hadn't she told him or given him some indication of what she was? Thinking over the words she spoke just yesterday told him she might know he was a shifter. She never said anything. He remembered the way she gently traced his markings.

Why didn't he notice hers?

You were too damn busy ogling her breasts. Breasts, which overflowed his hands, he discovered.

Houston wasn't sure what to do. He didn't want to scare her. Perhaps she would sense his presence and turn toward him. She would still be surprised. If he'd come in from a different direction, he would have been upwind. In that case she would have shifted back.

What if this panther wasn't Leah?

His breath broke then caught. He sipped air while his nerves stretched before finally seeming to unravel one fine strand at a time. He was suddenly angry at her deception. If she sensed what he was, she most certainly should have told him she was the same.

As patiently as he could manage, he waited for her to swivel her head. Instead, she stretched lazily, her backside rising into the air. She began to purr. Her unknowing actions were sending him over the edge.

He had to concentrate.

Only cobwebs along with dust filled his brain.

Crouching, he continued to watch her as she sinuously adjusted herself on the moss, making herself comfortable. He knew how the hot sun felt on his black coat. He wondered now how she would feel with sun bearing down on her. She wasn't black.

She was gorgeous in her cat.

As he watched and studied her, he wondered how long he could wait to reveal his presence. His breath hitched again. He swallowed what little hot air he could inhale. As he watched her with slow even breaths, he gradually began to calm. His heart no longer raced uncontrollably.

If he once had doubts about her being his mate, he was positive now that she was. For her safety, he would have to double his efforts to see her to the highlands and the shelter of his family. Michael could never possess her. If he did, she would die inside.

"Leah." His voice was throaty, filled with emotion as he called her name. He stepped forward then hesitated.

She turned, startled. It seemed she froze for a second then slowly backed away. If he gave her the chance, he knew she would bolt. There was nowhere for her to go.

"Don't run." He held his hands out in front of him feeling as if he was approaching a wild animal.

Almost as if the sound of his voice did stop her, she sat down. She was shaking her head, looking to the neatly piled stack of clothing near her sketchpad. He wanted to laugh. Didn't dare. She could not change back without being completely naked in front of him. When she heard his chuckle, she frowned at him.

"We have to talk."

Well, they did but it didn't appear she wanted anything to do with talking. What she wanted was to flee. He would have to leave so she could change.

He didn't want to do so.

Her eyes shimmered just as they did when she was human. Slowly, he walked to her. He understood she might be afraid of him even though she had no reason. If she didn't *ken* he was a shifter also, then she should be more afraid than ever.

He was sure she did know.

As he crouched down beside her, he waited. Needing to feel her, he stroked her back, touched her gently. Again and again, he ran his hand along her back. She purred softly arching to feel his hand just as she did when he ran his hands along her back when she was human.

"I'm not going to hurt you. You're beautiful."

Again, she arched against the pressure of his hand on her back as she nodded her head in understanding. He could imagine hearing her say she understood. She rubbed her face against his arm. The sensation shivered to the tips of his toes and back.

"You don't have anything to be afraid of. You understand that, don't you?" he asked as he continued slow languorous strokes on her back all the way to her rump.

God, how he wanted to do that when she was human.

Once more she nodded, looking to her clothing. He smiled wickedly understanding her thoughts. "You could change back. You would let me see you. Yesterday, we almost went that far. I saw your breasts. I think I could have removed all your clothing. In that case you would not have told me *nay*." He grinned as if he could read her thoughts.

Perhaps he could. She was telling him that was yesterday not today. Today you've put me in a compromising position. I don't know what to do.

"Did you know you've completely taken me by surprise as well as stealing my breath from me? Not many can do that. I never once thought you were a shifter. Look at you, there you are in your cat. You're so very beautiful. Someday perhaps we can run together, race over the wild hills in the highlands. Someday when it is not so dangerous. Do you like to swim? The *lochs* are delicious this time of year."

He laughed realizing by the way she moved she was angry with him. Perhaps he should be angry with her also. She kept secrets from him.

I kept secrets from her.

All along she knew what you were.

There was that. There wasn't a doubt in his mind she knew what he was capable of doing. He sensed she knew other things about him too. He meant to discover those truths.

"Leah, you could have said something. All this would have been avoided if you had. Ah, I understand. You were afraid of something. Not of me, I hope. Never be afraid of me.

"I'm going to give you some space. Nod your head if you understand." Actually, he wanted to stay here so he could watch. He felt as if everything between them changed with this newfound knowledge. They were kindred spirits.

She did nod.

"I'm going to leave for a couple of minutes so you can change into your dress. When I return, we'll talk." As far as he was concerned, she needed to talk. He needed to listen.

Her head bobbed.

Houston felt the cad. He didn't want to walk out of the clearing, giving her a chance to dress. No, he wanted to watch her. See her revealed one tiny moment at a time. There would be time for that. Slowly, he turned his back before starting down the overgrown path he used to get here.

Counting seconds to himself, he waited. One minute passed then two. He counted out another sixty seconds then returned.

When he stepped into the glade, her back was to him. It was long and slim. His gaze traveled to the sweetly rounded curves of her hips and buttocks. She was fastening the buttons on the front of her gown. He decided he would like to see her naked back as much as her front even though her breasts were deliciously round and rosy tipped.

His body hardened as his wayward thoughts took over. He shouldn't think along those lines right now. She had some answering to do before he could pursue another topic.

When she turned, "Houston..." Her voice wavered, floating on the slight breeze in the clearing.

"I never dreamed you would be a shifter, a panther. You're beautiful." He stepped forward, his hand outstretched. Gently touched the outline of her cheek. "Yesterday, you told me you knew what I was. Is that true?"

She nodded, "I did. That's why I didn't run when you entered into the clearing."

"Don't you think we should have talked then? This has blindsided me."

He felt a sudden rise of anger that she kept her secret along with what she knew about him. Secrets between mates weren't good. Perhaps she didn't understand who she was to him or how their lives were intertwined through eternity then beyond.

"I...I wanted to talk. I couldn't seem to form the words." She was keeping distance between them. "I was afraid."

He didn't like that.

"You were afraid of me? What the devil did I ever do to make you afraid?" His heart thundered with the emotions seething and rolling inside him. "How do we make this right?" He asked nonetheless he knew. The truth all of it was the only thing that would make anything right.

With a hesitant step back, she held her hands out as if she wanted more space between them. "No, Houston, I'm not afraid of you. At least not the way you think. I'm afraid of the way you make me feel. I'm afraid for myself because you're going to leave me. Your walking away is as inevitable as my next breath. I'm terrified I'm never going to see you again."

"I won't..."

He knew he had to leave her, however he meant to come back for her. The devil, she was a shifter. She kept it secret even when she knew that he was also a shifter. His emotions so muddled, he couldn't think straight. Didn't know if he was angry or merely frustrated with her reticence as well as the silence. He had to return for her. She was his mate.

"Don't deny it. You are leaving with no promises of returning. You're going to the highlands. Yes, you want me to go there then wait for you to show yourself. I've no way of getting there. You know that fact. So, what do you think I'm supposed to do?"

She was breathing hard. Her breasts heaved. She was magnificent. All he wanted was to hold and reassure her. Well, he wanted to make love to her too.

He wanted to pull her into his arms then kiss her senseless. At the moment, he didn't believe she would want anything to do with him. The need to understand all exploded in his mind.

With calm he didn't feel, he sat then patted a place beside him inviting her to join him. "Come sit. We both need to talk. There are some basic truths you need to understand before I do leave, but not forever. Perhaps there are some facts I need to learn about you before I can fill in the gaps I'm sure exist between us, at least in your mind." He didn't feel the calm he tried for. He leaned against the boulder near her secret hiding place for her sketches before patting the spot beside him.

She sat, her hands folded on her lap, a look of defiance on her lovely face. This was not going to be easy. When he closed his eyes, he saw her in her cat. She was so gorgeous. He inhaled Leah scented air into his lungs. He could not get enough of her. Perhaps they should join together first then talk.

"I..." She swallowed pushing her unbound golden hair away from her face. Her breasts rose and fell tantalizing in every way.

He wanted to run his hands through the length of her hair, feel the silkiness he recalled from the day before. "I?" he asked with a slow, lazy grin.

"Thought to tell you what I knew. Almost did yesterday. But then you know that. I was never good at keeping secrets."

"However, you didn't. Seems to me you're very good, almost too good."

He sounded harsher than he meant his anger showing in the tone he presented to her. That wasn't well done of him. With his words, she pulled away.

"No..."

"Leah, the devil, you're making this damn hard. Why? Why didn't you tell me when you saw my spots? Since you're a shifter too, there was no reason for fear." He was breathing hard, trying to stay rational. With every passing second, she seemed to be pulling away from him. "Why not?

"Now you're angry. I don't like arguments. Is that what you're doing, arguing with me? I can hardly think let alone speak to you when you're being nice, I'm so nervous now that you're angry..." she told him, her hands winding into the fabric of her worn dress. If she didn't take heed there would be nothing left in a few more minutes.

Trying to think more clearly, he squeezed the bridge of his nose. Let a rush of air out of his lungs. "I don't *ken* what to tell you. I'm not angry. No matter what you might think to believe."

If she ever saw him angry, she would understand the difference.

"What are you then?"

That was a good question. He didn't know what he was feeling other than complete stupidity. Yes, there was anger, perhaps more frustration at her seeming bashfulness.

"I'm not. It's just I've a need to know who you are what you know about me. It's more than just the fact I'm a shifter. Isn't it? You know more than that. I need to understand what you hold over my head."

That was the truth. He needed to calm her so she would talk to him. At the moment all he did was turn her into a pile of terrified nerves.

While he watched, she breathed deeply, her lungs filling with the much-needed oxygen. Beneath her gown, her breast moved enticingly with each breath she inhaled. He wanted to pull her into his arms for loving not talking. He wanted to trace the pink tips with his lips and tongue.

"It's true. I knew almost from the moment I first met you that you were a shifter. I could tell."

"How?"

"I'd seen you before, a long time ago."

His thoughts might be correct, nonetheless there was more to this story than she was saying. "In the highlands of course. You saw me as a cat or a human?" he queried, beginning to *ken* where this would go.

For so long he was sure he'd seen her before, positive that he knew her somehow from somewhere. He'd just never been able to narrow the facts down or pinpoint where that might be. He couldn't prove his suspicions.

"Where, Leah?"

"My mother and I lived in the highlands near McKenna land. There was a cottage near a *loch*. Yes, I like to swim but never as my cat. Mother made sure I understood all the problems that might happen to me if I was caught." She inhaled a breath of air, looked to the path he trudged up. "That wasn't the one we used yesterday. Although it would be better for my, our, purposes."

"I figured that out by the time I was half way up. It was hot and sweaty. Hasn't been used longer than the other one. There was barely anything anyone could name as a trail. So, Leah, go on with your story. You lived in the highlands. I've known that for some time. What else?"

"Father was a shifter, not mother. He died when I was about ten. We used to go places. Places where we never saw another living soul. We would shift and run with the wind. After he died, mother forbade shifting. By then, the Sassenach were combing the countryside looking for shifters. She told me no one would be stupid enough to shift then get caught."

He winced at her words. It wasn't stupidity that caught him. It was arrogance and the idiotic notion that he would live forever.

"I'm sorry. I *ken* you were caught in a steel trap left by the English. It was one that was close to my home. I walked there several times every day with the horrible foreboding that a shifter someday would find himself caught in the trap."

Houston nodded remembering all too well those days she spoke of. He couldn't remember the last time he shifted. It had been years. "If a shifter was caught, they would have to change to human, then they'd be stark naked."

He would have done that but a young woman came along and freed him. He didn't have to run naked through the heather to his clothes.

"Unfortunately, one day I found a gorgeous black panther caught in the Sassenach's trap. It must have hurt something fierce." Tears slid down her cheeks as she continued to recall that day. "It was you in that trap. When I saw you the day I brought Shadow to you, I knew. Even though I never saw you as human, I knew."

He nodded, brushed the tears from her cheeks with the back of his hand. "Yes, the stupid cat was me. If you had not come along, I would have shifted then hobbled back to my clothes. It would have taken me the better part of an hour to walk back."

"In your cat I watched you limp away. Was so very tempted to follow you so I could watch you change form."

"Wisely, you didn't."

"If there were more soldiers in the area, I could have created a diversion. Mother would have been so very angry. As it was, I did follow you for a few minutes. As the hour was getting late, I had to go home. Didn't want to lie to mother about where I was."

"Did you tell her you found me?"

"No. While she didn't want anything to happen to me, she cursed shifters."

"I thought she loved your father," he said feeling strange about her words as if something wasn't quite right.

"She did love him very much except she didn't like it when he shifted. Didn't like the fact I would have to deal with the problems created by what I could do. Mother feared I would never find my mate even while she hoped that person would not be another shifter."

His gaze settled on her waist. She moved closer to him. "Have you found your mate, Leah?"

He brushed his lips across her forehead before he pressed her head to his chest. Her heart beat hard against him. She closed her eyes as she leaned into him accepting his warmth.

"Have you, Leah?" He asked again hoping to hear the words. "Do you believe with all your heart you've found the person you're supposed to be with through eternity?"

"Maybe...not sure if I *ken* how a body's supposed to know. I've had no one to teach me those things."

"Come here," he said softly wanting to show her how he felt. Show her he was her mate. Show her he would never leave her behind. He now had an interest in her greater than ever before. Besides wanting a beautiful woman, he needed to discover his mate, everything about her. He'd waited so long to ascertain this small truth. He was thirty-one. Hell, Roby, his younger cousin, found his mate sooner. Crissie, another cousin found hers. She was barely twenty at the time.

"I *dinna ken* how I can get much closer," she said her voice soft with desire as well as passion.

"I need to kiss you." He pulled her onto his lap. She wrapped her arms around him. The soft curves of her woman's body pressed into him.

"Are we going to follow the rules?" she asked as she traced his lip with her thumb.

"God, I don't want to, but yes, yes we are at least this afternoon we are. Not for much longer though."

"I don't want to, either."

He kissed her deep and hard. His hand covered her breast. Her breasts were soft and firm, the tip hard, waiting to grow harder. He let his hand roam to the flare of her hips. She was perfection.

Houston didn't want to. He set her aside then drew her up to stand. He brushed wayward strands of long golden hair from her face, curling it behind her ears. "Leah, I know you are my mate. I'm not going to leave you here on this mountain with a crazy stepfather. I'm going to protect as well as cherish you for the rest of your life. You've got to believe me. When I'm whole again, we will wed."

"You sound terribly sure of yourself, Houston Stuart. How do I know you're not telling me a tall tale so you can have your way with me?"

"Tall tale?" he chuckled softly lifting her chin with a thumb. "You have to trust my word. Can you do that? Trust me?"

His voice was throaty and thick. The pulsing erection behind his trousers ached to be buried deep inside her sultry warmth. When he made love to her for the first time, they would be in a bed not the forest floor. The moment would come soon enough. With patience he would teach her she didn't have anything to worry about. Her future with him as a Stuart and part of the McKenna Clan was secure.

"I want to," she spoke softly. "I want to very much but I don't have a lot of faith in other people."

"People who have let you down?"

"Yes," she said agreeing with him as well as his assessment of her life. "My mother and father let me down because they died. Grizzly..."

"Grizzly just wasn't there for you. I'm going to make this right. Come to me tomorrow afternoon. We'll have dinner. I'll..." He didn't know what he was going to do. He wanted to make everything up to her. Nevertheless, at this moment it wasn't in his power to do so.

"I don't know. What if Grizzly is home?"

"You don't owe him anything. Come down the mountain. Say you will."

He didn't think he'd ever pleaded with anyone before. This was new to him. She was his mate. He would do anything for her.

"Yes..." her voice faded away.

Houston wasn't at all sure she would come. If she didn't come to him, he would go to her.

~ * ~

The next evening, Leah had second and third thoughts about going down the mountain to meet Houston for dinner. Her nerves were tied into tiny knots, twisting and coiling inside her belly with each ragged breath of air she sipped. On one hand going to him was everything she wanted. On the other she was terrified of jumping in over her head and drowning.

Is he truly my mate? To want a shifter goes against everything I was taught.

Houston told her she was his mate, his soul mate. How the devil did he know something like that? How did anyone *ken* the fact? While she felt drawn to him, enjoyed his company, loved the way he made her all jittery and nervous inside when he kissed her, there must be more to knowing if a man was her mate. When she first saw him, she thought she'd known him forever. Sensed a kinship with him that went beyond knowledge.

Brenda's lecture haunted her. What if he was just using those words so he could tempt her to his bed? *I want to be in his bed. He's the only man I've ever been attracted to.* He told her he wanted to make love to her in his bed not on the forest floor. She didn't know what to think or if her feelings were all a sham. All that flashed through her head were the rules linked to Brenda's worried expression the last time she spoke with her.

Leah could not get Brenda's look of concern from her mind. Every time she recalled the deep furrows between her friend's eyes, she grew more panicky.

This was happening all so unexpectedly and way too fast. She never anticipated anything to be like this in her boring always the same life. Together, the two of them broke most of Brenda's rules. She was sure Houston meant to break more of them if she saw him today, if she garnered the courage to actually walk up the steps to his apartment above his office. Leah knew she should turn around and walk home. *Nay* race home. Deep in her heart, she also knew she couldn't. She wanted to learn more from Houston. He wouldn't hurt her. She was sure of that.

Most of the night before she spent awake, pounding on her tiny pillow wishing she could ease the ache just thinking about him created. When she touched herself, ran her hands across her breasts, she recalled Houston's hands as well as his lips in those exact places. They were evocative, daring. What would she do if he did see her wearing nothing? She certainly wanted to see what he looked like beneath his clothes.

He would be splendid.

Seeing his cat again was more important than all those other feelings put together. She remembered the way he appeared five years ago. He was magnificent, so much larger than she was. When he moved, his muscles undulated with raw power. She touched her hand to her chest barely able to sip in a breath of air.

Leah understood she needed to talk with Brenda before she ventured to Houston's home. Brenda would give her the rules again. In the process, she would set her wayward mind in the right direction. She would have the courage to tell Houston no.

She would never have the courage.

She didn't want to stray form moral values learned years ago. Yet she did with every image, every recognition of his kiss, his scent.

Didn't want to risk anything when she knew he was leaving, despite his promises to return for her. He even told her they would wed. She wasn't at all certain if she believed him. If there were repercussions, she would be left alone to deal with them. Brenda would help after she lectured her.

Who was Brenda to talk?

She was a married woman.

Men, as Brenda told her, Hawk as well, had a way of promising one thing then doing something else entirely. Good lord, it was hard to clear her head of the musty sawdust filling the blank recesses. At least Brenda told her she wasn't the only girl ever coaxed into doing something she wanted though knew she shouldn't. Brenda had barely escaped being pregnant with her first child when she and Seamus married. It was just that luck was on her side.

Life turned out wonderful for Brenda.

Houston made no promises of marriage, just that he would come back for her. He told her what she wanted to hear when he said they would wed. What if that was just to get her to come down the mountain to his bed? When he put a ring on her finger, she would believe him.

Leah stepped into Brenda's cozy kitchen that was ripe with the scent of freshly baked pies. As of yet, she didn't know what kind, however the aroma made her stomach grumble in anticipation of eating the sweet treat.

"I'm worried about you, Leah Kennedy. After our talk the other day I don't know what to think." She set a slice of peach pie on the table for Leah. "Eat up. You won't get a piece of fresh baked pie for a while. This is the last batch until the apples are ready this fall. Can't be fixing too many treats or we'll all get fat.

"You'll never get fat, Brenda. The kids keep you so busy you barely have time to sit and rest a spell. You just keep losing weight. You should take better care of yourself." While Leah wanted to talk about Houston, she also wanted to delay the discussion for a short time. Her nerves were stretched so thin, nearly to the breaking point.

"I'll get right to my opinion as well as what I think about it. You know I'll say what's on my mind. You're going to see Houston. It's late. I'm assuming you plan to stay the night with him. That's a terrible idea, Leah Kennedy. You *ken* it as much as anyone. If you ask him to take you back up the mountain, he will."

Leah supposed it might be. It didn't matter to her. She was going to share the night with Houston, damn the consequences. She only wished she could tell Brenda that according to Houston, she was his soul mate. There were several things Brenda would retort back to her if she did. She grinned thinking about that.

"Now what has you laughing when we're talking about something as serious as you giving away your virginity to a no-account doctor who is leaving soon?" Brenda was tapping her fork on the plate glaring at her as her eyebrows drew together.

"I was thinking about something Houston told me as well as what you would say in return," Leah said still chuckling.

"You are listening to my lectures, just not heeding the important facts I'm telling you. I see. Well, if nothing else you are giving me practice for when my girls have their first beaus. I've come to the conclusion I can talk until I'm red in the face and you will still do whatever Houston wants. I'll pray that it is what you want also."

"Your girls might well do the same," Leah reminded her to be greeted with a scowl from her friend. "In any case, I'm old enough to sort all this out for myself. It isn't as if I haven't had time to think about what I want as well as what you've told me in pointed terms."

"You want Houston."

"Yes."

"What makes you think he wants you? What makes you believe he doesn't just want a quick romp with a beautiful, fey woman before he leaves here?" Brenda once again asked something she'd been asking herself since the first time Houston kissed her.

"He told me."

Brenda snorted, shaking her head before looking to the ceiling. "Men say what they know their women want to hear. I always fall for

Seamus even though I know what is going to sashay from his mouth before he says it. You, an innocent, don't stand a ghost of a chance when it comes to an experienced man such as Houston Stuart. He's probably had many affairs, all of them meaningless. What makes you believe this has meaning to him?"

Leah took a bit of grief from Brenda's words. She'd thought exactly the same but was choosing to ignore the images. "I like to believe I'm a woman capable of making a decision without being swayed by a man's sweet-talking words."

"Sex is powerful, leaves an innocent woman wanting something she can't put a finger on then once she knows the rapture that follows, she cannot say no. I understand I shouldn't be speaking of things like that to you. Nevertheless, maybe I should. Sex and love, toss in lust, it's all so complicated. As you don't have a mother to do it for you, I feel an obligation. You should love your man before you let him inside your body. Once you've done that there is no going back."

I do love him.

"You're right, of course. Even if I told you I love him, you would argue with me, wouldn't you?"

Brenda reached out taking both of Leah's hands in hers. Giving them a tender squeeze, she went on to say, "I wouldn't argue, not if you tell me that. What I would do is believe you. The question at hand is whether or not Houston returns the sentiment."

"He hasn't said so."

"Have you told him how you feel?"

"No."

Her stomach rolled. Telling wasn't something she intended. She did not want to make herself more vulnerable than she already felt. If he left then never returned for her, not saying the word would be the only way she could salvage her pride.

"Well then, perhaps you should do that tonight before he takes you to his bed, before he deflowers you. You should tell him then see what he says to you." Brenda sipped the tea in front of her, looking thoughtfully at her. "You've made up your mind. There is nothing I can say or do to dissuade you."

"Maybe. Depends on what he tells me. It doesn't have to be words of love. He just needs to reassure me he'll come back for me. If I had the money, I would go to the posting house. Take the first carriage to his home. He told me his mother and father would accept me, give me a job at the McKenna keep if I didn't want to take handouts, which I don't. Needless to say, money is something I don't have."

"If anyone sees you, if that cook of his finds out you spent the night, everyone in this tiny little village will *ken* the truth. She spreads gossip as if it was butter. Be careful."

"I will. I better go now."

The walk to Houston's office seemed to take forever. When she turned back to look at the house for one last time, Brenda stood in the door, her hand raised. Leah saw her mouth the words 'good luck' to her. She didn't know if she needed luck or not. What she needed now was courage to make the right decision for herself.

It was different when he kissed her and coaxed her to those incredibly raw, delicious feelings he could generate. She understood he wasn't going to expect her to take her clothes off then climb into his bed. The expectations stripped her nerves to nothingness, unknowing how he would proceed terrified.

"Where you going with your mind in the clouds?" Michael walked beside her, his hand possessively touching her shoulder.

"What?" Leah jerked away before she pressed her hand at her throat. "You scared me. What did you say?"

"That's what happens when you're walking down the street in a daze. Why don't you have dinner with me? I could treat you at the little restaurant where you and the doctor ate the other night. I'll even buy dessert."

"No. No, I couldn't do that. Doing so would give the wrong impression, Michael. I don't want anything from you now or ever."

"No? Is that any way to talk to your future husband?" he asked as he wrapped his arm around her, his hand settling on the curve of her hip. He squeezed as if she would welcome his advances.

Leah pushed away, feeling the first souring of her stomach. "Don't, Michael. I'm not going to be your wife. How many times do I have to tell you?"

It seemed to Leah he was trying to direct her toward the alley. She pushed against him, tugged his hand away from her waist. He put it back. "I don't want you to touch me."

"I'm getting tired of all your refusals. Tired of playing this game with you, Leah. Who else is going to marry you? Not Quaid or Ryan, certainly not the doctor as we all know he's leaving. Has he proposed? You've got your heart set on something you can't have. Wake up, Leah. All Houston Stuart wants from you is a quick tumble. You're nothing but a whore to him."

She gasped, stunned by Michael's accusations. There wasn't a bit of truth to his words, at least she hoped there wasn't. She hated all the doubts surfacing. Houston hadn't proposed. Just as she told Brenda there had been no promise of commitment. A promise was what she needed, a ring too. Either of those two things would change everything for her. She shook off the feeling of despair that seemed to settle around her heart threatening to grow. "That's not your business, Michael. I want you to take your hands off me." She pushed again.

"It is my business. I don't like you seeing him. Heard he went up the mountain yesterday. This time he didn't even use the excuse of stopping by the Fletcher place to see how the kids were doing. He's going to use you. Has he already?" Michael stopped in the middle of the street, his brows furrowed together. "That's it. He's already stolen what's mine."

"No, Michael, you've got everything all wrong. Not that I should say anything. I have nothing you can steal. I'm not yours. Just as I've told you countless times, I never will be."

Anger simmered, threatening to explode. She looked to Houston's office seeking someone to rescue her. The road was empty in both directions.

"You're going there...to the doc's office aren't you." He stepped back, his eyes blazing with the same fury as his tone.

She stiffened tilting her chin in the air. "I am. Not that I have to explain my actions or anything else to you."

"I was going to tell you it doesn't matter to me if you're no longer innocent as you should be when we wed. When he leaves you alone and increasing, I'll still marry you. I'll make an honest woman of you. Go on, do what you shouldn't. Don't think I don't care because I do. Though I'm willing to wait until he's done with you. That's how much I want you, Leah Kennedy. Don't you forget what I just said. It's a promise."

For a few seconds Leah watched as Michael strode away. His shoulders broad, his back straight, she saw the fury in his strides. Saw his fists clenched at his sides. She didn't know how she would ever convince that man she was never going to marry him.

Breathing deeply, she turned her attention back to what she was about to do, telling herself one small step at a time. What she needed to concentrate on was not making love but eating dinner. Getting food into her stomach without it curdling might prove a challenge. Leah did truly believe everything would fall into place as the evening progressed.

With unwanted hesitation coupled with weariness about what she planned with Houston, Leah walked up the steps to Houston's home. The sun sat on the horizon streaking the sky with glorious, mauves, pinks, oranges as well as a myriad of other colors.

She understood she was committed to this endeavor. What she couldn't comprehend was how it would end. If she had second thoughts, which she did, he wouldn't allow her to walk up the mountain in the dark. She would have to stay in Selkirk overnight, but where? With too many second thoughts assailing her, she couldn't pick up her hand to knock.

For a moment only, she turned away from the door, staring down the back steps she just walked up. Her breath caught in the back of her throat when she tried to let it out. An instant of courage was what she needed. She closed her eyes trying to see only Houston's smiling face and the way he always looked at her so tenderly with his clear silver eyes. She melted.

This was the biggest decision she'd ever made in her twenty years.

Facing the door for the second time, she started to knock. He must have heard her on the steps or some type of intuition told him she was there because the door swung open before her hand connected with the wood.

"Hello."

Her voice wavered with the tremors swamping her body. For a

moment, she was certain her knees would buckle. She held them tight.

"Thought I heard you. You having second thoughts?" he asked softly as he extended a hand to welcome her into his main living room. "You don't need to. I won't..." he broke off as if he wasn't entirely sure what he meant to say.

When she saw the fire, she remembered Shadow lying on the rug in front of the hearth. Recalled Houston's words that night, he would make him comfortable. She missed him so much. Tears stung her eyes along with her nose as she recalled the days they had together. She didn't want to cry. However, the fact of the matter was tears were inevitable whenever she thought of her dog she loved so much.

"It's alright." Houston pulled her into his arms, sensing her emotions, understanding the deep loneliness she felt since her dog passed on to another place. She wanted to believe where he went truly was a better space for him. "You're remembering Shadow, aren't you?"

She nodded as she leaned into him, her tears wetting his shirt. Even though she tried, she couldn't stop the memories or the tears. Her hands wrapped around his body as she absorbed his warmth. His scent spicy and all male filled her senses. His hard body pressed against hers, felt good and right. The heart beneath her cheek throbbed with vibrancy of life as well as all he had to give. His fingers around her waist squeezed before they pulled her closer. Next to her belly his erection was hard. He wanted her just as Brenda told her he did. She wanted him too. The sentiment wasn't all one sided.

"I'm sorry." She pushed away from him. "I didn't mean to cry. It's just that..." She sniffed back the tears that didn't want to stop.

He dried her tears with his thumbs. "You've no reason to be sorry. The dog was a precious being you loved with all your heart."

Yes, that was true. It seemed she heard or thought she heard more words. *I would love to feel that intense love from you. It's something every man would die to receive. It would feel as heaven.*

"Shadow used to be so bad, so very naughty. He was always trouble waiting to happen. He knew it too. The dog could not be trained to do anything. He would run when called just so I would chase him. That was something he liked best, the chase. He would never play ball with me because he would never bring the darn thing back."

His smile was tender when he looked at her. "Come sit down. Remember Shadow while I get you something to drink. Do you want tea or would you like something stronger? A glass of wine perhaps?"

"Yes, wine would be nice." She wondered if she should tell him about her visit with Brenda or the encounter with Michael. They were both in so many ways unpleasant. She didn't want to ruin the mood of the evening by pleasantries that weren't at all pleasant.

He handed her a glass of wine then sat down beside her, leaning against the arm of the couch. "What's on your mind?"

"I'm just nervous."

"Me too."

"You? You've done this before. Why would you be nervous?" She didn't understand. Thought he was fearless, practiced in the way of making love.

"Never made love to my mate or a virgin." His words were simple and to the point.

She didn't understand. Didn't think she ever would. Thoughtfully, she sipped letting the sweet tasting liquid slide down her throat. "How is it so different that you can say this is something you haven't done?"

"You talked to Brenda about tonight?"

He tilted her chin up so she would look at him. A flush of heat rose from her belly to her cheeks. She nodded.

"I see that you did. She doesn't approve. We both *ken* it's not her place to approve or disapprove. What we do here is all about you along with what you want. No one is forcing you. If you want to wait, we'll wait until I get back from Edinburgh."

Leah nodded again. "Your foot too?" she asked knowing he would be gone while it healed. She prayed the bones would heal correctly this time.

Houston grinned. The smile was a wicked grin, all male, one that made her forget all her nervousness.

"You did that on purpose." She was smiling now also, laughing softly as he placed his hand on her knee.

"What?"

"That smile is wicked. It helped me breathe easier." She tugged in air then held it close to her heart for the longest time.

"If my smirk helped you anyway then of course, I did it on purpose. I like looking at you, smiling, giving you pleasure. Want to give you more pleasure than you could ever imagine tonight. Again, if you want to wait, just say so."

He reached for her glass. After setting it on the table he framed her face with his hands. His lips passed gently across hers, once, twice then a third time. She remembered the other kisses, soft and sweet, hard and deep. All of them caused her body to flame with an aching need she couldn't define. His lips against hers did so now.

Tentatively as if this was the first time, she swept her tongue across her bottom lip, tasting him.

"That's it, Leah, relax. Enjoy me as much as I plan on enjoying you." He deepened the kiss, his tongue playing with hers as his hands shifted to her neck. Over and over his mouth molded against hers, his tongue dancing with hers until she felt the purr rise from deep in her belly.

He pulled away, running his thumb across her bottom lip. "Do you like perch?"

That was a change of topics if she ever encountered one. She was tempted to laugh. "Someone paid you with fish?" She did laugh as her nervousness began to vanish.

"Yes. You've got that right. My cook prepared it along with roasted potatoes and spring peas. It should all be very tasty. It's in the warming oven. We can eat anytime we are ready. There is more wine, as much as you'd like."

"Dinner sounds nice." She needed to stall for time while he seemed to want to proceed with his gentle, expert coaxing.

"Nonetheless, you want to talk first."

"Perhaps we can talk while we eat. Things happened today. I don't want to talk about them. However, you should know." She thought of Brenda then Michael. She wondered what happened to Grizzly and what would happen to her if he never came back.

"Sounds serious. This doesn't just have to do with Brenda, does it?"

"No."

"Michael?" His voice vibrated with anger.

~ * ~

Grizzly stumbled through the dense thickets. He didn't know where he was or why someone would have left him in this miserable place unless the purpose was for him to die. He never thought he had an enemy such as this. Last he recalled he'd been drinking at the tavern in a small village close to Selkirk where he lived. He'd been thinking about walking home to see what Leah made for dinner. His stomach rumbled when he thought of food. Food that he hadn't had for several days except he couldn't be certain how many days he'd been unconscious.

He woke, his head pounding blood pulsing in his ears, pain reeling. Hell, he didn't remember falling asleep. Didn't remember much of anything. That was how many days ago? He didn't remember. Could've been one day or a week for all he could recall. The way his innards felt it must have been at least a week. At this moment, his stomach was attached to his spine.

Enemies, he didn't have enemies, not that he knew of. Who would want him to die? Didn't have friends either. Fletcher hated him. Not enough to dump him in some godforsaken place to die. No, Fletcher didn't do this. He was too lazy. They were only enemies in pretense the fact gave them something to do.

Who then?

He owed money but not that much, nothing anyone would kill for. If he died, the men he owed wouldn't get anything from him or from Leah if they thought to collect from her.

Leah...what would she do if he didn't come back home? She wouldn't have a place to stay. That was one thing he promised her mother. He would never make her leave the house.

It didn't make much of a difference if he couldn't find his way to a village. The sun was setting for the night. The forest grew darker as he stumbled down the tiny godforsaken path in front of him. It got damn cold out here at night. Last night he thought he'd freeze to death. The wolves howling around him terrified every bone in his body until he shook like a leave floundering in a stiff wind. He didn't want to be some wolf's dinner.

The tree root caught his boot. Waving his arms, he tried to right himself. He stumbled, falling down the steep path, sliding, grinding in the rocky soil. Dirt and rocks clung to his teeth while he reached out his hands to stop his fall, his palms scraped raw. He grabbed at passing rocks and bushes. Slowly he came to a stop. He was breathing hard, blood on his lips, scratches on his arms as well as his face. He could feel the sting of the open abrasions.

"Hell and damnation!"

Face down he set his head on the dirt, copious tears falling across his cheeks until he was sobbing, his breaths ragged. This was not how he wanted to end his life. Not that he wanted his days to end anytime soon. Death in some place where no one would mourn his loss, no one even knew where he was. He certainly didn't have a clue as to his whereabouts.

Someone did though.

Someone who didn't want him to live.

Someone who left him here to die.

On unsteady limbs, he pushed himself to stand. Wobbling, one foot at a time he continued stumbling downhill. Silence of the night filled him with renewed terror. His heart pounded erratically. His nerves stretched so tight he was sure they would snap. If that happened, he'd be left with nothing. Wouldn't it be better to hear something? Some noise that would tell him he lived? Some noise that would tell him he wasn't an apparition haunting the night?

He tried to wet his parched lips with a tongue that held no moisture. Water...water...if he could find some, he would live. He had to find a creek or a pond even a river. Rain would be nice. He could tilt his head skyward and catch the drops with his tongue. Right now, a drink of whiskey might be just as nice. If he had to die, he might as well drown in liquor.

He stumbled again. Caught himself then tripped over something in his way. He landed in a small nearly dried creek. Life giving water trickled across the scrapes on his hands and face. He splashed his face and neck, scooped cool liquid in his hands then drank. Repeated the process. His prayers were answered at least one of them.

Ask and you shall receive. Isn't that what the good book preached? Maybe he should ask for more than just water. He needed the village of Selkirk or any other village to loom up in front of him. He needed food too.

The devil, his thirst was almost quenched. Though now he was cold and wet. There was just enough water in the creek to sip as well as drench his clothes. He rubbed his arms in a feeble attempt to make himself warmer. The gesture didn't help much. Honestly, he didn't think he'd ever be warm again.

Once more, he drank deeply from the small puddle of almost clear water. He knew if he followed the creek bed, he might find someone to help him. This was not a life-giving source of water though.

Keep walking, just keep putting one step in front of you, that will help you stay warm. Will get you that much closer to your goal. He wanted to live, he had to. He had responsibilities. He wasn't sure what they were at the moment. Nevertheless, he must have them. Everyone had responsibilities.

He wasn't certain if it would just be nicer to sleep. The water was here. He could sleep the rest of the night. In the morning when he could see his hands in front of his face, he could walk some more. He could find someone.

He didn't want to walk.

No, he needed rest.

The shuffle of footsteps behind him caused him to turn.

"Stick! What the hell are you doing here?"

He was pretty sure he knew. The boy was crazy.

"'Bout time you breathed your last old man. You won't hurt Leah ever again."

Chapter Seven

With curiosity as well as tenderness Houston watched Leah fiddle with her dress then the glass of wine she held. She was at turns nervous then shy, flighty as all hell. She looked at him beneath lowered lashes. He didn't have a doubt she wanted to be here. When he looked at her expressive face, he saw the hesitation flit across her fine-boned features.

She still wasn't sure about him.

Didn't believe his story about her being his soul mate. She was though. He had to find a way to prove that important fact to her. Had to find a way to make sure she trusted him.

"Was it something Brenda told you?" He didn't like everything that happened between them bound by another person's rules. They were shifters, mates for eternity. They weren't bound by the usual human rules. He wanted to take her fear away and replace it with the love he felt for her.

Ah, but Leah wasn't sure about this soul mate business. She'd grown up with a mother who despised shifters. Didn't want Leah to have anything to do with them. Her mother would have told her nothing about their kind. Perhaps she told her some things. However, Houston would wager they weren't kind.

His big body shuddered.

What if she didn't want anything to do with him because he was a shifter? The breath he tugged inside wavered along with his heart. Convincing her of something her mother spent a lifetime dissuading would not be easy. For this life as well as the ones to come, he needed to do exactly that.

"We talked. Brenda knows how I feel about you. She just doesn't want me to get hurt. I cannot give her the words that would reassure as well as put her mind at ease. It seems to me that if I jump in with both feet tonight, only time will tell if you're using me or not."

He supposed the same thing. He didn't have the words either. She might not believe his sweet-talk anyway. She had a mind of her own, that was why she came tonight. He understood her need for him simmered deep inside. He should tell her he loved her. He didn't think for one second she would believe the words. If he did, it might condemn him further in her eyes. Not enough time had passed since they met, since they kissed, since he caressed her soft white breasts. If he said something such as that, she might turn and flee. He had to pace this coaxing of Leah right.

"I'd like to find a way to vanquish all your fears. I don't have any ideas. What I do know is that I'll never knowingly hurt you. You're too dear to me, precious in fact. I've waited thirty-one years to find you and hold you."

He saw the way her eyes narrowed in question. He'd already said too much. What he needed tonight was to bind her to him in ways she would no longer question his words.

"That's the thing. I always believe you until someone else says something different. Brenda made arguments against this as did Michael. While I trust Brenda has my best interest at heart, I *ken* Michael does not."

"That's when you start asking yourself more questions. What else happened today?"

He felt the rise of anger. the sour taste in his mouth. He had enough to do to convince her without having to put aside other people's words. At this point, she didn't know what to believe or who to trust.

"Michael."

"I see.

She let out a puffy breath of air that sounded like frustration. When she looked at him straight in the eye, he saw the crystal blue clarity. "Don't see how you can when I don't. He still wants me. Still believes I will be his wife. How do I tell him it's never going to happen in plainer words? How do I keep him from slandering you?"

"Did he try to kiss you?"

Houston's jealousy kicked in. He didn't care what the man said about him. It was Leah he was concerned about. Leah was right, he didn't see anything. *Slandering me?* What the devil did that mean? He was beginning to dislike that young man with a vengeance.

"No, not this time. It wasn't dark and there were a few people on the street. They wouldn't have cared though. Everyone in town likes Michael, respects him too."

Houston paced across the room, abandoning his sitting position beside Leah. He was strung too tight to sit. Fear for her when he left was very real. He stopped in front of the fireplace, watching the flames leap and dance. For a few seconds, he thought of how much Leah meant to him, all the things he wanted with her including a family.

He had not told her any of that.

Telling her was not a possibility when she still harbored tenuous feeling about him. When she wouldn't accept the fact, she was his mate. When she didn't know if she loved him.

"Michael knew you were coming here this night, didn't he?"

"He guessed what we planned. That I was going to sleep with you. Michael told me he still wanted me to be his wife. Told me if I was...if I got with...with child, he'd still marry me. He wants me that much. Houston, I don't understand why."

Houston understood. Leah was the most beautiful person inside as well as out he'd ever met. Michael knew her beauty was more than skin deep even though the man had never traveled outside of Selkirk. Somehow, Michael was able to dismiss her fey nature as well as her poverty where others could not. He didn't want to admit to the fact. Nonetheless, there was more to Michael than he showed most people.

"Let's forget about Michael for the rest of the night. This evening is just about the two of us. We need to learn as much as we can about each other. Don't you think?" He sat down beside her again, refilled her glass along with his.

She smiled for him. His heart melted at the sight while his body hardened.

"I'd like to forget about him along with Brenda's disapproval too. Tonight, I don't want to think about right from wrong or anything accept you as well as the way you make my body pulse with need. You heat my soul to an inferno.

"Should we eat now or should I kiss you again? It's your choice. I'm pleased with either." While he was talking, he'd made the decision for her. He unfastened his shirt then drew it over his head.

Her eyes were wide, simmering with heat. The tiny sips of air she inhaled were ragged with desire. She ran her tongue between her lips, in the process opening them slightly. They were slick and moist, waiting for his attention. He needed to taste her, enjoy the sweetness. To be inside her would be a heaven he wanted to know. This was the way he'd always wanted to feel before he made love.

With her small fragile hand, she reached toward him, stroking his chest, running her slim fingers to the waistband of his trousers then up to trace his collarbone. The caress was soft, so very hesitant, unsure as well, the sensations stealing his breath.

"Is it too hot in here for you?" he asked while her gaze settled on his mouth. He knew what she wanted. She would have to wait a few minutes while he brought his seething emotions under control. When her exploring fingers settled on one of his hard nipples, the groan rumbling from deep in his belly couldn't be stopped.

She looked at him surprised.

He grinned, wondering now how she would answer.

"No..." she sighed softly as she turned her attention to his other nipple. "It is warm though. No, I am hot. It's because of you along with the way you look with your shirt off. Would you show me your cat?"

"After we make love. I wouldn't want to frighten you." He didn't fear showing her his cat just his completely nude body, his aroused body.

She stopped her hand falling to rest on his thigh so very close to his aroused penis. He groaned again. She smiled as if she understood. He was sure she didn't.

"How would that frighten me?" she queried softly. "I know you won't harm me in that form."

"I have to get naked in order to change. Are you ready to see me naked?" he asked. As he watched her and waited for the answer she would give, his nimble fingers began unfastening her gown, freeing her from constraint.

"Yes." She spoke so softly her voice paper-thin he could barely hear the words.

"I don't think you are. Soon, though, after we make love, I'll show you my cat form."

He was adamant with a promise to himself he wouldn't rush her. He spent so much time wooing her, wishing to take her into his bed. He wasn't about to ruin all the zealous preparation now.

Houston swept her onto his lap. Framing her face with his hands he kissed her hard and deep, his tongue sweeping possessively between her lips. Being inside her was paradise to him, a nirvana he needed to enjoy over and over.

"Houston." Her tiny voice brushed into him, filling him.

"You enchant me." He kissed her again and again. Her sweetness entered into his heart. She was his life. She would understand the concept after tonight. Leah would know how they were made for each other. Leah was made for him just as he was made for her. No other woman would do.

Her dress was open to his gaze. He knew from looking at her fully clothed she wore the bindings. The fact she'd run across Michael on her way here gave him reason to be thankful for the protection from other eyes they offered. He found the fastener before he slowly unwrapped her and watched the beautiful white globes burst free from their confinement. As cool air caressed her, the pink buds hardened, puckered nicely, begging. He touched each one with the palm of his hand.

"You are everything I'm not," she murmured tossing her head back, giving him access to more soft flesh.

"You're right."

She was sunlight to his darkness. He was hardness to her softness. Her words were true. She was summer to his winter. They were as different as night and day. Still, they were made for each other. Together they were a perfect fit.

Soon, she would learn that fact.

Soon, he prayed she would have no more reservations created by a mother who despised the fact her daughter was a shifter. A mother who found a way to taint her daughter's thoughts never understanding her soul mate was a shifter.

His hands roamed the sides of her body, cupped a soft breast. Held it, learned the weight of her. Caressed the curve of her hip. Traced the length of her leg as he slowly ran his hand beneath her skirts. Tender flesh met hard callused fingers. He found the sensitive spot behind her knees. Restlessly she moved, pressing down on his arousal. Her fingers wound through his hair before scraping across his shoulders while he divested her of all the pins holding her golden hair on top of her head. He ran his fingers through the soft length as the strands slowly floated to her waist.

"How do you feel?" he asked as he bathed her neck with kisses while one hand settled on her naked belly. With the touch she coiled against him, her soft breasts pushing against the hard wall of his chest.

"Different," she purred from the back of her throat.

"Different how?"

He sucked one of her large ivory globes into his mouth, sucking and pulling on the tender flesh, biting gently the hardened tip as she gasped in air. Waiting for her answer, he turned his attention to the other one.

Her fingers dug into his back. His muscles jumped from the touch. "I *dinna ken*," she wailed as his hand cupped the soft triangle between her thighs. "What are you doing?"

"Getting you ready to accept me inside you. Do you want me inside your hot sultry core? Tell me now." He had another question he needed to ask before he slipped inside the velvet sheathe she was gifting him with tonight.

"I *ken* I'm ready."

She jumped when he slipped a finger then a second one inside her. Her body shuddered as he touched upon the thin barrier she still possessed.

"Not yet, not quite yet," he told her. "Nevertheless, you are slick with your need. That's good, very good."

The devil, she was small and tight. He was afraid he would hurt her more than just in the taking of her virtue.

He lifted her then slipped her gown off. Except for her stockings, in a few seconds her clothes were piled on the floor. He cradled her in his arms. With fast, long strides he left the main room behind to find his bed. Gently, he set her down then rid himself of his boots then her stockings.

The next few minutes he bathed her naked body with kisses, his lips and his tongue finding tender, sensitive spots, places that sent her body rocking with need for him.

She was exquisite.

In a few more moments, she would be his.

"Houston!" she cried out for him, her body moving evocatively beneath his. He covered her mouth with his for a long hot kiss that sent her hips bucking with need for his body to fulfill the promise he created with his mouth and his hands.

"Honey, when was your last woman's time?"

Beneath him she froze. "Houston?"

He didn't want to stop to ask the question. He should have asked before he began this tender assault on her senses. "I have to know. Have to protect you. My question is important as to how I proceed from here." He hadn't wanted to embarrass her. So caught up in making this easier for her, he forgot the query until now."

"I..." She swept her tongue across her lips leaving moisture behind. He brushed a gentle kiss there sipping gently while she thought.

Two fingers were inside her, his thumb found the velvet hard pearl, touching caressing, flicking while it seemed her eyes crossed because of his question.

"I?" he asked, a small chuckle he tried to keep behind his teeth fell short of that mark.

"Three weeks maybe four. I don't keep track. Never saw a need. Three and a half weeks. Yes, that must be right." She cried out then as he found more sensitive spots.

Three and a half weeks maybe four, that was perfect. "Are you sure? You have to be certain."

"I should have one any time now." Her face was a brilliant red.

He felt nothing save tenderness for her, his mate. Wished he didn't have to embarrass her. As he lay above her, her long beautifully shaped legs spread for him. He would know heaven with her tonight. "Good,

162

good, I don't have to withdraw. There will be no chance of repercussions." Taking a second, he discarded his trousers. They fell on the floor.

Bending low he gently nipped her earlobe with his teeth. She rose against him, telling him she wanted him with every languid movement. He grit his teeth understanding he would have to move slowly.

With great care, he slowly penetrated her, eased his way inside. He felt the shifting of her muscles as her body accepted him. He was inside her silken heat. She surrounded him.

When he touched the small barrier he would dislodge, he stopped. Houston closed his eyes, willing his body to control. The air he inhaled was slow and deliberate. He would need to give her warning.

"This is going to hurt for a second. After that, I'll never hurt you again," he promised, understanding his words for lies. When he claimed her, he would hurt her one more time. She was a shifter. Would she claim him too? Perhaps when two shifters came together in the claiming neither would be hurt.

"I know. Brenda told me," she spoke softly, so softly he could barely hear. "When we did this, she wanted me to understand what would happen."

Ah, Brenda was playing mother in more ways than one. That was good, very good. She understood some of what was going to happen tonight.

"Are you ready?"

"Please."

Quickly, hoping to make this fast and as easy as possible for her, he thrust into her. Her startled cry stopped him cold. It was everything he dreaded yet at the same time breaking through the slim barrier was everything he wanted. He was her first as well as her last lover.

"You're mine now, Leah." *Through eternity and beyond, you've always been mine.*

"It did not hurt over much," she whispered softly as she began moving beneath him. Her leg wrapped around his buttocks as if she knew what she was doing.

Perhaps she remembered other times in their past.

Maybe it was instinct.

He didn't care.

The joining was magic to him, enchanting. His body throbbed as her passion entered into him. He cradled her. Rocked her as her body grew hotter and hotter. As she came closer to the rapture he wanted to create for her. He felt the passion building.

"Houston!" she cried out his name as she pulsed and heaved beneath his hard body. Energy flowing between them she cried out again as her tight vagina convulsed around him, as he felt the tremors he created drawing him to the rapture he wanted to give her. He drove harder into her, faster, touching her core as she continued to writhe and coil beneath him.

He spent himself inside her. His seed filled her. He was terrified of a pregnancy at the same time thrilled this day was nearly her woman's time. His seed would not take root inside her womb.

With his rod still deeply cradled in her liquid heat, he turned so she lay by his side. His fingers trailed up then down her spine. Whispering softly to her, he kissed her lightly on the lips then her nose.

"You're mine for all eternity, Leah. Nothing you say or question will refute that," he whispered to her as he felt his need rise once more. "You are made for me."

"I never thought..."

Softly he chuckled then made love to her again.

~ * ~

Leah never believed anything could ever feel so delicious and sinful at the same time. He was her light, her energy. She would give him her heart as well as her soul without asking. Never would she regret giving herself to Houston although she still wasn't sure about his claim they were soul mates destined to be together through all eternity. Even though she was a shifter that seemed a little bit farfetched to her ears.

She didn't understand they would be reborn again and again to meet each other in another time. One had to stretch the limits of their imagination to believe such a claim.

If she had this coupling to do over, she would, over then over again. When she turned, she saw him lying beside her, one arm tossed across his eyes to ward off the encroaching sunlight. He was breathtakingly handsome.

It was early, the sun just making an appearance on the eastern horizon. She told herself it would be prudent if she left before the village was awake. Prudent to be up the mountain and ensconced in her tiny home within the hour. With care, she could be up old craggy and no one would *ken* she spent the night at the doctor's home. Only Houston and she would know.

Lightly, she pushed a strand of his dark hair away from his eyes. She was tempted to run a fingertip along his jawline. He was handsome, so very strong. He still hadn't shown her his cat. It seemed through the night they were otherwise engaged so thoroughly she forgot to ask. The devil, she remembered all the times he made love to her; all the different ways he coaxed her. No matter what happened, if he never came back for her, she would remember this night as well as her first lover. She didn't want anyone else inside her body.

For her he was the only one.

One thought of Michael crossed her mind. She could never allow him to touch her so intimately as Houston stroked and kissed her. Could never allow this type of familiarity.

She couldn't.

Leah drew in a deep, shaky breath, her body trembling with the fear it might happen. What if she was presented with no choice? It was what her mother went through to survive.

Deep raw powerful foreboding washed over her while she gazed at Houston, her lover, her love, her life. She was terrified she would lose him. Terrified she would never know his loving touch again. She knew so little about him. Craved to learn more.

He was a physician trained in the university. In Edinburgh he would learn more about one of his major interest, obstetrics. Returning for her was a fool's dream she would hang onto until she turned old and grey. Again rumor had it he came from a powerful rich family. In any case he was learned. She couldn't read or write. His family would never acknowledge her. Whatever would he want with her besides the use of her body?

Suddenly, she was on her side, his chest pressed against her back. He was deep inside her. She found she was ready for him, moving while he thrust inside hard and fast, matching his body with hers. Moved until she cried out with the trembling, silver glistening of the rapture he generated.

It would happen soon. What she sought, what he gave.

That was the way the feelings had been some of the times last night. He would make love to her, leisurely tempting as well as torturing her until she pleaded for him to finish. He would laugh then tell her she needed patience. After that he would take her hard and fast never failing to lead her to climax as he poured himself inside her.

She sucked in a deep breath of air as his hand closed around one breast. "Houston!"

He thrust again and again. She felt him deep inside her, touching her deeply, filling her with raw feelings that spiraled higher always higher. Reveled in the knowledge he was one with her. She saw the light as well as the darkness. Saw stars shining as together they burst into flames.

Leah wished it wasn't so close to her woman's time. She wanted his child. If she were to become pregnant with his baby, she would hold part of him forever. A little Houston to love and cherish while she watched the child grow into a beautiful adult would be heaven for her.

She would never regret having his child. On the other hand, she would have trouble feeding a babe. Grizzly wouldn't want another mouth to feed. She was certain her stepfather would set her out on her arse if she showed up pregnant with no father to support her. Wasn't that what her mother did? Accepted the first man who wanted her so she could put food in her child's belly. When there was a child involved, a person could no longer be selfish.

Michael? Would she have to go to Michael when Houston didn't come back for her?

Fiercely, she pushed away the awful feelings that filled her, ripping at her heart. The perception she might have to do the same for a child's sake. No, he assured her she was safe. There would be no child.

My choice would no longer be mine to make. I would have to think about the precious wee life. The bairn. She shuddered.

"What is it, Leah? What's wrong?" Houston's warm breath so close to her, eased the feelings of doom sweeping through her. Erased the horrible thoughts for the moment at least.

His presence was strong, comforting as well. "I'm just glad there won't be a child."

"You don't want children?" he asked as he rose above her, tracing the length of her arm with a fingertip.

"Of course I do."

"Then what is it?"

"This child if we made one last night would not have a father. I couldn't bear that." She forced the moisture clogging her throat to vanish. "I couldn't bear having to marry someone just so I would have a roof over our heads along with food in our bellies."

"Of course..." His reply faded because of the hammering at his door.

Terrified Grizzly knew where she was and was going to break the door down, she brought the covers to her chin.

"What is that?"

"I'm sure it's nothing. I'll send whoever is there down the road to Hawk. Actually, he's officially their doctor now." Houston pulled on his discarded trousers before striding to the door.

"Houston!" The pounding continued. "Where the devil are you?"

When he opened the door, Hawk burst in. "What the devil do you want? Do you know what time it is?"

Sitting inside the bedroom, Leah felt as if what few precautions they took in concealing their rendezvous last night had just been shattered. Houston inadvertently left the bedroom door open. She knew her eyes were wide with alarm. Knew her body shuddered as she watched Hawk's gaze travel to her. Watched horrified as the realization that she was naked in Houston's bed sank into Hawk. If she could, she would have ducked beneath the covers however it seemed she couldn't move. At this point in time hiding would have done no earthly good.

"Hawk..." her voice trailed off into nothingness.

She jumped when Hawk sent a blow to Houston's jaw, knocking him backward a few steps. "You bastard! I knew this time was coming although I didn't think you'd be so obvious."

"I didn't deserve that, Hawk. Leah's my mate. I haven't done anything to her we didn't both want." Houston was rubbing his jaw as he looked into the bedroom.

She watched as he closed the door. Quickly, she rose, wrapping the sheet around her as she went to listen at the door. Her clothes, she remembered were strewn across the floor in the main room.

"She's innocent. You stole that from her, mate or not. I've never believed a shifter should do that before the wedding. You are going to marry her." The spoken words were a statement not a question.

One Houston didn't answer. She wasn't about to let Hawk intimidate the man she loved.

Before he could answer, Leah was on the defensive. "Houston has no obligations where I'm concerned." With the sheet wrapped tightly around her, Leah stepped through the door refusing to be a victim. Refusing to be talked about as if she was an item not a person. "We both understand I'm not, well I'm not educated. He needs someone who can read and write. He needs someone who can match his intellect." With as much dignity and modesty as she could manage, she picked up her clothes before she walked back to the bedroom.

When she closed the door behind her, she lay against it shaking. For a moment, she thought her knees would buckle. She closed her eyes, listening to the pounding of her heart.

Through the door she heard the men arguing. Assumed more of the conversation revolved around her. She was more than eager to return to the main room to disavow any conclusion about her welfare they might decide. She wanted to meet Hawk's accusation head on. It didn't sit right with her that they talked about her and around her when she wasn't there to refute the stupid male comments.

Within seconds she was dressed. "Now..." Head held high, she stepped into the main room. "You can tell me what this is all about. You," she directed her statement to Hawk, "did not come here to make assumptions about my relationship with Houston. It's none of your business. So, why are you here?"

Houston stood near the fireplace, arms crossed in front of him, his feet planted firmly apart. His dark brows were drawn together. She wasn't sure what he was thinking, only knew he would say nothing in front of his friend.

Hawk whistled softly, eyeing her up then down before he blushed. She was immediately self-conscious realizing for the sake of time she forgot the bindings. She was his to see.

"I'd stop ogling my mate if you know what's good for you. Friend or foe no one is going to look at my mate as if she's food for their plate."

Houston's voice sounded harsher than she'd ever heard him before. He turned to her. In a quiet voice, "Perhaps, Leah, you should finish dressing."

He didn't sound angry at her, just Hawk. She understood now she'd been in too much of a hurry to discover what had Hawk pounding on Houston's door this early in the morning. When she was back in the bedroom, not only did she wrap the binding around her, she also pulled her hair into a tightly unattractive bun.

When she stepped into the main room, Houston smiled with a nod she assumed was approval.

"Since you are here," Houston began, "there was an accident down the road toward Edinburgh. There are wounded people who need help. Hawk and I were going. You should stay here, wait for me. I would like to know you are safe."

She drew herself up, her shoulders squaring. "I can help tend to the less injured so the two you of can work on the people who need more, a physician. How many?" While she enjoyed tending to her wildlings, she'd always wanted to be able to give aide to humans. This was her chance. She held onto her breath praying Houston would agree.

"Thank you, but..." Hawk began dismissing her before even considering she might be helpful.

"You should go with us." Houston gave her his nod of approval. "You have talents in this area that need coaxing from you. Whether you understand your aptitude or not, you are a healer."

Her heart soared. "I'll get my cloak. It's somewhere around here." She was looking. Had no idea where Houston put the garment last night. There was very little she recalled about that time except for the hours they were in his big bed together. The thoughts brought heat to her face.

"What do you think you're doing?" Hawk turned to Houston clearly displeased by his invitation. "She will be in the way. We'll have to tend to her if she faints."

"I won't faint," she blustered, angry with the man she thought was her friend. "Well, you *ken* that for a fact?"

"You know as well as I do, she has remarkable skills. It's time she put them to use on something other than animals." Houston seemed to mean what he said. He looked at her with a gentle smile along with another nod of what she thought was encouragement.

To Leah it didn't appear Houston would back down.

"She's a woman."

"I noticed," Houston said, his voice taken on different note as he slanted a heated gaze in her direction. "Do you have the buggy?"

"Yes, as well as my horse."

"I'll take the buggy with Leah." Houston was putting together bandages along with splints. He pulled painkillers from his shelf along with bottles she didn't know what they contained.

"What can I do?"

"Take this to the buggy then come back for more." He was working quickly yet with a practiced grace. Houston knew what he was about.

"I've supplies in the buggy too. I'm leaving. For the record, I don't approve of a woman tending to men."

"What if there are women there? Do you approve of a woman tending another woman?" Leah asked sarcastically all the while knowing this was the way men thought.

She might not be able to read or write. Nonetheless, there were a lot of things she did understand as well as anyone else.

She felt as if the purpose in her life became clear. Houston told her they were made for each other. Perhaps there was more to his words than she assumed earlier. Perhaps if she could help him with his practice, they could find a way to be together.

If he wanted her to help this way, perhaps he didn't just want her in his bed. Maybe she meant more to him than she assumed. She made two trips to the buggy. On the third trip they both carried satchels of supplies.

"How many are hurt?" she asked thinking Houston must have known before he packed supplies.

Maybe when she was dressing, they hadn't talked just about her.

"There were six people in the carriage plus two drivers. Don't know if all are hurt but..." his tone changed again, this time it was filled with concern.

"Some might not have survived?" she asked as she thought of her animals she'd not been able to heal. That was the hardest part of helping the injured, seeing them leave this world for a better place. She smiled though as she remembered all those that made it.

"Yes," he said his voice tight, strained. "Since the messenger didn't say, Hawk had no way of knowing."

She put her hand on his arm, feeling the strength of the man, sensing the genuine concern for the people radiating from deep inside. "Even if we lose some, it will be alright. God's will, I'm thinking. It's the only way I can come to terms with the senseless death of an animal. While I understand it's not the same for a human, I have to think of a death that way."

Houston placed his hand on top of hers. "It's so real. If you don't want to come with me, you don't have to. I'll stop and let you down."

"More than anything I want to be with you helping. For the first time in my life, I feel a real purpose."

"Good, I want you with me too. Want you to know how much confidence I have in you in your abilities."

His gently spoken words meant everything to her. They rode in silence. The sun rose above the forested hills casting light on the road. Nervous energy assailed her, her fingers winding in the folds of her gown. Nearly twenty minutes later they rounded a curve to see the carriage tipped over. Hawk strode between patients pointing seeming to give directions. She thought he might be separating the people who were not so badly injured from the ones who would need his along with Houston's skills. One body lay off to the side covered with a cloth.

She understood the man passed on to another world. Leah hoped it was heaven where he went, perhaps as some believed a better place. The breath she drew in for courage wavered in a thin stream as she let it rush from her lips. This was real, very real. She swiped her sweaty palms on her gown.

Houston seemed to notice the hesitation she was feeling. "You can stay in the buggy if you like. Just because you came along doesn't mean you can't have second or even third thoughts about lending aid." His voice was edged with tender concern, the glint in his eyes told her the same.

She flashed him the biggest smile she could manage under the current circumstances. While her hands trembled, she had second thoughts as well. Nevertheless, she was determined. "No, I can do this. I want to do this." Not waiting for help she climbed from the buggy.

In four long strides, Hawk stood beside her. "You *ken* I didn't want you here. Now I'm pleased you chose to come along. There is plenty for you to do. Those four have minor injuries, which you can easily tend to. If you want to continue in this vein, how you handle yourself will be your first test. Take a satchel of the bandages with you. If you need help, give either one of us a call. I do believe you know what to do."

"Thank you," she murmured realizing Hawk just had a huge change of heart.

The man must have realized his as well as Houston's talents would be better used with the severe injuries. Since she was here, there was no reason to keep anyone from being tended to with immediacy.

Leah went to work with her patients. A little boy had a cut over one eye that was bleeding profusely. She washed the injury with the water Houston brought then bandaged the small slash. When she finished, she found him a place to sit near his mother who broke her arm. Houston worked on the woman. With her good arm, she wrapped it around the little boy who tried valiantly to keep from crying. Leah found candy in Houston's bag. She brought a piece for the little boy. He smiled then told her the confection was delicious.

There were scrapes and bruises, a sprained ankle, which she wrapped. When she finished, she found a rock she could place the foot on so the injury was elevated. There was nothing she encountered she couldn't handle.

Exhausted yet strangely exhilarated, Leah stood back for a moment looking at her patients. Moving from one person to the next person, she checked on each one's condition, offering water. None needed the pain medications Houston brought. When she was satisfied she'd done all she could, she turned to Hawk and Houston.

Hawk was mounting his horse. He smiled then tipped his cap to her before he turned toward Selkirk.

Houston shook his head, a dark brow arched as if he wasn't sure what to say. "There is nothing else we can do here. Hawk is going for wagons to help these people back to our offices. I'll be busy all day as well as into the night. You can stay or go up the mountain. It's up to you. I would like you to stay though." Tenderly, he ran his knuckles down her cheek. "You did well for your first time. I didn't have one doubt about your abilities. Thank you for your help. You're a natural. I guess I never truly realized what you did for your wildlings."

Moisture welled up threatening to break through her quiet resolve to keep her emotions in check. "For the first time in my life I felt needed. If you don't need me, I'll go to Brenda's. She always needs help with the children. While I don't want to tell her about last night, would it be alright with you if I speak of it today?"

"Yes, we do need to keep last night between us. I'm thinking we need to talk about what happened last night as well as this morning when Hawk burst in and saw you. There will be repercussions we can't avoid even though we know Hawk won't say anything."

"I suppose we do."

She thought about the feelings, the pleasure. She thought about her hopes and dreams. She was almost sure at this moment in time he meant what he told her about returning for her. Still doubts assailed her. She was afraid, now that the night of pleasure was over and in the process he got what he wanted, he would forget what he told her. He never promised, a promise meant everything to her. He would move on with his life, never giving her another thought. She couldn't bear life if he did. Deep in her heart, she didn't expect miracles. It would be a miracle if he did come for her when he finished his business. Men like Houston didn't commit to women like her.

"Don't look so worried," he spoke softly, tenderly caressing the line of her jaw. "We just need to sort some things out before I head to Edinburgh, you and me. You need to know what I want to happen. What I expect from our relationship." He massaged his temples as creases formed on his brow. "It's so new..."

Turning her gaze from his she stared down the road. She didn't want to talk about expectations or the future. "How long do you think it will take Hawk to get the wagons?"

"You're avoiding the topic. I'll accept that for now. Hawk won't be gone too long though. He alerted several people in the village before we left. They should be ready as soon as he gets there, so maybe another thirty minutes or so. It won't take him long on his horse. The carts will take additional time."

"I'll go see how my patients are doing."

Unable to sort through her fears, she rose. Houston followed. The boy was smiling now. His mother's arm had been splinted. It would need to be set. The others she cared for were all doing fine except for one lady whose attitude was the problem.

"When are we finally going to get decent care? You're not a physician, not even an apprentice I dare to say." The lady stared at Leah. "What if I die from what you did? What then?"

"You won't die from a scratch on your arm. You might have a scar to show for your adventure though. It will give you something to brag about the next time you have tea. It will make the other ladies jealous." Houston stood beside her defending Leah's work.

"She doesn't have the right to work on me," the lady persisted bitterly.

"Of course, she does. This woman is my apprentice. She's truly quite skilled more so than most men I've worked with."

A bubble of happiness started in the pit of her stomach then worked its way to her heart. He thought she did well. She drew in a breath of air before turning to gaze into his silver-gray eyes.

"I mean that," he said softly as they walked from the woman.

~ * ~

"Houston wants me to stay in the upstairs apartment in his office when he's gone. I don't know what to do. Don't know where Grizzly is. It's just not like the man to leave and not come home. It's been a week."

Fears for Grizzly flooded her. She didn't need him to survive. As long as she possessed the house up the mountain, she would be fine. However, she didn't wish ill of anyone.

"I don't think living in that apartment is wise. After the accident the entire town knows you stayed the night at his office. You were seen leaving with Houston just as the sun rose. Now, after you tended to the people in the carriage, there is more talk. None of it good for your reputation," Brenda murmured softly, only concern in her voice. "I just don't know what to do with you."

Leah understood there were no recriminations. After all, Brenda had not been a model of propriety herself. "Just keep talking to me and stay my friend. I *ken* I'm going to need one soon."

At the moment, Leah felt alone as well as abandoned by Grizzly. She thought someone should look for him. With no one to ask, she wasn't sure what to do, afraid he was gone for good, never coming back. She hadn't seen Stick in over three weeks. Actually, she couldn't remember the last time she spoke with him

Her life was taking on too many changes.

Too much was happening.

Houston should be her rock. He was leaving. Nothing would ever be the same again. She fought the sudden rise of tears. Fought the feeling that made her feel sorry for herself.

Battled them with all her heart. The tears still rose, spiking her lashes with moisture, clogging her throat despite swallowing, pushing them down to wherever they came from. The last thing she wanted was to cry.

Brenda leaned forward, moisture in her eyes, "Honey, I'll always be your friend. Whatever you decide I'm here for you. Whatever happens I won't abandon you. Staying in his office will only create more talk. If you don't have a place to live, having a roof over your head might, however, be for the best."

"That's just it. I'm torn. Feel as if I've been ripped in half. I don't know what to do. There are things I can't tell you. In any case if I did, you wouldn't believe me or...you would think I'm crazy. Houston doesn't want me to live on the mountain alone. Says even with Grizzly there he's afraid for me."

The breath of air she drew in stayed in her lungs burning while she held it waiting for Brenda to say something.

"You *ken* I'll always listen to you. Might disagree nonetheless, I'll always listen. What I do agree with Houston is that it's not right for you to stay on the mountain by yourself. You can always bring your things to the guesthouse. We could put you there for a short while but not indefinitely. Maybe Houston will return for you. Though I get the distinct feeling you don't believe he will."

With a heavy sigh Leah searched for words, "I know though this is just too...too different for normal people to believe. Your guesthouse is for guests not tenants. I don't have the coin to pay you either. An imposition is not something I intend to be."

Brenda's brows slowly drew together. "You're not going to tell me you're a witch or a fairy or some such nonsense?"

Leah almost laughed. "*Nay*, I'm not going to tell you anything except it's closer to some such nonsense than you can imagine."

"Well, I'm glad I am to see you smiling. Why, if I didn't miss my guess, you almost laughed. We could use a little more levity today."

"You have a way of cheering my heart."

Leah knew her thoughts were deep, troubling, bordering on depression. Her life choices were frightening. She couldn't count on anyone except herself. She had no idea what to decide.

Perhaps she could count on Brenda. She didn't know for sure. Brenda didn't want to see her hurt. She believed with all her heart Houston would hurt her.

Maybe he hurt her already and she just wasn't willing to acknowledge that fact.

Chapter Eight

A week passed. To his regret, he saw Leah occasionally. This was not the way he wanted to spend the last week in Selkirk. Had little time to be alone with her or talk over things that required saying. Houston understood she needed reassurance. All he could do though was to keep telling her his intentions. What he could not do was convince her to trust him.

She had to believe in herself first. Leah had too many doubts about her abilities. Her healing skills were unmatched. The day of the carriage accident she proved herself. He was certain he could teach her how to set human bones as he recalled the sparrow hawk at her refuge.

When he first saw the animals she took care of, he didn't think much about what she did other than how much she cherished all living things. Now, he realized her abilities went far beyond the norm.

Today he had to talk to her. Had to find the words to make her understand his intentions. He looked all over town. She must have gone home. He didn't like it when she stayed there alone. She knew how he felt, but nonetheless did so anyway. With a feminine shrug, she asked him where she could stay where no one would talk about her. He didn't have an answer to her question.

He passed the Fletcher place, waved to Mrs. Fletcher. Thought of Grizzly who he was certain that for one reason or another wasn't coming back. It was best if Leah understood the fact. She might hope he wouldn't return. Houston didn't truly know.

There were things he could do for her if she would agree. He could bring her to Edinburgh with him. She could live in his townhouse. There were enough rooms a person could get lost. Even if they didn't share a bed, there would be talk. Her name would once more be fuel for gossip. Edinburgh was a large city so few would even care. Unfortunately, she would.

She wouldn't agree unless he married her. At this point he didn't think she would agree to a marriage even though he understood she wanted that very thing. Right now, it wasn't prudent for him to marry. Before he made a commitment, he needed to be a whole man. Wanted to know his foot was healed. When that was done, he would propose.

He had every faith in Hawk's talents when it came to bone setting. Houston saw him perform what some would call miracles. If he accomplished the breaking of five bones then setting them again so they would heal straight, that would also be a miracle.

When he reached the small building Leah called home, he tied the reins to the railing before setting off on the easiest path to her refuge. He wasn't about to battle brambles just to reach the place. If Grizzly wasn't coming back, the location no longer mattered.

Houston hoped when he stepped into her sanctuary she would be in her cat form. He wanted to see her that way again before he left.

Sunlight glistened off her long golden hair as she sat on a rock sketching. No, she wasn't in her cat. He still hadn't shown her his cat. Even though it wasn't sensible, he would today if she asked.

Leah looked up when his shadow drifted across her. His heart caught in his throat. He didn't want to leave her alone in this isolated spot on the mountain. Didn't ever want to leave her alone. While he was away from her, he would do nothing except worry.

Sitting down next to her, he set her hand in his. "Put your sketches away. We've important things to talk over that can't wait."

"You're leaving."

She turned from him doing as he requested, tears in her hauntingly beautiful blue eyes.

He heard the muffled sob as she stuffed the sketch into its satchel. Hurting her hurt him. His heart broke at the sound of her anguish. The need to take all the pain away swamped him.

"Yes, I'm leaving as soon as we finish here," he whispered as he pushed flyaway strands of hair behind her ear.

He wanted to kiss her. Didn't dare.

"I've scarcely seen you the last few days." Her voice was barely there, her words paper-thin, reedy.

"Too true. Regrets are paramount in this case. If I could I would have done everything different. Would have spent every second with you. There were things I couldn't put off."

"I understand."

She gazed at him with red-rimmed eyes. This wasn't the first time she cried. Only the first time he saw as well as heard the tears.

"No, I don't think you do. I've the feeling you're telling yourself you weren't important to me and that's why I couldn't spend time with you. It's not true." He spoke softly wishing he could make her understand.

Only time would tell the true story. He would have to be patient with her.

He'd not been with her, not slept with her although every moment he was ensconced in business he was thinking of her. She wouldn't believe the words if he spoke them.

She turned to him, touched his chin, "You're an important person. I'm only me, a fey creature is what the villagers call me. You will go on to be a brilliant physician. I know that as surely as my heart continues to beat."

"Not any more important than you, Leah. Brilliant is not something I strive for, just knowledgeable so I don't hurt those who come to me for help."

"You're too modest," she spoke with such reverence.

Houston needed to pull her into his arms, waylay the fear she felt. Again, he knew that feat was impossible. The thought tore at his heart. All he could do now was look to the future while praying she wouldn't do anything foolish.

"No, not modest." He paused then, sliding his sweaty palms along his pants. This was the hardest conversation he'd ever had with her. Everything he said was important. "First, let's talk about Grizzly. Has he been seen? Have you seen him or heard of his whereabouts?"

She rearranged her skirts spreading them around her, smoothing her hands down the length. He wanted to buy her new gowns, dress her in clothing that wasn't threadbare.

When she looked at him, tiny diamonds of moisture spiked on her dark lashes. It always amazed him for one so fair her lashes were long and dark. She blinked away some of the wetness before slanting him a wan smile.

"I don't believe he is alive. He would have turned up here. Three weeks, Grizzly's been gone all that time. No one in the village cares enough about him to search, not even Seamus will take the time."

He shuddered at the thought of her only kin passing away without a trace. Without a body it was hard to mourn. He didn't know if she would mourn Grizzly. Nonetheless, he did deserve a burial, everyone did. "What will happen to his land, to the home where you live? Do you know if this hovel will still belong to you?"

She wouldn't want to move. If Grizzly adopted her, this place should be her inheritance. If he didn't, who knew?

"I always thought the house along with the land would be mine. Houston, I *ken* you don't want me to stay here by myself. It's my home. I've nowhere to go. If I don't inherit the place, I won't have anywhere to live. Can't stay at Brenda's and Seamus' guesthouse. They use it. Besides I can't pay rent. Without the little cabin, I've nothing."

With every second passed, fear for her circumstances grew. "What I would like is for you to come to Edinburgh with me. You can live in the townhouse my family owns with me. I can protect you."

"Oh, and your family would be thrilled to hear you've a woman living with you, wouldn't they? The people you know as well as work with would talk about me behind your back. You couldn't bring anyone to your home because I would be there. The bad things about this situation you propose keeps growing."

"No, my mother and father along with my brothers would make sure I was reprimanded. They would put me in my place. However, I would know you were safe as well as protected. I wouldn't have to worry about you." He grinned as he thought about their words to him. "When I tell them you're my mate, they will understand."

Mate, not wife. The difference clouded his judgment, his heart, all that he was and wanted to be.

Houston didn't understand why he didn't spirit her to the church, after that marry her this instant. Yes, he did. He wanted to do this right with his family and friends around him in attendance and as witnesses. He wanted her to have a fine wedding gown, flowers, a cake. Most of all he wanted to be whole when he married her. When he looked at his foot, when he limped, he felt half a man.

"Even if you can live with that I cannot. For your family to look at you with scorn in their hearts because of me is too much to bear. We have no choice except to let this momentary passion for each other go."

Her fingers wove in then out of the dress she wore, another threadbare gown. When he could, he would fix that. If she allowed it, he would fix it now.

"If this place, humble as it is, is not yours, what will you do? You refuse to allow Brenda to help you. You've turned down the apartment above my office. Now you won't accept a place in Edinburg to live. Would you take money to travel to the highlands to live with my parents? You know I will gladly give it to you."

"Your solutions give me the label of your mistress or whore. I'm not as intelligent as most people. However, I certainly understand what those arrangements mean. I won't denigrate you or myself that way."

Swearing softly, he paced the perimeter of her sanctuary; taking in the scene, understanding this place was part of what made Leah so special. This situation was far too difficult, more difficult than he ever believed it should be. She was too damn stubborn, set in her ways. He would never think of her as his mistress or a whore. "You don't understand that I will make everything right. You just have to be patient."

"I have to follow my heart. While I'm willing to wait, in the process see what comes my way, it shouldn't be too hard to figure something out for myself if the worst-case scenario happens. Don't think anyone will evict me. Until Grizzly is found dead or alive, I'm safe. You needn't worry about me."

"You're most likely right about that. I'll still worry." His long breath of air whooshed out in a soft sigh. He wasn't getting anywhere with this.

"Grizzly will show up." She spoke the words though he wasn't sure she meant them.

He didn't think the man would ever show up. "Did Grizzly adopt you?" Before he thought, the words popped out. He had to know the truth. It could change everything.

"Mother thought so. At one time I had the feeling he didn't. I always called myself, out of stubbornness, Leah McEwen, my birth name. Grizzly got angry one day then insisted I use his last name, Kennedy. It was then I thought he adopted me. Mother and Grizzly kept arguing about it though. To answer your question, I'm not sure. Probably not, Grizzly was too lazy to do anything that would take time away from his drinking."

"If you weren't adopted, someone else might show up to claim this home, the land. What will you do then?"

She lifted her fragile shoulders; too delicate to be left on her own even though Houston knew she possessed a will of iron. In most cases she could take care of herself. "I don't know. You understand I've nowhere to go."

"I understand nothing of the sort. You've got my family to go to, he persisted. You have to remember they will provide a home for you. I'll write them as soon as I reach my townhouse. They'll look for you."

"No!" The single word exploded from her. She shook her head over and over. "No."

"No?" He tugged in a breath of air, ready to shake her, needing for her to see things the way she should. He should just write the letter. It would be for her good.

"Don't write. Don't anticipate the worst when we don't know if he's truly gone. Let me wait and see."

"That's fair."

He didn't like what she asked of him. Wanted to take care of her before he left. Things dangling left unchecked irritated him.

She smiled then her bottom lip tucked endearingly beneath her teeth. "We agree on something."

"There's something else."

"Yes. What more could there be?"

Putting off leaving until he cleared this up was not possible. Still, he needed to head down the mountain before the sun sank below the horizon. He didn't want to ride in the dark. Wanted to reach Edinburgh as soon as possible.

"Listen, I've left directions to my home in the highlands as well as the townhouse in the city with Hawk. You know you can trust him. Go to him if there is even one problem. Go immediately if Grizzly is found dead. We both understand that might well come to pass."

She nodded. "Yes." She lifted her shoulders, her eyes imploring him, "What good will that do?"

"If anything happens you have money to go to my family home. Hawk is keeping the coin for you. If anything happens, have Hawk send a letter to me. He'll write me if nothing happens just to tell me how you are doing."

"If I write, Hawk will know what I say. There would be nothing private between us."

"Yes, he'll also know what I tell you because I intend to correspond every day. You can go to his office. He'll read the letters to you. Perhaps he will also help you learn to read if he has the time."

"He tried before and was never successful."

"Yes, well, you can explain what we learned. You just see things backward. It's nothing that should get in the way of your learning. Since you've made so much progress already you might be able to read some of my letters if I keep them simple. Maybe I'll write two. One you can use to help you learn then one with more details."

"Compliments I don't deserve," she murmured softly. Still, she smiled. "You did all the work. You figured out what is wrong with me. No one else could do that."

"Leah, Leah, whatever am I going to do with you? Nothing is wrong with you. You are smart as well as shy, reclusive yet willing to try new things. I want you in my life forever."

He realized he couldn't live without her. Before, when he knew she was his mate, he accepted the fact she would obviously stay with him, live with him, bear his children. Now, however, he understood the powerful feelings he had for her. God, he loved her so much he was bursting with it.

"Just not yet...in your life"

Tenderly he placed her hands in his, drawing her to her feet. His hands around her waist now, he pressed her close. "Just not yet," he agreed with her. "The timing isn't right unless you want to come with me. I think you've made it perfectly clear how you feel about that. If I had time right now, I'd make love to you again. Show you how much you mean to me. Leah." He brushed hair from her face, his fingertips lingering on her cheek. "While I've never been celibate, I've had sex with women. However, I've never made love to anyone except you."

"I want to feel you deep inside me," she said softly tears still clouding her eyes.

"Don't tempt me. I want that too."

She couldn't possibly understand how much she enticed him. *Nay,* she couldn't understand. Because he didn't entirely.

Slowly, he lowered his head. His lips were so very close to hers. He felt the soft puffs of air as she exhaled each tiny breath. Knowing it would be a couple of months before he could hold her, kiss her again, he shaped his mouth across hers, traced and bathed her softness with his tongue. She moaned softly, purring, wrapping her arms around him, sliding her hands to his nape. As she stood on tiptoes, her breasts pushed against his chest. She gave him everything he could ever want.

"Make love to me," she said as she pulled away from him for a fraction in time.

"Can't risk it."

He was shaking his head, knowing if they did, he would surely get her with child. She shouldn't have to endure more humiliation at his hands even though he never intended any of it. They were lucky the first time. Chancing it a second could be disaster for her.

"I *dinna* care. Want your child. More than anything." Her breaths came in panting gulps. Once again, he lowered his lips to hers, swept them with moisture, plunged inside reveling in the sweet taste he encountered.

"You will increase with my child someday. Patience, sweetling, patience and all will be yours. I promise. I care too much for you to give you more shame than I already have. I don't want to leave you pregnant."

His hands cupped her buttocks, pulled her so she would feel the heat of his erection.

She was his heaven.

He was leaving her.

He would give most anything if he could take her with him without causing more shame. His purpose was true. He planned it before he arrived in Selkirk, before he met and bedded his mate. For him this quest was far too important to forget. He would learn so much. So much that might help Leah when she did have a child of his. Would aid her when she was giving birth.

"I have to go. Walk me down the mountain or at least to your home." His hand rested on the hidden curve of her breast. He wished he could feel the soft flesh. Wished they weren't bound.

"You could stay the night."

"No, that wouldn't be wise or prudent. Walk with me. Promise me you will let me know if you need me. Come to my family home if there are problems. Promise me."

"I cannot promise...people will talk about you. I cannot bear that."

"Promise me. Leah, you have to promise. I won't be able to leave if you do not. The money is there for you if you need it. I don't give a damn about what people say or think about me. It's you I care about."

She smiled for a moment but the smile wilted. "You *ken* that is what I want. Don't want you to leave."

"Promise me."

She didn't. He couldn't wait for her any longer. They walked to the home where she would stubbornly remain as long as it was hers. He kissed her quickly on the forehead before mounting his horse. Without the promise he sought, he rode out of her life.

As he left, he felt her gaze burning his back. Knew she cried again. Would do anything in his power to make this different. Tears slipped from his eyes. He shouldn't have given her a choice.

I'm a bastard.

Hell, he tried everything he could think of, stubborn woman. He could have married her. As he started down the road to Edinburgh, waves of foreboding washed over him. Fear for her pooled in his gut. He felt as if he saw things he shouldn't, feared things there was no need to fear.

He tried to tell himself she had Brenda and Seamus to look after her along with Hawk to protect her.

What did he miss? There was something niggling in the back of his mind. He'd thought to cover all the potential difficulties that might face her when he found her in the refuge.

He missed something.

~ * ~

Leah would keep him forever in her heart. That day when he left, she'd never felt so forlorn and alone. Even when her mother passed on, she'd not been so devastated. With Houston's departure part of her died.

As the days swept by, she sunk farther into despondency spending more time at the sanctuary. She walked the forests. Found animals that needed love as well as patching. For her, love was in abundance. She needed to shower anything that would accept that love with tender loving care.

Hawk rode to the house every other day or so with letters from Houston. They were simple letters telling her what he was doing and learning. The man he studied with according to Houston was a brilliant physician ahead of his time. Leah told him the man couldn't possibly be as brilliant as he was.

He sent letters she could read. Hawk helped her with the words she didn't know. He never spoke of love or commitment. Always, he reminded her about his mother and father, Brenna and Alistair. Always, he told her to rely on him along with his family if she needed anything.

At the end of each letter, he would ask her if he could write his parents and tell them about her. Always she declined.

She wanted to hear words of love which were never part of the letter. She liked to tell herself that was because Hawk had to read the letters to her. After all, that reason was why she never told him how much she loved him.

Liar.

She didn't tell him because he didn't return the emotion. If Hawk wasn't writing the letters from her, she would have said so many different things. She would never have spoken of love.

Hawk left after the month to tend to Houston's foot. He was gone a fortnight. Without the daily visits, she was lonelier than before. She didn't know she could be lonelier. There were no letters to be read to her or for her to have written. She spent more time sketching the animals as well as an inordinate amount of time tending the small vegetable garden behind the house.

Grizzly still didn't make an appearance. It seemed as if he vanished from the face of the earth. She stifled a sob as she began to count all the changes in her life since January when Shadow died and she first truly met Houston. The differences were enormous.

Michael walked up the mountain at least once a week. He kept his hands to himself. However, he never failed to ask her to wed him. She always told him the same thing. As the days slowly passed by everything was the same yet different.

Hawk returned with good news. Houston's foot was healing nicely. The surgery was successful. There should be no more limping. He was recuperating in the highlands. It wasn't too long after that she received a letter asking her to join him.

There were no words of commitment or love. As Brenda told her, he just wanted her in his bed. He was selfishly using her love for him. If Brenda would have encouraged her just a tiny bit, she might have gone.

Hawk looked at her as if she was foolish for believing there ever would be a commitment. It seemed to Leah everyone thought they knew Houston better than she did.

Perhaps they were right.

"Hello." Brenda stood at the back door, drying her hands on a dishtowel, smiling at her. "It's a beautiful day outside. The sun is shining. Seems it's been raining forever. Glad to see you come down from the mountain to see someone besides Hawk. What's got that dour expression painted on your face? Bad news? Someone find Grizzly?"

"No, can I come in and just sit awhile. Need someone to talk to even though I can't say why."

Desperately, she needed to talk to Houston. Needed to tell him things he should learn from her.

"Of course you can come inside. I'd never tell you no. I want you to remember we're friends. I won't judge no matter how bad it is," she told her as she put a pot of water on the stove to make tea. "There is nothing like a good cup of tea to cure whatever ails a body."

Leah felt as if Brenda guessed her news. She didn't know how the woman would know, maybe because she'd been through it so many times herself. Leah was both pleased and fearful. She was sure she was pregnant. She had all the symptoms she'd seen Brenda go through before each of her children were born.

She had to tell someone.

As she lifted her shoulders in a hopeless shrug, she said, "Others will judge." Leah hadn't meant to say those words. She was relieved though that she did because Brenda would guess then she wouldn't have to actually tell Brenda she was increasing.

Brenda's face took on a different expression. To Leah she looked surprised then worried. "Just that one time?" she asked.

Leah assumed Brenda knew the answer. Brenda was her confidant. She pretty much told her everything. "Yes."

"Thought you told me Houston said it would be safe. It was the right time of the month."

Brenda's question shook her to the soul. He had said those same words. The last thing she expected was to be pregnant. It was her fault though.

"It was my mistake. I've never truly paid attention to my..." she swallowed hard still embarrassed talking about woman things even to the woman who was the closest person she had to a mother. "My cycle. I'm not regular. I told him three or four weeks then was positive it had been nearly four weeks. Because of that he didn't use any type of protection. He would have if I'd told him differently. He didn't want this to happen to me."

Brenda drummed her nails on the table. "I'm not regular. That's why Seamus has so much trouble trying to figure out when to as well as when not to protect me. I guess you're no different. How do you feel about a wee one growing inside you?"

"Happy," Leah told Brenda honestly. "Happy, except I know when the people see my condition there will be other feelings. I'll feel ashamed even though I truly don't believe I've anything to be ashamed of."

"Does anyone else know?" She arched her eyebrows.

"No. I'll have to tell Hawk soon. I believe he's already guessed. He keeps staring at me with this unusual expression on his face. Sometimes he'll start to say something then he'll clear his throat then say nothing."

"He's only been back a few days. Did he tell you anything about Houston and the surgery?"

"Says it went well. Other than that, he read a letter to me. Houston is recovering. He's still saying he's going to come for me. When he does, we'll talk. Says he doesn't know when. He doesn't want to rush the healing and in the process damage Hawk's work."

"That man needs to be here today, not a second later. He's not treating you right." She was shaking a finger at the back door. "Well, he knows. When I see him next, I'm going to tell him just exactly what I think of his actions or rather his inactions."

For a moment Leah thought she might laugh. In her defense, Brenda sounded so fierce. Brenda's blustering did build her confidence. To have someone who was on her side was everything she yearned for. Still, she had to bow to reality. "Houston isn't coming for me. We both understand that fact. Don't get upset over it. I'm not good enough for him." Leah wished what she said wasn't true. It was just that she couldn't let her hopes get the better of her. Her emotions lately had been so far out of control she didn't know how to handle them. It seemed she cried all the time.

"That man told you he would be here."

"He did. I never truly believed him. He has a purpose in life that doesn't include me. If he doesn't see that now, he will. I don't want to be a burden to him, one he can't get rid of. He's wise not to make a commitment to me." Everything she said was the truth. She just didn't know how she was going to survive on her own without him.

"Oh, honey, you can't keep thinking that way. You're a loving caring person who would make any man a fine wife." Brenda picked up the teacups. She paused half way to the sink. "What about Michael?"

Leah lifted her shoulders slightly unsure where Brenda's line of questioning was going. "What about him? He certainly isn't going to be my husband even though he's still saying different. Since Houston left, he's become more and more persistent. Walks up the mountain now almost every night after work. He got another promotion. It's only been a few months since the first one. He tells me his father is pretty much through working. Says that he wants to sit on the front porch and watch his grandchildren."

"That old man doesn't have any grandchildren."

"That's Michael's point."

Brenda cleared her throat as she seemed to think about what she was about to say. "If you don't want him, don't lead the poor boy on. He seems to think you would be willing to be his wife. Everyone has heard him talking, even Hawk."

Brenda set the cups in the sink before walking back to the table.

The knocking on the kitchen door startled them. "Brenda, Leah you in there? Been looking all over for you. Even rode up the mountain."

"It's Hawk," Leah said apprehensively. This wasn't normal. "Whatever do you suppose he wants here?"

"Guess we'll have to open the door and welcome him inside if we want to find out. "Maybe Hawk has another letter from Houston. Perhaps it says he'll be here in the next day or two."

"There was one this morning," Leah sighed softly, confused even more about her feelings coupled with what exactly they meant.

Everything Houston told her she wanted to come true. Several times she'd been tempted to use his money so she could go to the highlands. Nothing waited for her on her mountain or in Selkirk. "There wouldn't be a letter tonight though. Not unless something bad happened."

Brenda opened the door. "Hello, it's a fine spring day now isn't it, doctor Hawk. What do you want with Leah? We both *ken* you're not here to talk to me."

"It's exceptional. Always straight to the point. Is Leah here?" He stepped into the room.

"Now, what do you need with the young lady? She told me a letter arrived this morning."

"No letter. I wish that was why I'm here. We think we found your stepfather, Grizzly."

"You did?" For a moment her heart forgot to beat. She clamped her hands together waiting for more words.

Hawk cleared his throat as he jammed his hands through his hair after that into his pockets. For a second, he looked out the window. When he returned his gaze to her, "I need for you to identify the body."

When Hawk started talking, Leah stood, her hands clasped tightly in front of her. His words hit her hard. What he told her suddenly resonating, she slumped to the chair. "You want me to do what? I can't." She couldn't bear to see a dead body, especially not Grizzly's. She remembered finding her mother. "No, no, God no."

"I'm sorry. I should have told you to sit."

She wiped tears from her eyes trying to control her emotions that seemed to be seething out of her control. "What if I don't want to? It's been so many weeks, Hawk. I don't..." She had no more words.

"You're the only one who can for sure."

"Now that's not true." Brenda stepped in front of her. "You don't need this poor girl to go through any more trauma. There's not a reason in this world that Seamus or Mr. Fletcher can't do the duty. Leah doesn't have to be put through any of that stress. In her condition..."

Leah shot Brenda a look when she started to confirm what she was sure Hawk guessed. She wanted to tell Hawk. Planned to tell him this morning except she was too excited about the letter. There hadn't been one in several days. She'd been so afraid Houston was losing interest in her just as she suspected all along that he would.

"Suppose you're right. Why don't you stay with Leah? I'll go down to the newspaper, see if Seamus can come with me to the undertakers." He turned to Leah. "You and I have something I'm thinking we need to talk about. I know it's none of my business, but Houston...well, we'll talk. Come by my office before you head up the mountain."

"No, I'm going home now."

Leah didn't want to talk to Hawk. She knew what he was going to tell her. It wasn't his business. He would have to let her decide for herself what was best."

"Identifying Grizzly won't take more than a few minutes. Go to my office now and wait for me. I'll be right there. You won't have long to wait."

With that announcement he left, the door banging shut behind him. Just like a man he expected his command to be obeyed.

"I'm not going. If he wants to talk to me today, he'll have to ride up the mountain."

Leah felt adamant about not seeing Hawk. She didn't want to apologize or listen to a lecture. She needed time to think about the repercussions of Grizzly's death. It seemed her tiny world was slowly falling apart around her.

"I'm sorry I let that slip. It wasn't well done of me." Brenda apologized.

"He knew. What you said only served to confirm his guess. It's not his business. I don't want to confide in him. He has a male point of view I don't want to listen to. Now that we know what happened to Grizzly, I'll have to make a few more decisions. I discovered Grizzly never officially adopted me so the house isn't mine to live in. Don't know what will happen to the old shack or if anyone wants it. If someone does turn up to claim the home as well as the land, I'll have to leave."

"Everyone thought he did. You took his last name," Brenda said as she watched her. Her littlest gave out a long wail easily heard. "I'll be right back. You just stay here until I get the baby."

Tempted to leave, Leah sat down, her heart caught in her throat. All the feelings of doom assailing her since Houston left returned full force. She was sure she would no longer have a home. She would have to make hard decisions in the next few weeks. Her hand rested on her belly. She was just beginning to round with the *wee bairn*. Her breasts were larger. Her morning sickness was usually short, over with before the noon hour.

All that could change.

When Brenda walked into the room, Leah did stand. "I need to go now. Have to get my thoughts in order before I have the talk with Hawk I'm sure he's itching to have. I know what he's going to say. If I don't leave now, he'll come by here then he'll make more demands."

"What is that? What is he going to tell you?" Brenda challenged. "That you should write Houston. In the process tell him about your condition?"

"Yes, he'll also tell me that I should use the money Houston left to travel to his home. I can't do that. I just can't. I won't tell Houston in a letter that I'm carrying his child. That he was wrong about the safety of what we did."

"Why not? Houston asked you to do that very thing."

"He doesn't truly want me. He doesn't love me. Those should be enough reasons. I don't want him to feel obligated."

"Perhaps he would want to have a hand in the raising of his child," Brenda challenged her again.

Her words hit her hard in her belly. Leah didn't have one reason to think Houston would not want to keep his babe with him. He would come for the child. Would make sure the child stayed with him, despite the fact she was the mother. That was why she wasn't ready to tell the man.

"You're right of course. I have to tell him. I suppose you would say writing a letter would be the coward's way out." She let a little stream of breath slide past her lips.

She was a coward.

"No, in this case it would be practical as well as prudent. I understand where you're coming from. I did tell you I was increasing before Seamus and I wed. Well, I didn't want to make him marry me because of the child. I wanted him to marry me because he loved me. I'm expecting you feel about the same. Well, am I right?"

"Very much so. Oh, if he told me he loved me before he left, I'd go to his family home without blinking one eyelash. Wouldn't hesitate for a second. The fact of the matter is that he didn't. I'm going home now. I've a great deal to think about before Hawk confronts me, before the entire village knows I'm in the family way."

"Houston should be here to share the shame. I've a mind to write to him, tell him what I think he's doing to you. He knew all along you would be ridiculed."

"Brenda, it's alright."

"No, it's not!"

"He wanted me to leave when he did. Told me I could live in his townhouse in Edinburgh. Told me I could go to his family. I chose not to do either of those two options. He didn't like me to be here alone, unprotected. I chose to stay. He understood I'm a grown woman who he couldn't force to his way of thinking."

"Why didn't you?"

Helplessly she shrugged, her shoulders trembling with the movement. "As I told you before, he doesn't love me. I'd be a burden to him. It's not something I wanted to do."

"You don't think of yourself enough. Now, you just sit tight until you've got your priorities straight then you march yourself to Hawk's office and do the right thing."

"Brenda," she spoke softly her voice wavering. "That's just it. I don't *ken* what the right thing is. I've no idea. Seems everyone knows except me."

"You can't just sit there and expect to know what is right when your emotions are in upheaval. They are a tangled-up mess," Brenda persisted. "Maybe Hawk can shed some light on what you should do. He's a man after all as he must think a bit as Houston does."

"No," Leah was shaking her head. "If he comes back, tell him I'll be in to talk to him first thing in the morning. Tell him I have to have time to think."

"You're making yourself sick with all this worry. Cannot be good for the wee little life growing inside you."

No, it wasn't good. At the moment, nothing seemed good or right. Her stomach rolled as she stood up. She was so very tired. The way she felt now, her home seemed miles away.

Maybe she should go see Hawk.

If she did that, it would be dark when she reached home.

As it was, she would make it up the mountain before the sun hid itself behind the trees. She sucked in a huge gulp or air.

"I'll see him in the morning. If it's all right with you, I'll stop by after I've talked to him, tell you what happened. Maybe the visit will help me decide."

"If that's what you want. Truly, you should let someone help you. You cannot do this all on your own. You've the child on the way to remember."

She understood that all too well. Since Grizzly was gone there was no income, no way to buy staples she needed, no one to provide meat, not that Grizzly did much hunting or that she wanted to eat the animals. She did understand all God's creatures served a purpose. It would take a few more months for her vegetable garden to supply enough for her to survive. It seemed she was living on borrowed time.

No way, no way would she let the *bairn* inside her starve. No way! Leah clenched her fists determined to make sure she did what was right for her child. What was best for her no longer mattered. It was up to her to provide for the tiny being she carried inside her. She could no longer think only of herself. She had important responsibilities to attend to.

She didn't know how to provide.

Didn't know where her next meal would come from.

The breath she held inside her threatened to erupt as endless bad scenarios flooded her brain. Caused her to waver with the next step. It had been two days since she'd eaten anything except a few roots and the scone Brenda offered last time she was there. If she'd said anything, Brenda would have fed her. Would expect her for at least one meal every day.

She was too proud, too stubborn to say anything.

Feeling dizzy as well as weak, she leaned against a post. With her eyes closed she breathed in the wonderful aromas from the restaurant. What stood out was the fragrant scent of freshly baked bread. Her stomach rumbled hungrily.

I have to get up the mountain before dark.

Don't have anything to eat there either.

I can rummage tomorrow morning in the forest. Can find something to fill my stomach.

She knew how futile that was. It wasn't the right time of year for anything except the mushrooms and a few spring peas, perhaps onions. She would never touch the mushrooms. For a few more seconds she rested, inhaling the much-needed air she needed before she made the slow trek up the mountain. At her best it would take fifteen minutes give or take. Tonight, she was sure the trip would take at least thirty minutes.

This wasn't going to be easy.

No, she might not make it past the Fletcher place before dark.

~ * ~

"What are you doing standing out here all alone? A pretty girl like you shouldn't be alone." Michael stood in front of her smiling as if he wasn't watching her dissolve right in front of him. Her nonexistent breath coupled with a heart thundering beneath her chest stole rational thought from her muddled head. "Heard they found Grizzly's body on the mountain somewhere. I'm sorry for that. You must be devastated. If you're lonely, I'm willing to help. Hell, I'm willing to help any way you'll let me."

That was true. She was lonely but not because she missed him. She hated herself for that feeling. Hated the fact she didn't care for Grizzly. It wasn't right not for her to mourn her stepfather. True, she needed help. She didn't want to have to ask Michael. Didn't want to be beholding to him.

"How did you hear? I was just told a little while ago."

One hand on her chest she blurted out the words. It seemed it had not taken long for the news to spread past Hawk, Brenda, Seamus as well as herself.

"The whole village is talking about his death." He set a hand above her head on the pole she was leaning on. His gaze raked the length of her leaving her skin prickling. "You alright. You don't look so good."

"Just tired." *Hungry and sick too.* "Otherwise I'm fine."

"You don't look so good," he repeated as if he didn't just tell her that. "Are you heading up the mountain? I could take you up there if you want. Got my horse saddled." He looked down the road. "You can ride in front of me. I'll keep you safe."

It's the last thing I want.

Don't know how I'll walk that far.

Don't want Michael alone with me at the house.

"I'm fine. I'll be up there before dark. Don't need help."

She did though, needed food more at the moment than a ride to her home.

"Not the way you're looking right now. Kind of sickly if you ask me. Come on, promise I won't bite, at least not very hard." He laughed at his joke then took her hand. "I've got a basket packed with fried chicken, lots of those vegetables you like so well. Ma made some bread this afternoon she sent over for my dinner. I'm willing to share if you like. I'll take you home then we can eat. Maybe you'll have a thank you kiss for me when we're done."

Her stomach rumbled its despair at her treatment of it seeming to smell the delicious aroma.

A thank you kiss? Nay.

She needed to say a resounding no to his proposition. Didn't know how to do that when she was so hungry, when he offered to feed her, offered her a ride when she could barely put one foot in front of the other.

"Come on, Leah. Let me help you. I won't hurt you." He placed her hand in his then led her toward the waiting horse. "You'll feel a whole lot better after you've had something to eat."

She smelled the food again.

He set his hands on her waist and helped her mount then he was behind her, his arms wrapped around her.

He wasn't Houston.

No, this was Michael. She didn't want anything to do with the man. She was riding in front of him because he offered food along with a way home that didn't involve walking.

He had food with him.

She could almost taste it.

She felt his body shift against her back as the horse wound its way up the narrow winding road to her home. He didn't talk much. She tried to hold herself away from him. Exhausted, she failed to do so. When they reached the house, he slid from the horse. She wasn't sure she could get down without help.

He didn't give her a choice. His hands around her waist, he easily lifted her then held her close as her body slid down the length of his. She felt his arousal against her belly. Wanted to scream for him to go away then thought of the food.

She wasn't going to do anything to send him down the mountain until she filled her stomach. The devil, she was just like her mother. Was slowly becoming her mother. She was taking what a man offered so she could live. No, so her child could live.

Her mind warred with the needs of her body.

Her stomach growled again.

She could eat with him this one night. He couldn't mean to stay.

"Should we go inside?" he politely asked as he offered an arm smiling as if he knew she wanted his attention.

"Yes, Michael, thank you for taking me home. You *ken* you can't stay the night. After we eat you have to go home. It wouldn't be proper."

He chuckled softly. "Leah Kennedy is talking about proper after what she's done and the condition she's in? Let's eat then we can discuss other things, other more important things."

He wasn't Houston.

He now had her exactly where he'd wanted her for such a long time. The food was delicious. For the first time in a very long time her body felt satisfied. He wasn't going to tell her now that he fed her she owed him the use of her body. She prayed he would not.

"What did you want to talk about?"

"Us."

Chapter Nine

Even though Leah protested, Michael stayed the night telling her even for a man riding down the mountain in the dark wasn't the safest thing to do. He slept on Grizzly's bed while she tried to sleep in her little nook. Michael snored. It was almost as if Grizzly was here in the bed instead of Michael. The man would make sure everyone in town knew he spent the night with her. The fact was one more mark against her reputation, against her ability to make a decision for herself.

Michael asked her to marry him again.

She refused. With each passing day as her situation became more dire, the refusal was growing harder and harder to say. The next morning, he waited for her as he meant to take her to Hawk for the upcoming lecture. Leah had a pretty good idea what the discussion with Hawk would entail.

Her heart in her throat, she waited for his help to mount the horse. He chuckled as his hands circled her waist.

"You're so tiny, Leah. My hands go around your waist easily. I wanted you last night. You should thank me for my restraint. I can wait for the wedding night." He touched his lips on the back of her neck. She shuddered.

He wasn't Houston.

Her back stiffened when he mounted behind her, drawing her close his hand resting possessively against her belly. He had no right. Last night, he wasn't nearly so bold. Every day he grew more confident that she would finally say yes. She supposed he had every reason to see her that way as her circumstances grew steadily worse.

In the village they passed by several people who waved. Quaid and Ryan saw them and came up to speak to them. It seemed to Leah he planned this. Everyone would be talking about them.

She drew in a long breath of air, cleansing herself. They stopped in front of Hawk's office.

"When you're done here, you come by the store. I'll treat you to breakfast. Heard your stomach grumbling all the way down the mountain. Will you do that?"

He sounded hopeful not confident this time. She couldn't give in to him so easily just because he offered her something to eat.

"No, but thank you. I told Brenda I would stop by her place. We need to chat, girl things."

"I see. Then come for lunch. You need to keep that little one you're carrying from starving to death. I'm just the man to help you do that. You're going to stop telling me no pretty soon. You just wait and see."

She sucked in a deep breath of air, turning to him her emotions seething. "Does everyone know?"

"No but they will. I'm going to tell everyone who asks the *wee* one is mine even though it isn't. You're going to change your mind, Leah. I'm a patient man. I'll see you for lunch. We can discuss the wedding, when and where."

It was in her mind to tell him when hell freezes over. Instead, she bit her tongue to keep the retort where it belonged, behind her teeth. She was not so far gone yet that she'd agree to marry him. When reality finally hit home, she would though. Maybe Houston would come for her after all. Maybe hell would freeze over.

Except for the brief ride, Michael kept his hands to himself. He was what some would say a perfect gentleman. His actions last night as well as today didn't change her opinion or the fact she didn't want him for a husband. Didn't want him to touch her intimately. If she'd never known Houston, felt his arms around her, she might have been able to accept Michael into her life.

She might not have a choice.

At Hawk's she flipped her leg over the horse before he could dismount. Landing on both feet she gave Michael one quick glance before striding to the office. With her hand raised to knock on the door, it opened.

"You're a stubborn *lass*," Hawk told her ushering her inside then into the examining room.

The puppy Houston once tried to give her jumped around her begging for her attention.

She bent down. She rubbed his head then his belly. She wanted to ignore what was happening. "What is this?" Panic welled in her veins. This wasn't what she expected. "What are you doing?"

"Only going to give you a quick exam."

She didn't know what that entailed. However, she certainly wasn't going to let him examine her. "No!" Her fists clenched by her sides, she stared at him.

"Don't be afraid. The exam is actually quick and pretty much involves questions."

"Nothing else. I'm not taking my clothes off." Her body shook as she tried to tell herself he was a physician. If Houston were here, she would let him do whatever was necessary. The baby needed to be healthy.

He wasn't here.

"First, all I want is for you to sit here. Can you trust me? Houston would want his baby as well as you to receive the best medical care."

She gulped air then nodded. "I believe so. Don't want you touching me though."

"I understand. As you get farther along, I'm going to have to see where the baby is, if the head is turned, if it has dropped. I'll have to feel your lower body."

"Dropped?"

"Today, since you're so skittish let's just decide when the baby will be born give or take the *bairn's* plans." His voice was gentle, soothing.

She sat where he wanted her then drew in a deep cleansing breath of air. "How did you know? Brenda knew and Michael as well."

"It's very simple, Leah. You're so willow thin the tiniest bump shows. Either you're gaining weight in the most peculiar of ways or you are pregnant. Now, the first time you slept with Houston was the night before the carriage accident. Is that right? The end of February?"

This was too personal. Heat flooded her. When she slept with Houston was no one's business except hers and Houston's.

Still, she nodded her head in answer. "Yes. It was the only time. He left several weeks later. Well, more than several."

"So," it seemed Hawk did some mental calculations, "We can expect the child sometime late November or early December. What are your plans to keep the baby healthy? You're alone up there on the mountain. You don't have a viable income. How are you planning to manage?"

The earlier flush of embarrassment drained from her face. She knew she paled with the realization she couldn't manage. She didn't have any plans. Didn't know how she was going to do so.

"I see you haven't given any thought to that. Leah, it's one thing to be stubborn and refuse help when it's just you to worry about. Unfortunately, you've passed well beyond that point in your life."

"I know." Her voice shook, tears threatened.

She pushed the sorrow aside. She didn't want to cry.

"Do you also understand that Grizzly's brother surfaced when news of his death became the talk of the town, the talk of the countryside? The man owns the land that hovel you call home sits on. He wants the land. Has no use for what he calls squatters. That's you, Leah."

She swayed slightly, the room spinning at the news. It was the worst she could have heard. Did everything just have to keep getting worse?

"No..." she moaned, the sound seeming to come from the back of her throat.

"If you won't except Houston's help, you have to let me help you." Hawk waited for a few seconds watching her. "Or Brenda's. You're not alone in this world. You don't have to meet every challenge head on then damn the consequences."

"Don't want to be a burden."

"Why don't you let Houston decide that? Write to him. Tell him you carry his child. He'll do the right thing," Hawk said even though she didn't hear much conviction in his words.

Anger surfaced. "That's the problem. I don't want him to do the right thing by me. I want his love. He doesn't love me. If he felt anything for me, he'd be here. I'm not going to impose myself on him or make him feel guilty or obligated to me."

Hawk turned from her, striding from the room into the main office. She heard his swear words. Felt the feelings of loss thinking about Houston always created deep in her heart. She knew he was furious with her for refusing anyone's help.

She couldn't though. She just couldn't impose on the only people she cared about.

Hawk was standing in the doorway now, his voice taking on the frustration he showed. "The man loves you. The devil, he's your mate. You are made for each other, both healers. Tell the man."

"Why hasn't he come for me as he promised? I'm sure his foot has healed by now. You told me the surgery went well. From what he told me before he left, I would have expected him."

"I don't know."

"There is only one conclusion I can draw from that. I have to be realistic. He lied to me about his intentions."

Truly, she didn't know if she said the words to convince herself or Hawk.

"I suppose you do. If not on the mountain, then where are you planning on living?"

"I don't know."

She thought about Michael. Was the man a last resort? Could she bear to commit herself to him for the sake of her child?

"The man wants you off the mountain by tomorrow morning. I'll ride up there with you today. Help you with your things. We can take my buggy unless you have more than would fit in it."

"No, there is nothing there I can use if I don't have anywhere to live. Just a few pieces of clothing."

"This is absurd. There are places for you to live. Stubborn, that's what you are Leah Kennedy, stubborn."

"McEwen, Leah McEwen now since Grizzly never bothered to have the papers drawn up that would have protected me from this."

Once again, she felt the slow rise of moisture in her throat. She didn't want to cry.

"Leah McEwen."

"I can't pay you for this visit or the birth. I've nothing to give in place of coin."

It seemed her true circumstances just hit home. *I've nothing.*

"Don't you think Houston will pay?"

More anger surfaced.

"He would I suppose."

She sucked in a wobbly breath thinking of what Houston might say or do if he knew about her condition. He deserved to know. She had to tell him.

"There is no suppose about it. He would. If you don't tell him about this pregnancy, I will write him myself."

"You understand I can't write him. Besides, he shouldn't learn from a letter," she said as she realized what she was telling Hawk.

"Go to him. The money is here, waiting for you to use the groats. If you won't write the man, go to him. You can always come back if that's what you feel is the best."

"I..." She swallowed the lump of tears forming in her throat. Drat, all she did anymore was cry. "I don't know where he is."

"By now he should be home. He should be home," he repeated then waving his hand in the air. "Should be on his way to get you. He gave you his address as well as directions. Where are they?"

She bent her head. Stared at her feet and the old boots she wore. Soon they would have to be repaired again. There was no money for that. She remembered what Michael told her.

*No, no, no...*she wasn't going to become her mother. Wasn't going to go to a man because she had no other choice. Wasn't going to lie in a man's bed so she could eat.

I love Houston.

"In my satchel in the refuge. Am I going to be able to go there tonight? All my sketches are there too. I'll have to let the animals have their freedom. Some aren't ready. They'll die." A new batch of tears slid down her cheeks.

Stop feeling sorry for yourself.

"I'll take you as soon as I can. You'll come back with me."

"No, if it's my last night at home, I'm going to stay there. After that I don't know where I'll go."

"Very well, I'll bring whatever you want down the mountain when I leave. Where will you be?" He spoke softly now that a few decisions were made.

She would have to make another one soon. She would have to tell Michael she would marry him. The lump of tears she fought grew. Her stomach soured.

"I'm going to see Brenda then I'm eating lunch with Michael."

Leah watched the narrowing of Hawk's eyes, the disapproval written so clearly on his handsome face. Hawk knew how she felt about Michael. He also knew her feelings for Houston.

"I hope that isn't what I'm thinking."

It was.

"Before...Michael wants to marry me, unlike Houston. I have to think of the *bairn*, just like you told me. I will, however, tell Houston before I actually marry Michael. It's only right."

Hawk jammed his hands through his hair, leaving the long strands endearingly disheveled. "You've other choice than to bind yourself to a man you despise for the rest of your life. We're not talking about weeks or months. We're talking about forever."

She stiffened even though she understood Hawk's words as well as the truth of them. "Not that I see. If you'll excuse me, Brenda will think I changed my mind about stopping there. I will ask her if I can use her guesthouse for a few nights. Do you think Houston would be angry if I used that coin he gave you to pay Brenda and Seamus rent?"

"Yes. I won't allow that to happen. The coin is for travel to his family home. He would be furious with me if I allowed you to use it differently. Besides, you just told me you would go there to tell him about your condition."

"I *ken* it was for only one way."

"There was more than that. Nonetheless, I doubt if it was enough to get you home as well."

"I see. I could loan you the extra money so you wouldn't feel stranded on McKenna land if things don't go your way. Houston would pay me back. Though if you get there and talk to him, I don't have a doubt you'll need the extra money."

"I thought to buy a new gown for the travel. I could hardly go meet his family in what I own."

She plucked at her skirts, wishing to be more presentable when she introduced herself to his mother and father. During the time she spoke with Hawk, she made up her mind about two things.

The first one was that she would say yes to Michael the next time he proposed or perhaps at lunch.

The second was that she would go to Houston then tell him she was pregnant. She would have to also explain that to Michael, in the process hope he would understand the trip was the honorable thing to do.

She knew all along Houston deserved to know. After that she would return and marry Michael. He would give her child all the love he deserved. She didn't know why but she was positive the child was a boy. The thought stopped her, sent doubt rushing through her head. What if he didn't love the baby? What if he resented the child because he would be Houston's?

Shivers of fear for her baby wracked her body. What if the child was a shifter? Oh, no, no what if he despised the baby for that reason?

Hawk's voice intruded on her thoughts. "I'm sure Houston would be happy to pay for a gown also. If he isn't, I'll have no problem. I'm just happy you're finally thinking straight. Whatever you do, don't tell Michael yes until you see Houston."

"Next time he asks I'm going to say yes. Houston will only want to marry me because of the child. As I told you before, that isn't what I want. I've made up my mind."

Leah walked out the door realizing the life looming in front of her was not something she wanted, not something she could enjoy. What waited for her was bleak. She would have to make the best of her decision.

For the sake of the child.

"Well, that took longer than I thought," Brenda greeted her at the door. "You've been with Hawk all this time? There must have been a lot to talk over."

"I've been kicked out of my house," Leah told Brenda as she sat down at the kitchen table. "Can I use the guesthouse?"

"Of course..."

Leah interrupted. "I'm going tell Michael yes as soon as he asks again. We're having lunch. So far every time I see him in private, he poses the question."

"Perhaps that's for the best," Brenda said softly reaching out to take her hand in hers. "Houston hasn't come back here for you. He might not ever. The last letter you told me about didn't mention his return."

"It is. Why do I feel as if my heart has been ripped from my chest? I don't know if I'll ever smile again. I cry all the time."

"It's ripping apart because you love another man. I can't bear to think of my life if I had to marry someone other than my Seamus so I could put food in the child's mouth."

"I'm going to the highlands to talk to Houston with the money he left for me. I'll tell him about the baby. Hawk said he would help me pay for a new dress. Will you go with me to pick it out?"

"Yes, I'd be glad to. What if Houston tells you he wants to marry you?"

"It's all I've dreamt of. Nevertheless, I'll tell him no. I'm not the right person for him. He'll do better with a woman who is his equal. He would only ask because I carry his child. If he loved me..."

I'm his mate.

"If he loves you, he won't settle for that excuse," Brenda said softly the concern etched clearly in her eyes.

"You're right of course. You see he doesn't love me so that's not going to be an issue."

If she could love him enough for both of them...she did love him that much, maybe more.

The knock at the door surprised them both. Leah had been so deep in her thoughts about seeing Houston one more time she didn't hear Michael's steps up the back porch. He was persistent. He came for her.

"You ready for lunch?" he asked as Brenda let him into the kitchen. His smile seemed boyish to Leah. In front of him, he clutched his hat in his hands.

"Yes, we've a great deal to talk over this afternoon."

"Did you have a change of heart?" he asked grinning as if he understood she finally relented and would agree.

"In private please, I would like this to be between the two of us, no one else." Leah would have to hear some promises where the baby was concerned before she actually told him yes.

She wasn't going to agree to the proposal unless she felt satisfied what Michael told her earlier was true.

He would have to reaffirm his promise to raise this baby she was carrying as his own. She would settle for nothing less.

As it turned out, Hawk came for her before she could say anything to Michael. He appeared impatient to be gone. Leah promised to meet Michael the next day at this time. In some respects, she was relieved. She wasn't in a hurry to make a lifelong commitment to a man she didn't love.

"You can't stay the night at the house," Hawk told her when they reached her home. "That's why I interrupted your lunch. Grizzly's brother is up there right now, intends to stay there. We need to get this taken care of. Did he ask you again?"

"No, we didn't have time to talk. Seems he always finds me when I'm starving. All I did was eat. All he did was grin at me. He understood I've finally relented."

Hawk helped her into the buggy. By the time they returned, the street lamps were glowing. He pulled up the buggy in front of Brenda's home.

"You going to be alright?"

"Yes, I'm fine." She clutched the satchel with her drawings as well as the direction to the Stuart home to her chest. It had been so hard saying good bye to her wildlings as well as the one place she enjoyed.

"Does she know you are coming?"

Well, she knew she would be there tomorrow. When she asked Brenda, Leah didn't know that tonight she would need a roof over her head too. "Yes," she lied to Hawk.

He set her things in front of the guesthouse. Lamps were lit giving the tiny home a soft comforting glow. That was good for her lie to Hawk but bad news for her tonight. She would have to find a safe sheltered place until tomorrow.

It was only one night. She could find a protected place to sleep.

"Leah, what are you doing out here in the cold?" Michael asked.

Just when she thought she was at the lowest point she could go, things got worse.

He held out his hand. "You can stay at my house."

~ * ~

Houston ran. He shouldn't have shifted. Knew better. However, the pull to change was too intense now that his foot healed. Finally, after five long years, he was a whole man. Shouldn't have to prove that to himself. Yet...yet the person he needed to prove it to was Leah.

He'd gone to his grandfather's home deep in the highlands to find the peace he craved as well as to heal. He finished his studies from his apprenticeship, jotting notes to himself along with theories to be tested when he had the opportunity. During his stay in Edinburgh, his knowledge increased tenfold.

Now in his cat form the chance of anyone seeing him was next to nothing. When he shifted, he didn't believe he was risking his life. Despite the warnings from all the elders, he decided against their sage advice giving in to his whim.

Just when he thought to turn back, he stopped, the hair down his spine standing on end. A few shadows danced around the trees. He caught the scent of man. Acting quickly might serve him well.

Sassenach!

He wasn't in the open yet he understood the ever-present danger presented in the here and now. Had to make his way to a safe place, a place where he could wait out anyone searching for him, anyone who thought they saw a black panther loping through the highlands. The hunting lodge where he was staying was too far away as well as too in the open for him to return without increasing the risk.

The cave where he, his brothers and cousins often stashed clothing and firewood for emergencies such as this one was close. It had been eons since he'd been there. He knew Riley and Kit came here from time to time. He could only hope there were provisions of some sort since he didn't know how long he would have to wait. His cousins were all wed now. He doubted if they ever visited unless it was for a retreat away from their children.

In that case they would have little use for the cave. His brothers would use this from time to time.

Keeping to the shadows, dancing around the rocks Houston gingerly made his way to the safe retreat. In the summer the cave was always pleasant. At the moment he was glad of the early morning fog rising off the ground. It would help conceal him to the searching eyes.

When he saw the opening, he gave a silent prayer of thanks. The fact he'd been foolish along with stupid pulsed in his mind. He understood carelessness could get a man in deep trouble. He shifted before he walked inside, unsure of himself. The thought of another person inhabiting the cave never crossed his mind until now. The devil, he was stark naked.

Presenting himself naked to just anyone wasn't appealing. It was better than the alternative. He didn't want to spend the rest of his life pacing inside a cage in London entertaining countless Englishmen ogling him with the hope that he would turn into a black panther.

His prayers were answered. No one was present. Padding quietly to the far end of the cave, he discovered a pair of trousers and shirt. Quickly, he slipped them on. They were a bit large. They must have been Alistair's. He was the largest of all of them. He found soft leather moccasins nearby. Ever since Roby and Kit spent time with the natives in America, they favored the soft shoes over boots whenever they could.

So, he wasn't the only one who gave into the need to run. He didn't think he was. Precautions were taken though. He doubted if anyone else ran alone. A few minutes later, he sat in front of a fire with a piece of deer jerky to satisfy his rumbling belly.

All he did was think about Leah.

What she was doing.

How she was feeling.

He wanted to feel her warmth as well as her softness in his arms. Her lips shaped sweetly beneath his were an aphrodisiac calling to him.

When he stripped in order to run this evening, the thought of her loping along beside him thrilled every sense he possessed. He knew he would always be tempted to take the risk.

Not when it was her life at stake.

Perhaps the future would bring something better for their kind. Perhaps the Sassenach would leave them alone. Go back to England. Give up the notion of shifters as gossip, tall tales told around a campfire. As far as he knew, they'd never caught one. He stood quickly when he heard the noise in the front of the cave, his hand to the knife stuck in his boot. Dressed, he truly had no reason to fear the Sassenach soldiers. This could be a man looking for shelter.

It would not do well for him to be caught here yet there was nothing that could be proven. He was no longer naked or in his cat form. A million excuses flashed through his head.

"Well, big brother seems as if you couldn't resist the lure and temptation that seems to plague us all. Glad I found you before the soldiers who are prowling around here."

"Kit, what are you doing? This is a quite the distance from the family home."

Houston was thrilled to see his brother. He realized he'd been lonely. It was time to return for Leah. He had one more task to accomplish before he could do that. Quickly, they embraced.

"Is that anyway to greet your brother? I came looking for you. Seems you've got several letters waiting for you to read. Thought I would bring them." Kit reached into his bag to grab the posts. He handed them over.

"Hawk?" Houston asked his heart racing because he knew they were from Leah. Hawk always signed his name on the missives. Leah did not, even though he knew she could do so.

"Why would he write you so many letters? Seems strange if you ask me." Kit looked from the letters he was holding to his face as if trying to discover what he was thinking.

"Nothing strange about it," he murmured reaching for the letters wanting nothing more than to be in the privacy of the lodge so he could read them.

Lately, she'd been vague. Instead of talking about the sanctuary and the new animals, she rambled not saying much of anything. Sometimes the sun was shining. Sometimes it was raining. She spoke of Brenda's children, never of herself.

One of Kit's eyebrows arched upward clearly disbelieving. "As you say."

His brother didn't believe a word of what he told him. In his brother's place he wouldn't either. "It's about all the things I learned during the apprenticeship. I relayed the information to Hawk. He writes with questions. We both want to put the information and newfound knowledge to use. Nothing unusual there."

"I see." Kit grabbed a piece of jerky before sitting down by the fire. "When are you coming home for good? We miss you."

"Sold my practice to Hawk although you should know that. I haven't kept secrets. Plan on making a quick trip to Selkirk to pick up something very important then I'll return. Planning to set up a practice in the village." Yes, he was going to pick up the woman he loved, his mate. She might protest. It was what she often said in her letters. He could find a way to dissuade the nonsense she spouted about not being good enough for him.

"Something important? Does it have anything to do with those letters you're holding as if they're burning your hand you want to read them so badly?" he queried with a bland note to his tone coupled with a broad smile.

To Houston his brother's questions didn't sound innocent at all. "Give me another week up here to finish the healing. Don't want to rush anything. I'll be down then."

"Alright, have it your way. You always were one to keep secrets," Kit said. "Are you planning on staying here the night? Or would you like to go back to the lodge?"

"Back to the lodge if you brought a horse for me. I'd like to take a detour and retrieve my clothes if that's not too much trouble." Houston rose, dusting off his buckskins. With his foot, he covered the fire with dirt. "I'll have to restock the cave tomorrow." Yes, he would do several things after he read the letters, after he decided how he was going to ask

Leah to marry him. It would have to be very special, perfect in every way.

At the lodge, Kit rummaged through the cupboard and supplies until he found a bottle of brandy. He'd already set deer steaks frying on the stove. Potatoes and onions occupied the same pan.

Houston settled down to read the letters. Hawk usually sent them in order. She started with the death of Grizzly. As the letter continued, he grew more concerned about her. She left out too many pertinent facts.

She didn't answer any of his questions concerning her wellbeing. Instead, she avoided them, telling him about Brenda and the children again. The littlest one could toddle now. She was so cute.

How Hawk set Tommy McAlister's bone.

"Hell!"

"What is it? Something you don't like about a procedure?" Kit asked failing to hide his all-knowing grin behind his teeth.

"Something like that," Houston muttered.

Dark rage filled him. What the devil was she doing letting Michael take her up the mountain? She ate dinner with him. Didn't she have anything to eat?

"Perhaps it's time for you to return home," Kit pointed out for a second time. "You wouldn't be swearing at what Hawk writes about medicine."

Houston slanted him an enraged glare. "I can't. Not yet. I've got company coming. Can't leave until he gets here and I can make my excuses." He set the stack of letters on the table unwilling to read more at the moment. Didn't want to give away too many feelings. Kit's guesses were most likely very close to the truth.

Striding outside he leaned against the porch railing, watching the end of the day, the gloaming, so beautiful in this part of the country. He didn't know what to do about Leah. Hawk wouldn't let any harm come to her. Wouldn't let Michael insinuate himself into her life. Would Hawk have a choice if Leah made a bad decision? He tugged in a long draught of heather filled air. He needed to shift again. To run and run until he couldn't breathe.

Kit appeared, handing him a full glass of brandy. "I could stay here and give your excuses. You could pick up whatever you left in

Selkirk. You'd do that for me if I needed help."

Houston respected the offer. He also respected his obligations. The man would not be thrilled to be considered second to anyone. Leaving his younger brother to placate the man wouldn't do.

"Thank you," Houston spoke through clenched teeth. "I can't. It won't be too much longer." Surely, nothing that bad was happening that couldn't wait a week.

"If you change your mind." one of Kit's eyebrows rose in conjecture, "I'll be happy to stay for you. What is it you're not telling me?"

He wasn't telling him he was afraid the woman he loved was about to have no options left. With Grizzly dead, her circumstances might be dire. He had to get to her. It would take a week probably more to get to Selkirk from here. He was beside himself. He didn't know what to do.

He drank long and deep. The burn down his throat felt good. Helped him think. God, he needed to think. He needed to figure out what he had to do. Imposing his problems on his brother was not his way.

"That's exactly it. There are things I'm not wanting to tell anyone. Things I have to take care of before I make them public."

He recalled the way she felt in his arms, the way she looked all stretched out in the sun while in her cat. The way her breasts tasted, the scent of her provocative and ethereal.

"You're in love. There are problems in paradise," Kit laughed. "Glad I'm not in love. Too many difficulties even though eventually I hope to find my mate. Of course, I'm assuming this woman is your mate."

Houston wouldn't confirm or deny. He grunted then walked down the steps needing distance from his brother's prying eyes as well as his questions.

"I could help, always good with the ladies. Want me to pick her up for you?" The question was followed by a soft chuckle.

If his brother was hedging for a fight, he was coming mighty close with those words. "Stuff it. That's exactly why I'd never ask you for help."

"That bad?" Kit followed him. "Don't mind a friendly fight if it helps clear your head. If it makes you feel better."

"Nothing tonight is going to clear my head. Maybe I'll get lucky and my visitor will arrive sooner than expected."

"Maybe you won't. Looks like you're wound up tight," Kit said over his shoulder while he returned to the cabin.

Houston sat down on the steps, his glass dangling from his fingers. He needed to read the rest of the letters. Needed to understand what Hawk wasn't saying.

From what he read of Hawk's letter, she was staying in Brenda's guesthouse refusing to come here, refusing to stay at the office, unable to stay in the hovel up the mountain. He knew she didn't have money. Knew also she was too damn stubborn to accept help.

Hawk talked about Michael asking her to marry him just about every time she saw him. Hawk also alluded to the fact he should get his butt to Selkirk to make things right for her. If he waited too long, he might not be able to do that. Might be too late.

He was sure Hawk wasn't telling him everything. It was just like the man to hide facts from him. Perhaps it was more like Leah to explain to Hawk there were certain things she didn't want him to know.

His gut rolled, curling within itself.

"Dinner's ready," Kit called from the front door.

Hunger would be nice. A few hours ago in the cave, he thought he could have eaten the whole deer. Now the pain in his stomach had nothing to do with food.

"Coming. I'll be right there."

When he entered the room, he stole a glance at the stack of letters thinking he should read through Hawk's scribbling in hopes of seeing the underlying truths he wasn't catching when he read Leah's thoughts. What the devil weren't they telling him?

He felt uncomfortable with Kit's gaze boring into him. Knew he should tell him something. It wasn't the right time to share his feelings about Leah to anyone. He wanted to wait until she agreed to marry him. Should have done that before he left for Edinburgh. He just didn't think there would be so many complications.

Grizzly's death was the biggest problem. His demise seemed to have set off a chain reaction making Leah's quality of life worse. If she would allow it, Hawk would take care of her until he could come for her.

That was the major roadblock. She was too stubborn and independent to allow anyone to take care of her.

Why the devil would Michael persist in asking for her hand unless she gave him a reason? She loathed the man. Well, maybe loath wasn't the right word to use where Michael was concerned. However, he knew she didn't want to marry him.

She would only do so under the direst of circumstances.

What could that be? She always told him she would never be like her mother and give herself to a man she didn't love. Perhaps she didn't love him either.

He didn't think that was the case.

"A penny for your thoughts?" Kit asked as he ate. "You've got that deep brooding look on your face that tells me you're not going to be good company tonight."

"What does that mean?"

Houston looked up from his plate of food. He was scowling at Kit. Kit did nothing to deserve it except offer to help.

"Believe I'll head home first thing in the morning. Your company stinks."

"Best you do that. I'm sure I'm not going to get any better the next few days when I want to be somewhere I'm not."

How many days passed since Hawk and Leah wrote the letters? More like weeks. Hell, something worse than having to stay in Brenda's guesthouse could have happened to her.

Kit finished the meat then cleaned up before retiring for the night. Houston sat back on a chair by the fireplace the letters in his hand. He poured over them, wishing he could find the hidden meanings Hawk scrawled into them.

He couldn't.

Half muzzled, he stood on the porch staring at the night sky wondering how Leah was fairing. Something was dreadfully wrong. He knew it deep in his gut, was also sure he heard her calling out his name.

"Thought you went to bed," Houston spoke to Kit who now stood beside him.

"No, worried about you."

"Don't be. I'll figure everything out. I'll be down in a couple of days. Think I'll meet the man who is coming here instead of waiting. I've spent enough time recuperating. Thanks for knocking some sense into me."

"There truly is something wrong." Kit ventured.

"Yeah, I believe so. Just don't know what it is. Thank you for coming here. I needed to see the letters from Hawk more than..."

"Ah, but I do believe you just about gave something away you didn't want to. This time I am going to bed. I'll be out of your hair tomorrow. Don't wait too long to figure things out with your lady friend. It might not be prudent. Hate to see you lose something you love before you have a chance to possess, it big brother."

That was part of the problem. He already possessed her. Once would never be enough. He wanted to yell. A fight would be nice. Unfortunately, his brother didn't seem to want to engage any longer.

Hawk would have. The man understood what a fool he was. Understood the injustice he did to Leah.

He took her virginity.

He left her alone to face the gossip.

He was a bloody bastard.

~ * ~

"Whatever has happened, it has Houston tied into knots," Kit told his father when they sat down that afternoon for a whiskey. "It could be funny."

"You don't believe there is humor in his discomfort?" One of Alistair's eyebrows rose asking a million questions in the process.

Kit was shaking his head, feeling grim as he thought on everything his older brother failed to say. "Not this time. He's tied up so tight I don't think he'll ever loosen the knots. Sure it's a woman who's done that to him?"

"Did he tell you anything else? Is the woman his mate?"

"Houston wouldn't even admit that it is a woman who has him

worried. Tied in knots and tight lipped." Kit felt sorry for the brother he always looked up to. For some reason Kit was sure that same brother was shirking his duties when it came to this woman.

"I remember when I first figured out Brenna was my mate," Alistair mused seeming to think back in time. "Seems she figured it out at the same time. Couldn't keep my hands to myself. Bedded her as well as claimed her that very night. Made up some fool excuse. Thought Connal would kill me when he found out. Got lucky though, he was so involved with his problems he didn't have time to worry about his little sister.

"You saying Houston has bedded her. If he has there might be repercussions that Houston doesn't know about. Can't believe he would leave a woman, his mate, to fend for herself under those conditions."

"Not with Houston, he wouldn't take that chance. He would use whatever precautions at his disposal to keep that from happening. Can't believe this woman is increasing."

"True, he would. Accidents can happen even with a man as astute about females as your brother. Happens when the physical part of lovemaking takes over the mind. Always happened with..." Alistair let the rest of the words fade away.

Kit understood what his father wasn't saying. The two of them, his mother and father, still had this way of looking at each other, a smile, a glance sometimes a nod of the head. After the interchange they would disappear upstairs for hours.

Kit wanted that for himself. He drew in a long deep breath of air as he thought on the complexities of love.

"I suppose all we can do is let this play out," Kit murmured.

"Pick up the pieces when everything goes awry." Brenna strode into the room, Riley behind her. "Houston is in too deep, you're saying?"

"You think things are going to go awry for your oldest son?" Alistair asked while he poured drinks for the newcomers.

"Maybe, maybe not. Nevertheless, you saw him when he passed through here weeks ago. He had secrets then just as he does now. It didn't seem he knew what to do with himself."

"That's the way he was yesterday. Even though he understands he shouldn't delay a moment longer, he feels obligated to wait for this other physician. At least he decided to go see the man instead of wait for the man to come to him. Believe he figured out that he might not have time to procrastinate any longer."

"Wish you could have read the letters," Riley said as he held up his hands in his defense. "Understand that would be a huge breach of propriety. Still wish we had more insight into the manner of the problem."

"No, we don't," Kit said. "Our big brother isn't in the confiding mood."

"So, we have to wait. I could ride to Selkirk. Do some snooping. Perhaps I could find out what ails our big brother."

"Boys no, all that ails your brother is the fact his mate is not with him. I'm sure he's been an absolute fool believing he can leave a woman alone for this long, in the process not suffer some consequences. All we can do now is be patient and supportive." Brenna paused, her glass half way to her lips. "If we think it might be necessary, then of course you can ride to Selkirk one or both of you. Hawk would be pleased to see the two of you.

"Houston might well be furious," Alistair said thoughtfully.

"Might also be grateful," Kit pointed out as his gaze turned north toward the hunting lodge.

Chapter Ten

Leah swallowed the lump in her throat, her legs threatening to buckle while she stood in front of the huge oak door. She pushed her sweaty hands down the front of her brand-new dress. True to her word, Brenda helped her pick it out. True to his word, Hawk paid for the gown telling her Houston would reimburse him. Leah wasn't at all sure that was true. Nonetheless, she couldn't show up at his family home in one of her dilapidated, well-worn gowns. Hawk also bought her the second part of the passage she needed to come here. He paid for her way back to Selkirk. Unfortunately, after paying for lodging as well as food, she didn't have enough left to make it all the way to Selkirk. Somehow, she would find the means though. Finding the home was not difficult. Seemed everyone knew where Houston Stuart's family lived.

Thankfully no one asked her too many questions.

After several seconds of debating, her heart pounding unmercifully, she knocked on the door. When no one answered right away, she thought to leave. Felt a moment's relief. It was short lived. No, she couldn't leave. She owed Houston the truth and prayed he was home. If he wasn't home, she didn't know what she would do. Her heart thundering even more wildly beneath her ribs, she waited.

This had all become such an incredible coil. Two weeks ago, she told Michael she would marry him when she returned from giving Houston the news about the baby. She promised him as he promised her he would take care of the child as if the *wee* babe was his. She believed him, at least as far as she could. If the *bairn* turned out be a shifter, she was sure he would consider his promise null and void. At that point he might even put her back on the street. With her thumb she wiped away a lone tear refusing to allow these people to see into the depth of her despair. It seemed all she'd done since she became pregnant was cry. She never cried.

So lost in thought, she didn't hear the door open. The voice on the other side startled her back to the present. With a little nervous gasp, she stared wide eyed at the man.

"Miss? May I help you?"

"Miss Leah McEwen, is Houston here? I'd like to speak with him."

Needed to speak with him. She held her hands in front of her clasped tightly so the man wouldn't see her shaking. He probably could anyway.

"He's not presently home," the man said his voice soft. He seemed as if he cared.

"Oh." She didn't know what to do now. This was her worst nightmare. She tried to peek around him to see if there was anyone else she could talk to, not that she would know what to say if she did see his mother or father.

"Who is this?" A deep masculine voice boomed from behind the man Leah assumed was their butler.

He had a butler. She didn't even have a home to call her home. At least not yet, not until she married Michael. She would have a home, nothing like this one.

Houston had servants.

The butler turned, still soft spoken went on to inform the man behind him, "Says her name is Leah McEwen. Wants to speak to Houston. Told her he wasn't home."

"Well, let her in. If she's Houston's friend, we need to treat her with kindness. Don't you think?"

"Of course."

"She must be tired, maybe hungry too. It is nearing the dinner hour. My name's Kit by the way. Come in. Make yourself at home."

Politely he smiled at her, his charming grin reminding her of Houston.

She stepped through the door, looking down the hall then up the huge stairway leading to the second floor. Everything was polished and clean. She thought of her tiny home, the one that was no longer hers. A catch of despair clogged her throat. If she believed earlier they weren't suited, this all put a huge emphasis on the fact.

Kit placed his hand on the small of her back, guiding her into the spacious home. "We're just having a drink before dinner along with a bit of pleasant conversation. Would you like a drink?"

She was gently pushed along. Again, he reminded her of Houston except he was more vibrant, more verbal. He seemed to smile a great deal more than Houston. He was laughing now. She didn't know if she wanted to drink with them.

"Yes, please."

"Leah, this is Alistair and Brenna Stuart and this is Riley. Houston's family, if you haven't guessed as much, which I assume you have, since you are here to see my older brother."

She didn't know if she should curtsy or just say nice to meet you. The protocol was beyond her education. Everything was beyond her learning. She settled for both then "I don't mean to intrude on your family. There is something I need to speak with Houston about then I'll be on my way. No need for..."

"You must share dinner with us," Brenna spoke softly. "If you are Houston's friend, then you are ours also. We'd like to get to know you better."

This was not what she anticipated when she decided to do Hawk's wishes. She needed to tell Houston what she came here to do then leave. The wedding was planned. She was expected. She didn't have time to linger.

"Thank you, I couldn't impose on you. Do you know when Hawk will be here?" she asked as she looked from one to the other. All seemed to sport knowing smiles.

"Don't know," Kit said as he lifted his broad shoulders. "Last time I saw him he was indecisive. Told me he had to wait for a physician so they could go over important information. Told me he'd be down then and that he had something important to pick up in Selkirk."

Was he talking about me?

Of course not, ninny.

"Oh." She studied her hands for too many seconds before she looked up to meet smiling, sincere eyes. "Can I go there? Where he is? It's really important. Have something to tell him he needs to know. After that we both can get on with our lives."

The palms of her hands were sweaty. She couldn't hold the glass she was given without shaking.

"You are such a dear," Brenna said, her eyes shining with some unspoken knowledge. "You don't have anything to be nervous about as I see that you are uneasy. However, you couldn't possibly travel into the highlands by yourself. I'm certain Houston wouldn't even like it if you were accompanied by one of his brothers. You can wait here until Houston decides to come home. It will be much safer."

"I know the highlands. At one time I lived there. Everything would be fine."

"No, no, no, you must stay, wait for him."

She stood, tipping over the chair she'd been sitting on. "I couldn't possibly do that. My wedding is soon, well...as soon as I get back...maybe two weeks. I would..."

Kit righted her chair, "Sit down. Finish your glass of sherry. We can discuss what you are going to do over dinner."

"You can stay here, wait for him to return," Brenna said, offering her a spare room in this great house. "Until Houston returns if you wish. We would be pleased to have you stay with us. I could use the company as the boys are always so busy with their lives these days."

"No, more gossip, more people talking about me, about Houston. I cannot. It would hurt him. Can't do that to him." She tucked her bottom lip beneath her teeth blinking back tears of shame as she watched these people who knew nothing about her make decisions affecting her life.

Brenna looked at her as if she knew all her secrets, knew she carried her son's child. They would condemn her if she married Michael, giving their grandson to someone unworthy. She knew it as surely as she knew her heart would keep beating.

"Sit down," Riley stepped forward a warm hand on her shoulder gently pressuring her to do just that. "Relax. Why don't you tell us what you want Houston to know? We can relay the message more easily than you. I would start out first thing in the morning. You might even get back to Selkirk in time for that wedding you just mentioned."

"I couldn't. Can't tell anyone except Houston. Private, it's very private. Just between the two of us." Her face drained of blood. She swayed slightly catching herself before she slipped. Falling to the floor in front of his family would embarrass her further.

"Of course you can stay with us," Alistair agreed as it seemed he too guessed all her secrets.

"*Nay, nay,* it's something for me to tell Houston, only Houston. It's private, just between the two of us." She set the crystal glass on the table next to her chair. A crystal glass, she'd never even seen one let alone held one or drank from one. Dear God, what had she gotten herself into?

"You look exhausted, dear. Would you like to take a short nap before dinner?" Brenna asked, her voice a soft melodic sound in the dark recesses of her thoughts. "We do want you to stay for a meal. After all, you're a friend of Houston's. We would be remiss if we didn't extend the courtesy. Why, he would never forgive us if we sent you back to your lodgings without having you stay for dinner."

Before she could put one sentence together, she was ushered by Kit up the steps. She found herself in a room with a large bed. For a moment, she assumed it was a guest room.

"This is Houston's room. He's rarely here. Make yourself comfortable. I'll come get you when it's time for dinner."

Before she could say *nay*, Kit vanished out the door. *He would come get me when it was time for dinner. I am to lie on Houston's bed to take a nap. I won't be able to sleep.*

Unsure, frightened she was in way over her head and floundering, Leah plopped down on the bed, Houston's bed. She pulled a pillow close. It carried his scent. She knew she would never forget it.

More tears followed.

She shouldn't be here, should have never done this in the first place. What would they say when they discovered her truth? She should walk down those steps and out the door to the inn.

She should.

Before something else happened she couldn't undo.

Instead, her stomach rumbled hungrily. She ate sparingly on her way here needing to save the coin for her trip back. She didn't have enough. They offered a free meal, one she should never turn down, for the baby's sake.

For my baby's sake.

Her hands rested on the gentle swell of her belly. She was usually so flat. Would he know if she saw him? Did his parents know? They certainly acted as if they knew. How could they?

She rose then, paced between the door and the window. At the window she stopped looking down on the same scene Houston would have seen while he was growing up.

Kit along with Alistair strode down the street away from the house. Evidently, they had business somewhere. Wasn't partaking of the before dinner drinks. She wasn't sure. However, she was suddenly afraid she broke up the family gathering.

Riley walked in the other direction. It seemed a puzzle to her. A few minutes ago, the family appeared to be enjoying each other's company.

Now they weren't.

Until she showed up.

No, she wasn't going to intrude further. She would wait. Have dinner with them then say polite goodbyes. She could be on the next coach back to Selkirk tomorrow morning.

The knock on the door startled her. "A pot of tea for you?"

"Tea?" She paused wondering what she was supposed to say. "Well, yes...where did Kit and Alistair go?"

"Don't know. In any case it's not my business. I'm just the upstairs maid," she curtsied then left the room.

Upstairs maid?

Once again Leah found herself staring out the window. What she saw gave her more reason to wonder what was going on in the household. Kit was riding north. Wasn't that where they told her Houston was?

They couldn't mean to keep her here. She would miss her wedding. Michael accepted her promise to return and marry him.

Made for Houston

What was she if she didn't keep her promises?

What kind of person would agree to marry someone then just up and change her mind?

Brenna expected her to nap. The devil, there was no way she could sleep. Her nerves were stretched so thin she thought surely they would snap. A cup of tea would be nice. When she poured the tea, she saw lemon as well as milk. She put a bit of both in her tea, sugar as well.

She never had sugar or lemon.

More factors that meant nothing to these people that made her stand out as completely wrong for Houston. Perhaps it was a good thing she made this journey. She had more and more reasons why the two of them didn't suit. It wasn't just the fact she could barely read and write. They came from two very different worlds.

Alistair returned, his arms full. When she looked a second time, he carried her small valise. *Nay, nay, nay*, they weren't going to allow her to stay at the inn. Her hands fisted by her sides.

Riley returned.

There was no sign of Kit.

Finishing her tea, she lay back down on the bed, thinking of Houston. Indulging herself for this short amount of time couldn't be wrong, perhaps not too wrong. To think about Michael right now was something she couldn't bear, not while she was in Houston's home, not while his mother and father were acting so sweetly to her, not while she was lying in Houston's big bed.

They must know just by looking at her, she wouldn't suit their son. Alistair and Brenna would help her leave in the morning. They were just being nice, nice people just like their son.

Leah didn't know when she fell asleep, dreams of Houston floating in her head. She woke when the door opened.

"Leah? I've got something for you. Didn't want to wake you. However, dinner will be in a few minutes. I wanted you to try these dresses on. I think they will fit with a few modifications," Brenna said, her voice soft.

Sitting up, Leah pushed flyaway strands of hair from her face. "Oh, I fell asleep. Dresses?"

226

"You did. I'm glad. You looked so tired when you first got here, dark circles and all under your eyes. Houston would be so upset if we didn't make sure you were well rested."

"What did you say earlier?" Leah thought she heard mention of a gown. Something else that didn't make sense.

"I brought you two new gowns, well, they aren't new. They were once mine. I had them fashioned so they would fit you. Though I've made sure a seamstress will see them before everything is finalized."

"No, no I don't need gowns. I have my own." She started to stand.

Brenna held out her hands to stop her. "Don't be alarmed. Your gowns were threadbare. They would not withstand the carriage ride home. You must have a few things to wear more suitable than the gown you have on at the moment. We wouldn't want you traveling to Selkirk with nothing on."

"I can't accept your generosity. Bring my dresses back, please."

"Houston would never forgive me if I allowed a friend of his to go nearly naked. These will do fine. I've spent no money so there is nothing to reimburse. Lord knows I've more dresses than I could ever wear. I was planning on taking them to the church to give away. Now you can have them. Here," she held a daffodil yellow confection out to her. "Try this one on."

"I cannot."

"Of course you can dear. I'll help with the buttons down the back of the one you're wearing." The fabric binding her breasts was undone.

Brenna sipped in a surprised breath of air.

Before Leah could inhale a few deep breaths, she found herself standing in front of Brenna with only her worn chemise covering her. She wasn't at all sure if she'd ever been this embarrassed in her entire life.

She didn't think so.

The dress was slipped over her head. A woman she hadn't seen before stood in front of her taking little nips and tucks in the gown.

"This will do nicely," the lady murmured.

"Do you want her to try on the second gown?" Brenna asked.

"No, this will do as a pattern for me. She is truly quite thin."

Leah knew she wasn't going to stay thin. When she did increase,

Michael would take care of her. She would have enough dresses so that she wouldn't have to worry. Michael promised. She didn't care about the gowns though. She just wanted to make sure she had enough to eat.

Finally gaining a bit of raw courage, "Can I have my old gowns back?"

"I'm sorry dear, they aren't fit for anyone to wear especially not one of my son's friends. I burned them."

"You did what?" For a moment the room swirled. Quickly, she sat down on the bed hoping to steady herself. She was so very dizzy she had to put her head in her hands.

"Yes, don't be too distressed. Now you have two more perfectly wearable dresses."

"Thank you..." Leah had no idea what else to say.

These people overwhelmed her from the top of her head to the tips of her toes. Houston was nothing like his mother and father.

"You're perfectly welcome. Now, put your other gown on. Do you need help?"

"No," Leah said watching as the dressmaker unfastened the dress. Again, she was left wearing nothing but her worn chemise. She looked longingly at the bindings. Slowly, she wrapped them around herself. His mother would surely see the evidence that she was increasing. They would know.

"As soon as you're all buttoned up, come down to dinner. We'll be in the drawing room waiting for you."

Brenna was out the door before Leah could say anything. Desperately, she needed to protest.

~ * ~

"How did Leah take your highhandedness?" Alistair leaned back in the chair his legs stretched out in front of him, a glass of brandy in his hands. His smirk amused her. One of his brows was arched in question.

Better than I thought she would," Brenna laughed softly. "She truly is a dear. Believe she was too shocked to say anything. After she comes down, we'll have to stop her before she gives the gowns back. In any case, they will never fit me after the dressmaker is finished with them. She is so willow slim. Do you know that she binds her breasts?"

"Wonder what Houston thinks about that?" Alistair asked.

"Except for the obvious swell of her belly," Riley said laughing as his mother shot him a glare that she meant to say he shouldn't be staring so at his brother's mate's stomach.

"It is quite obvious even to those of us who have never seen her before," Alistair murmured. "Was she terribly angry when you told her you burned those old worthless gowns of hers?"

"Don't understand why Houston didn't do something about what she wore. He has the money. Did he want her running around in clothing that was practically see through?" Riley asked sipping on his drink as he turned his attention to the opening into the hall and the stairs. "I certainly wouldn't want my mate to be seen like that by other men."

"I've a feeling she wouldn't accept help. Wonder what her story is along with why she isn't engaged to our son. She told me she once lived in these parts," Brenna said as she too directed her attention to the doorway.

It wouldn't do to be caught talking about her when she did find her way downstairs.

"Stubborn, just like Houston," Riley said choking back his laughter. "He found someone who could match him. Do you think she's a shifter?"

"Know she is," Brenna spoke quietly. "Saw the faint marks on her chest when she changed her clothing. It won't do, won't do at all for her to marry someone who isn't a shifter. The man would never be able to raise Houston's son. Would never understand. In addition, the knowledge would give him far too much power over both Houston as well as Leah."

"Houston won't allow anyone but himself to raise a child of his," Alistair said. "Just as I wouldn't. She'll have to make a decision. Wonder why she hasn't thought of that."

"No man would," Riley said looking out the door. "I wonder how this other guy convinced her he would treat Houston's child as his own."

"Don't think she would agree to a marriage if the man did not convince her," Brenna said. "This is so not right. Don't know what we can do to change that if she won't agree to stay here."

"She doesn't have enough money for passage home. Hawk must have wanted to make sure she would stay with us," Alistair said thoughtfully. "Her small valise was all she brought with her. I checked the coin she had left in her purse. There was not enough there to get her to Selkirk, only about half way."

"What will she do? She doesn't seem the type to melt with adversity," Riley said as he once again stared up the steps.

"She will probably get a job which will give Houston time to get here," Brenna said. "Or she'll decide to walk. We can only hope for the latter then pray Houston will understand the necessity to hurry home."

"She can't do that!" Riley's furious voice shocked Brenna. She turned to him wondering what he would say. "I'll go with her. Make sure she stays safe. My brother's future wife shouldn't travel alone. She shouldn't have to walk. I'll also make sure I stand in the way of the marriage until Houston can find his way to Selkirk. He still owns the office. So, I'll bed down there."

"Fine idea. I'll feel so much better if you are with her, to protect her," Brenna said finally relieved her son's future might be brighter than she thought a few hours ago when Leah proclaimed she had every intention of binding herself to another man. "Won't have so many misgivings."

"She'll be furious," Alistair pointed out with a chuckle. "She believes wholeheartedly she can manage on her own. Has no idea all the pitfalls along with dangers awaiting a lone woman."

"Probably furious, yes," Riley agreed. "I'm more worried about Houston being furious than that little wisp of a female he's fallen in love with. She's a fey creature, breathtakingly beautiful."

"Failed to provide for her to the extent that she agreed to wed another man," Brenna said angry with her son as she watched Riley nod in the direction of the stairs, "Leah..."

"Thank you for the gowns, Mrs. Stuart."

"Brenna."

Leah inhaled a deep breath. "In any case, I didn't mean to sound rude. I'm used to doing with little to nothing. Not used to people I don't know being so generous."

"You do know us. We're Houston's family. That makes us friends."

"He did tell me how wonderful you were. I just wanted to talk to him. Didn't want to feel beholding to anyone. Didn't expect you to invite me for dinner or give me new things to wear."

"There is no reason to feel that way, beholding," Brenna took her arm, ushering her into the dining room. "We're always pleased to do things for Houston's friends."

When they were settled, the trays of food brought into the room and served, Brenna stopped eating for a moment her fork in hand. "Why don't you tell us how you met Houston? Believe we'd all be interested in the story."

Leah cleared her throat before starting. To Brenna she didn't look at all sure of herself. "I..." She drew in a long deep breath of air her eyes widening while moisture seemed to well in deep blue pools. "I brought my dog to him. Wanted him to cure Shadow even though I understood deep down he was dying. I needed to give him one more chance before I had to say goodbye."

"Did he cure your dog?"

Brenna understood how much Houston loved animals. From what Leah said, it didn't sound promising. Thought of his wound the one he could never quite come to terms with. Remembered the young girl he told them about who rescued him from the steel trap. He told them she touched his heart. Thought there was something more between them. Dismissed her ideas because she was so much younger. Her gaze shot to Leah again.

"No. Shadow passed on that night. It was his time to go. Houston did promise that my dog would feel no pain. He kept that promise and buried him the next morning when I was able to come down off the mountain to help him."

"You didn't live in the village?" Brenna asked suddenly realizing there was a great deal more to this woman's story than what initially met the eye. For some reason her mind kept going back to the girl who rescued him that day so long ago. She would be Leah's age now.

"No, I lived with Grizzly along with my mother until she passed away. After that it was just Grizzly and me."

Leah went on to tell the rest of her story, leaving out the part where she fell in love with their son. She told them about her sanctuary as well as the wildlings, the sketches she enjoyed drawing. How Hawk told her she could make the sketches into a book. That now without his help or Hawk's that wouldn't be possible.

With more answers there were more questions. When her throat was too parched to talk more, she sipped her wine.

"So, Grizzly wasn't your stepfather after all," Brenna said, her voice bitter, her thoughts spiraling to places she shouldn't travel. "You should not have stayed with the old man."

Brenna yearned to wrap this tender young woman in her arms as well as protect her until Houston could. Evidently her son had the same inclination. After hearing her tale, Brenna had every reason to believe she was truly Houston's mate.

They were made for each other.

Leah just didn't know it yet.

Perhaps Houston didn't either. He certainly didn't act with her best interest at heart. She would have to have a serious discussion with her oldest about how a woman should be treated.

She would have to do everything in her power to keep Leah here. If that didn't work, she would indeed send Riley with her.

"Grizzly never claimed me as his. He told mother he did. He never signed the papers making me his stepdaughter. That's why I lost the house. Why I have to..."

Brenna couldn't help the tightening of her fists beneath the table. Alistair watched her closely. She understood he feared for her, feared she was getting too emotionally involved with the young woman who could easily break their son's heart if she proceeded with her foolishness.

"Lazy bastard," Riley said gaining raised eyebrows and dark shuttered looks from both his mother and father.

"Riley's right about Grizzly. All he cared about was his whiskey. He wanted me in the home to cook his dinner. That's all I meant to him. Sometimes he went to work. Sometimes he ended up in the next village drinking himself into a stupor. The only reason he was able to keep his

232

job is because Seamus refused to fire him."

"Free labor," Brenna murmured wishing she could change all the bad things that happened to this lovely young woman including her son's seeming abuse.

It appeared her son bedded her then left her with promises he hadn't kept yet. He'd had more than enough time to keep those vows. No wonder she was willing to commit to another man. She had nothing left. Survival for her along with her babe was most important to her.

"Who is the man you're marrying when you return to Selkirk. Don't remember if you told us his name," Alistair continued the questions as he kept a steady gaze on her as well.

Leah visibly flinched at the mention of giving over the man's name. Brenna was sure this was not a love match. "Michael, Michael McConnal."

Her voice whispered from her lips. The sound was reedy and thin. Her eyes grew vague, clouded over when she spoke his name. Shadows of deep despair grew in her eyes.

"You love him that much?" Brenna asked knowing the answer without looking into Leah's eyes for confirmation.

Leah was playing with the napkin she'd set on the table. Her eyes focused on her plate. She'd eaten little. It was probably because of the interrogation. Brenna regretted that now. Nevertheless, she couldn't turn back time. She had to change the stilted atmosphere.

"He's been a gentleman. Nice to me," Leah told them refusing to look and meet her gaze. "He's been asking for a long time now."

"That's not love," Brenna's words turned gentle.

She didn't want to frighten her into running away. Her intentions were to keep Leah safe and sound in the family home until Houston could get his arse down the mountain to rectify this horrible situation he single handedly created.

"No, it's not but...but I don't have a choice."

The distress in Leah's voice alarmed Brenna. However, she understood why it was there and so poignant she felt tears well in her eyes.

"Why don't you eat? We can talk later when you've finished. I believe our questions must have put a damper on your appetite. If done to me, I would have also lost the desire for food."

Brenna leaned back, watching Leah while sipping her wine. She rose from the table meaning to give Leah more distance, beckoning Riley to stay and entertain if he could. He would know what to say when she did not. She nodded at Alistair who joined his wife.

Riley nodded as if he understood what she wanted. "Tell me more about your wildlings?"

He watched as the smile on Leah's face grew. His mother wanted him to put her at ease. She was so very thin, such a beautiful fey creature with eyes the most incredible shade of blue he'd ever seen. If given the chance, he could drown in them. Supposed Houston did that very thing when he stared into them. She did need to eat. Riley poured himself more wine then topped hers off.

"What would you like to know?" she asked with a dreamy look in her eyes, crystal clear blue eyes.

They were compelling eyes. Ones Houston must have not been able to refuse. For a moment Riley wished she was his mate even though he wasn't ready to settle down nor did he register intense feeling for her. Perhaps that was his brother's problem. Houston had been single for so long, he didn't want a wife, especially a fey one.

He didn't believe that for a moment. All their cousins found their mates. He'd heard Houston tease but at the same time saw the emotions in his brother's eyes.

The desire to possess what they did.

"Anything you'd like to tell me. You said you healed them?" Riley questioned.

"Mostly birds; some small animals. I'd find them in the woods then bring them back to the refuge to keep them safe. With the birds I was able to mend broken bones as well as wings. It was hard to let them go."

"I imagine so. Did you grow so close to the animals?"

He thought he'd never met a more caring person, except perhaps his oldest brother. They were made for each other, perfect in every way possible.

"Enough to want to give them names."

"You didn't."

"No, I would not have been able to let them go if I did." She smeared butter on a biscuit then honey. Her plate was almost empty. That was a good sign.

He served his purpose for the time being. The morning meal would be big, would have to tide them over until dinner the next evening if she persisted in leaving. "I can understand that. Names always make things more personal."

"Do you shift?" She asked as she set her fork on an empty plate. Her smile telling him she was thinking of something else. "I only saw Houston's cat once. He is so big and powerful."

He jerked at her question. Evidently, she knew about his brother. It was obvious she would have questions about Houston's biological family. He wasn't sure how much Houston told her. She did deserve honest answers.

"Everyone except mother are shifters." He waited breath held deep in his lungs. "You?"

Riley saw the wistful little smile, heard the soft wisp of air filter through her lips. "Yes, but I'm not big and black. I'm not at all like Houston. Mother hated father because he could shift. She tried to ignore the fact that I was the same as my *dah*."

It was time to plant a few seeds of doubt in her mind about this McConnal fellow. "You cannot possibly expect a man who is not a shifter to raise a child who is. Can you? He might act the same as your mother."

At his words she visibly flinched. "You have a point. What choice do I have? You heard my stor..." Leah stopped, covering her lips with her hands while she closed her eyes.

"You were going to tell my wayward brother you are increasing with his child," Riley ventured to challenge her with the truth she sought to keep secret. "He doesn't know yet."

Moisture filled her eyes. "No, no, that's not true. I..."

"Don't deny the obvious. You just unwittingly confirmed our guesses. He's done wrong by you. Indeed, though it would not be right. You can't return the favor by marrying the wrong man. In the process making your baby's life a living hell. That wouldn't be right. You have to have patience. Trust in Houston. Trust the one you love. The man who loves you."

Her suddenly white face worried him. Riley didn't know how far to go with his comments or insinuations.

Tears slipped down her cheeks. "I...I don't know what to do. Needed to tell him. That's why I came here. He doesn't love me, you see. He's never said so. Now, I have to go home and face the consequences of what I did. With the child involved, I don't have the time to wait."

"You can stay here. You know that. Brenna has told you. Houston I'm sure has suggested this scenario. I'm confirming. Wait for the man who holds your heart in his hands." Riley reached out to hold her hands. He wanted nothing more than to reassure. "He will do the right thing if you wait."

"He doesn't love me."

"You don't know that."

"If he loved me, he would have returned before this. My visit is just...just to..."

"To what?" Riley asked letting her hands go free in order to pace the length of the dining room. "We should go to the parlor."

He was sure he could think of no more reasons for her to stay.

"I should return to the inn."

"You don't have a room there. Alistair and I brought your things here. You will stay the night in the Stuart house, in Houston's bed."

He felt sure his words were far too harsh.

"I can get the room back," she said looking toward the door.

"You can't. The innkeeper won't give you a room. Alistair made sure of that when we brought your things here."

Riley advised his father against that very thing. He insisted it was the only way to ensure she stay the night before traipsing off on her own. Settled into the Stuart home she would be easier to keep a watchful eye on.

"That was underhanded," she murmured as tears slipped down her cheeks. "I wouldn't have expected anything less. From the moment I entered this home it seemed to me you all had an agenda."

"Yes, our intent was keeping you here until Houston came home."

Leah had been pushed too far. Riley knew that for a fact. He hoped Brenna understood too. Now it was time for the gentleness she deserved.

"It's not going to happen. Tomorrow, I'm going home."

He held out an arm, "Let's go where it's more comfortable. You can sit by the fireplace. While you watch the flames, you can sip a glass of wine or tea, whatever you prefer. I promise I won't say anything more unless you ask."

"You're not going to change my mind."

"No, I don't believe anyone except Houston could change your mind."

Riley hoped Kit made it to the hunting lodge before the sun set. The sooner Houston come after Leah, his mate, the sooner Leah's life would be set on the right course.

When they walked into the parlor, they were alone. Riley realized his mother and father still had hopes he could convince her to stay.

He could not.

What he did wonder about was what she would do when she discovered the fact she didn't have enough money to go all the way to Selkirk. He supposed the best thing at the moment was to let her know the truth.

It wasn't wise to put off the inevitable and risk even more anger. That was exactly what he was doing simply because he was a coward. He didn't want to see the look of despair on her face as well as in those beautiful eyes of hers.

"Your mother wants me to stay here until Houston decides to come home. That could be months away." She accepted the cup of tea he poured for her, holding it in one hand.

"Pretty sure he'll be back in a day or two, probably one."

It would take Kit most of today and into the night to get to the hunting lodge. Houston might not rush out the next morning. If he did, they would both be back late tomorrow evening. That was if everything went as planned. They certainly wouldn't take unnecessary risks.

"She does. Would that be so hard to do?" Riley queried her watching the play of her features.

"Yes, no, I might be late getting back to Selkirk if I did."

"Would that be so bad?" He was smiling now, feeling that perhaps he was making a tiny bit of progress. "Would your fiancé not wait for you if you were late. Would he refuse to wed you?"

Her eyes narrowed, the blue darkening turning stormy. "He would wait. At least I think he would."

"Then you'll stay here two days. That will give Houston the chance to get here, change your mind about marrying this man who is not like you, who is not your mate."

She gasped, "You know too much, you guess... No, I'm not going to wait. I'm leaving tomorrow whenever there is a coach south. I promised him."

The determination in her voice surprised Riley.

"If I did so, it wouldn't be fair to Michael."

"What about what is fair to Houston along with the child? Have you thought of that? Doesn't the father of your child deserve more consideration than a man who means nothing to you except food in your belly?"

He'd lost his patience along with the control he was usually known for. His anger began to simmer.

"That's why I came here. Consideration," she said, plucking at her skirt her gaze focused on the blue and white Aubusson carpet in front of her. "That's why I stayed for dinner. Told all of you my life story."

"Ah, I do believe you left out some pertinent facts," Riley went on to say.

He stood by the fireplace, leaning against the bricks, his arms crossed in front of him trying for an air of nonchalance he didn't feel.

"What would that be?" Frown lines formed across her forehead. Her expressive eyes gazed at him, compelling him to give away more of what she needed to know.

"Again," he paused in thought. "I've only a guess. Something you said earlier, something that might be leading me to an untrue conclusion. I would hope you wouldn't lie to me."

She stiffened.

He grinned.

"No, I don't suppose you do. You leave out information though.

Isn't that a lie by omission?"

His smile grew as he watched her squirm. He didn't want her to squirm even though he needed the truth.

"What are you talking about?"

"You told me you heal animals, wildlings. Didn't you?" He tried to see beyond what she was telling him.

She nodded but failed to answer. He sat down across from her chair. "You are the fey girl who freed Houston from the trap that mangled his foot. You saw him to the hunting lodge, well, followed him to make sure he would stay safe. You even held off a Sassenach patrol that would have surely caught him in his panther form or naked. Even then he understood how special you were to him."

She was shaking her head. Riley saw the truth in her eyes. He guessed correctly just as he was sure his mother had also. This woman was the right age. She appeared now older but much the same as Houston described her at the time. He would do everything in his power to stop this so-called wedding to McConnal. Riley was also certain Houston knew for a fact Leah was his savior from that long ago day.

Leah didn't confirm or deny Riley's statement. Once more her gaze returned to the floor. The rug seemed to fascinate her.

He played his last card, one he hoped would keep her here in the safety of the Stuart home. "What if I told you that you didn't have the needed coin to go all the way to Selkirk?

If it was possible for her to pale farther, she did. She drew in a loaded breath of air. "I will go as far as I can."

"Then?" the question was a fair one. One she should consider before she made a decision.

"I'll walk."

"That is precisely what I was afraid of. You cannot do that unprotected. I'll go with you. Make sure the fair is paid in its entirety."

"No," she held up her hands. "No, you cannot do such a thing. I would not want to owe you. I would have to ask Michael for the coin. He might not want to do such a thing."

"You can't stop me with a word of protest. It would take a hell of a lot more persuasion to do so. You don't have the strength for that. I will travel with you."

"I don't suppose I do."

Her angry voice resonated in the softest spot of his heart. Truly, he didn't want to cause her discomfort of any kind. This was such an impossible situation.

~ * ~

Houston looked up from the papers he was reading to see Kit at the door. He heard the pounding hooves. Didn't expect his sibling who was here only a few days before to reappear.

"What do I owe the honor of this second visit?" Houston said, his voice low, harsher than he meant it to be. His brother seemed different his expression shuddered.

"You have a visitor," Kit spoke as if he kept a secret. "At home. Mother is doing her best to entertain."

Houston remembered times when they were growing up when Kit wanted him to guess rather than telling him what exactly was happening.

"You going to tell me? I don't have all day. Was making plans to go home then on to Selkirk."

"Might be too late for you to pick up that something you left there," Kit said as he sauntered to the brandy bottle then poured them both a drink. There was laughter in his eyes. "Here, you might need this."

"Don't want a drink now." Houston settled the papers he'd been looking through into a satchel. "Have to put this in order so I can leave."

"Good, I might need more than one drink before we're finished here tonight." Kit sat down, stretching his legs out in front of him, his expression smug.

"You never answered my question."

"What was that?" A lopsided smile curled on Kit's face. "Don't seem to remember. Care to ask again?"

"What the devil are you doing here?" Houston was rapidly losing patience. He was packed. All he wanted at the moment was to go to bed so he could get up at the crack of dawn. He needed to show Leah he was keeping his promise.

"Relaying a message that's all. Mother sent me. Couldn't refuse. You know." Kit sipped. His eyes narrowed as his brother watched him. "If this wasn't so darn important to you, I'd drag it out."

"Message from mother. That's frightening. Kit, if you don't tell me soon, I'm going to shove my fist down your throat."

Houston rose. Stood over his brother, his fists clenched tightly at his sides.

Kit sipped again carefully watching his brother's hands. "Told you that you had a visitor, didn't I?" he asked blandly schooling his features, seeming to enjoy the fury he should try to avoid at all cost.

"Yes."

"Had something to tell you. Wouldn't tell us so I can only conjecture. We all guessed. Hoping that by now mother has ferreted out the truth."

Houston's brain traveled in a million different circles. The devil, he was talking in rhymes. "Yes," he gritted out again.

"It was a lady. Told us you were her friend. Had something she wanted to tell you, only you."

A lady?

Leah?

That was impossible, or was it? Perhaps she finally decided to let him help her.

That brought him to attention. He needed to ask who it was. At this moment he wasn't thinking straight. "Is she waiting for me? Is that why you came?"

"If you hurry, she might be there when you arrive. Very determined lady, she is. Said since you weren't there she was going home. Had a wedding to get to," Kit said, watching him over the rim of his glass.

Houston stalked to the bottle of liquid fire, poured himself a generous amount then sat down.

"Who? Did this lady have a name?"

"McEwen was her surname. Do you know her or was this just a ruse the lady used to get herself a free meal?"

Houston expected the name to be Kennedy, prayed the name would be Leah Kennedy. Something surfaced between the cobwebs in his brain. He remembered her telling me the name that was hers before Grizzly sauntered into her life.

"Leah..."

"You do know her." Kit was laughing at his expense. There was no other way to describe the merriment on his face.

He nodded thoughtfully thinking of all the possible reasons why Leah would come to the highlands. The only one was that she wanted him in her life. "When I knew her, she went by Leah Kennedy."

"That was months ago."

"Too many," he agreed, at the moment wishing he'd gone to her sooner, set their relationship down the right path. Truth be told he'd been afraid she'd tell him no. She never did believe she was good enough for him. "So, did she tell anyone what she wanted to tell me?" Despite the late hour, he was ready to start down the mountain.

"No, but we all guessed. There wasn't a doubt in anyone's mind that..." Kit seemed to enjoy letting his statement hang in midair.

"That what?" he was stabbing his hands through his hair, waiting.

"She's increasing. Also..." Kit paused dramatically as if he waited for the coming reaction.

Houston's face drained of blood. He swallowed hard. *Impossible. Anything was possible.*

"Oh, and she's getting married in less than two weeks. You should do something about that since we all *ken* she's your mate. No, can't let your mate marry someone else then raise your shifter child."

Kit was groping. He couldn't possibly know she was pregnant or that she was a shifter. Leah would never tell him such a thing.

Chapter Eleven

Houston paced. He paced more. The seconds ticked by at a turtle's pace. His gut rolled as he stood by the window watching and waiting for the sun to rise. Echoing from the room above, he heard Kit's snores. Understood he needed to be sleeping. It wasn't to be.

Why would she agree to marry Michael McConnal? It had to be Michael. There wasn't anyone else who asked her. He tried to sort through the facts. Nothing made sense. Grizzly died. Either Brenda or Hawk would take care of her. She didn't need to resort to marriage to a man she didn't love.

She was stubborn to the core.

Wouldn't accept charity. Didn't believe she was good enough for him. He understood that all too well.

When he was there, she also refused his help. Wouldn't agree to living in his home above his office even when he was gone. Brenda would allow her use of the guesthouse.

Not for forever.

He'd been gone too long, way too long. He was a selfish bastard, thinking only of his needs when the woman he loved was in peril.

Selfishly, thinking only of himself, he left his mate to fend for herself when he was positive she would do well. Obviously, he was wrong.

If Kit didn't rise in the next few minutes, he was going to leave him behind. There was almost enough light. By the time he saddled his horse there would be plenty of sunlight. According to Kit she intended to leave today. He prayed his mother would find a way to keep her at the house. Deep in his heart he understood Leah's need to be independent.

She never took handouts. Always lived within her means.

He left her with no way to do that.

Hindsight told him he should have returned with Hawk after the surgery. Who better to help him mend than his mate? She tended the wounded. Had a gentle hand. Knew and understood what the sick and helpless needed better than anyone.

He'd not wanted her to see him less than a man.

Stupid, selfish bastard.

"You ready to go?" Kit's footsteps thundered down the stairs from the loft above.

Houston couldn't read his brother's expression. "Been ready since last night."

"What are we waiting for then?" Kit strode out the door toward the stable whistling as if he didn't have a care in the world. Houston understood he did not.

It seemed his brother was as eager to get on the trail as he was. He prayed she would be fine, hoped also that she would weather the coach ride back to Selkirk with no problems.

He recalled the carriage accident the night after he made love to her. Hell, he should have claimed her that night. Should have made sure he bound her to him. Why did he wait?

Didn't a baby bind a woman to a man?

That night he thought...well, hell, he thought she was safe from conceiving. That night he didn't think.

He supposed in Leah's case a baby did not bind him to her. She would always fend for herself, do things her way despite the apparent difficulties. He had to reach Selkirk before the marriage to Michael could take place. Had to find a means to make her believe he loved her.

He loved her.

She wasn't just his mate. He loved her more than his life. Why he never told her the words he couldn't say. Needed to say those words as soon as possible. So much about the way he conducted his fledgling relationship with Leah was remiss.

The breath he inhaled coupled with the realization he failed her in too many ways staggered him. Did she love him? Apparently not since she couldn't wait a few more days to marry a man he knew she didn't love.

If she showed him her cat, what would Michael do? How would he react if he saw her as her panther; all golden, sleek and beautiful? The thought did nothing to calm his splintering nerves. The man might well turn her into the Sassenach for the reward they offered. Leah couldn't, shouldn't trust Michael, not with her life or their baby's life.

The ride to his home lasted an eternity. When he and Kit rode into the stable, the sky was darkening. The hour was late. He knew he had to rest as well as eat. He couldn't continue at this pace for another day without sleep nor could he ride in the dark.

"It's going to be fine," Kit told him slapping him on the back as they strode to the house.

When they walked inside, the entryway was deathly quiet. The tick of the grandfather clock, creaking walls, all sounds that set his nerves on edge. A few seconds later both Brenna and Alistair strode from the parlor. It seemed they waited up for him.

"Thank God, you got here so quickly. They, Leah and Riley left this morning. You should be able to catch up to the coach before they reach Selkirk."

"Riley went with her?" he asked as he flung his coat over a chair.

The fact his brother rode with her lifted a huge weight from his shoulders.

"Yes, he plans on doing everything he can to waylay the wedding until you get there. She's a stubborn little mite. I do like her spirit though. She will be a good mate for you if you ever catch up with her. Don't understand why you waited so long to visit us," Brenna said softly. "Now, you eat your fill then go on up to your room to sleep. Kit will go with you in the morning."

A tray of food was brought out as well as wine. It was delicious. He hadn't eaten since the night before. His stomach rumbled and churned for more reasons than just hunger. He needed to focus. Had to find a means to convince her he loved her. What would it take? What words could he use to make her understand she was good enough, more than good enough for the likes of him. He was just a man after all. Wealth did not make a person better than the next.

"You should tell her," Kit said as if he was reading his mind.

"Tell her what?"

Houston knew what his brother was thinking. He wholeheartedly agreed. It was a matter of finding the privacy to explain his feelings. He wasn't about to blurt out the words in a sudden rush. She'd never believe something like that.

"You love her. It's written so clearly in your expression as well as your eyes every time her name is mentioned. It's a conundrum you need to figure out before you barge into her wedding to voice your opinion. Although that scenario would be better than standing back and watching her ruin her life as well as the child's life she is carrying for you."

"My only hope is that I arrive before the nuptials instead of after." He didn't know what he'd do if she said her 'I do' to Michael McConnal. It was the worst possible scenario. If that happened, he would just have to pray they didn't consummate the marriage. In that case, he would do whatever was necessary to keep them apart while he sought an annulment.

"You will be traveling faster than a rambling coach. I would bet you reach the carriage before it gets to Selkirk. If that is the circumstance, you can whisk her away where you can explain your bad behavior," Brenna said laughing as he narrowed his brows at her. "You have to admit whatever you did to make her run to another man was not well done of you."

"We will have to stop to change horses," Kit said from the far corner of the room. "They do have one day head start."

"We won't be taking our meals at the inns along the way," Houston said thinking he would just pay for something as they passed by then eat as they rode.

"You think the coach will stop?" Brenna questioned him. "I've been on some where they give the riders enough time to see to their needs and that is about it. Nothing more then they hightail it out bent on keeping to whatever schedule is important to them. Would rather ride and sleep in the woods than ever get back on another one of those coaches."

"Riley will make sure she has food."

"Yes, I'm sure your little brother will do that. What I'm saying is, don't count on catching up to that coach before it reaches Selkirk. Your horses will have limitations. You can't ride them too hard for too long. You both know that. I'm sure Kit will be the voice of reason here."

"I'm sure he will," Houston said blandly. He looked at his brother as he raised a glass in salute to him.

"If your finished eating, go get some sleep. I'm sure I won't see you in the morning. The two of you will be up then gone before I am," Brenna said as she watched her son stride up the steps to his room.

"He botched this one up royal. Had only himself to blame." Brenna turned to Kit. "You will take care of your brother. Make sure he does nothing stupid." She paused for a moment before continuing. "I pray this venture is successful. I can't imagine if I would have had to live my life without Alistair." She looked to her husband, lifted her glass as Kit had just done.

"I would have found you. After that I would have made you come to me," Alistair said softly, "I would have never acted as stupidly as my son. If I recall the very night I realized you were my mate, we finalized our union. I claimed you that evening. Wasn't about to allow another second to pass before doing so." He turned to Kit. "To you, I hope you have more common sense when it come to your mate than your brother."

"No one could have less than my brother," he muttered. "That fey creature who is his would have melted for him if he gave her reason. When she spoke his name, it was evident she loved him beyond her life. Anyone with half a brain could see that."

With so many thoughts penetrating his brain coupled with the recriminations he forced on himself, Houston strode up the steps to his room. The moment he stepped inside, he knew Leah had been there. When he pulled back the covers, held the pillow to his heart, her scent lingered. She touched him as no other. Moisture clogged his throat, welled in his eyes. He had so much accounting to do where she was concerned. He prayed she would give him the chance to make up to her the last months.

Quickly, he disrobed. Thinking of Leah in this bed with him he closed his eyes. His thoughts were not conducive to sleep. It seemed he did sleep. When next he opened his eyes, the room was light. The sun was not fully up yet. He dressed, shoved an extra pair of buckskins along with a shirt into his saddlebag. By the time he reached the kitchen, Kit was there drinking coffee.

"What took you so long?" His little boy grin was still wickedly devilish.

Houston ignored the question as well as the grin. He didn't want to give his brother more material to bait him. He poured a cup of coffee before sitting to gulp down a breakfast of eggs and bacon. He grabbed a loaf of bread to stick in his satchel.

"You ready?"

"Thought you would never ask."

"I'm hoping to catch up to them by tomorrow sometime."

They each took two extra horses. Even with the extra mounts they would have to rest. In the process give the horses the same consideration. If Houston had it his way, he wouldn't stop. Kit wouldn't either.

Even though Kit teased, Houston understood his brother knew what all this meant to him, to his future life. His brother would do whatever necessary for him. Would go to hell and back if he had to do so.

By the time the two men stopped for the night, the horses were spent. Houston cared for the horses while Kit booked two rooms at the inn then ordered dinner to be sent to Houston's room.

The fair was hardy, filling. It was delicious. They each drank a pint of ale. Houston ordered a bath. At every bend in the road, he hoped to see the lumbering carriage. Even if they met up with a carriage, they couldn't be sure it would be the one they wanted. That day they passed two that were going to Edinburgh and one to Glasgow.

The next day went much the same as the first. Houston felt the first fears that he might be too late even though he knew Leah and Riley were not in Selkirk yet. Not anywhere close. She would have at least a day after arrival before the wedding could take place. He reassured himself that Riley would do everything in his power to slow that process.

When the third and the fourth day passed without confronting the carriage, Houston's heart sank. They did everything possible to catch up to the vehicle. How the devil could that coach travel faster?

It was on the sixth day their efforts played out. When he saw the carriage, his heart lodged in his throat. They were so close to the little village this one had to be the one.

"What do you think?" Kit asked as he stared down the road. "Do you think that's the coach we're looking for?"

"I pray it is, also hope she'll forget all this nonsense and come with me."

Houston was certain it wouldn't be that easy. He had explaining to do, a great deal of it. He wouldn't be surprised if she opted to stay on the coach. Instead, he was tempted to pull her in front of him then ride off down the road with her. Kidnap her if that was the only way to get his point across. He didn't want to give her a choice even while he felt certain she would eventually choose him.

Kit chuckled softly seeming to empathize with him. "For your sake I also hope that it will be that easy. She's a stubborn lass. Sure, I don't have to tell you that."

They pulled astride the coach. "Need to talk to someone inside if you don't mind," Houston said even while he understood he would likely be refused.

"Can't do that. Got to keep to the schedule. What's so important that's got you wanting to stop the carriage?" the man asked with a chuckle. "Wouldn't be that fey little lady riding inside. Over the last few days heard some of the conversation between her and the man she's traveling with. You got some axe to grind?"

"Yes, it is the lady. The man she's with is my brother." Thank God it was because if it wasn't someone he trusted implicitly, he might have to kill the poor bloke for no other reason except he was there.

"Well, we'll be stopping in about five hours. You can talk to her then." He pushed his hat back before turning his attention from the road. His dark eyes roamed over him, stared at him hard.

"There's no way to change your mind?" Houston queried thinking he could get inside the carriage without it stopping with Kit's help. He could change places with Riley. It certainly wouldn't hurt for him to have a couple days to talk with her. He understood he would have to plead his case before she would agree to be his wife. He wronged her.

"Nope."

The man pushed the horses harder. It was clear to Houston why they didn't catch up sooner. If every driver drove this way, he wondered why there weren't more carriage accidents.

The coach hit a rock in the road. Houston heard the tiny scream from Leah. Heard soothing words from his brother Riley. His heart lurched just as hard as the vehicle.

She was taking her life for granted by riding in this thing. Riley should have taught her how to ride a horse. She would have fared better. If that happened, he would never have caught her.

"How about if I change places with my brother. You won't even have to stop."

At this pace he understood it might be foolhardy to do something such as that. He didn't see a choice.

"*Dinna* matter to me. Not stopping even if the wheel runs over one or both of the two of you. Got to reach the inn before it's too dark to see my hand in front of my face. We'd be there now if we didn't lose a wheel a back down the road."

Houston tried to swallow the lump of fear lodged in his throat. "Was anyone hurt?"

"Not too bad. The lady got banged up a bit but the man fixed her up. Bandaged the scratch on her arm. Maybe a few more bruises for the both of them."

The baby?

Kit was riding alongside the window next to Riley. Houston heard him speaking, "You up to trading places with our big brother. Believe he's got a death wish. Even though I understand why."

"Anything is better than riding in here. Not only am I claustrophobic but I'm also a bit seasick. Don't ever want to do this again."

"How's Leah?" Houston took Kit's place, peering into the small space where they were riding.

Leah, her face pale as snow was leaning against the opposite wall, her eyes closed.

"Both she as well as the baby she's carrying are doing fine. At least I believe so. She hasn't had any cramping. Doesn't seem as if she is going to lose the *wee* one to this wild ride."

"Just how did you get so smart about babies?" Houston asked pleased to hear the news.

"Listen to you, always listen when you talk about birthings. You haven't been around much lately but..."

"I'm going first. Just swing the door open for me. Keep it that way." Everything would be fine as long as they didn't hit another bump in the road.

Not too many minutes passed before he was inside the carriage and Riley rode his horse. The brothers agreed to continue ahead to get a room then wait for him. He would do his best to convince Leah she didn't want to marry Michael McConnal.

Once he was inside, Houston pulled her into his arms. She snuggled against him as if she belonged there. Hell, she did belong with him, next to him for the rest of their lives. He wouldn't accept anything less. She would marry him not Michael McConnal.

When he studied her, her eyes were rimmed with shadows. She appeared exhausted. When he calculated how far along she was, he came to the conclusion she was three and a half months into her pregnancy. She might be sick in the mornings. Tempted to rent horses at the next stop, he considered the possibilities until he had to put that from his head.

He stroked her back. She moaned softly pushing herself against him. He certainly hoped she didn't think it was Riley. His hand possessively roamed to her slightly swollen belly. It had to be her stomach that gave her away to his family. She was so parchment thin that the smallest swell would announce her condition to anyone who cared to look.

Her lashes lay gently across alabaster cheeks. She moved slightly, settling her hand on his chest.

"Houston?" she murmured softly as she rubbed her cheek against him.

"It's me," he said, pulling her closer, feeling a low grumble of desire coming from deep in his chest.

"Good, I'm glad."

Would she be happy when she woke and found herself wrapped up tight in his arms? Kissing her softly on the forehead, he prayed she would be, prayed now that he found her again all would be well.

I still have to convince her of so many things.

He went over the list in his head while he wondered what he should conquer first.

His brothers would beat him to Selkirk. They would help in every way they could. "Ultimately, this was up to him to make right. He had made so many mistakes.

It was dark when the carriage finally slowed. Lights from an inn shimmered down the road. In his arms she stirred.

Her voice soft, "Houston? Is it truly you?"

~ * ~

Leah blinked twice then pushed away from the man she loved. He held her hands against his chest, a small grin on his too handsome face. Her heart fluttered. "How did you get in here? I *ken* the driver wouldn't stop for any reason. Did you..." She wasn't at all sure how his presence beside her was possible. "What did you do with Riley?"

He laughed softly, pulling her closer when she pushed farther away. "You wouldn't believe me if I told you. Riley is just fine. Kit and Riley rode on ahead to secure a room for the night."

"Oh, I *dinna* think you should be holding me close like this. I'm almost a married woman," she said her words wavering as she spoke them.

They held no conviction. In truth, she wanted him to hold her like this forever and ever. Telling him no was hard.

"Of course I should hold you. I'm the man you love. Aren't I? The fact you're not wed yet gives me every reason to change your mind since I vehemently protest the marriage you planed to the wrong man. Perhaps holding you close, showing you what you'll be missing if you don't marry me is the way to go about convincing you."

"Yes, but it's not that easy. Even as we speak people are doing things, planning a wedding that is supposed to take place soon. I gave my word. I...I cannot go back on it." Breaking a promise was not something she would do lightly. Yet spending her life with Michael was also something she should give more consideration now that Houston knew about the baby, now that he followed her.

Did he want the baby or her?

Houston cut her off with a wave of his hand. "Tell Michael McConnal you changed your mind. Tell him you love me as well as the obvious fact I've come back for you. Tell him you don't need him to feed you as well as our child. Tell him you don't need him so you can have a roof over your head. Tell him I will provide all that is necessary."

She wanted to do that along with so much more. She didn't understand why she needed words of love from Houston when she didn't from Michael.

She should be satisfied. Houston showing up here was more than she ever expected.

"I've given him my promise to marry him. What would you have me do? Go back on my word? Brenda is fashioning a wedding dress for me."

Tears filled her eyes, threatened to spill forth. This was not what she expected. The last thing she could handle was waking up in Houston's arms for the remainder of the journey. If that happened, she would never be able to go through with the marriage she planned.

"Yes, that's exactly what I want. You and I are soul mates. We have to be together in this time to move on to the next when we pass from this world. If I don't claim you, this will be the end of us. The marriage isn't as important as the claiming."

"I don't want Michael to touch me the way you do. I would tell him no." She thought that would be enough. It wouldn't. If she married Michael, he would have the right to have her in every way. She would be Michael's not Houston's. Michael would own her. She didn't know if she could bare that. Just thinking about his touching her sent shivers of despair coursing through her.

"Michael is not going to accept half a marriage. He would force you if you refused him. If you wed him, you will have to let him bed you. You would let him inside you. Is that what you want?"

"No, he wouldn't. He's been patient and caring. He hasn't demanded anything from me. He's not going to take what I'm unwilling to give." The horrible feeling of isolation filled her. She understood if she wed Michael, she would give up her soul. *Never my heart.* "I've no choice now. You waited too long to come for me. To keep your promise."

"I'm not going to let you make a mistake that will ruin both our lives."

He dipped his head, swept his tongue around the tender shell of her ear. She trembled then felt his response against her.

"You should stop."

"Why?" he asked unemotionally.

"Because I don't think I could say no to you if you continue. Houston, I want you. I need you. I made a promise I need to keep. You would sway me away from values I hold dear."

"You're mine, Leah. Your virginity is mine."

"It can't be."

He growled low in his throat. "Let me prove to you how suited we are tonight when we stop. It won't be much longer. If you make love to me again, how can you give yourself to that man?"

"I promised..."

"Is that all? I can assure you any man, Michael included, would rather you break your promise at the altar than endure a lifetime with a woman who doesn't love him and never will. Right now, he believes you will learn to love him. You and I both know that will never happen."

"Michael knows I don't love him. He still wants me."

"That's because he thinks time will change your feelings. He's wrong. You will always love me, no one else. It's written in the stars."

"Do you love me?" She asked the one question she didn't think he could answer.

Silence permeated the distance between them, tears flowed. He could not build a bridge with promises, only love.

His silence told her way too much.

She understood he didn't love her.

So be it.

When they arrived at the inn, Riley and Kit had booked two rooms for them. She walked into the large room with a spacious sitting area as well as a bathing room. She saw steam rising from the water. For the entire journey Riley treated her to a bath every night along with a hot meal. She understood she didn't have the coin for any of those things. Still, she allowed him to do that for her.

"You take your bath, Leah. I'll wait out here."

Houston kissed the tip of her nose, nothing more. She wasn't sure if she was disappointed. She only had a couple of days left to be with him before she married. She also knew she would end up in his bed if not tonight then the next one. One more time with him would have to last her the rest of her life.

The bath was hot, soothing her aching muscles. For the first time since Houston left Selkirk, she felt relaxed. Tension left her body as she soaked and listened to his quiet boot treads in the hallway. She understood she should sit down with Houston, talk about the baby. Since Riley knew she was increasing, she was sure Houston would know as well. It was in her best interest to bring up the subject. They would have to figure something out.

Finishing, she donned one of the gowns Brenna had made over for her. The fit was amazing, the cloth so fine and smooth. She'd never owned a dress such as this one, never would again. That thought left a bittersweet taste in her mouth.

"You through with the water?" Houston asked.

His voice startled Leah from her daydreaming, dreams she could never hope to have. "Yes. It's all yours."

"Kit and Riley are going to join us for dinner. Hope that's alright," he spoke from the bathing room.

"Of course," she murmured softly while she listened to the sound of his clothing hitting the floor. He would be naked now. She was tempted to look.

"Help yourself to the wine," he called out.

She did. Drank half the glass then topped it off. Leah sat in front of the fire, staring at the one bed, the one big bed in the room. He would want to share that bed with her. She needed to be strong. Didn't have any idea how she could be. During the trip she never shared a room with Riley.

Of course not, you ninny.

No, you wouldn't...he wouldn't think to do so. It was Riley who expected her to sleep with Houston.

So true.

She looked up. Houston stood in front of her, his shirt off, britches partially fastened while he towel dried his hair. He was grinning.

"You've no idea how beautiful you are."

Her breath caught in the back of her throat. This was nothing new. She'd seen him before. She'd never seen Michael.

"Y-you're naked."

He paused, the towel still in one hand as he brushed it across his hair. He looked down then up his long body, caught her gaze with his. "No, don't believe I am naked. You've got me confused with someone else."

"Practically naked," she amended looking away for a moment yet unable to stop herself, she looked back, thought to reach out and touch him. Pulled her thoughts along with her hand back, keeping herself away from temptation.

His eyes shimmered as his smile grew. Once more she felt she'd been cast under his spell. Why didn't she feel that way about Michael? Why couldn't Michael's smile steal her heart the way Houston's did? She knew if Houston decided to make love to her tonight, she wouldn't tell him no. She wanted one or two more times with him before she cast her lot with another man.

"He doesn't deserve you," Houston told her as he continued to watch her. "Did you pour me a glass of wine?"

"No, but I will." She rose.

He put out his hand to stop her. "I'll get it."

Leah closed her eyes, unwilling to live in a past she couldn't have. If she watched the play of his muscles across his back, she would sink farther into the depth of depression threatening her. Either that or she'd find herself tempted to seduce him.

If she allowed herself to dream, she could see herself in the fine home where his parents lived or one just as fine where just the two of them would live with their child. She wasn't up to his standards. Settling for a man she didn't love was something she would have to do.

He sat down beside her. His presence, the scent of him, the heat all were unmistakable. She'd known his love once.

"You should dress," her voice wavered, the words a thin wobble holding no command. "Your brothers will be in here soon. What will they think?"

"They will know this for what it is. You and I are sharing a room. They will conjecture what will happen tonight." He brushed a kiss on her forehead. His breath floated across her neck then higher. "There is one bed. Two people. What conclusion would you come up with?"

"We cannot sleep together."

Still there was no force to her words. He would know she would not deny him.

"We can," he murmured as his tongue curled around her ear, his teeth nipping.

She quivered, pushed away from him. His hand wrapped around her waist pulling her closer, giving her no space of her own. To save her soul she could not tell him no. One more time, she wanted to feel him move within her more than life itself.

"You cannot think to get away from me so easily, Leah." His large hand rested on her belly. "You carry our child, one that was conceived in love. One who will most likely be a shifter."

"I understand that."

"If you wed a different man, you will condemn us to separate lives through the rest of eternity." His hand traced a line down her arm then back up. "Do you want to live without me forever into eternity?"

"You don't know that."

She was sure he would tell her he meant to take the child from her. He would do just that if she wed Michael. He had the wealth as well as the power, connections also. She knew that just as surely as she knew her heart would keep beating, knew it just as surely that she knew she loved him with all her heart.

"Can you risk the possibility? Can you believe that you can sacrifice this life then believe we can find each other in another? I for one don't want to take that chance."

His subtle coaxing was taking its toll on her. She shuddered when one bold hand cupped a breast. He swept his thumb across her nipple. She sucked in a deep breath of air, tempted to turn into his arms in the process let him make love to her. So very tempted to give up on her promise to Michael while making new ones with Houston.

"How would a man who is not able to shift deal with a child who can? I've seen enough children of shifters to know that they cannot be kept from experimenting with their abilities. The secret could not be kept from the man you are willing to wed. His or her life would be in danger from the first moment they discovered their unique abilities. Michael would be no different in his reaction to something he can't possibly understand."

"You don't know that."

"I do." He stood almost as if he knew his brothers would be outside the door waiting to be allowed inside.

The knock on the door didn't surprise her. While Riley and Kit walked in, she thought about Houston's words. They weren't anything she hadn't thought of before. She didn't want to believe what he said was true. The other night at dinner, Riley told her the same.

She did believe.

Where she grew up, she was the only child or person with the ability to change form. She had no idea what she did or how she acted when she was a toddler. Her father would have encouraged her, helped her learn about herself. The mother she adored would have done the opposite.

"We're here," Riley grinned as he waltzed into the room, Kit behind him, both sporting huge grins.

"What's for dinner," Kit asked as he looked under the covers on a couple of dishes, "or have the two of you eaten it all?"

"You tell us. You ordered the food or is it just the meal of the day?" Houston slipped on a shirt as he pulled up chairs around the table.

"They didn't say" Kit shrugged broad shoulders as he stood

behind the chair. They seemed to be waiting for her.

Houston pulled a chair out she assumed was meant for her. She didn't want to eat. Swallowing would be difficult with the men in front of her believing what they thought was going to happen in the bed tonight. Her stomach rolled even as she walked to the chair Houston held out for her. Michael never did anything like that. It was another point against Houston. Inbred gentility, an aristocrat, even though he'd told her several times he was not a lord. He was a real gentleman though.

She sat. Stared blindly at the meal in front of her, her fingers twitching beneath the table. The wine seemed better than anything else. She downed her glass wishing it had been larger. *Nay*, she would have to persevere through this night as well as the next. It wouldn't do to show him how weak she was or how easily he could sweet-talk her into his arms.

With the few tender caresses before his brother's arrived, she was ready to do his bidding. She understood what he wanted was to convince her to go with hm by bedding her.

She was lost.

"You're not hungry?" Houston leaned toward her, enclosing her free hand with his.

The warmth of the touch encompassed her, pushed inward, heating her to boiling. She tried not to look at him. If she stared into the steel grey of his eyes, she would be lost to his world.

"You need to eat. Keep up your stamina for another ride in the coach with the mad man as your driver," Riley wisely pointed out.

"For our child," Houston said.

She looked at him, her eyes wide, melting beneath the heated gaze she sought to ignore. A breath of air caught in the back of her throat. His eyes were gentle yet commanding. She understood what he wanted.

"For our child," she agreed then tried to eat.

One small bite then another entered her lips then slipped down to fill her belly. He topped off her glass. She sipped this time understanding she would need all her wits about her when Riley and Kit left.

Riley spent so much time talking to her while they rode toward Selkirk. The man had so many reasons why she should not marry Michael linked with why Houston was the only man for her.

The thing was, he didn't have to convince her. She understood the facts. Understood things Riley didn't. Riley didn't comprehend why she wasn't good enough for his brother. He told her so many times Houston wasn't good enough for her. She deserved better than a man who was so slow to keep a promise his mate agreed to a marriage to another man.

"We're going now." Riley kissed her on the forehead. "Good luck tonight, little one. Follow your heart and you'll have no regrets."

No matter what she chose she would have regrets. Following her heart would not be difficult. If she let Houston have his way, she would betray Michael's trust. If that happened though, she would have another wonderful night in Houston's arms before there would be no more. She never promised Michael that she wouldn't make love with Houston.

When they were alone, Houston stood by the door, his back against it, seeming to study her. A slow smile grew. She felt such tenderness for him. He was a good man, gentle to a fault.

"You look exhausted. Those dark circles under your eyes will go away if you get a good night of sleep."

He pushed away striding toward her. He picked up both the bottle of wine along with the two wine glasses. After he set them on a small table by one of the large brocaded chairs facing the fireplace, he came back for her.

Scooping her into his arms, he strode to the chairs.

"Houston!" She balled her fist then hit him on the chest not knowing what he intended. He was highhanded in thinking he could do what he wanted with her without a thought to asking.

He grunted. "We still have things to discuss. I'm not going to stop until you agree with me. You will decide to be mine. I should claim you tonight. If I do, at least in one way you will be mine."

"You cannot. I won't let you," she murmured even while her treacherous body seemed to mold against his. "What is claiming?"

"When we make love, my claws grow then they mark your shoulders for all to see who you belong to. Even if you decide to marry Michael, you will be mine. It is something I have to do before it is too late. Your obstinacy in this matter terrifies me."

She shuddered, wondering at the pain. It was something her mother should have told her about. Might have if she lived long enough. Probably not, her mother would have done all in her power to keep her from a shifter.

"Was your mother marked by your father?" he asked as he slowly stroked her arm.

The caresses generated heat as well as other feelings she'd been aware of since the first touch of his lips upon her.

"I don't know." She didn't want to think about any of this. In any case she would have a devil of a hard time while he continued his explorations.

He handed her the glass of wine. She closed her eyes trying to remember if there were any marks on her mother's shoulders. There were few times she saw her mother without clothing. She didn't want to admit anything to Houston. Wasn't sure why.

Houston went on to say as if trying to encourage her. "My mother has four just above each shoulder blade as well as one on top of her shoulder. I noticed when I was still small and asked her about them. She told me I'd have to wait until I was older to learn what went on between mates. You father would explain everything then. Think, Leah..."

She did then, closing her eyes once more. It seemed all she could think about was each stroke of his fingers along her arm. The way his chest moved with each breath of air he drew inward. She knew if she let herself lean her head against him, she would hear the beat of his heart. Always she felt one with this man.

"I think so, maybe. Perhaps that is why she hated shifters so much."

Reaching up she touched his cheek with the palm of her hand, felt the day's growth of beard. Marveled in their differences.

"I've heard from my mother as well as others that if you are not a shifter the pain is worse, far worse than the taking of the mate's innocence. I'm content to know it won't be that way with you. Don't ever want to hurt you again."

He was reminding her of her lost virginity. She willingly gave her innocence to him. "You haven't been listening to me. I haven't changed my mind. Won't even if you claim me tonight."

"You still plan on wedding a man who can't give you what you need, what you deserve?" he swore beneath his breath.

Leah didn't know what he said. The words must have been Celtic. She was certain he was angry, furiously so. "I don't fit in your world. I'm too different. Michael and I have that in common."

"That's something else we need to discuss. You will fit. Did anyone say different when you were with my family? Did you spill the wine in your crystal glass? Did you make snide remarks at the dinner? No." He tapped his chin. "You must have belched when you finished the meal." He smiled at the small giggle she couldn't hold back before he continued. "I don't care how you grew up or that we were raised differently. We are also raised in a very similar way."

"No, but..."

"...but?" One of his dark eyebrows lifted, challenging her with what seemed to be everything he possessed.

She plucked at her skirt, nerves stretching so thin she was positive they would snap. "There are so many things that we don't share. At your home I drank wine from crystal glasses. Never seen them let alone put my lips against them. This dress." She paused, sucking in a blast of air for more courage. "Even the dress I bought special to see you and your family is not as fine as this hand-me-down. Your mother said it would go to the needy if I didn't except. I'm needy. There is no other way to describe my circumstances."

"I'm more needy than you. I need you right now in so many different ways on so many diverse levels I'd be unable to list them." With a finger on her chin, he turned her face from her mesmerized gaze at the fire to meet his.

"I yearn for you right now. Crave for you to admit that we are made for each other." He placed tender kisses at either side of her mouth. Tugged gently on her bottom lip imploring her to open for him.

Unable to help herself she did what he begged for. She tasted the wine lured by the warmth he presented to her, she met him, explored when he backed off, retreated when it seemed he needed to venture inside her. The slow purr rumbling from her belly gave credence to the raw passion he elicited from her. His scent flooded her. She would never forget all that he was, all they might have been.

Breathless yet determined she pulled away from him. "Houston."

"What?" He placed light nipping kisses along her neck while it seemed he waited for her to speak.

"You have to stop?"

"I don't have to do anything unless you want me to. Do you truly want me to stop, Leah? Or is it your conscious speaking for you. What you believe you owe Michael does not exist."

He did pull away. Did give her space to collect her thoughts and feelings. "You, your family have servants; a butler, a cook a...Houston, without you I would be one of those servants.

"Perhaps. Doesn't change the fact you're meant to be my wife. I want to give you everything you desire including me."

He handed her the glass of wine, leaning back watching her intently. "You will tell Michael you're marrying me not him."

~ * ~

Michael paced his sitting room above the store. Quaid and Ryan watched him grinning at his immense discomfort. Where the devil was Leah? By his calculations, she should have been here two days ago. They were getting married tomorrow afternoon.

What if she changed her mind? Sweat beaded on his forehead as well as the rest of his body. He wiped his moisture-ridden palms on his trousers.

He should have never allowed her to visit Houston's family. He could have stopped her. They must have waylaid her kept her on McKenna land so she couldn't return here.

"Why don't you bed Betsy or Marie? Get the tiny fey creature out of your system. You'll be a lot more fun to be around," Quaid suggested laughing.

"I promised not to see either one while she was gone," Michael said feeling heat rise to his cheeks.

He'd never promised any woman anything before. This time he

was certain the vow was the only way to make sure she came back to him. "In return, she promised to come back and marry me."

"You promised the girl you wouldn't see anyone else?" Ryan asked seeming truly amazed. He let out a roar of laughter. "I do hope this is not the way of your future."

"No!" Michael waved his hand in the air. "It was more than that, I promised myself not just her. It was the only way to get her back."

Both of his friends let out a second round of raucous laugher. "You wanted to save yourself for a woman? For that otherworldly creature who is so different from everyone else she has people laughing behind your back? You *ken* she is not good enough for you. She was raised in a hovel. Not that the fact makes her different. She just is."

"Yes, I did just that" Michael growled low in his throat as be began to doubt himself. There were other reasons though. Important reasons. "You two better not be among those laughing at me. She promised she would come back after speaking with Houston. Leah promised to marry me. It's what I want." He pointed his thumb at his chest several times to emphasize the point he was trying to make.

"Never understood what you saw in her," Quaid said still laughing so hard he had trouble getting the words out.

"She's too thin. Doesn't have anything on top worth a man's hands," Ryan added, "Marie would make a better wife except for the fact she's slept with every man close to her age in the territory. No one wants to wed a whore even if she's wealthy and pretty."

"Doesn't have hips a man can hold on to, when..."

"She does have the longest legs imaginable. Ah, that's what you see in her..." Quaid seemed to realize something. "You want those long skinny legs wrapped around you when..."

"She's beautiful. You're both right. She does have something I want. As soon as she's mine I intend to collect."

Michael smiled then. It was the first time since Leah left that he felt happiness slither through him. Leah was worth a small fortune. That fortune would be his.

As soon as they were wed, he meant to turn her into one of the English patrols in the areas. Oh, she didn't know it yet. He'd seen her shift. Somehow, he would find a way to trap her when she was vulnerable. He would make her shift for him. Coax her into the deed or force her if he couldn't do it any other way. She would never shift back if she didn't have clothing nearby. He would see to everything. The sight of her in her panther form, pacing a cage gave him reason to howl with laughter.

At the moment he wasn't positive how to do it. Perhaps he should wait until that brat of hers was born. The child might also be a shifter. There would be two shifters for him to collect the bounty on. He could hold the child over her head. That was the way he would force her. She would do anything for that brat of hers.

Ha! He bet the doctor didn't know any of this. What would he do if he found out Leah could change her form? He wouldn't want her so much. *Nay*, he would give her to him without blinking an eye. That's what he would do. More than just being fanciful, she was a freak.

Now all he had to do was marry her. Brenda played right into his hands by encouraging her to wed him. He would always be thankful to that woman. He rubbed his hands together anticipating the outcome.

"What is it you want so bad?" Ryan asked sounding curious now, all humor having vanished.

"I'll let you know as soon as the time is right. Think I'll wait until the child is born before showing my hand."

Chapter Twelve

Houston didn't want to coax and seduce Leah to his way that night. Didn't want to claim her when she was in his power because of sexual needs. He didn't have another choice. This was a do or die in the attempt situation. This was a dire condition for both of them even though she didn't understand. When his brothers left the room, he said a silent prayer heavenward.

"More wine," he asked smiling at her, remembering all the sweetly tender spots to kiss her.

She was the most caring person he'd ever known. She needed to learn how to care for herself first.

She nodded holding her glass out to him. "I'm sorry I've disappointed you. Truly, if I could change this, I would."

He would allow her the lie tonight but not again, not when she met Michael before the sham wedding they planned. Houston intended to be with her. If she still persisted in marrying that man, he would object. Telling everyone the babe she carried was his, was not a plan he relished. If she let this wedding go that far, he would do more including describing the tiny mole that was on her right buttocks. If she still persisted in the sham, he would embarrass her farther. He would tell her beforehand so she could weigh her options.

"Change is inevitable." The sensations coursing through him were strange. Houston still had a feeling in his gut Michael meant her harm not a life of love as man and wife. He didn't know why. Didn't believe the emotion was jealousy talking although he had to admit jealousy played a part in his emotions. No, the feeling came straight from his gut. When all the other young men in town made fun of her, why did Michael of all people want her?

He was certain. It wasn't for the same reasons as his. His mind catapulted into worst- and best-case scenarios. She was so beautiful all the young men should be vying for her attention.

They weren't.

He'd come across her in her cat form unexpectedly. She'd been surprised. What if somehow, Michael saw her shift? His belly turned acrid. He didn't want to think the man would betray her that way. Her future as well as their child's was in dire straits if his thoughts were true.

There was a hefty bounty on a shifter's head. It wasn't just in the highlands, the posters advertising that reward were hung throughout Scotland. "No!" His fist collided with his palm.

She jumped, seemingly startled by the one word bellowing from him. "Houston?"

He tried for serene calm. "Sorry, didn't mean to surprise you. I was thinking."

"Not a good thought I assume?"

He lifted his shoulders, unwilling to tell her his mind unless it was as a last resort. Without discussing this with his brothers, he was positive he was right. Didn't like the fact the thought belittled Leah. Houston was positive Michael wanted to marry her for what he could get from her.

"Do you mind if I leave for a few minutes. I've got to speak with Kit and Riley. You can get ready for bed, or sip more wine. I'll join you later."

The look on her face, was it relief? He wondered if she believed he wouldn't join her in bed if he left for a few minutes. After his discussion with his brothers, he felt sure there would be no choice for him.

"Perhaps I'll do both. It seems I need the wine to fall asleep."

Her smile beguiling, he almost turned around.

"Don't go to sleep without me," he said as the door closed behind him.

If he had to put off her claiming until the next night he would. This was too urgent to leave unspoken. If his gut wasn't churning as well as the hairs on the back of his neck standing on end, he would wait. This was too serious to leave unsaid another moment. All their lives as well as their parents' well, hell the entire clan could be at risk.

With the knock on the door and the following come in, he stepped into the room. His brothers each had a pint in hand.

"Trouble in paradise?" Kit asked, the crease lines along his brow told of different thoughts.

"You *ken* I wouldn't be here if it wasn't important." All his thoughts rumbling around in his head, he sought the words.

"We both know where you'd rather be," Riley laughed nodding his head in the direction of his room. "If my mate was in the other room, it would take something powerful to get me away."

"In bed with my soon to be wife, claiming her." Houston stuffed his hands through his hair.

"Why are you here?" Kit challenged getting to the point of his visit.

"Michael has nefarious purposes where Leah is concerned. After a few things she told me, I've come to the conclusion he knows she is a shifter. I *dinna* want to believe this. Nonetheless, he could want to collect that bounty on our kind. If she is involved, it would threaten all of us."

"Why would you think that?" Kit asked.

"Because Leah is so different from all of the other females in the area. From what Leah has told me, he's bedded most of them. She is the only one he hasn't actually slept with," Riley paused as his gaze traveled to Houston. "Until recently he never favored her."

"He promised not to bed another woman while she was gone so she would keep her promise to him to return," Houston added. "I still haven't convinced her to break her promise. However, I will even if I have to tell her my thoughts. She understands the child she carries will be a shifter. If what I'm thinking is true, Michael will wait until the babe is born then turn them both over to the Sassenach for the money they will bring him. He will use the child to make her comply with his wishes. The only loyalty that man possesses is to himself."

The stunned silence told Houston more than a reply would have. It seemed neither of his brothers had an inkling of what to say.

"Should we stay with you or ride ahead?" Riley asked. "I hate leaving the two of you."

"At first light ride on, talk with Hawk. Listen to him. He might have some insight into this situation. I think he was as baffled as I was when Michael turned sweet on Leah then started asking her to marry him. Even when I still lived there while everyone in the village knew she was sweet on me, he persisted."

Houston found himself pacing while thoughts of kidnapping Leah and riding home swept through his head. He meant to give her a chance to turn down Michael's offer on her own. If he failed to convince her, he'd do whatever was necessary to save her life as well as his child's.

"We can be there late tomorrow afternoon if we ride hard. Maybe by midday," Kit said. "We'll get up as soon as it's light then be on our way."

Houston sipped air, needing it desperately, his emotions in upheaval. "She cannot wed that man."

"Other than Hawk no one can learn about the things we talked about here."

"That's obvious."

Leaving his brothers discussing this new information, Houston strode to the room to see Leah. He understood what had to be done. When he entered a candle was burning near the bedside table casting light across her face. The smudges under her eyes were still evident.

He promised himself once he claimed her, he would leave her to sleep. The task would be difficult. She was so precious to him. How had he let their relationship get so far out of hand? Fool, he was a complete idiot where Leah was concerned.

Because, you didn't think. Thought she would fall into your waiting arms. Forgot she was a woman with an independent mind.

Yes, she was that. He loved her all the more because of that fact. His mother was much like Leah. He didn't think she gave Alistair any of this trouble. If she did, the pair didn't talk about it. At their age, they were still a loving couple. Too many times he barged into their room catching them in a compromising position until they bought a lock for their door. He wanted his relationship with Leah to be just as loving. It would be somewhat different though simply because they were both shifters.

"You're not sleeping." Houston strode across the room removing clothing as he walked. By the time he crawled into bed with her he was naked. She was clothed from her chin to the tips of her toes. The barrier wouldn't last long.

"Neither are you," she murmured, the quilt coming nearly to her eyes.

"Do you want me so much that you couldn't fall asleep thinking about me?" he chuckled wishing that was the case. If it was, he'd be more than happy to oblige.

"Yes, that doesn't mean I'm going to change my mind."

The need to both laugh and cry at her statement flooded him. While he was content, she wanted him, she left him frustrated with the need for her to think differently. To forget a vow made when she had no roof over her head or food in her belly.

"Your promise has to be broken before irreparable damage can take place," he murmured as he slipped into bed beside her.

He shouldn't have blurted those words as he came to her bed intending to make all her problems disappear until morning.

"What?" she started to sit.

"Hush, don't get up. I mean nothing, at least nothing that matters at this moment. Do you want to make love to me? You can seduce me, coax me to do whatever wickedness you can think of. Touch me anywhere. Didn't you want to do that once?"

She laughed. The sound was soft and sweet exactly like her. "I wouldn't know how to go about doing something like that."

"Think hard, *lass*. Sure you can figure something out."

His hands framed her face while he hovered over her. He felt the sweet whisper of her breath as it fanned across his face. He stole air from the room, catching the scent of wildflowers.

Pushing up on her elbows she rose above him. Set her lips on his. They were moisture slick, soft as rose petals. Candlelight still bathed her face. Her eyes shimmered with clarity. She understood what she did here, wanted and needed him as much as he did her. A breeze entered into the room from the open window. He pulled the covers higher needing both the cooling air as well the comfort from the warmth of the heavy quilt.

Heat between them would rise tonight become an inferno if he had his way.

Shudders swept through him as the mercuric touch of her fingers danced across his chest. She played. Dreams of her body next to his for the rest of their lives created a divine havoc within him.

The dance grew bolder, the play more intense, hotter sweeping across him lower and lower until the back of her hand brushed across him intimately. He sipped air, straining for the control he needed. He clasped her hands in his, bringing them over her head.

"Perhaps I should lead this dance for now. You're too good at what you do," he whispered as he showered her neck with kisses leaving his mark behind.

Her answer was a soft purr. He needed nothing else.

He kissed her again and again reaching for the stars and the moon as his lips molded across hers, took them sweetly into his mouth bathed them intimately.

"You wear too much." He stroked her, lent his tongue to every part of her he could find. The buttons to her nightdress were unfastened. With a little help from her, he swept it over her head.

Flesh against flesh he continued his pursuit of her pleasure, of their pleasure. The soft contours of her body pressed against him, enticed and enchanted. He sipped here then there. Brought her nipple deep into his mouth sucked and laved as she arched to meet him.

"Please, Houston. I love you so much..."

He paused at her words, understood she could not love him more than he did her. Yet so caught up in the moment he failed to say the words to her. His body shook with the need to possess her as he moved lower to her woman's mound. Her belly was slightly larger from their babe. He caught her scent, the muskiness of woman coupled with the light flowers she loved so much.

She was soft, swollen and slick with her passion. The desire he found in her ran hot and deep, raw and delicious.

Slowly, he found the heated core that would welcome him into its depth. Velvet softness surrounded him. They were made for each other. No one else would do for her or for him. When her body coiled tightly, he needed to scream, howl his delight drive into her so hard and fast she would cry out his name. Instead, he held still, hovering over her, gritting his teeth against the temptation to end this so soon. This connection was primal.

"What do you want, Leah?" he asked as he joined his lips with hers, pushing his tongue inside her as he would do the same with his penis.

"You, Houston, only you. I want you."

Her voice was whisper thin, in need of him. He knew it. As did she.

"All I want is you, Leah. Change your mind. Don't put your life in Michael's hands."

Beneath him she stiffened as if he slapped her. He did not. He was desperate, in need for just that. Slowly, he moved within her, teasing her, tempting her but not fulfilling her need.

"I'm going to claim you now. It might hurt. I've truly no idea." His lips met hers. He found the tiny nubbin, her clitoris, deep in her wet slick folds. When he felt her body come to life, the small tremors coursing through her, his claws grew.

When she cried out her frantic release, his nails scored her shoulders. She met him arching as he thrust inside her again and again. Tears wetted her cheeks along with her eyelashes.

When it was over, she lay beneath him so still it frightened him. He pushed moist hair from the sides of her face.

"Houston... Oh God, we cannot go on like this."

He was suddenly terrified of what she might need to tell him. "Like what? What happened?"

He needed to learn everything. "Leah...?"

"I saw us. Just as you told me we've lived through other times. I don't know what to do now? Except now I *ken* you are right about everything."

For a moment he felt as if he'd won. "You have to marry me," he spoke softly still pleading his case. "It is the only way to make our lives right."

Her tears turned to sobs. "I cannot. I promised Michael."

"You owe no allegiance to that man." His words gritted from him as he was more certain than ever the man meant to sell her for the bounty. Michael wanted her for the money she would bring to him.

"Come." He pulled her to a sitting position. The candlelight still shone on her as her breasts moved sweetly. "I will clean you up."

"It didn't hurt, not much. It was a bit like getting pricked by tiny needles," she told him resting one hand on his chest.

He chuckled softly, "So, my claws are no more than tiny needles. I should be offended."

"But you're not. You're glad you didn't hurt me." She smiled, touching his mouth with a fingertip, trailing it along his bottom lip.

That was the truth. The pain he caused when he broke through her barrier was more than he imagined. He'd never made love to a virgin before. Naked, he padded to the basin then filled it with water. With the soft cloth set nearby, he washed the blood from her slender shoulders. This moment was too precious for words.

He did not convince her. He would have to tell her everything.

How would he live his life without her, if she refused to come with him?

When he was finished, he poured them both wine. "Drink this then we both need to sleep unless we want to miss the coach."

"I would not mind missing that mad man's coach. Another day's ride..."

"You have no words. We could ride horseback the rest of the way. It would not be as fast. Nonetheless, we would still arrive in time for your wedding."

He was barely able to say the words that could haunt him for the rest of his life.

"You could. I couldn't unless you wanted to go that far with me sitting in front of you."

Fond memories of those times she rode with him surfaced. "You recall those few trips we made up the mountain with you sitting on my lap? That would be pleasant for me. Would the ride be as pleasant for you?"

She looked down, must have seen naked flesh to her waist.

Gasping slightly, she pulled the quilt to her shoulders.

"Would it, Leah?"

"Y-yes."

The small flare of color to her face fascinated him. She blushed so shyly. "You're bashful. I've touched every part of you, more than once. I intend to do the same tomorrow night. What do you say about that?"

She smiled sweetly, however it didn't reach her eyes. "I will remember riding in front of you for the rest of my life along with everything you did." Her voice so wistful the sound brought moisture to his eyes.

"You could change that."

"I know..."

For the first time he felt hopeful she might do just that. "Leah, you don't want to hear this. If you force this, I will do anything and everything to stop your wedding. Even if it means embarrassing you, I cannot allow your promise to a man who doesn't deserve you in the process ruin our lives."

"I didn't..."

"I promise. There is no way in hell that man will ever call you wife." Houston didn't want to sound so harsh. He understood how difficult this was for her. For the time being, the only way he could make it easy was to go along with her plans.

Her plans be damned.

"How?" She lowered her lashes. "How would you embarrass me?"

"I'm not going to say, simply because my plan would embarrass as well as frighten you. I don't want to do that not unless you force me to do so by stepping in front of a minister with the intention of committing your life to McConnal."

She leaned back against the headboard, closing her eyes. For a moment he thought she might spill her wine.

"Can we ride the horses tomorrow?"

~ * ~

Leah sat in front of Houston all the way to the next inn. They didn't make it as far as the coach. Nonetheless, it would be easy enough to ride the remaining distance to Selkirk and still get there in time for the wedding. A wedding Houston intended to stop. He was beginning to change her inclination to keep a promise made under duress. When she agreed to Michael's proposal, she'd been so hungry so deserted she didn't feel as if she had an option left to her. It was easier now that she had food in her stomach.

Thinking about Michael touching her in the same way Houston did sent revulsion flooding her body. She closed her eyes, refusing to think about the man.

What would Houston do to stop things from coming to the promised conclusion?

Anything, he told her. She needed to know what anything meant.

"How are you doing?" His lips brushed across her nape then higher to her ear before tugging gently with his teeth.

She shivered, unable to stop thinking about Houston's words. He was leaving her in the dark about her, their future. "Better if you would tell me what you plan."

"I will have to soon if you don't tell me what I want to hear."

He gave her no quarter while they rode even going so far as to stroke her intimately. She wanted him to hold her, keep her safe throughout the night. She knew she didn't want anything to do with Michael McConnal. Could not live the life she once thought would be her only salvation.

"If you don't stop this nonsense, that man will be doing this to you tomorrow night. Do you want that, Leah?"

"No, you *ken* I don't."

Sobs welled into her throat. This was untenable. She had no idea how her life came to this. One moment it was just as it had been for five years, the next chaos broke out.

"I just don't have another argument to give you. Well, I do but as I said, I have to wait. You..."

"You have to tell me. If it's something I should know, you can't leave me in the dark. I have to have all the facts to make the right decision."

She was leaning against him, her legs spread wide. Two fingers were deep inside her while he gave attention to the silken knot of pleasure. She felt her body begin the slow spiral where she would lose all control, where the pleasure would swamp her. He was deflecting, stalling so he didn't have to tell her. In this situation, she was powerless to stop.

"Tonight. I promise I'll tell you tonight then together we can decide what to do. I won't force you."

"I'm glad. I need a reason to break my vow. Only you can give that to me. Please, Houston, give me a solid reason."

Houston thought he'd given her more than one good reason. Well, he now had an even better motive. "Despite the fact you are too stubborn for your best interest, I admire your loyalty to the agreement you made as misplaced as it was. I wish I could figure out a way to trap that man in his scheme without having to tell you what I believe as the truth. The last thing I want is to put this on your shoulders. You are more desirable than any woman I've ever known."

"Stubborn, am I?" She poked him in the chest. "No more than you."

"If I was not so stubborn and pigheaded, you would end up in that other man's bed tomorrow night. Don't know any other man who could be told no a thousand times and keep on trying to change a woman's mind."

"Thank you." Her voice was soft, held a hint of despair. "I pray now that doesn't happen."

"I guarantee you after you hear what I have to say, you will have no qualms. You will feel no reason to break the contract you made. I understood the danger in telling you, which is why I've put it off. Understand we will have to give a good reason to the minister without letting that man know what I inadvertently figured out."

"Now will you tell me?"

The day had been long and tiring. "This is my last card. I pray when I play it you will completely understand."

She watched as he sought air for courage perhaps. Breathing deeply, he began. "You should play it. At this point you've done much to change my mind. Think hard about the questions I mean to ask you. You always disliked that man. You recall this, don't you?"

She nodded, her eyes wide questioning all he said.

"This gut feeling is something animals use to survive to live another day. Even cats and dogs have this response to people they believe will do them harm. Do you believe in what your gut is telling you? Did the fine hair on your arms or the back of your neck ever seem to prickle when he was around you?"

She pulled her lips together in her thought. The way his eyes seemed to bore into her it appeared he wanted to know what was inside her mind. "I hope you can be honest now that so much rides on your memory."

"When you look at me that way, I see knowledge, recollection. I might not have to explain everything."

"Always. Always I've had this feeling of doubt. Lately, I blamed the feelings on his friends. I never liked them either. Was I so wrong?"

"Listen to your instincts. McConnal hasn't changed. One can't hide their true nature forever. I *ken* I've said this before. If you marry that man, you will make the biggest mistake of your life."

"You're still not telling me everything or anything. Do you mean to make me figure this out on my own? I'm confused."

She wasn't going to let any of this go unanswered. The truth needed to be told. He would have to tell her everything. She sensed there was much more to what Houston was trying say.

"I didn't want to have to say more. I hoped you would come to the same conclusion without me telling you."

"You will say more."

"Suppose I have to," His shoulders rose in what appeared to be a shrug of indifference she felt sure he didn't feel.

She framed his face with her hands. "I trust you more than I've ever trusted anyone, even my mother who always held something back from me. You are my friend as well as my lover. Please..."

It seemed the plea was all he needed to finish the story. "You recall the signs we see every day about the bounty on shifters?"

He waited. She needed a few seconds for her to think about what he said.

Leah didn't seem at all sure where he intended to go with this. "Never paid a lot of attention to them," she murmured. "While I know what I am, mother was able to erase a lot of those feeling from my head. Sometimes I forget how different I am. What does that have to do with Michael as well as the promise I'm getting closer to breaking with each passing word you say?"

"Do you also remember the day I stepped into your sanctuary? The day I saw you as the sleek golden panther you are?"

"That's a day I'll never forget." She kissed the palm of his hand as she watched his eyes simmer with what she recognized now as raw passion. "You still haven't shown me your cat."

Her body trembled with her need for him. "I'm tempted now to scoop you into my arms then take you to the bed waiting for us." He paused, distractedly running his hands through his hair. I have to see this through. If you are still willing, we will have all night to explore each other."

"I need you. I believe you know how willing I am."

He sucked in air again, watching her intensely. "It's my belief that sometime in the last year or so that man saw you shift. He knows what you are."

Her startled gasp left sweat beading on his forehead. He watched her eyes as they captured the meaning of his words. Moisture coated her lashes leaving tiny diamond prisms she tried to blink away.

"He knows...? *Kens* I'm a shifter? Why hasn't he said anything?"

"I believe so. Why else would he suddenly and so very ardently pursue you? He's always been a man to avoid matrimony. Found his delights in willing women a lot of willing women. Such as Betsy and Marie along with all the other willing ladies in the area."

"You believe as soon as he puts a ring on my finger and I say the words he will sell me to the Sassenach."

"No, what I think is closer to the truth is that he'll wait until you give birth then sell both you and our child to the English. When your child is born, he will have more leverage over you, a *wee bairn* to blackmail you with."

For the first time since she accepted Michael's proposal, she gave in to her emotions. Under these circumstances with this knowledge pounding in her head, she could never say the words of commitment. Houston was right on all counts.

"I've been such a fool." More tears welled in her eyes.

"Look," he pointed down the road there is the inn, "we will have time to rest and make our own commitments to each other."

~ * ~

The next day they made good time. By ten o'clock they were in town. Houston stopped at his office first. They both hoped his brothers would be waiting for him along with Hawk.

She wanted to confront Michael, tell him they would not wed this afternoon or ever. If she did, Houston would be furious. Still...

He could never understand how hurt she was at the deception as well as the fact she'd not seen through his lies. She'd been so desperate. All she'd wanted was to be able to protect her child. This was her life she needed to put to rights. It was up to her to tell Michael she had no intention of wedding him.

Houston would disagree claiming her life might be in danger if she did this alone. He might be right. She swallowed the lump of fear in her throat when she watched the brothers walk down the road to Hawk's office.

They were making plans without her.

She left a note for Houston telling him where she would be as well as what she intended.

Leah fisted her hands, determined to see this through to the bitter end. She would, of course, tell Michael she knew his plan. That might be tantamount to admitting she was a shifter. She would tell him her decision without saying much more than Houston asked her to wed him. She wanted her husband to be the man who sired the *wee* babe she bore inside her. That knowledge would have to suffice as her excuse.

With hands fisted along with a few extra breaths of air, she started down the steps then toward the McConnal store. He might be getting ready for a ceremony that wasn't going to take place.

Halfway there with numerous misgivings, she turned back. This impulsiveness of hers was ill advised. She understood. She saw Quaid and Ryan pointing at her and laughing.

Anger simmered deep inside.

The two friends might be part of Michael's plot, might also plan her's as well as her child's demise at the hands of the English. She had to go through with this. Had to get the day over before she lost all nerve.

She longed for Brenda's advice. Advice she couldn't receive simply because her best friend didn't know her truth.

The balance between trust and friendship when one had abilities that went beyond the norm was delicate. Leah supposed she never trusted Brenda enough to divulge the secret her mother thought should be kept to herself for the entirety of her life.

It wasn't until she met Houston that she felt comfortable as a shifter. He made her feel special. Deep down, even if Michael didn't mean to give her to the Sassenach, she would never feel comfortable around him.

When she entered the store, one of his employees sent her upstairs. If not for the decision she made yesterday, she would have spent the evening here. The shudder sweeping through her sent a wave of insecurity through her. She should have waited for Houston.

She meant to turn around. She did then whirled when she heard her name.

"Leah, whatever are you doing here? Don't you know it's bad luck for the bride to see the groom before the wedding?" Michael asked as he stood at the top of the steps, shirtless with his trousers half fastened. He smirked at her.

"I..." She swallowed the fear rising from her belly. This was not wise of her.

"You couldn't wait to see me. Well, come on up. Maybe we can share a few intimacies before tonight. What do you think? A kiss or perhaps something more."

"No," she murmured shaking her head as she looked over her shoulder hoping to see Houston or one of his brothers.

"No what?" he suddenly sounded angry. In the next instant he tempered his voice. "Come talk to me. Is something bothering you? I'm so pleased you kept your promise as did I."

Her feet dragging, she did his bidding. This was what she came for, talk, to tell him the wedding wasn't happening today or any other day. She was going to marry Houston. He would understand.

"Michael?"

She stepped inside his private rooms. The door banged closed then she was in his arms, his mouth sealed on hers. She pushed at his chest, beating on him with her fists, struggled in his embrace, violently until he stopped. Lifting his head, he stared into her eyes.

His brows were furrowed together, clearly displeased. "What are you doing here? You should be at Brenda's dressing for the ceremony."

The little sips of air getting into her body weren't doing her any good. The room tilted, spinning around as she tried to steady herself. "There isn't going to be a ceremony," she blurted out relieved she finally said the words that had been tormenting her.

"Stop teasing, you promised to marry me." he said, stepping closer to her, his hands on her shoulders. His grip tightened until she cried out. "You're mine, Leah, not Houston's. He abandoned you."

"Michael? Don't!"

"Don't kiss the woman who's going to be my wife in a few hours? Don't touch her and taste her as someone else has done? You will be my wife. You're lucky I've forgiven you." He moved back from her, cold anger simmering in the depth of his eyes. "You slept with him."

"No! Don't do this." She pushed away from him, her body shaking as she further realized the stupidity of what she did.

He pulled her against him, his hands roaming, exploring her body, touching her places he had no right. "If this is true, I'm going to have you on the floor right now. I've waited for you. My patience was always what kept me from taking what I wanted. You made a mistake coming here, little bitch."

Beneath his questing fingers, the fastenings on her gown were falling apart. Cool air caressed bare flesh. His hand cupped her breast, squeezing until once again she cried out at the pain he inflicted.

"Stop!" She struggled kicking at him. Her gown ripped as he tugged on the material. The torn fabric pooled on the floor.

"Yes, Leah. You'll feel me inside you. You will know what you'll be missing. Right now, right here, I mean to collect everything that is due me. Your body along with the bounty."

"No!" She panicked. With no alternative, she shifted. In her panther form it was the only way she would have the strength to evade his advances. Her claws raked across his bared chest once then twice.

He cried out. Screamed in rage. "Whore!" Blood dripped from his chest while she stood frozen to the floor watching him.

Her feet as well as her mind were motionless. Underneath her ribs her heart thundered, blood pounding in her ears willing her to shift back. *Shift!*

Michael stared at her, his face mottled with his fury. "You'll pay for this, little freak."

Change back!

A voice reverberated in her head. She heard her thoughts. Understood she had to act fast before he could find some way to corner her. Her worst fears would come true.

Change now!

She did so. Found herself shivering without a shred of clothing left to her. Quickly, she searched the floor groping for the torn pieces of her dress. Found the gown that was frayed. Quickly slipping what was left of it over her head, she fastened as much as possible.

Michael was on his feet then. He shook his fist at her. "You little hellion. I will trap you. Don't underestimate me. I've seen you twice now."

Leah backed toward the door. The only way he would catch her would be to make her shift again. She had to leave. Racing for the door, he beat her to it. His hand slapped the door closed before she could squeeze through the narrow opening. The weight of his body left it shut. He grinned at her now, appearing confident she was under his power. He would be the one to command and dictate.

Once again, she backed from him. Terror swamped her, filling her with dread, "You can't mean to do this. Please, Michael. I'm not what you think. It's your imagination working. You just want the bounty so you've imagined things. You haven't seen anything."

"Quick speaking won't get you out of this. I do mean to have everything. The promise of your body, your child's, too, if the babe is a shifter. If not, I don't care what will happen to him. You along with the brat will help me turn a tidy profit."

"No..." There was nothing more she could think to say. He could have her body anytime he wanted. Next time, he'd be prepared if she shifted. He wouldn't leave anything to chance. She played her last card. He would take her now.

"You can be my whore until you make a mistake. If you try to fight me by shifting, I'll have you exactly where I want you. Now, you'll never be my wife." He was wiping blood from his chest with some of the fabric from her gown that was shredded when she changed form.

Houston, where are you? Why didn't I listen to you?

"Leah!" Her name followed by the roar shook the walls of the room. She said a silent prayer.

Houston.

He came. Tears rolled down her eyes while she watched the door burst open, slamming against the opposite wall. Riley, Kit, Hawk; they were all behind Houston.

Houston's fist caught Michael's jaw, blindsiding him. The solid punch crumpled him to the ground. When he sat up, he rubbed his chin where the blow connected.

Leah was in his arms. "Don't ever touch her again. I'll kill you if you do." His voice shook with fury she'd never seen before.

"You don't know what she is," Michael grinned as if he meant to impart knowledge that would make Houston leave her. "If you knew, you wouldn't defend her so ardently. You would give her to me."

"I do know exactly who and what she is," Houston spoke softly, his gaze riveted on her. "The most beautiful caring person I've ever known. Leah is the woman I love with all my heart."

"You love me?"

Her heart forgot to beat for a moment. She reached out to him, touching his jaw. Instead of finding herself in his arms, she slumped to the ground.

"We'll take care of Michael. Make sure he understands the consequences of pursuing this further," Kit said, "Take her home."

Houston scooped Leah into his arms then did just that. He found smelling salts in his office. When she woke, she was lying in his arms on his big bed.

"You love me?" she asked softly, her hand touching his cheek. She never believed he loved her, would ever love her. "Did I hear you right?"

Tenderly, he brushed tendrils of lose hair behind her ear. "Have I never told you that before?"

"Not to my recollection."

"Well then, I will have to make sure I tell you every day and every night from now on. I love you, Leah McEwen. Love you with all my heart."

~ * ~

Fear was not an emotion Houston was used to. When he read her note, he found his heart stuck in his throat. She would have walked blindly into his trap. She would have never thought how easy it would be for him to make her shift. Now, at least, her defense would be his word against McConnal's, his brothers along with Hawk's.

The tale would remain in Selkirk unless Michael was foolhardy enough to venture to McKenna land. There the clan was powerful. He would never succeed in any endeavor against a McKenna relative. If anything, the patrols would increase. The clan was used to that. They would recover.

"McConnal will never receive any bounty money." Houston kissed her forehead, relieved this was finally over.

"I fainted. I've never done that before."

"Yes, and what do you think it does to a man's ego to find the woman he loves has fainted because he told her how he felt?"

"I love you too," she spoke so softly he had to bend close to hear the words.

"I *ken* it."

"Then," she paused, touching his chin with the tip of her finger. "Can you find me something to wear? I believe we will have company soon."

"Ah, the pounding on the stairs. I'm sure they are here only to see how you are."

"That might be true. Still, do you want others to see me like this? Even though they did when we were at Michael's, I would rather not repeat the performance."

He was grinning now, couldn't help himself. "The door is closed. However, since the small bag you packed before you left McKenna land is sitting in the corner, I'll be happy to dress you."

She hit him on the shoulder. "Tell the truth now. You'd rather undress me."

He chuckled softly looking at her, knowing the veracity of her words. The sound of more voices coming through the door from the main room stopped him.

"That sounds like Brenda." She jumped from his arms as well as the bed before rushing to the valise.

He sat back resting against the headboard, enjoying her naked rush. When she got to the point where she needed help, he pushed away from the bed though he couldn't help placing a few kisses on strategic places.

"We've a lot of explaining to do without mentioning the bounty or the fact you shifted in Michael's arms then left ten beautiful claw prints on his chest."

"I will simply tell everyone my nails did that to him."

"Yes, however, if one looks at the scratches then compares the deep cuts to your nails that will not be believable."

He watched her carefully. "Allow me and my brothers along with Hawk to make the explanations. We've been doing this most of our lives. It's easy enough to talk around what people think might have happened in addition what truly did."

"McConnal will spread his story to anyone willing to listen," Leah said softly. "He was furious to be denied all his plans."

Epilogue

Houston and Leah watched their little shifter experiment with his abilities. They laughed when the boy changed one way then back only to do the same again. In his cat, he was black as midnight, just like his proud father. Houston was pleased, a very proud papa. When he told Alistair they wanted to come to the lodge for a few days to be by themselves, he protested. "You're taking my grandson away" he told them and "what will you be doing next? Moving away?" Like Crissie, the Laird's youngest?

It took him longer than expected to reassure his father, telling him the planned to be away for only a week. He needed time with his wife. While the wedding and ensuing months had been peaceful, the two of them needed to reassure their love for each other. The house and practice Houston wanted was still in its developmental stages. While the new home and office were only half finished, the practice was prospering.

Leah leaned into his arms. "He is too precocious. Were you like that?" she asked turning to look at him.

Her eyes shimmered with passion they couldn't act on, at least not until the little one found his crib for a nap. That would be in about two hours. The dog Houston tried to give her leapt and barked around the little boy. Hawk gave her back to them after they wed. Sadie was her name.

"I was worse, a little hellion I was told," he chuckled softly nipping at her ear followed by kisses down her neck to the spot where he felt her blood pounding wildly.

The boy in his cat form was on his lap. "Seems the lad wants some attention. Doesn't like his mum getting all of my caresses."

"No, I don't suppose he would. If he's just like his father, he doesn't want to give up time."

"He's almost a year old. Should we be thinking that we should have a little girl who looks just like you?" Houston asked as his hands explored tender spots, erotic spots that he knew would leave her spineless giving the promise he was up to anything she wanted.

Leah let a long breath of air escape from her lungs while she stroked Sadie. "It's too soon. He wouldn't even be two years old when the next one is born. I don't have the energy to have an inquisitive toddler as well as a baby to take care of."

"Alistair is having trouble living it down that while he sired the first of the McKenna-Stuart, clan he has only one grandchild to show for his endeavors. Connal lords it over him whenever they are together."

"Well, that is not our problem. Seems Riley and Kit could help out with the grandchildren."

"They haven't found their mates yet," Houston said laughing. "They have to find a woman who is made for them just as I have done."

"You're right, of course. You've told me too many times to count I was made for you, made just for Houston."

"I was made for you also, made for Leah that I was. It's a proven fact. We fit each other perfectly in every way."

The years were good for Houston and Leah. They had three more children; two more boys along with one precious girl. The Sassenach continued to plague the highlands. Yet, in the ensuing years, the troubles became fewer. Their children were able to run and roam if they were careful. Still, there were members of the clan McKenna who wanted more freedom, more space. Some moved to America, heading west for the wild untamed lands that existed there. Some settled in Texas, some in the Sierra Madres.

Some of the children from both the Stuarts as well as the McKennas were part of those who left the highlands. So far away, it was hard to visit. However, they never lost track of the clan, which continued to grow and prosper.

Coming Soon by the Author

at

Rogue Phoenix Press

Say You Love Kit

Chapter One

Scotland 1651

Aila MacDuff felt desperation to the tips of her toes. Frantic to get as far from Inverness as possible, she spurred her bay mare forward. Every few seconds, she looked over her shoulder in hopes no one trailed her. Silently, she prayed.

He would come for her, follow her to the ends of the earth unless she could reach the Kinnel Stones before he caught up to her. She gambled that the man would never risk his life by following her into the huge boulders. She'd been riding now for over an hour. All the joints in her body ached. The pins she held her hair in place with were gone, vanished along the trail. Her heart thundered in her throat. What few nips of air she could press into her lungs burned painfully.

Eilig Henderson, the Earl of Gadby, a man with no heart, killed her mate. Aila hated him despite the fact or perhaps because of the circumstance he was her betrothed. The contract was drawn up two days after she was born, before she could say yes or no not that her father would have allowed her to voice her opinion. The MacDuff wanted to form an alliance with the lowlander, a man who could bring more power and wealth to him. She was his means to do so. The Henderson's paid dearly for her. Her father thought his daughter would be pleased to become a countess since Eilig was an earl. The fact the man was twenty years her senior also didn't make a bit of difference to the man who sired her. For her father it was about what he could gain. She couldn't bear the thought of lying beneath a man she despised while he heaved and grunted over her. While she wasn't certain exactly about lovemaking, she heard the servants talk.

Aila hated them both, her father as well as the earl.

Two days from Inverness the store of food she brought with her was almost depleted. She still had a loaf of bread along with a small wheel of cheese. The nights in the forest were terrifying even though she was able to find relatively safe places off the trail to sleep. The first eve of her hasty escape, she discovered sleeping with one eye open was just a phrase used. A few hours after she drew her tartan around her shoulders, she was fast asleep, awaking with the rising of the sun.

Well, at best, the following night's sleep was elusive for her. Without possessing a mirror to look, she knew there would be dark circles beneath her eyes as well as forest debris in the curls of her hair. When she jabbed her fingers through the length some pine needles along with leaves fell to the ground. If her calculations were right, she would only have to spend one more night in the woods.

The devil I pray that is so.

Once last night when she was tucked neatly beneath a bush, the pounding of hooves passed by her echoing in her ears. Certain the man on the horse was the earl or one of his minions; she scrunched as far into the thorny bush as she could scratching her hands as well as her face. Her heart pounded so loud, she felt certain he would hear.

Did Eilig *ken* where she was headed? He would never think of the Kinnel Stones. Would never believe she might want to live in a different time perhaps even a different century.

If he did, her prayers had not been answered.

Craig MacLean, her mate, told her what to do if something happened to him. She cried copious tears, begged him not to confront the earl. He heeded none of her begging as he told her they had to wed in this lifetime if they were to move on through eternity. If something happened and they did not wed before one of them passed on, they would never see each other again. They did not have the time to marry. Craig was killed before they could do so, before he could claim her or take her virginity. Truthfully, she didn't understand much of what he told her. Didn't understand about being his mate for all of time. All she comprehended was that she loved him with all her heart. She didn't want him to die. Didn't want to never see her love again.

"Promise me, Aila. Promise that you'll go to the Kinnel Stones," Craig said, his voice soft. He kissed her then, lightly on the lips. The kiss was soft and sweet, holding so much promise. The slight caress was their last.

She tried to savor every second. He pulled away to look at her, framing her face with his large hands. She tried to speak, tried to say the word he wanted to hear. All she could manage was a nod of her head.

"Meet me in the tavern in Inverness close to the castle. You know which one?" Gently, he brushed his lips across her forehead then lower to her lips. She craved for him to make love to her. Desperation flooding her, it seemed she understood this would be the last time she touched him, the last time he stroked her so tenderly.

Again she nodded. She swept her tongue across her lower lip wishing he would deepen the kiss even though she understood the pressing urgency of their situation.

If Eilig found them together, he would kill Craig. The sixth sense, the feeling Craig was going to die swamped her again and again. What Eilig would do to her when he found her, she had no idea. What she did understand is that his retribution would never be pleasant. She pictured herself locked away in an upstairs room in his mansion in Edinburgh.

Tears streamed down her cheeks, empaling her lashes with their wetness. Craig kissed her again, a deeper more demanding kiss, not one she would have liked. She yearned to feel his tongue deep inside her mouth. It wasn't to be.

"Aila," he spoke to her again, "when you go to the tavern, bring a small valise as well as food for a three day ride." He pulled out a pistol. "There is one bullet. Use it on Eilig if you have to keep him away from you. If I'm not at the tavern, it means your betrothed murdered me. Do you understand what I'm saying?" His dark brown eyes searched her, delved into her as he gazed at her.

"Y-yes, no." She shook her head, wisps of hair spilled around her face. Angrily, she brushed them from her face.

He smiled; the dimple on one side of his face tempted her to touch him. "If I'm not there wait no more than fifteen minutes. Ride to the Kinnel Stones, with luck along with destiny on our side, the stones will take you to the place where I'll be, my next life. Do you *ken*?"

Her hand rested on his chest. She sniffed back the moisture wishing she could do this without tears. "I'm afraid."

"I know. I wish I could do this with you, sweeting. You *ken* I cannot. Beyond, in another time, I will be there. Nonetheless you'll discover me in a different body. There cannot be two of us." He paused, looking toward the castle in Inverness. "Take your horse with you through the stones. You will need the little mare when you come out. Trust in your judgment, trust that the stones will take you to the right time for us to reunite."

"How will I know when I find you? Will you look like you? What will your name be?"

"As to knowing when you find me, well, I suppose you will sense the connection. The feelings will be the same as when you are with me, when you are in my arms. I'm certain I won't look like me because I will be born of other parents. My name won't be the same either."

She rested her head against his chest soaking up the strength of him, his scent his hard body next to her pressing against her. "I love you."

"Our love will carry through time. Trust me." He squeezed her shoulders. "I must leave. Heed my advice, Aila. Don't tarry at the tavern more than fifteen minutes. I'm sure the place will be safe for a short time. I doubt the man will *ken* where we would meet or that after my demise that you would dare defy him. He will expect your complete compliance."

Torn, terrified, afraid to move from the spot where she stood, Aila watched the man she loved while he walked away from her. She understood all too well he wouldn't survive the earl's men. The Earl of Gadby never played fair. He would kill him. She knew that beyond a doubt. Craig didn't stand a chance to survive the upcoming encounter.

Aila didn't know if she possessed the strength to do what Craig asked her to do. What she did understand was that she wasn't going to go through life the earl's wife nor would she live through the following years without her mate. The Kinnel Stones was her only option.

Vanquishing her terror would not be an easy task. Riding alone to the Kinnel stones would be difficult. Nonetheless the undertaking was something she would do. She didn't want her love to be disappointed in her.

As expected, Craig did not meet her at the tavern. Now, she wrapped her tartan around her, pulling the fabric close to warm her. She ate the last of the bread along with some of the cheese. With her eyes closed, she craved sleep.

When she woke, morning sunlight filtered softly through the brambles hiding her. Her mare grazed nearby. Bent over at the nearby stream, she splashed cold water on her face before sipping the cool liquid. She filled her leather bag with the water.

Straightening her shoulders, she prepared for the last leg of her journey. Well, she thought this part of her ride would be the end. What if the stones didn't send her anywhere? If they didn't, she would be right back where she started. No, if they didn't send her someplace different, she would try to ride to Glasgow, perhaps hide out somewhere in a tiny village. The earl would never search over long for her. He would seek someone else for a wife another means to gain in wealth and power.

By the time the sun reached its zenith, she stood in front of the stones. Several deep breaths didn't give her the courage to walk into them. Her hands shook, nay all of her shook. All her life she heard stories about people vanishing when they stepped inside those stones. She also heard stories of bad men being sent through to another place and time. Before now she never believed the tall tales. At this point in time, she needed to believe she wouldn't die when she stepped inside the circle of boulders.

Slowly, with hesitant steps, she walked toward the towering stones. Before she stepped inside, she patted the mare on the nose, whispering to her more to soothe her nerves than the mares.

"This will all be fine. Nothing will happen to us." She didn't believe her words. It seemed neither did her mare as she balked at entering the eerie scene.

Aila continued to whisper encouraging words. The horse began to move with her, shaking her head as if saying no. Inside, white mists floated around them. At times she could see stones, at other moments she could see nothing except the fog surrounding them. Chanting sounds swirled around them, women singing seeming to lead the way. From time to time, she felt as if something pushed her, directing her in one direction then another. The scent of jasmine surrounded her, filled her, gave her courage. She didn't understand. At one moment she felt certain she heard her mate's voice soothing her, telling her how brave she was calling out to her. She was brave. Would survive as well as prosper with him by her side.

The devil, she didn't feel brave. There was no courage in her heart. She swallowed hard, wishing for this to be over and done. The songs didn't end, the mists didn't cease swirling around her. Wayward strands of hair danced across her face, tickling her nose. She swore, pushing the damp hair behind her ears. As the moments lasted and lasted with no termination in sight, she thought each nerve she possessed would undoubtedly snap.

With her head resting against her horse's muzzle, she thought this was now the end of her. At this desperate moment the white mist began to clear. Her eyes wide open now she gazed at the open field in front of the Kinnel Stones, dazzling sunlight blinding her. This was the same field where she stood before she entered, fear holding her frozen for a few seconds before she managed to conquer the terror. From here she willingly walked into the mystery surrounding these giant edifices.

She blinked several times, questions rushing through her head. Was she still in the same time? Had she accomplished nothing by walking into the stones? All this appeared the same to her. The grass seemed longer. Well, that was a stupid thought. The clouds were different. At the moment the sun blazed overhead. In front of her a rabbit hopped across her path.

What to do now? *Put one foot in front of the other.*

The sun would go down in about two hours. She needed to find a place to sleep. Ah, should she travel back to Inverness? No, she could not. If this was still sixteen-fifty-one, the earl would find her. So, making up her mind, she decided to do as Craig told her, follow her instincts. She would first travel south then toward Glasgow. If nothing else, she would find some way to begin a new life. She lined her cloak as well as her valise with coin. Before she found work, she wouldn't starve.

I can do this.

Aila sat down on the grass to eat the last remaining cheese. What was this day, still the third day since she left? What was the year? At least she knew she was still in Scotland. To her ears the laugh she emitted did not sound real. This was so ludicrous she couldn't stop laughing. She laughed until there were tears in her eyes, until the moisture slid down her cheeks, until the laughter turned to raspy giggles. Finally, she stopped, wiped the wetness from her cheeks. Reality hit home.

I'm searching for a man. I don't know his name or what he looks like. I'm supposed to know when I meet him. Of course, he will also ken the truth about me. Ha!

Looking to the stones, she thought for a moment life might be more secure if she returned to her time. She assumed that wouldn't be possible, as she didn't believe she had a choice in the matter. The power of the stones would rule.

Heading off in the direction she came from she rode until she thought she should find her favorite bramble bush. It wasn't to be. She realized as she rode that everything looked different. Yes, this was still forest, still bushes on the sides of the roads. The trail she rode didn't appear familiar either. This was not the way back to Inverness. Her gut instinct had indeed taken over. Inadvertently, she rode south as she planned.

Just as she had done before she followed a stream. Dismounting she resigned herself to another night among the trees. Another night passed. She woke to a slight drizzle coupled with misty fog. For a moment, she thought she might have walked back to the Kinnel Stones.

Hours later she found an inn, The Black Hound the sign read. Horses were tied in front. Perhaps she would be able to rent a room for the night. She had the coin. In her cloak she rummaged for what she thought would be enough groats to pay for a room along with a meal. She tugged in a deep breath of air staring at the porch then the door. She left her mare tied next to a large stallion.

With hesitant steps, she walked up the steps to the porch. Raucous laughter reverberating from the inside met her, gave her reason for her steps to falter as she determinedly set one foot in front of the other. This was another test of her strength to her courage.

Her heart lodged in her throat. Her breaths were short pants. This was not something she would ever look forward to doing. *Craig.* Her mate could be inside that room. Might be sitting on a chair sipping a cold glass of ale. He might be one of the men singing and laughing.

She wouldn't know him if she saw him. He wouldn't know her if he saw her. What was it Craig told her? A sixth sense would lead her to the man, her mate.

Wiping her sweaty hands on her dress, she reached for the door, pulled on the heavy wood. When she stepped inside, everyone turned to look at her, the men, the barmaids, the man at the bar. The boisterous laughter and conversation rocked to a roaring stop. Silence greeted her. A prickle of fears rushed up her spine. She wanted to turn, to run, to hide.

While she gulped air, she determinedly set her chin in a haughty position then stepped forward telling herself she needed food, a hot bath as well as a safe place to sleep. More than anything she didn't wish to sleep on the forest floor again. Each footstep seemed to take longer than the last. She reached the bar then tugged in a deep breath of ale-scented air so strong she nearly gagged.

"You the new help?"

"No..." She continued to look around her, to search out the faces staring at her. A hand squeezed her fanny. She yelped then jumped away. "Stop!"

"You're going to do real well for yourself here. Can I be your first?" the man who touched her asked.

The devil, what was he talking about? His leering grin sent another rush of fear up her spine. She pushed exploring hands away from her. Trembling nerves threatened to make her run. She drug more air into her lungs, then, "Stop!" She swatted to no avail. Someone squeezed her breast. Cold revulsion swept through her.

"You can't just sashay your pretty backside in here teasing a fellow. You got to give something in return. I'll take you upstairs. You can give it to me."

No, I don't.

In a softly spoken voice, she turned to face the men finally understanding what they were asking. "I'm not for sale to any of you. All I want is to spend the night here alone. After that I'll be on my way." She hoped they understood what she meant.

They didn't.

"You can spend your night in my bed. Won't cost you a penny."

"No! You're all wrong about me." She shook her head backing against the bar holding her arms out in front of her as if the gesture would stop a man from taking what they thought she offered. When she felt the wood bump against her back, she turned to face the man selling drinks.

Hastily, she began to speak. "I'd like a room. I've coin. Also want a hot bath along with a meal." Her hand shook when she clasped the money in her pocket. The coins burned hotly against her skin.

The man stared at her, his eyes hard, accusing eyes. "The men are right. Your coming in here is only going to mean trouble. Why don't you give them what they want? Don't want any fights. They'll pay you for your service."

"I'm not for sale," she repeated firmly at least she thought her voice was strong. "I just want a room. That's all. Nothing more." At the moment thoughts of food and a bath vanished out of her mind. Swaying slightly, she was so very exhausted. Aila wasn't at all certain she could walk up those steps even if given a chance. "I've money."

"The inn is full. There are no more rooms. You should have been here a few hours ago. Lots of travelers this time of year." His voice was harsher than she thought it should be.

No rooms? Where would she go? The thought of sleeping on the cold hard ground again left her feeling miserably alone. Well, she could certainly buy some food. That would be good. He couldn't refuse her food.

A hand pressed on the small of her back. The whisper of words caressed her cheek. She felt a shudder of pleasure murmur through her. The scent of man touched her senses. For some reason the sensations floating around her didn't frighten her nor did they create revulsion in the pit of her stomach.

"Play along with me, sweetheart. I won't hurt you. Trust me." The man turned her. His length pressed against her, heating her. He was tall, broad of shoulder, handsome as the devil himself.

When he smiled warmly at her, his silver blue eyes twinkling, she felt as if she'd been cast into a spell he skillfully wove around her. Felt as if she'd known him forever. Tenderly, his lips found hers, a soft brush of lips, the slightest touch of his tongue. He held her buttocks in his hands, cupped pressed her against him. Now his strokes were more intense. He swept his tongue along her lower lip, tugged with his teeth. She gasped. When she did so, he pushed inside. Craig never did such a thing. The room seemed to turn, spinning around her. With knees threatening to buckle she clung to his shoulders her fingers digging into him.

His hands roamed across her hips finding purchase at her waist. His gaze riveted on her eyes. "I've missed you, little darling. Come, let's get something to eat. I'll protect you." He turned to the cheering men in the room. He waved his hand in silent salute. "She's mine. This little lady is mine. I was looking for her. She must have taken a wrong turn in the road."

He was presupposing as he guided her to a table in the corner. In any case, she didn't know what to say, as things for her seemed to have been going from bad to worse. She didn't want to go with this man yet she didn't believe she had much of a choice. She could hardly stand at the bar while the other men tried to take things she didn't want to give. Aila had the bizarre thought that she would most likely give this man anything he asked for.

After he made sure she sat near him, he motioned to one of the maids serving the inn. The laughter along with the talk picked up again. With this man's claim upon her, they lost interest. His large male hand rested on her thigh as if he took possession of her. She supposed the show was now over.

Aila watched as a buxom young woman sat on a man's lap, his hand down the bodice of her gown. The lady laughed, swatting his hand away. "Now, Deargh, you've got to wait 'til my shift is done." He kissed her hard, his hand staying where it was beneath the fabric.

Aila gaped at the pair, her mouth open. She turned to look at the man who brought her to the table. His grin slanted her way felt as if sunshine caressed her face. Trying to adjust to these surroundings she turned away.

Panic settling in her stomach, she glanced another look at the man who rescued her. His grin still felt as if sunshine stroked her. He nodded at the couple who were fondling each other. She wondered what it would be like to have a man touch her so. Heat flooded her face. She pressed cold hands to the fire building on her cheeks.

The devil, she'd never seen anyone so handsome as this man. His eyes twinkled merrily seeming to change from silver to blue. His shoulders were broad, his waist narrow. His hand on her leg large. She stared at him for the longest time, down his chest back to his mouth then his eyes. Craig wasn't this beautiful. Her body flamed to life in much the same way it did when she looked at her mate. Still, this time it seemed to her she flew hotter and higher than ever before.

This man wasn't her mate. Couldn't be. She wouldn't just walk into the first inn she encountered then find her mate sitting at a corner table.

He could be.

No, Craig said I would sense that he was if indeed he was. She couldn't think straight. She didn't know what to say. Her body so scorched, she couldn't sense a thing.

"Two ales," the man told the barmaid holding up two fingers. "Are you hungry?" He was laughing at her, knowing she stared at him. He squeezed her thigh. She yelped. His grin grew hotter.

"Famished," she croaked. Heat flared anew tempest soared. What the devil was he doing to her?

"For me or food?" he asked boldly as if he did that sort of thing every day. Not waiting for an answer to the absurd infuriating question, "Bring us bread and cheese, a platter of meat also." Turning to her, whispering close to her ear. "We'll taste each other later." The tip of his tongue touched her ear. He nipped.

She jumped, her body tingling with reverberating sensations.

"You arrogant..." she bit back the words. Aila wasn't about to lose out on a free meal by insulting this man further. She didn't know how long her coin would last. She was hungry, for food, not for him. Furiously angry with the man, she kept that last word she almost uttered behind her teeth.

He cocked a perfectly arched black eyebrow. His smile broad. "Beast? Is that what you were about to say?"

"Beast," she agreed her arms crossed in front of her. "Exactly."

She finished with emphasis.

He squeezed again, stroking higher then back to his original resting spot on her leg. "You should be nicer to your savior," he told her, his voice deep, darkly smooth, reminding her of slow gliding honey. His smile was bold as well as smug.

She wondered what his lips would feel like pressed tightly against hers instead of the light strokes he sent her way when he first encountered her. Nevertheless, she wasn't about to let him get away with his smug and arrogant demeanor. "Savior?" she retorted forgetting she wanted to keep him happy at least until she was fed. "How can you call yourself my savior? I was in complete control of this situation." God, how she hated the lie. She was anything but in charge.

The way he held his body spoke of superior confidence. She might be inclined to call the posture arrogant.

He tossed her a smoldering look. Without a moment in the interim he barked a hoot of laughter. "Whatever you might think, I saved you from the men in the room who weren't about to let the new tender morsel that sashayed her pretty little backside into their masculine domain leave without a taste of that sweet delight she inadvertently offered." Seeming to put emphasis on his point, he stared at her lips then her breasts.

Aila squirmed beneath his bold perusal. She'd never encountered a man anything like this one.

She supposed she deserved the scrutiny having done the same to him. Unable to stop her next retort, defiantly she tilted her chin upward once again proclaiming. "I had everything under complete control."

"If you say so." His lips twitched as if amused at her confession.

Clearly, he didn't believe her. She needed to make certain he would. "I do."

"Should I leave? You could demonstrate exactly how you would be able to sashay out of the main room without finding yourself upstairs beneath one of these men. The feat would be intriguing to watch. If that were about to happen, I might be persuaded to come to your aid again…perhaps not. Depends on what you might want to offer me in return for my services." He didn't say the words, his smirk did. He was simply asking her if she wanted him or them. The choice was blatantly obvious. If she had to choose, he won hands down.

The flush of embarrassment rushed to her face needing to let him understand how she felt about his suggestion. "You're crude."

"Honest," he retorted quickly. "I will treat you gently as you deserve to be treated."

"I'm a lady. I wouldn't allow something like that to happen. Wouldn't allow men to just have their way with me. I won't allow you to do so either. You're too presumptuous by far." Craig told her too many times to count that her station in life wouldn't stop a man who wanted her from taking what she didn't offer. Also told her she should always guard her temper. The annoyance she so easily exhibited could garner her a wealth of trouble. While he enjoyed watching her in a rage, most men would not. If she angered them, they would put her in her place. Wherever that was she didn't know. Craig didn't tell her. She supposed now that since she was in a different time, she wouldn't have a station. She was no longer a lady. That fact didn't bother her at all. If she wasn't a lady, there would be no expectations about her behavior.

The arrogant man leaned back, his arms crossed over his chest, still grinning still showing off his even white teeth. She understood he was about to take umbrage as to her claim. "Hmm...a lady with pine needles as well as leaves in her hair." He squinted those silver blue eyes at her as if in complete concentration. "Do I see the top of an acorn in those bright red strands of hair? Quite the fashion now days, don't you think?"

Sucking in air she decided to ignore his comment. Since he baited her, she thought a change of subject might help. So, she blurted the first question that popped into her head only to immediately regret the query, "What year is this?"

His masculine all-knowing smirk widened before he sat forward, his forearms on the table his eyes ablaze with laughter, "Are you trying to sidetrack me? Just when the conversation was getting interesting, you ask something ridiculous. Is this a game to you? What exactly do you play at?"

Yes, she guessed to someone who knew the answer to her query, she would seem crazy. She still wanted to know. At the moment it seemed prudent to her to continue. She tilted her head a bit to the side.

After that to ease the ache of three nights sleeping on the forest floor, she ran her hand along the back of her neck, the soreness increasing with the zealous interrogation. So exhausted, she was having a devil of a time keeping her wits. She lifted her shoulders in what she hoped was a devil-may-care shrug. "I was just curious if you knew."

He hooted with laughter, his eyes alight with amusement. "If I knew? What the devil are you talking about? It's seventeen-fifty-one. The month happens to be March if you would like to know that also, March first to be exactly precise. The time is, he pulled out a pocket watch, four-thirty-three in the afternoon not morning. Are there any more questions? Within reason or even beyond reason, I'll be delighted to answer anything you wish to enquire about."

Swallowing the lump in her throat, she realized Craig's ploy worked. The Kinnel Stones took her forward one hundred years to the day. She prayed she would not have to look over her shoulder to make sure her betrothed wasn't following her. With that thought fear ricocheted through her. Perhaps for her purposes she should allow this man to become her savior in all ways. She was exhausted from traveling alone, from constantly looking over her shoulder.

The barmaid set the tray of food he ordered on the table before handing them each a glass of ale. Looking at the food her mouth watered. Her stomach rumbled loudly enough to catch his attention.

"Help yourself," he said softly, his eyes taking on a soft silver hue appearing concerned for her. "Thought you looked hungry. Understood the hunger wasn't just for me. The way you kissed me though… could give a man other ideas."

Refusing to give credence to his unfinished statement, she remained quiet. They ate in silence for a few minutes. Ravenous, she ate until she finally felt satisfied. The food along with the ale was delicious. Replete for the moment, she leaned back.

"When was the last time you ate?" His question didn't truly surprise her after the amount she just devoured.

Feeling as if the bottom was about to drop, Aila didn't want to answer so she changed the subject to something more palatable. She didn't want him to feel responsible for her. Didn't want any man to feel protective of her until she found her mate. This man was not her mate. He wasn't anything like Craig. That was who she was looking for, someone who would at least act like the man she loved. Craig didn't posses any of the characteristics of this particular male. He definitely wasn't arrogant or over-confident. Craig never wanted to control the situation. He was always pleased to allow her the last say. The man she knew from one hundred years in the past would never kiss a woman he didn't know.

"What is your name?" She thought as long as they were having this strange conversation she would like to know who she was speaking to.

One of his dark eyebrows tilted upward. He sat back sipping his drink, eyeing her critically as if he heard all her unique convoluted thoughts. "Good question, you go first?"

She didn't want to answer him. Understood she should. So, she waited for what she wasn't all that certain.

~ * ~

When the woman stepped through the door of the inn, Kit Stuart knew he'd never seen a woman so beautiful. She was so damn beautiful, his mouth dropped open, his breath caught in the back of his throat while a tiny bit of drool slid from the corner of his mouth. For the longest time she stood framed in the doorway. Midafternoon light set her fiery red hair in glowing flames surrounding delicate features. He wondered if her temperament fit the color of her hair. Understood he'd enjoy her temper. All the men in the room had the same reaction to her beauty as he did. Way too many minutes passed while he stared at her, stared until he was spurred into action by the chatter around him.

By the words he overheard, the lady would end up in someone's bed tonight. The thought of this woman in another man's bed was untenable. This evening, he damn well meant to make certain the only bed she slept in was his. The devil, she was tall. Although she was thin, her womanly curves were generous. The way the fabric of her dress curved around her breasts, he could tell the tender globes would overflow his large hands. The violet shimmer of her eyes also caught his attention, the color unusual. Unique as he believed she would be.

At his first approach, he wasn't positive how he would handle the primary meeting. Several ideas plummeted through his thoroughly male brain, all of the notions completely sensual. Perhaps he would save her from the lecherous uncouth men in the inn then she would be his. He watched her waver, stagger a bit. Either she was intoxicated or she was exhausted. She stopped briefly. Saw her tilt her tiny chin just so as if she meant to proceed brashly through the sea of men. To get through the pack of male animals, wanting her she would need more than brazenness to succeed. He deliberated about what exactly it was she wanted here.

Kit always treated his lady friends gently, reverently, with the utmost respect. Women were important in all things even though they were the weaker sex. His heart beat harder than he was used to when he saw a beautiful woman. Of course, he'd never seen the likes of one this dazzling. His gave drifted over her exquisite features once more. His body hardened with the immediate sizzle of lust.

What the devil was she doing in these parts alone, unescorted? Whoever was responsible for her should lecture her little rear until she couldn't sit for a week. These were bold thoughts from a man who would never lay an angry hand on a woman's backside or any other part of her anatomy. In time, he would discover why she was alone. Rushing her to reveal private as well as intimate facts about herself was not his style.

During the last month, the Kinnel Stones seemed to call out his name. Comprehending that fact was beyond him. Nevertheless, once or twice a week he made his way north to the stones. He would stay at this inn, The Black Hound Inn each time. He didn't understand. After he stayed a few nights, riding the area, searching for some elusive thing, he would continue on to the McKenna hunting lodge. Perhaps this woman with unusual eyes was the reason for his travel. If she wasn't the reason, she was definitely a bonus.

This week was no different. His parents thought he was actually bordering on crazy especially when he couldn't give them a reason why. His actions puzzled him just as much they did his mother and father. This instance, however, he might find a tiny reward in all the travel. He would have a softly beautiful woman for the night.

The woman was beautiful, her hair a fiery red, her flesh a soft ivory with no apparent freckles. He wouldn't care if her nose sported a few, as he believed kissing each one would be quite intoxicating. With not even a word from her, she was generating an inferno of need inside him. Her smile twisted his heart in too many different direction to keep count.

His fingers drummed on the table as he waited for the answer to his question. Even in her state of dishabille, his gaze was drawn to her breasts along with the sweetly seductive lips of hers; moist now with the ale she sipped. His mouth watered to taste every gorgeous inch of her. Beneath his scrutiny she moved slightly. Squirmed might be a better word. Hell, she stared at his mouth then his chest. She gazed lower. The table was in the way of what she seemed to want to see. There wasn't a doubt in his mind her sightseeing would have stopped at his crotch. Now it was his turn to squirm. He needed a change of direction.

"Believe I asked you your name."

The woman lifted her delicate shoulders as if she was thinking why not placate this man. "Aila."

"Beautiful name." Not as breathtaking as the woman, yet nice enough, "Aila what?" he queried hoping to reap more information than she seemed willing to put forth.

"Why?"

Because, he thought warily, he wanted to know who he was going to make love to this evening. This was his turn to heave his shoulders upward a disgruntled feeling in the pit of his stomach. "Why not?" This was far too soon for him to give out clues to his intentions for the evening. Although he was certain she would figure out his plans in time. There was the question of her willingness even though she eagerly returned the earlier kiss.

Kissing wasn't making love.

She let out a long puff of air, sending the tiny leaf still attached to one strand of her curly hair near her eyebrow upward for a brief moment. He wanted to pluck the acorn top out of her hair so that he might feel a strand or two. Wished to know if the silken strand would heat his skin. Her gaze turned to the door before she relocated her sights on his mouth. Slowly, she ran her tongue across her bottom lip, a tiny pink one. His blood was fired and hot, a lightning strike to his loins. He'd never experienced such an intense reaction. If she wasn't an experienced lady, she was certainly acting like one. At first sight she seemed almost virginal.

"Aila MacDuff," she finally told him her finely created shoulders rising then falling, causing her breasts to sway slightly against the lavender muslin of her gown. Her gaze shifted to her hands that were wrapped around her glass of ale.

"Now." He leaned forward, wresting her fingers from the glass before clasping them in his hands. They were cold hands, trembling inside his warmth. He looked more closely at her. She seemed to be shivering. He didn't know what to think. "Was that so hard?"

Visibly she bristled, wrenching her hands back to settle them in her lap. "Your turn."

He grinned uncertain why exactly he was egging her on. His name around here was no secret. Every man in this room knew he was part of the McKenna clan, second son to Alistair Stuart. He wondered why this woman needed to ask.

"Why should I tell you something you know? Every person in this room *kens* who I am. That's why they let you alone when I claimed you." Claimed her...he had in a way. She couldn't possibly be his mate. He would sense the fact. Houston, his brother, knew the moment he saw Leah. He needed to take care before he did something stupid. His older brother had botched everything up when it came to his mate. At the time, he promised himself that wouldn't happen to him. Taking this second by second seemed imperative.

Her eyes darkened perceptibly then turned purple with seeming anger. She shook her head, the ragged strands of red hair dancing around her shoulders. The acorn popped out. One hand emerged from her lap. A finger pointed at him. He felt certain if she could reach him, she'd be prodding him in the chest with that skinny little finger. Damn, the finger wasn't skinny, no, it was long and slim, he wanted to taste the tip, sample that part of her, yearned to sample every sweet part of her.

"I *dinna ken* your name, you ass."

For a moment, her language startled him. He sat back, revising his opinion. The unexpected smile erupted on his face, the hoot of laughter coming next. He liked the sound of the words coming from behind her lips. Still, grinning, he watched her breasts sway with her apparent fury, knew at that moment she would be passionate in everything she did.

"Ass?" He sent an eyebrow upward knew the gesture would

irritate her too. Something inside him enjoyed every part of her including the passion, the fury he could so easily provoke.

"Yes!" She sat back crossing her arms beneath those tempting globes of hers, sending them up toward the heavens. He wondered what color exactly the tips would be. Well, they were high enough the rounded parts peered more openly from the cut of her gown. The corsage wasn't low; the sweet sight came because of her actions. If he gave her cause for more annoyance, perhaps the crests would show. In that case, he would discern the color. The thought was intriguing.

After a moment of consideration, perhaps he decided where she was concerned he was an ass. "Everyone in these parts of the highlands knows who I am. You should also know my name."

"I don't."

"Well then, let me introduce myself."

Before he could finish with the polite, at least he believed his words to be polite, she blurted abruptly, "It's about time."

Taken aback, this time he kept his laughter behind his teeth, "Kit Stuart, your savior as well as at your service."

"Was that so hard?" she asked her breasts heaving her chin tilted defiantly. "A name is just a name, hardly something to hold behind the owners teeth."

He let his head fall back hooting with laughter amused more than he could remember. She was definitely one of a kind. "Eat some more. When you are sated, we will pursue this conversation in a more private atmosphere."

"I couldn't eat another bite." She stared hard at him her lips thinning perceptively, her eyes widening as if she suddenly understood what he was telling her. "Private atmosphere?"

This was where he needed to proceed with caution. "Do you plan to stay in the common area of the inn all night? I can assure you Mr. McIntosh will not allow something so brazen. There are no rooms available for you to rent. I suppose I assumed you would rather stay with me than one of these other men. Perhaps you would like more twigs, as well leaves to adorn your person. Was I wrong?"

"I guess you're the lesser of the evils I'm presented with at the moment. Another night on the cold ground is not acceptable either." She stood up so quickly the chair behind her toppled to the ground with a loud bang, garnering the attention of everyone in the room.

After the crash, all eyes turned toward them. She shivered rubbing her hands along her bared arms. Kit held his hand out to her. In the other hand, he clasped her small valise as well as her cape. Aila didn't appear to know how to proceed. She had the appearance of a trapped animal caught between two opposing forces. Yes, Kit thought she might truly be walking to her destiny. The more time he spent with this elusive creature the more certain he was that in some capacity they would share the next few months together perhaps even longer. One fact for certain flashed into his brain. She would never bore him. The very nature of how she affected his body gave him good reason to set aside any and all notion of acting the gentleman.

Kit had never been stared at in the manner she now looked at him. Yes, he was tall and broad. His buff breeches were tailored specifically for his broad legs, sturdy legs he liked to think. Some of the women he'd seen intimately used other words to describe him. Next to him she felt fragile, uncertain at best. Her future now was held in his hands, his rather large hands. He liked that feeling knowing his protection of her would come at a small cost to her.

He would make sure Aila enjoyed the time they would have together. The cottage about a mile from his parents' house would do fine for her home. He would fix it up to her liking. Kit enjoyed the idea of her becoming his new mistress. Several weeks ago, he dismissed his mistress in Inverness. She bored him to tears. There was nothing there for him. He didn't' enjoy the day and a half ride just to see her. He'd felt reckless. His need to find something more in life tore at him. As his older brother found his mate, he yearned for the same. Houston and Leah had a child now, a boy who was just turning one. The young lad was also experimenting with shifting.

Well, the time was too soon to make assumptions about Aila. Just because he wanted to be her savior didn't make him the man who she would travel with through eternity. No, not for one moment in time did he belief she would become more to him. His parents told him he would sense the connection. What he sensed about Aila was that he wanted her now. Tomorrow would be too late.

At the foot of the stairs, she hesitated. While he'd thought earlier that she was so exhausted she wouldn't be able to walk up those steps, reality seemed to be intruding. The ale along with the food probably helped give her a bit of strength. At the moment, she wavered. He wrapped his arm around her waist supporting her in the endeavor that should have been easy for her.

"Let me help you." He smiled into her upturned face. "You're as weak as a newborn kitten."

She leaned into him, allowing him to ease her way up the stairs. When they finally entered the room, he bade her sit.

"Your bath is ordered along with a bottle of wine. You've a few things to tell me tonight if you can remain awake." He paced the room, waiting for the hot water to appear. The conversation he intended could be delayed until she was able to refresh herself perhaps, remove the pine needles adorning her hair.

Her gaze followed him while he strode around the room. Occasionally, her stares would linger on the bed. He wasn't going to sleep on the floor in his room, neither was Aila. He was certain she did not wish to broach that subject this instant.

Before the water arrived, he spoke softly to her. "I'll return in fifteen minutes. You will answer some of my questions."

She flashed him a gaze that told him when hell freezes over. He chuckled as he opened the door to servants bringing the steaming hot water. Her eyes widened in seeming pleasure. To know her thoughts circling inside her woman's brain would delight him.

He would have liked to stay to watch. That would have been too highhanded for even him. Striding down the steps to the common room, he looked over the patrons. The time had grown late. Most of the customers left to go to their homes. A few of the men, who sought favors from the barmaids after the bar closed, lingered.

When he stepped onto the porch fresh air assailed him. Unable think of anything to do while he waited for her, he strode around outskirts of the inn. Having more thoughts about Aila as well as how she got to the inn, he made his way to the stable. His ebony stallion was tethered in one of the stall. Kit stroked his nose.

Whispering to the horse, "I wonder where she came from as well as wear she is going. She is closed up tight. No matter how different she is she will have to come to trust me. I've the sinking suspicion she has no one. What the devil was she doing asking about the year?" He needed the answers, not his suppositions.

He spotted a beautiful bay mare in the stall next to his stallion. Giving his attention to the horse, he stroked her nose.

"It's the ladies mount," the stable boy told him as he approached. "She paid me to brush her down then give her his feed."

Kit nodded, understanding a tiny bit more about the lady. She had some money. He wagered, though she didn't have a lot. "I will pay you when we leave. Whatever you do, don't accept coin from her."

"Whatever you say." The boy shrugged.

At this time Kit wasn't all that sure what he wanted concerning Aila. On one hand, he wanted to make certain she would rely on him for all her needs. On the other hand, he didn't want her to pay for anything understanding she would run out of funds soon enough if left to her devices. Once that happened, she would lean on him for her support.

She needed coin of her own. He didn't want her to possess one groat. At odds with his thinking, he groaned deeply.

If she had the means, she might leave him. That wouldn't do at all. After he left the barn, he stared in the direction of the Kinnel Stones. A peculiar feeling washed over him. The sensation rippling through every part, dancing in his head as if there was something he didn't understand. He turned to the light shining from his room. Her silhouette moved through the space. She finished her bath.

He supposed the time had come for a confrontation of sorts. He would bathe first though. The water had seemed *verra* appealing.

Stopping only to order more hot water, he eagerly two-stepped his way up the stairs. He knocked softly on the door before entering. She stood by the window, dressed in a virginal white nightdress, her fingers winding through each other.

"Nervous?" he baited her hoping to see her eyes flash with anger, changing color at the same time.

She held her bottom lip beneath her teeth he suspected to stop it from trembling. Her eyes flashing dangerously. "Of course, wouldn't you be? This isn't something I would do under normal circumstances."

She was right. The situation was anything save normal. "Wouldn't I be nervous? Hmm...no, I'm not in the least bit anxious. In fact I'm looking forward to the next weeks with you." He pulled his shirttail from his breeches. "Especially tonight."

"What are you doing?" Ignoring her he walked to the door. More hot water was brought into the room. He waited until the servants left to speak again. "Taking a bath."

"You can't!" Her panicked voice reached him.

He turned, thoroughly relishing the moment understanding what her answer would be. "Why? Certainly you've seen a man's body." His shirt on the floor he divested himself of his black boots. Ah, he wiggled his freed toes. "Yes, that feels very good."

"You will be quite naked is why. As a matter of fact, I haven't." Her indignation charmed him.

He hooted with laughter. He wasn't at all certain he believed her. "Never take a bath wearing my clothes. Is that what you would wish."

Her hands were now fisted tightly, settled on her hips. The gesture pulled her virginal gown tight across her breasts. Inwardly, he groaned. He saw the taut hard nipples he thought to uncover later, perhaps not tonight. Nonetheless, he would see all of her soon.

"If you don't like the look of me naked, you can close your eyes."

His entire length of him burned. Prudence told him she might faint if she witnessed his totally aroused body. "You should go sit by the fire. Your hair should be dry before we go to bed. Wet hair is unpleasant," he told her his voice gruff with the need the vision of her created in his head. He didn't wait to see if she obeyed. Turning his back to her, he divested himself of his clothing. He slipped into the water. A long sigh of pleasure left his lips.

Quickly, he washed then dried. He donned clean clothes before he padded to the chair next to hers.

"You," she swallowed, "you are not a gentleman."

"Did you peek?" He chuckled, liking the way her mouth quivered with the statement. She probably didn't. He felt a nagging need to tease as well as question. "Do I meet with your approval?"

A rosy glow painted her cheeks. She'd closed her eyes for a few seconds while he studied the dark lashes fanned across those bright pink cheeks. She did have a few very faint freckles across the bridge of her nose. The sight was endearing.

"No..."

"I think you did. Admit it, tell me you gave into your curiosity and took a quick look at me." His chuckle was softly teasing. "Did you like what you saw?" Kit didn't believe for one instant she would admit to anything. Nonetheless, he wanted to see the spark in those beautiful violet eyes when she denied his accusation. It was easy to see, she was not adept at lying.

"You have taken a lot for granted." Visibly bristling, she told him instead, a sickeningly sweet smile plastered on such sweetly kissable lips he lost all train of thought.

He handed her a glass of wine believing now was the right time to discuss their future, at least tonight into next morning. She should understand exactly what he intended for them. "Aila, you've no place to stay this night. You should thank me instead of glare at me as if I'm the devil incarnate. After all, I'm doing you a favor."

She sighed softly, her breasts moving delightfully beneath the nightgown that did more to reveal than she could possibly be aware of. He was certain she believed the fabric concealed her enchanting female charms. "I know." She twirled the stem of her glass watching the dark red liquid move within. "I will pay you half the cost of the room."

"Don't want money from you. You can trust me." Gently, he stroked her cheek then continued the light touch along her neck until his fingers rested on the rapidly beating pulse at the base. He was pleased with the result of his light caress. "Tell me what you are looking for."

"No, no..." She was shaking her head. "If I tried to explain my circumstances you wouldn't believe me. You would call me a liar or believe me crazy. I cannot. No, no..."

"Try me." Kit felt a very real need to not only coax her into his bed but to also gain her trust. "I won't judge. I would never consider you to have lost your senses."

She squirmed pressing the length of her gown down her sides. His breath caught in the back of his throat. His heart raced. By the expression on her face, he felt sure he wouldn't like what she was about to say. The next words rushed from her lips. "All I can say is that I'm looking for someone, someone who will be *verra* dear to me in the ensuing years. If I don't find him, I *dinna ken* what I will do. I've no one here, you see." With that said, she turned from him to gaze at the leaping flames in the fireplace.

At her statement, Kit's heart lodged in his throat, leapt with anger it didn't seem he could tamp down. "Him?" He didn't like the way that sounded. Not if he could help it, she wasn't going to search for a him, for another man. She was his.

"I shouldn't have said that." Touching her fingers to her lips, she looked away from him, the length of her hair brushing against her gown covering her more thoroughly than he appreciated.

He needed her complete cooperation. "Shouldn't be honest with me?" he queried, his antagonism growing still. This blind rage was an emotion he'd never met with before. "While you are with me you won't be looking for anyone, especially some man." The need to comprehend more rushed within. Wanted her to tell him the man's name so he could shoot him. No, he'd rather strangle him with his bare hands.

"Who is it that you are looking for?" He tried for a calm soothing voice. If she saw his anger, she would never confide or trust.

She drank down half the glass of wine. A small film of dampness coated her lips. When next she looked at him, moisture clouded her eyes violet hued eyes. Her words erupted in a thin wail. "I don't know."

That was passing strange. There was more here than she was saying. "So, any man will do." Kit didn't understand the blazing fury he felt at her words. "Am I any man? Will I do in a pinch?" He wanted to shake her until her teeth rattled, until she would admit to wanting him as much as he wanted her. Until she realized he must be the man she searched to find.

"No."

"No what?"

Breathing in deeply, she seemed to brace herself before she could say her next words. "You're not any man." A long pause followed while he willed himself to let her finish. "I *dinna ken* what you mean by do in a pinch."

His Aila was too damn naïve. She had no idea what the havoc she created in him or what exactly he wanted with her. He needed to believe her. He understood that was a good thing. Again he tried to tamp down his pressing fury coupled with the deep possessiveness simmering too close to the surface. "Do you know the man's name?"

"No."

Kit didn't understand anything. He could only make assumptions he didn't like. "So, you would give yourself to this unknown man instead of spending the next few weeks and months with me, under my protection?" He felt incensed, enraged that she didn't want him. He didn't understand nor did he comprehend what to do about it. Something like this never happened to him before.

"Yes."

"You won't! Not for as long as I live!" Kit still didn't understand where the fury came from. This woman was his. She belonged to him. No way in hell was she going to search for another man! He would tie her to their bed if she tried. There was no reason for his anger. All she did was state a fact as she saw it. There was more to this. She wasn't telling him everything.

He stuffed a breath of air into his lungs before jabbing his hands into his hair. She stared at him, her mouth slightly open her eyes so wide and violet, the sight stole the last remaining air in his lungs.

He needed to go for another walk. *Nay*, he needed to shift then run as his cat. Settling for a walk would have to suffice.

~ * ~

Eilig Henderson, the Second Earl of Gadby, paced the dark airless room he called his office. He killed the bastard Craig MacLean before he could shake Aila's whereabouts from the man's closed lips and defiant eyes. This was a hell of his making. He no longer knew what to do. The chit could be anywhere in Scotland. Hell, by now she could be headed anywhere in the world. Ships left the Inverness port every day. All Craig told him was that she was beyond his reach, that he would never lay his hands on her. Beyond his reach, what the devil did that mean?

Where in tarnation was he going to search for her? One of his spies told him she headed west into the most desolate part of the highlands. The man followed her for two long nights and three days. He must have passed by her on the second night of his surveillance. His hireling wasn't even positive the woman he followed was Aila. All he could tell him was that the woman had bright red hair. This woman might have been a decoy to lead him astray. Traveling west would not bring her to the port of Inverness.

When the man least expected to see her, believed he lost the woman he followed, he came across her riding in front of him. Where she was headed he certainly had no idea. Now, following her was more difficult. The land was barren of trees. He had to stay at least a curve or two even a hill behind her. When he would crest a hill, he would wait until she moved on always west.

What he finally saw stole every last bit of air from his body. Aila MacDuff, if the woman he shadowed was Aila, she would not ever be the earl's bride. The woman along with her horse walked into the Kinnel Stones. That was a place haunted by tales. No one who entered there was ever seen again.

Curiously, he approached the stones where she entered. White mist swirled inside the stones. The fog so dense he couldn't see her or the mare she brought inside with her. Soft chanting filled the air around him the sound compelling him to answer urging him forward. Quickly, he backed up not wishing to be tempted further. He waited for over two hours before he turned to leave. The news he had to impart to the earl would not be taken well.

When he heard the tale, Eilig's fist hit the table hard while he thought about all that his spy told him. He rehashed every word in his brain. Memorized what the man said. His fortune was in dire straights if he couldn't retrieve the woman. He needed an heiress, a rich one to pay his gambling debts. He also needed her fortune to repair his two homes. He would bed her until she bore him a son. After that he would find a means to divest himself of his unwanted wife. She was a fey creature. Most likely there would be little to no enjoyment in bedding her. He didn't care. The use of her body for the time it took for her to conceive a male child would have to satisfy him.

As his wife, she was his to do with what he pleased.

Nonetheless, what he understood at the moment was that he would need to risk everything to follow her into the Kinnel Stones. The man told him she did not come out of the stones. He waited and watched for her to emerge. What if the rumors about that bizzare place were true? If he followed her inside, he might not ever be able to return.

Nothing mattered in the present, if he didn't get her back. If he didn't wed her, returning to this time wouldn't be worth his wile. His life was in shambles, his estates falling down around him. This was his one chance. None of the other eligible women would have anything to do with him. Their doting parents understood what he could not give their daughters. Understood his vagaries. Aila's father didn't care.

Eilig made the only logical decision he could make. Two days later after setting his estate in order, he set off for the stones, a small valise in hand. He had enough money to see him through weeks of searching for the woman who threatened his very existence who if not found would make his life a living hell. He prayed the funds he left in the Edinburgh bank would still be available to him in whatever year he surfaced. When he unearthed her, he would drag her back through the stones. At that time, he would pray they would end up in the right year as well as the right place. He would keep her locked up until she agreed to marry him.

Sitting atop his horse a few feet from the Kinnel Stones, his life flashed in front of him. For a moment, his heart ceased to beat. Sweat ran down his face. He stared at those huge stones for far too long dreading the irrevocable step he was about to take. His courage vanished. He swore to himself. If he didn't return with her, his life was over. For him there was no choice, no choice at all.

Heaving a deep breath, he placed one step in front of the other until he was inside. His horse reared. He kept the reins tightly in his fist, as he would need the mount when he stepped outside the stones if he lived to step outside.

Black instead of white mist circled around him. Evil, wicked chanting pushing, dragging him to bump into stone after stone until he was bruised from the beating he was undergoing. The noise he encountered sounded malevolent, even to his battered senses. Soundly pushed from behind he hit a stone. He groaned at impact.

Suddenly everything stopped. He felt as if he'd just been whisked away. The blackness evaporated as if hit by a scalding sun. He blinked several times while he stared through the space between the stones. His heart skipped a beat. He was suddenly free to make his decisions.

It was as if he went nowhere. Even with that sensation assailing him, he understood he'd been pushed to another time. The same field of heather sat in front of him. Rolling grass over hills looked the same as when he walked inside the stones. He didn't know what to think.

He was alive! Eilig Henderson slid his hands along his thighs wiping away the moisture. In all his life he'd never been in such an ordeal, the black mist, the chanting, the pushing coupled with the clawing. All the while he expected to die. Now he stood on the other side of the Kinnel Stones. His horse nickered softly beside him.

The sky was dark, black as sin. It must be night of what year? He stuck his hand in front of his face. It was the barest shadow. This was not the time to be wandering in the highland crags. He knew first hand there would be *reavers* afoot. For him sending men to steal from the English crossing the borders of Scotland had been a fine way of making extra groats. *Reavers* could also be found in the highlands.

His stomach rumbled hungrily. Hesitantly, he placed one foot in front of the other.

He decided he could be anywhere in time. Could be in the same time. At least he was in Scotland, not some foreign country where he wouldn't know the language. He tugged in a deep breath of air feeling a bit of courage surge through his blood stream.

Where would Aila go?

What would a woman alone as well as frightened decide? Eilig tried to put himself in the frame of mind of a young terrified woman. He couldn't. What he did decide was that she most likely wouldn't head back to Inverness. She would find herself in the same pickle as he was. No, just as he didn't *ken* what the year was, she wouldn't either. She wouldn't want to risk him finding her if she'd not moved on in time.

Aila was no fool. She would head south then west so she could lose herself in a small village or even a larger city such as Glasgow. She held a two-day head start over him. She was a woman. A woman would encounter problems that would never plague a man. He hoped he got to her before she lost her virginity. Her innocence was his to take from her. Her maidenhead didn't belong to another man. Craig MacLean was a fool for not sampling her.

He grinned then set his horse on a path he prayed would lead him straight to Aila.

The next evening he rode up to The Black Hound Inn. He handed his reins over to the stable boy. With confidence that he would discover she had been here, he sauntered up the steps then into the bar. He found a table in the middle of the room. After all he didn't wish to hide. He wanted to discover if the flame-haired violet-eyed woman had come this way. If she hadn't he'd have to think on her destination again. Perhaps he should head west if he didn't ascertain anything new.

He grinned when he discovered she came this way. His grin turned to a scowl when the little barmaid sitting beguilingly on his lap told him she went with Kit Stuart two mornings before this. Anger furrowed in his heart when she told him that Kit's family was powerful, also that he came from a wealthy clan. While he wasn't a Lord, the family held an immense amount of land. She finished by adding to what she previously said that they were rich as Midas.

Well, he would have to tread carefully. Would need to consider each move he made.

Connal's Eternal Love
Sweet McKenna Book One

A few days shy of All Hallows' Eve Connal McKenna, Laird of Clan Chattan stands on the parapets of his castle. Bonfires line the hillsides while his clan prepares for the upcoming festivities. Drawn by the whispering of the wind, Connal McKenna feels a strange restlessness in his soul. Setting out to discover the wickedness that is calling to him, he discovers his mate. With gentle words and sensuous kisses, the auburn-eyed highlander conquers his mate, the beautiful, defiant Wynnie Adair who he comes upon during an evening ride. She must ultimately put her trust in the only man who can save her from the ruthless plans of her father and succumb to his gentle coaxing.

In Brady's Arms
Sweet McKenna Book Two

Forced to run from the only home she knows, beautiful, headstrong Lillian Townsends seeks shelter in the wild highlands where the McKenna clan live. Trying to avoid a betrothal contract signed by her stepfather to an aging lord, she is desperate to find a means to sidestep the inevitable, including a marriage to the oldest son of the laird. Lilly is enamored of the young lord who pursues her with unrelenting determination flashing his devilishly handsome charms. She is hard pressed to resist.

Besotted from the first moment Brady McKenna sees Lilly, he is determined to find a means to coax her into his arms and bed. With only the promise of carnal pleasure as his mistress, Brady relentlessly pursues the woman who has unwittingly forged a place in his heart. She is like no other woman, proud, defiant and enchanting. Despite his father's advice to stay away from her, he cannot. He boldly seeks her out and makes her his own.

Nobody but Walker
Sweet McKenna Book Three

The Highland Lass...

She was brought up, adored and loved by a doting mother and father ardently protected by her brothers. She was everything sweet and innocent until she was faced with betrayal and an unexpected and out of wedlock pregnancy. When she gave her love to a man who couldn't return her passion and commitment, she was left devastated and furious. Faced with the loss of her child if she didn't comply to his demands, Crissie McKenna followed him to Belfast then on to his country home to discover he was already married.

...The Irishman

Stunned to find out his one and only encounter with the woman he wanted to love forever created a child, Walker Endicott, Earl of Briarwood, claimed his child as his only heir. Walker threatened all her previously held values even while he thrilled her senses. From the moment he first saw her to the second she ran after him begging him to make love to her, his captivating masculinity held her fascinated. In his arms she would know tempestuous passion, bitter despair, and a soaring joy that would humble them both before the power of love.

Roby's Moonlit Night
Sweet McKenna Book Four

Once she'd been a pampered child with high expectations for her future blessed with love. Then she became an innocent pawn in a terrible game of greed and power. Now, with a noose around her neck, Pippa was to hang before she had the chance to unveil the men who drove her from her home, before she had the chance to live.

Roby McKenna was a man blessed with endless charm and wit. While he searched for his eternal love across the Atlantic in a new land, he would have to come home to find her. His silver blue eyes could sparkle with amusement or harden to steel gray with displeasure. He had all the women a man could want or need. As he grew older, mistresses were not enough. A quirk of fate brought him to the gallows, a spark of destiny made him claim the condemned Pippa as his bride.

My Sweet Broc
Bad Boys Book One

He's a bad bad boy...

Broc Wallace is a fun-loving rake who never thought any beautiful woman could melt his heart. He lives life in the present enjoying the camaraderie of his friends and the pleasures of his mistress. When Bliss races into his life, he is ill prepared to deal with her secrets or give up the tenor of his life. When the truth is revealed, he finds himself unable to forgive and forget the betrayal.

...but she's sweet for him

Bliss MacTavish knows she's playing with fire when she refuses to tell this bad boy her name. He tempts her with sweet whispers of seduction knowing her innocent nature will be unable to refuse all he yearns to give her. Deciding to follow her heart, she finds the repercussions more than she bargains for when she gives herself to this bad boy.

Crazy for Cam
Bad Boys Book Two

He's a bad bad boy...

Lord Cam MacEwen, Viscount of Rosehill, tries his best to be proper and court the lady of his dreams in the acceptable way. The feat proves impossible when the lady in question uses every means at her disposal to tempt him. He fights his jealousy for another man as well as the need to make her his own, finally giving in to her irresistible passion.

...but she's crazy for him.

Chelsea MacTavish wants the bad boy she fell in love with and kissed just before her eighteenth birthday. With feminine wiles and irresistible allure, the sensuous lady plans to best Cam at his game of hearts and make him forget his need to court her properly.

Falling for Flynt
Bad Boys Book Three

He's a bad, bad boy...

Fascinated by Hope's loss of memory yet haunted by her sultry beauty, Flynt is irresistibly drawn to the stoic miss—and into her troubles with the sultan who wants her for himself. When he discovers she is the sister of his best friend, his pride keeps him from pursuing her and making her his.

...but she's falling for him.

Raised in a harem but now penniless, alone and without her memory, Hope must discover a way to remember all that she has lost. She finds a way to continue with her life as a servant in Flynt's home. The first sight of Flynt steals Hope's breath as well as her heart. Can she overcome her fears and give herself to the man she fell in love with.

Dancing With Donal
Bad Boys Book Four

He's a bad bad boy...

Once a bad boy always a bad boy, Donal Chamberlin's carefree ways come crashing down around him when he meets the ravishingly beautiful Daryl MacTavish, the innocent little sister of one of his best friends. He is determined to win her heart as he sets his sights on marriage and an heir. His past gets in the way of his quest when a woman he once loved threatens Daryl's life.

...but she's dancing with him.

Daryl has seen the control her sister's husbands hold over them. She yearns for a life where she makes decisions for herself. No man will have power over her. But no man kisses her the way Donal does. No man can make her forget all her goals leaving her helpless to give up her dreams. Yet Donal is determined to dance through all the barriers she thrust in front of him, pursuing her until she says yes.

Loving Leslie
Bad Boys Book Five

He's a bad bad boy...

Leslie Stewart, Duke of Southcliff is stoic, set in his ways, a spy who is used to having his life well ordered. He expects life to continue on in this perfectly conventional fashion. He assumes his bad boy status while keeping mamas and debutantes at arm's length. An heir is needed but Leslie has every intention of finding a woman who doesn't covet his wealth and tittle. He is irresistibly drawn to the headstrong young lady who becomes more beautiful as she develops into a woman.

...but she is loving him.

When Leslie kisses Lacie MacTavish, she knows even at the tender age of fifteen this is the man of her dreams. Forced to wait until she comes of age, Lacie withdraws into herself. Now she is eighteen and Leslie has returned from a mission for the British Government ready to claim her as his bride. She refuses him and he must find a way to seduce her and in the process create a burning passion within her, which she cannot deny.

Pleasing Arie
Bad Boys Book Six

He's a bad bad boy...

Arie Demir has never been denied anything in his life. He takes what he wants. What he undeniably yearns for is the beautiful redheaded spitfire he sees in a restaurant in Glasgow. At every turn, she confuses him by disputing his power over her. Alison refuses to accept the fact he owns her. While Arie tries desperately with patience and tenderness to drive her wild with new sensations, his scorching kisses ignite the fires of her very soul to make her understand he is all she will ever want.

...but is she pleasing him?

Alison Fletcher never expected to find herself kidnapped and sold to a whorehouse then bought by a Turkish sultan to become his slave. She vows to never surrender to the arrogant man who believes he owns her. She is stunned by the magnificently handsome man who awaits her compliance. Unexpectedly, she finds Arie the lesser of all the evils. The hidden depths of his mesmerizing dark brown eyes hold her into their power; his muscular embrace makes her weak with desire. She is his to do with as he wishes.

Graham's Wicked Kiss
Bad Boys Book Seven

He's a bad bad boy...

Graham Chamberlin is stunned to find three young boys dangling from the trees lining the drive to Runningmead Manner. On further inspection, he is astonished at their obsession to protect a young woman who has been brutalized by her pimp. The woman he discovers hiding in a third-floor attic room is gravely injured. He takes the silver haired stowaway under his wing. Clearly, Graham's new guest is a lady with many secrets. He is determined to unlock all the mysteries surrounding her.

...But she can't resist his wicked kiss.

The years since Ria left the convent where she was raised have been a nightmare. Her secrets are dangerous—as is the powerful man determined to find her. Handsome Graham Chamberlin is clearly a gentleman with secrets of his own, but staying with him could mean the difference between life and death for Ria. With each passing day, her handsome host turns Ria's convalescence into an increasingly sensual escape. Now her greatest challenge may be imagining anything less than a future in his arms.

Feeling Etienne's Love
Bad Boys Book Eight

He's a bad bad boy...

Etienne Dubois is the son of a wealthy vineyard owner who craves the excitement of putting his life on the line. Working with the French government and as a confidant of King Charles X give him reasons for living. An encounter with a beautiful young woman in a plush bordello in Paris has him rethinking his roguish ways. Etienne never expects to become a father especially from one encounter with an innocent prostitute who whispers his name and has him rethinking his well-ordered life.

...But she can't help feeling his love.

Elisa Moreau, the only daughter of Angelique Moreau, the owner of an exclusive bordello in Bordeaux, France, has loved Etienne Dubois since she was six. Unfortunately, until an unexpected encounter at a brothel in Paris puts the two of them in the same room, Etienne doesn't even know she exists. Confused but wanting Etienne and this chance meeting to never end, Elisa gives herself to the man who has held her heart in hands for what seems like her entire life.

All I Want Is Link
Bad Boys Book Nine

He's a bad bad boy...

Merry Stewart is wildly unpredictable. Left alone to run wild over the Bordeaux and Scottish countryside she becomes impetuous and daringly bold. Over the years, she's found she can bedevil her softhearted brothers into allowing her exploits to go unnoticed. As a young woman she has learned she can do as she pleases when she pleases. Now, Merry has set her amorous sights on the Duke of Weston—a man she has never met but has every intention of marrying. No other suitor will satisfy her—especially not the exceptionally striking, horse breeder, Devlin Mathews.

...she's the woman of his desires.

Posing as commoner Devlin Mathews to escape a potentially fatal confrontation, Devlin is enthralled and infuriated by the audacious, duke-hunting dark haired vixen. Bedeviled at every opportunity, he finds dealing with the tiny she-devil exasperating as well as intriguing. Without revealing his true identify, the infamous rogue pledges to thwart Merry's plans to wed the man of her dream-never imagining the bewitching strategist would turn out to be the only woman he would ever dream of marrying.

Devlin's Angel
Bad Boys Book Ten

He's a bad bad boy...

Merry Stewart is wildly unpredictable. Left alone to run wild over the Bordeaux and Scottish countryside she becomes impetuous and daringly bold. Over the years, she's found she can bedevil her softhearted brothers into allowing her exploits to go unnoticed. As a young woman she has learned she can do as she pleases when she pleases. Now, Merry has set her amorous sights on the Duke of Weston—a man she has never met but has every intention of marrying. No other suitor will satisfy her—especially not the exceptionally striking, horse breeder, Devlin Mathews.

...she's the woman of his desires.

Posing as commoner Devlin Mathews to escape a potentially fatal confrontation, Devlin is enthralled and infuriated by the audacious, duke-hunting dark haired vixen. Bedeviled at every opportunity, he finds dealing with the tiny she-devil exasperating as well as intriguing. Without revealing his true identify, the infamous rogue pledges to thwart Merry's plans to wed the man of her dream-never imagining the bewitching strategist would turn out to be the only woman he would ever dream of marrying.

Foolish for Piper

The pickpocket...

Piper has spent her life surviving the streets of St. Giles Parish in London, a den of iniquity and crime. Masquerading as a boy she escapes the whorehouses the young girls are sent to as they come of age. The day she encounters Brett MacLachlan begins the same as every other one. When she picks his pocket, she has no idea her life is going to change irreversibly.

...and the mark

Handsome aristocrat Brett MacLachlan has come to London for his amusement only to find his world turned upside down by a thief and her dog. From the moment he spots her, Brett knows there is something intrinsically wrong. In his arms, Piper discovers passion and joy. Yet secrets of her past haunt her, and a scar will tell the true tale as well as her identity.

Taylor's Destiny

She traveled to another time and place to change destiny...

Enjoying a day of sailing, Taylor Maxwell never expected after a suffering a concussion she would wake up in another century. A resilient independent woman in the twenty-first century, the blond beauty is ill prepared for life in the 1800s. Her first sight of the naval captain who rescues her makes her heart stop, giving her hope for her future.

His life is transformed by a woman who appears from nowhere...

Born to a life of ease, Reid Stewart defies the dictates of those born to aristocracy and chooses a life of adventure in the navy and as a spy for the crown. When he discovers a nearly naked woman on the bow of small sailing ship, his heart warms. His love for Taylor and his need to protect her from a man who pursues her might cost him his life as well as hers.

Caitlin's Duke

She played a fiddle in an Irish pub...

Caitlin O'Shea Is the most beautiful woman Roc Leighton has ever seen. With her blue violet eyes and long black hair she captivates him. In turn he mesmerizes Caitlin. Caught in the power of his gaze as he watches her, she is wise enough to know he desires her but will never give his heart to her. Caitlin has vowed to never be any man's mistress.

And fell in love with an English Lord...

Roc knows the first time he watches her play the fiddle and dance around the pub, she will be his next mistress. Despite her protest, he will find a way to convince her that her place is with him. While Caitlin's determination to keep her vows, fate takes a cruel turn and she is forced to seek refuge with Roc.

Catching Meara
Book One in the McKenna Clan Series

Meara Thorton was a feisty, world-class computer hacker—cornered by the FBI and shockingly given the chance to be their newly acquired technical analyst. Brilliant and intuitive, yet aching with the loss of everyone she has cared about, her restless heart led her to discover a love she fought and a world she didn't know could possibly exist.

Sweet Sexy Sadie
Book Two in the McKenna Clan Series

From the first time Sadie's eyes met those of Brody McKenna in the hot Sierra Madre Mountains, theirs was a potent attraction—not gentle, slow, and easy, but hot, hard, and all-consuming. The daughter of a dysfunctional family, Sadie had dreams no man could wrench from her with hot sex and an all-consuming passion. She'd challenge this alpha male with all the strength she possessed. But her red hair, fiery temperament, and indomitable spirit obsessed Brody...and he knew he had to find a way to show her he was more than he appeared and convince her to make a life with him.

Sweet Misbehavin'
Book Three in the McKenna Clan Series

Cast adrift after fleeing the home of Jokul, the ice demon, Atantsi, a firestarter, grew to womanhood as she moved through time to keep the demon from finding her. Though stubborn and courageous, she was ill prepared to use powers she had not been taught. Her first sight of the intoxicating Carr McKenna left her breathless, and her second encounter gave her hope for a future she never thought she had.

A playboy, a second son and a shifter, a man who thought his life would be carefree, Carr McKenna was shocked to discover the woman he'd paid as an escort is a firestarter who is running for her life. He is the leader of all the McKennas around the world and that he has multiple powers. His passion for Margo and the need to defend her might cost him his life as well as hers.

Sweet Talkin' Sugar
Book Four in the McKenna Clan Series

Lyonesse McKenna, was dreaming, or was she? From the instant Lyn saw Deacon McClain across a black jack table in a crowed Las Vegas casino the unmistakable attraction sent Lyn's senses flying into overdrive. Her family of shapeshifters believed in soul mates. She'd always been skeptical yet she couldn't help but question the way her heart sped when he looked at her.

When Deacon appeared in Las Vegas he knew his first job was to save Lyn from a Sea Demon, but the next order of business was to convince her he would someday mean more to her than she'd ever expected. But her stubborn nature and unbendable spirit consumed Deacon...and he had to chase away all the demons real and imagined in order to win her heart.

Sweet Surrender
Book Five in the McKenna Clan Series

Ripped from her family at the top of Infinity Cliff, Kimi McKenna finds herself thrust somewhere into the future. Dark elements threaten to destroy the earth unless Kimi can work together with the white witch to stop the destruction. Confused by her mate's role in the conspiracy, she refuses to acknowledge the connection. But amidst raging fire and attacks on the people she is coming to hold dear, she allows Maska O'keefe into her heart.

Maska O'keefe has loved the beautiful shapeshifter for years. Unable to save her life years ago, he vows to watch over her as he is given a second chance to convince her that even though he is a witch and not a shifter, they are indeed soul mates. Kimi's divided loyalties between her family and the cause she is now a part of will determine their relationship. Only the part she plays as the messiah can bring this to a conclusion in the final battle.

Dakota's Bride
The first book in the Lakota/Pinkerton Series

When Emma St. John received her brother's letter imploring her to escape her stepfather's vengeful scheme and to trust Dakota Barringer with her life, she was willing to chance it. But the handsome, brooding riverboat owner Emma found in Natchez a danger of another kind. For Emma soon found herself surrendering to an unrelenting desire.

Raised by the Sioux when his parents were killed, Dakota had been betrayed once before by a white woman. He wasn't about to trust another, especially one claiming that her stepfather, a powerful U.S. senator, had framed her as a murderess. But he couldn't let Emma's intoxicating effect on him. Now Dakota would risk his very life to protect the innocent beauty who had seduced him with her tender love.

My Angel
The second book in the Lakota/Pinkerton Series

A BEAUTY IN BUCKSKINS
When her father decided to send her to a finishing school back East, Angela Chamberlain refused to be confined to stuffy drawing rooms. Instead, the daring spitfire who could shoot like a man and ride like the wind longed for a life of adventure and romance—and she knew exactly who could give it to her. Devil Blackmoor was a hired gun with a dangerous reputation. But Angela was willing to go to the ends of the earth to capture the handsome devil's heart.

A DEVIL IN DISGUISE
He'd come to America looking for excitement, but Devil Blackmoor got more than he bargained for when he encountered a

beautiful rebel who answered his kisses with a wild innocence that touched his very soul. Yet standing between them were more obstacles than either ever dreamed. For Devil had strapped on a gun for the wrong man. And that made Angela his enemy. Now he'll have to choose between his duty and the woman he loves more than life.

The Locket
The third book in the Lakota/Pinkerton Series

The year is 1894. Seeking revenge for crimes against his family, Misha Petrovich follows a path that leads straight to Ariel Cameron's boarding house in Mist Harbor, Oregon. A family heirloom in Ariel's possession leads Misha to believe she is guilty. The locket has been handed down to the oldest girl in the Petrovich family for generations. Ariel is innocent of wrong doing, but her father is not. Misha is torn by his feelings for Ariel and his need for restitution against her father. Knowing that the relationship between them is fragile, Misha does everything in his power to protect Ariel's father. His efforts are to no avail when her father is shot. Ariel comes to realize Misha's steadfast courage and determination to protect her and her father despite what has happened to his family. Ariel's love and devotion heals Misha's heart.

The Talisman
The fourth book in the Lakota/Pinkerton Series

Running from a marriage that lasted one night, Dr. Moriah McKeown discovers the land she has settled on is coveted by determined and lawless men. Yet the proud young woman who once vowed never to abandon her home has second thoughts when her adopted children are threatened. Her only recourse is to enlist the aid of a dark, dangerous gun for hire.

Haunted by the past and a betrayal he will never forgive, Ian Civanovich uses his fast gun and his reckless courage to forget the faithlessness of a woman in his past. He will trust no female—nor will he rest until the threat hovering over Moriah McKeown is put to rest.

Forever His
The fifth book in the Lakota/Pinkerton Series

Struggling to come to terms with the part she played in Jacob St. John's death, Etta Barringer resigns from Pinkerton Agency and seeks peace and solace in a Rocky Mountain Cabin.

Jacob has vowed to discover the reason Etta has betrayed him, sold him out to his enemy and left him for dead.

Isolated in their cabin, they discover their love for each other and learn to trust. But the trust is shattered when Jacob learns she is married to his sworn enemy; the man who left him in the desert to die.

Allura's Secret
Twelve Dancing Princesses Book One

Allura McClellan is horrified by her father's decision to take out an ad in the Times awarding her to the man strong enough and smart enough to win her hand and uncover her secrets. She's an intelligent young woman who takes great delight in the freedom allotted to her by her father. She's well aware that marriage would effectively curtail the adventures she's shared with her sisters and cousins.

Hunter Gray is nothing like the other men who've arrived to vie for Allura's hand in marriage and everything that goes along with it. However, he is the first to refuse to concede defeat and pursue her despite her attempts to disguise her true appearance. It's her temperament that is of more concern to him than her looks. Hunter has worked all his life with the hope of someday owning his own land. Now that it looks like there's a very real possibility that everything he's ever wanted is within reach nothing is going to deter him – including Miss Allura's disagreeable disposition.

Amorica's Wager
Twelve Dancing Princesses Book Two

Amorica Hepburn was sent to London to find a husband. Finding a man was the last item on her agenda. With her two cousins, Amorica wagers she can dissuade her suitor before the others. Despite her efforts she discovers a chemistry that cannot be denied. Suddenly she is the arrogant man's wife, pledged to a marriage neither desire. But swept off to his ancestral home above the Dover cliffs and into his strong embrace, Amorica is soon possessed by a raging passion for the husband she had vowed to despise...

Damian Andrews couldn't afford to trust the emerald-eyed spitfire who happened upon his secret. Amorica's hatred of all men of his kind only inflames the war that rages between them. Still, he can not control the intense desire his stubborn bride inspires, or make her surrender to his will until he has conquered the headstrong beauty on the battlefield of love...

Ravyn's Marriage of Inconvenience
Twelve Dancing Princesses Book Three

A REGAL BEAUTY

When the duchess decides to wed her to a wastrel and a fop, Ravyn Grahm takes matters into her own hands and declares her engagement to another man. Instead of fessing up and telling her great aunt what she has done, she goes through with the pretense. Ariec Lakeland is the bastard son of an earl and has a dangerous reputation. But Ravyn is willing to do most anything to keep the duchess from discovering the lie.

A DEVIL-MAY-CARE SMUGGLER

He'd bought land in America, looking to put down roots and end his life of adventure, but Ariec Lakeland got more than he bargained for when he encountered a beautiful heiress who made a promise she didn't want to keep. But the promise could not be undone and standing between them were more obstacles than either ever dreamed. Ariec had made plans to spend the rest of his life in America and that was at odds with Ravyn's plan of living in England and running her father's estate. Now, he'll have to choose between his dreams and the woman he loves more than life.

Christel's Sunrise
Twelve Dancing Princesses Book Four

He Made Her An Offer...

Life has thrown Christel McClellan some experiences that could have devastated a less determined woman. Beautiful, self-assured and fiercely independent, she is trying to forget the loss of her stillborn child. But is the child alive?

She Couldn't Deny...

Life is carefree for Ryder MacLaren who loves to see what is on the other side of the sunrise. Laird of Clan MacLaren, he is wealthy, handsome and happily unencumbered...until stunning Christel McClellan enters his life. When he hears her story, he believes the child she thought dead has been sold to a wealthy buyer.

Storm's Passion
Twelve Dancing Princesses Book Five

SHE MADE A PROPOSAL...

Life strikes Storm Graham a shattering blow when she learns her father has bartered her to a man she detests. Storm is beautiful, self–assured and fiercely independent, and refuses to be a pawn in her father's schemes, yet she can find no way out of this bargain made in hell. Going on the offensive she asks the wealthiest man on the eastern coast of England to marry her, never believing she might fall in love.

HE TRIED TO REFUSE...

For Hadden Johnston life has provided everything he ever wanted, including a sanctuary for homeless children. He is wealthy, handsome and happily unencumbered...until stunning Storm Graham marches into his life and proposes a marriage of convenience. Yet this type of marriage to a woman who inflames his senses is far from acceptable. If he's going to be tied down, he will move heaven and earth to have this woman warming his bed.

Gotta Have Fayth
Twelve Dancing Princesses Book Six

A regal beauty with raven hair and piercing blue eyes, Fayth Graham is unwilling to parade herself in front of the wealthy Lords of England during the season. Seeking a means to dissuade any man wishing to wed her, she seeks a way to ruin herself for marriage. When she unexpectedly meets a man with sparkling gray eyes and an infectious grin, she decides this is the man who will keep her from agreeing to obey.

He returned from six months at sea, looking for a few nights of pleasure with a willing lass, but Jarret Kinsley got more than he bargained for when he met a beautiful debutant who responded to his kisses with a wild innocence that touched his heart. Yet the obstacles looming between them might rip them apart. Both had vowed never to marry, so when consequences of their dalliances got in the way, Jarret would have to choose between the life he's always desired and the woman he loves more than life.

Ella's Pleasure
Twelve Dancing Princesses Book Seven

A WHISPER OF PLEASURE

Ella Hepburn was an auburn haired debutant from the harsh Scottish coastline—a wild innocent to be seduced and tamed. A spirited beauty, she captivated Drake Montgomerie's jaded heart—while succumbing to the smoldering desire she felt for her unyielding suitor.

A WHISPER OF DANGER

In Drake Montgomerie's glittering world of money and privilege, young Ella discovered passion and desire could overcome everything she'd been taught to resist—entangling Drake, the heir apparent, in a lethal coil of aristocratic family intrigue. But grave peril would only nurse the sparks of a love that knew no limits and a magnificent ecstasy that would not be denied.

Eveleen's Seduction
Twelve Dancing Princesses Book Eight

A WHISPER OF SEDUCTION

A brutal attack on Eveleen Hepburn's cherished island off the Scottish coastline leaves her shattered and bewildered. Learning a man she once trusted can kill as easily as he can breathe even though the deed saves her life, creates questions that need answers. An innocent beauty, she enchants Logan Maxwell's cynical heart—giving in to the raging passion she feels for her mysterious suitor.

A WHISPER OF INTRIGUE

In Logan's Maxwell's world of espionage and privilege, young Eveleen discovers truths about herself she never expected, and a need for passion and love can overcome all her fears if she learns to accept certain truths. She finds herself entangled in a lethal battle for land that was once owned by French nobility, taken from them during the revolution and sold to Maxwell. But grave peril would unleash the flames of love that simmers, creating a magical union that cannot be refuted.

Tavia's Deception
Twelve Dancing Princesses Book Nine

WHISPERS OF DECEPTION

When her father decides to send her to London for her season, Tavia Hepburn resolves to see the world instead. The raven haired beauty decides to disguise herself as a lad and find employment on a ship bound for Barcelona as a cabin boy. But she never bargains on finding passion and love to a red haired sea captain who rescues her from certain death.

WHISPERS OF MURDER

For James Macmurra, the world is black and white until he meets a young debutante, who turns his world upside down. He's unable to deny Tavia's intoxicating effect on him. In a match tense with obstacles, unwillingness to divulge secrets, and unforeseen peril, irresistible desire and passion grows into undeniable love. James would risk his life to shelter and protect the innocent debutante who seduces him with her sweet love.

Larena's Fascination
Twelve Dancing Princesses Book Ten

WHISPERS OF FASCINATION

Fiery, free spirited Larena Graham never wanted to marry a duke. She is thrilled to be in love with the fourth son of an aristocrat, Gavin Broon. But when it seems Gavin ignores her, she set her sights on politics and bettering human life. Unsuspecting intrigue and a plot against her, she continues her dangerous plans despite Gavin's wishes.

WHISPERS OF TRUST

Gavin has every intention of properly courting the beautiful Larena until he must leave the city in order to put his affairs in order. Returning to London, he finds the woman he means to make his own is embroiled in political protests that could lead to a prison ship. Larena must learn to trust the handsome Scotsman whose most pressing mission is to protect her and keep her from harm.

Tira's Education
Twelve Dancing Princesses Book Eleven
WHISPERS OF EDUCATION

Learning how to build ships is Tira Hepburn's only dream until she meets Jamie Lundin and her world is turned upside down. With her raven black hair and vivid green eyes, she tempts Jamie and pushes him to defy his vows. She never bargains on finding an irrevocable love and a passion to a man who cannot fulfill her dreams despite his burning desire for her.

WHISPERS OF A BARGAIN

Arrogant and self-assured Jamie is brought up short when Tira captures his heart. All his carefully made plans are put to the test when he decides to teach her the art of ship building if she will spend a week with him alone on his ship. He is unable to deny Tira's intoxicating effect on him. When Tira leaves him behind unwilling to live with him without the benefit of marriage, he races after her. Jamie will risk everything to shelter and protect the innocent debutante who seduces him with her sweet love.

Aidan's Love
Twelve Dancing Princesses Book Twelve

Whispers of Love

Aidan McLellan has loved since she first set eyes on him as a young girl. Spontaneous, wild and eager to grow up, Aidan haunts his waking thoughts day and night, insinuating herself into his life. With her fiery red hair and sparkling sapphire eyes, she seizes Blade's heart even while he tries to resist the innocent child until she becomes a woman.

Whispers of Courage

Blade has waited what seems a lifetime to claim the woman who captures his heart as a little girl. Claiming his inheritance before his younger brother takes what is rightfully his, Blade must convince Aidan of his sincerity after years of avoidance and wed her before his father dies so he can return home, securing his rightful place. Everything is put to the test when his life as well as Aidan's is threatened by the man who once called him brother.

Don't Hustle Letty
Good Girls Book One

She's a good girl...

As tempted as Scarlett was, she had too many secrets to let someone enter her world—secrets that would send any reasonable man to the farthest ends of the earth. Bobby was far from reasonable and despite her desperate attempts to hold him at bay, he would not let her past destroy their future. With her escort service, Scarlett used men and their insatiable lust for women to capitalize on the means to survive and prosper. She vowed to never wed, to never put herself in the control of a man.

...nonetheless he has other ideas.

Lord Robert Munroe, with his newly acquired title of marquis goes to Scarlett's for training on how to comport himself. The marquis, better known as Bobby, knows how to pick a pocket as well as get into a bloke's home to steal them blind. What he doesn't know is how to be a gentleman. When he sets his sights on the prim Miss Scarlet, Letty, to his way of thinking, he decides she is the woman he wants to call his wife. He tempts all that she is with sweet words and tender coaxing until she is unable to refuse all he hopes to give her.

Twelve Days to Love

When Archer Steele shows up at Calanthe Durand's failing plantation with an alligator over his shoulder, Cali thinks she's never seen a more handsome man. During the war she had to defend herself and her servants from both union and confederate soldiers. Independent and self-sufficient, she vows to never marry.

But Archer Steele has different ideas. The first time Archer sees Cali in town, he feels an instant attraction. He decides he will do everything and anything to convince the beautiful Miss Durand he is worthy of her love. During the weeks leading up to Christmas, he gives her twelve gifts in hopes she will fall in love with him. Yet they are faced with challenges they must overcome before Cali can commit to a marriage.

Door to Heaven

Jessica Lawrence is the stepdaughter of a woman born in the twentieth century transported back in time to the year 1868. An acclaimed suffragette, she raises Jessica to believe in the equality of women. Jess Law believes everything she was taught, and when the time is right she becomes a private investigator. Courageous and impetuous, Jess finds danger in her quest to save all women from white slavery. Her passionate mission results in a wedding to Roc Newman, a man she knows can steal her heart...

Roc can't trust the sapphire-eyed spitfire who invades his home in search of secret papers and knocks him flat with her karate moves. Jessica's refusal to obey his wishes serves to inflame the war between them. Still, he cannot control the intense desire his reluctant bride inspires, or make her surrender her independence, until he has conquered the headstrong beauty on the battlefield of love...

Rebel Heart

HER REBEL SPIRIT DEFIED HIS OUTSIDERS SOUL...She was velvet and silk, eyes the color of a summer storm and amber hair. Victoria DeMontville, because of a promise and a codicil to her father's will, was forced to marry one man to protect her from another. She hated Cameron Savage with a fierce passion. But to hold on to her genetic research and find a cure for the deadly Signe virus, she must pretend to love the enemy at her door, come with weapons of fire to melt her icy heart...

HIS OUTSIDERS TOUCH IGNITED RAGING PASSIONS... He wore a mask, disguised as the Phantom, a true legend come to life. Even as war and debate over new genetic research engulfed them all, he would find his greatest adversary in the beauty who'd branded him an outsider and barbarian, the woman he was born to possess, his soul mate.

Safari Moon

Solo St. John, a wildlife photographer, is preparing for a trip to Alaska. Suddenly, Solo finds women of all sorts invading his privacy, his home and his office, all cooing nonsense words and blatantly throwing themselves at him. Solo doesn't know why, and he has no idea how to rid himself of the persistent women. He finally decides to beg a favor of his best buddy Nyssa Harrington.

In love with Solo for the past ten years and knowing he doesn't return her feelings Nyssa doesn't want to talk to Solo. She knows if she accepts his phone call, she will not be able to resist the temptation to hope again.

Straight to Heaven

Running from demons, Alexandra McMurdie stumbles into Forbidden Ground where up is down and elements of nature are contested. Though a strong independent woman in the twenty-first century' she is unprepared for life in the 1800s. Her first site of the formidable James Lawrence makes her heart skip a beat, giving her cause to reconsider her desperate need to find a way home.

Born with a silver spoon, James' life was torn apart during the War Between the States. Moving west he vows to put the life he once knew in the past. When he discovers a half-frozen woman near Gold Hill, his heart begins to thaw. His love for Alexandra and his need to keep her from a man who has pursued her through time might cost him his life as well as hers.

A Valentine's Anthology

The Lending Library-a fantasy by Christie L. Kraemer
Faeries try to fit into the human world when the forest where they make their home is destroyed by a mysterious enemy.

Chasing Rainbows-a contemporary romance by Genene Valleau
An eccentric aunt, an inventive uncle, a mother who wears poodle skirts, and a brother who wears pearls provide a hilarious backdrop for the courtship of a young woman who yearns for a "normal" family.

The Gift-an historical romance by Christine Young
A man and a woman on opposite sides of the Civil War get a second chance at love after one final battle returns soldiers to their war-torn homes to rebuild their lives.

A St. Patrick's Day Tale
Christine Young, C. L. Kraemer, Genene Valleau

Tumble through time...
...to Ireland in 1817, when tensions are high between Protestants and Catholics and fae people guide the fate of villagers. A lovely Catholic lass stumbles upon the weakly ritual fisticuffing between Irish lads. She falls into the lap of a handsome young Protestant. Family ties, grudges, and two conniving faeries threaten their budding love. But the faeries outsmart themselves when they hijack a time machine that has mysteriously appeared in their forest and are whisked to...
...Eugene, Oregon in the 20th century, amid a property feud between the local faeries and night elves. The conniving faeries from Olde Ireland try to stir up more mischief. However, a warrior gnome

convinces the magic folk to control their own destiny, and forces the intruding faeries to take refuge in the time machine again, spinning their way toward...

...A modern day castle in western Oregon. An eccentric inventor is determined to reclaim his wayward time machine and save his beloved wife from her latest misadventure. If only they can travel safely past the black hole...

a May Day Anthology
Christine Young, C. L. Kraemer, Rosemary Indra, Genene Valleau

Highland Miracle — Christine Young
HURTLED THROUGH TIME, Sean Michael Sterling, landed in the midst of a May Day celebration he didn't understand, assuming the role of Laird Sterling.

ILLIGITAMATE CHILD OF NOBILITY, Reagan Douglas searches for a way out of her half brother's house.

Defying the Odds — C.L. Kraemer
The night elves on the hill aren't happy without their magic. They concoct a plan to punish those who were involved in the act that rendered them almost human. Meanwhile, Uther, the rogue night elf, has returned to woo the Librarian to be his eternal mate.

Love in Bloom — Rosemary Indra
When childhood friends reunite it takes two fairies and a matchmaking daughter to help them admit their true love for each other.

No More Poodle Skirts — Genie Gabriel
After drifting for years in the innocent age of the 1950s, a woman struggles to join today's world by finding a career and a new love, with some help from her zany family.

Once Upon a Christmas Moon
Christine Young, C. L. Kraemer, Genene Valleau

TWELVE DAYS TO LOVE

When Archer Steele shows up at Calanthe Durand's failing plantation with an alligator over his shoulder, Cali thinks she's never seen a more handsome man. During the war she had to defend herself and her servants from both union and confederate soldiers. Independent and self-sufficient, she vows to never marry. But Archer Steele has different ideas. The first time Archer sees Cali in town, he feels an instant attraction. He decides he will do everything and anything to convince the beautiful Miss Durand he is worthy of her love. During the weeks leading up to Christmas, he gives her twelve gifts in hopes she will fall in love with him.

BOOTS AND BLADES

An ancient evil from the old country has arrived in the high desert of Oregon. Gnome children are vanishing then re-appearing, showing various stages of traumatization. Tiamoon, warrior gnome, will put her skills to use alongside Killian, a handsome warrior, also in need of a cause.

CHRISTMAS PAWSIBILITIES

With their world destroyed and their space ship malfunctioning, the dogizens of Planet Canid have little choice but to crash land on Earth. They face tortuous experiments at the hands of the Geeks in Green...or they can trust an eccentric inventor and his zany family to deliver the Canine Queen's puppies and help them celebrate new lives.